# THE PRESIDENT'S CAT
Guram Odisharia

# THE SHORE OF NIGHT
Daur Nachkebia

**Central Asian Literatures in Translation**

Series Editor: **Rebecca Ruth Gould**
(School of Oriental and African Studies, University of London)

Editorial Board:
**Erdağ Göknar** (Duke University)
**Jeanne-Marie Jackson** (Johns Hopkins University)
**Donald Rayfield**, Professor Emeritus (Queen Mary University of London)
**Roman Utkin** (Davidson College)

# TWO NOVELS FROM THE CAUCASUS

## THE PRESIDENT'S CAT
Guram Odisharia

Translated by David Foreman

## THE SHORE OF NIGHT
Daur Nachkebia

Translated by Felix Helbing

BOSTON
2024

Library of Congress Cataloging-in-Publication Data

Names: Nachkebia, Daur, 1960–author. | Odisharia, Guram, author. |
   Nachkebia, Daur, 1960–Bereg nochi English. | Odisharia, Guram.
   Prezidentis kata. English.
Title: Two novels from the Caucasus / Daur Nachkebia, Guram Odisharia.
Description: Boston : Academic Studies
   Press, 2024. | Series: Central Asian literatures in translation
Identifiers: LCCN 2024012518 (print) | LCCN 2024012519 (ebook) |
   ISBN 9798887195605 (hardback) | ISBN 9798887195612 (paperback) |
   ISBN 9798887195629 (adobe pdf) | ISBN 9798887195636 (epub)
Subjects: LCSH: Caucasian fiction—Translated into English. |
   LCGFT: Novels.
Classification: LCC PK9040.T86 2024  (print) | LCC PK9040  (ebook) |
DDC
   891.73/5—dc23/eng/20240508
LC record available at https://lccn.loc.gov/2024012518
LC ebook record available at https://lccn.loc.gov/2024012519

Copyright © 2024, Academic Studies Press
All rights reserved.

ISBN 9798887195605 (hardback)
ISBN 9798887195612 (paperback)
ISBN 9798887195629 (adobe pdf)
ISBN 9798887195636 (epub)

Book design by Tatiana Vernikov
Cover design by Ivan Grave

Published by Academic Studies Press
1577 Beacon Street
Brookline, MA 02446, USA
press@academicstudiespress.com
www.academicstudiespress.com

# Contents

| | |
|---|---|
| Foreword | 7 |
| The President's Cat: A Novel<br>*Guram Odisharia* | 13 |
| The Shore of Night: A Novel<br>*Daur Nachkebia* | 253 |

# Foreword

*Erik R. Scott*

The union of these two books in one volume is not an accident, nor simply a consequence of the fact that literature from the Caucasus all too rarely reaches the English-reading public. These two novels, though written by different people and in diverging literary styles, are interwoven by their shared setting, common concerns, and the unique friendship of their authors, a Georgian and an Abkhaz. Guram Odisharia's *The President's Cat* and Daur Nachkebia's *The Shore of Night* are best understood as composing a double book. The book's two parts can be read separately, but they arguably produce a more profound impression when read together, in dialogue with one another.

At first glance, their dialogical relationship might not be readily apparent. Odisharia's novel is whimsical in form and content. Some chapters read like overheard anecdotes, others like the toasts for which the Caucasus region is famous; some are long and circuitous, others are nearly haiku-like in their brevity. The novel's characters are lively, and its setting is lush. *The President's Cat* is the radiant day to the dark desperation of Nachkebia's *The Shore of Night*. Nachkebia's novel, in contrast to Odisharia's work, takes the form of one uninterrupted chapter, even as the lives of its characters lie in fragmented ruins.

8 | Erik R. Scott

Running between the two novels is the war in Abkhazia, which began with armed clashes in August 1992 and concluded with the fall of the capital city of Sukhumi to Abkhaz forces seeking to separate from Georgia in September 1993. The war decimated what had been one of the most vibrant and multiethnic corners of the sprawling Soviet Union. It turned seaside resorts, bustling port cities, grand hotels, and botanical gardens into zones of destruction. In *The Shore of Night*, set after the war, Beslan no longer recognizes Sukhumi. The street which he walks down "no longer resembles its former self" because "more than a year of continuous shelling and bombing has distorted it beyond recognition." The war killed thousands on both sides and led to the expulsion of around 250,000 Georgians from Abkhazia. Among those displaced by the conflict was Guram Odisharia. In the fall of 1993, the Georgian writer was forced to journey over 50 miles on foot through the treacherous Sakeni-Chiberi mountain pass to seek safety. Along the way, he witnessed the deaths of several of his companions as a result of cold and starvation, a tragedy he chronicled in an earlier work, *The Path of the Persecuted*.

The two novels speak to each other across the vast chasm opened by the war. *The President's Cat* expresses wry but heartfelt nostalgia for what was lost when the war began. At the novel's center is Sukhumi, the "biggest and smallest city in the world." It is a city home to Abkhaz, Georgians, Armenians, Greeks, Jews, Ukrainians, and Russians. A city whose subtropical climate allowed for the cultivation of "the December peach (from America), the wild strawberry tree, the honey tree (from China), the Rodop lemon (from Bulgaria), the Volkameriana lemon (from Italy)." A city located in the Caucasus that also served as a gateway to the wider world, where foreign sailors and tourists journeyed across the Black Sea to bring jeans, chewing gum, Elvis Presley records, and Coca Cola.

And yet, it is a place that remained little understood by those who visited it, let alone by those who ruled it from Moscow.

Odisharia does not shy away from the contradictions of this strangely Edenic place under Soviet rule. The book's main character, Mikhail Temurovich Bgazhba, is a dissident of sorts while still serving as the First Secretary of the Autonomous Soviet Socialist Republic of Abkhazia. Bgazhba lives "according to his own rules" but operates comfortably within the system. He boasts, charms, cajoles, and sometimes lies to carve out a degree of autonomy for Abkhazia, but also to get his own way. He represents, in Odisharia's description, a postwar generation, one "torn by mutually exclusive aspirations, a generation of dreamers and pragmatists: lyrical romantics and devotees of comfort." Beneath the veil of enchantment Bgazhba casts over those around him, one can sense tensions: between Moscow and the Caucasus, between nationalities, between men and women, between political responsibilities and moral obligations, between life as it is and life as it is told in Bgazhba's stories. But for most of the novel, these disturbances remain only hinted at, so much so that when conflict breaks out, no one can understand "how the war had crept up on them, insinuated itself into the city, how the rumbling and bellowing had started."

Nachkebia's *The Shore of Night* plunges us fully into the war and its desolate aftermath. The world described by Odisharia has so completely vanished that one wonders whether it ever truly existed. War-torn Abkhazia staggers the mind: Adgur and his compatriots die randomly, meaninglessly, leaving an unfillable emptiness in the hearts of those still living; the once bustling city lies partly abandoned and in rubble; an aging communist stalwart, Mancha Satbeyivich, spends his days searching in vain for a hidden conspiracy behind the tragic turn of events in old issues of *Pravda*. As Beslan, the novel's main narrator, observes, "the feeling that dominates my heart is that this is all made up, it's unreal, that we've found ourselves the victims of mass suggestion." But occasionally he is struck by the opposite view; perhaps the Soviet Abkhazia he thought he knew was only a mirage, and the war represents an intrusion of reality. He observes, "Abkhazia has never been as real as it is now, on the verge of trouble."

Both novelists explore these contradictions in a polyphonic manner that calls to mind the choral traditions of the Caucasus. *The President's Cat* employs numerous narrators, voices, and tones. *The Shore of Night* weaves together Adgur's journal and Beslan's ruminations about it. Both works embrace the messiness of personal experiences over clear-cut political ideologies. Abkhazia, a small republic, is an intimate place where nearly everything is personalized, in peace as well as in war.

It is not surprising, then, that Odisharia and Nachkebia's personal biographies are closely entwined. Odisharia was born in Sukhumi in 1951; Nachkebia was born a little later, in 1960, and further south, in a village in Abkhazia's Ochamchire district, but he moved to Sukhumi in his youth to attend boarding school. Odisharia gained acclaim as a journalist, editor, and writer; Nachkebia received a degree in physics before pursuing the same careers. Both worked for the Writers' Union of Abkhazia before the war and formed a close friendship. What is surprising is that their friendship survived the war, Odisharia's displacement, and nationalist pressures on both sides of the conflict that made meaningful Georgian-Abkhaz dialogue almost impossible. Yet their connection endured, and the two books in this volume were published around the same time in 2007. After publishing these novels, Odisharia and Nachkebia took up political posts in close succession: Odisharia became Georgia's Minister of Culture and Monument Protection in 2012, while Nachkebia was appointed as Abkhazia's Minister of Education in 2011. Both then left their posts in 2014: Odisharia resigned after opposing a plan for gold mining at a prehistoric site in Georgia; Nachkebia departed after pushing back against creeping Russian influence in Abkhazia. Years later, and in a political climate that has only grown more acrimonious, their personal bond remains.

This double book is steeped in the particularities of Abkhazia, but its themes have resonance far beyond the Caucasus. The way the war in 1992-1993 devastated Abkhazia's urban spaces, ripped apart its multiethnic communities, and left a legacy of trauma in its wake anticipated the conflicts in the region that would soon follow: the war in Chechnya in 1994–1996, which reduced Grozny to ruins; the return of fighting in Abkhazia and South Ossetia amidst the Russo-Georgian War of 2008; and Russia's war against Ukraine, which began with incursions and the annexation of Crimea in 2014, escalated with the full-scale invasion in 2022, and continues unabated at the time of writing. Odisharia and Nachkebia, each in their own way, gaze into the face of war and do not shy away from tallying the losses it has caused in their native land. But both novelists also attest to the irrepressible glimmer of human creativity and the power of empathy, even in the darkest of times. Thanks to the careful and thoughtful work of the translators, David Foreman and Felix Helbing, these two novels from the Caucasus tell us of a lost world that was and urge us to imagine a better world that might still be.

# The President's Cat

## A Novel

*Guram Odisharia*

# The President's Cat

# 1.

It was the time of year when the monkey puzzle tree blooms. In other words, May.

At the same time, the pawpaw and the bitter orange begin to bloom and the tulip tree as well.

And the hawthorn also. However, sometimes the hawthorn unfurls its buds a bit later.

But that May was wondrously strange . . . Although perhaps no different from all other previous Mays, except people do not usually retain the previous May in their minds and hearts as long as the current May.

But we will leave the hawthorn in peace. Imagine, even the soap trees and may apples were in bloom, although strictly speaking, both ought to have waited till June or even July.

But all the same . . . It was truly an unusual May running a riot in the Sukhumi Botanical Gardens that year.

It was a May in conjuror's guise.

The alyssum and the cosmos, which generally bloom all the year round, chose May to go kind of crazy for some reason, literally exploded in flowers, intoxicating the tourists.

That's the way it was.

In short, that year´s May again pulled off all her old tricks splendidly.

And *he* . . . *He* sat calmly without saying a word and kept staring at the fallen amaranth flowers, bright red, like little balloons or heaps of precious adornments magnified for television.

In the garden it was already drawing close to noon, but in the foliage, one could still hear the cautious rustle of a young morning breeze with a good night's sleep behind it.

And the twittering of birds as well.

"How many people are unaware of the existence of amaranth," he thought sadly. "And how unfortunate that they don't know . . . And how nice that they don't know."

That day the amaranth had a particularly sharp fragrance.

"A strong scent . . . That means there'll soon be a brief shower," he continued in his unhurried reflections.

He was wearing a white lab coat. And all the others were in white coats, too. The board of studies was in session. There were twenty-two of them along with invited guests.

The paper was by a senior scientist from the Institute of Tea and Sub-Tropical Cultures. The author was from the "Lemon Group," and on this occasion his talk was about frost-resistant types of lemon. He was a typical scientist—bespectacled, bald, calm—in a word, the incarnation of orderliness and respectability, a faithful husband and good family man, a model citizen and patriot.

Half an hour had passed since the paper had begun. And there was just as much time to go.

Mikhail, Mikhail Temurovich (he, who was contemplating the amaranth), had wanted the session that day to be held outdoors. A long table had been set up in the fretted shade of a pecan tree and intertwined palm canopies.

He loved the green cool of the Botanical Gardens, penetrated by the sun and wafted by the blue-green sea and the garden breezes aiming to embrace you in secluded nooks.

The President's Cat | 17

He took a sip of tea. He sampled its taste. As a rule, he preferred tea without sugar, but that day he had added half a spoonful.

The sugar was Cuban. Cane sugar. White. Whiter than white. Maybe that was why he put the sugar in because it was from Cuba. There was a reason for it.

He drank the tea while listening to the garden and the speaker.

When the speaker from the "frost-resistant lemon group" had finished, silence fell.

That is, only the voices of the garden could be heard.

A minute passed, then another . . .

Everyone was looking at him. What would the boss say?

And he said:

"Everything was fine, esteemed colleagues . . . But I cannot fail to note at this point that, while you were developing your scientific argumentation, over there on that tree, on its left branch, a male thrush swooped down on a female three times . . . And all three times successfully . . . That's why there were feathers occasionally floating down on our heads, esteemed colleagues."

And the breeze wafted his words around the garden, like the seeds of some wondrous plant.

And at that very minute, it was as if not only in the garden, but somewhere high up there in the sky, a burst of laughter rang out from the members of the board of studies and invited guests.

And because the majority of those sitting in the shade of the pecan and the palms were women, the silvery laughter of the women predominated, pleasantly arousing and masking the guffaws of the men. Although the reason being probably not just their numerical supremacy.

That May his hearing could easily distinguish the ringing laughter of one of them from the rest.

Indeed, for him the magic force of her ringing laughter easily prevailed over the combined energy of all the others' laughter.

That laughter belonged to a woman with a bold glance.

"One of her ancestors must have been a brigand," he had earlier thought regarding this woman.

Yes, yes, that was it, aggressively tender and tenderly aggressive, such was this beauty of Balzacian age (Well, what else is there to add? You can imagine the rest yourself).

When the merriment died down, everyone noticed both the branch of the pecan and the ruffled thrush sitting on it. His female partner was nowhere to be seen, but nobody doubted that he and he alone was the very thrush which had quite recently caused the foliage of the pecan to loudly shake three times in a row, and for some reason only one person had noticed it.

In short, only after these words did everyone apprehend the voices of the garden, as if someone had suddenly switched on an old radio from childhood.

The pecan foliage rustled ironically.

In the city on that day, there was neither a single space nor a single second for a single tear of grief.

Yes, it was exactly at the time when the monkey puzzle tree bloomed in the Botanical Gardens.

And many people, simply a multitude of people, knew nothing, neither of the amaranth nor of John Fitzgerald Kennedy's cat . . . However, back then even he himself knew nothing about this cat, because at that time only the plaintive squeak of the latter's distant forbears, the one of his grandmothers and great-grandmothers, explored with a pink tongue the mystery of a Sukhumi sky festively sprinkled with stars.

For this was even before the completion of the scientific work which he later published as a separate volume and entitled *The Thrush as a Songbird.*

And besides . . .

And in particular, it was still such a long time before the war in Abkhazia and yet just a stone's throw away from it, just a few decades and just a few seconds . . .

# The President's Cat

In the eighth decade of the twentieth century, thirty years after the death of Stalin, the Soviet Union, which had defeated fascism during the Second World War at the cost of twenty million of its citizens' lives and covered an area comprising one sixth of the planet, began to experience long anticipated quakes.

Its gigantic steel framework could no longer be held together by any special bolts, however painstakingly manufactured and embellished by the pentagonal symbols of the "Quality Mark."

Nor by splendid military parades...

Nor by oaths, convictions, promises...

Nor by the efforts of the KGB behind the scenes...

And away it all unwound, undermining the foundations of the New Babylon.

I well recall the way some maintained that, putting everything else aside, the USSR was bound to collapse for the simple reason that it was founded on the blood of innocent children, of Alexei Romanov and his sisters. And not just on their blood, on the blood of many other children as well.

And so it unfolded.

Much has been said about this and the like in the recent past. Much will be said in the future, too.

In a word, in the homeland of communism, a new, incomprehensible, and "different" period was budding, growing, gathering strength, preparing to explode in a stormy florescence.

The communist party, which one deluded genius termed the "honour and conscience of our era," appointed and removed the leaders of the Union of Socialist Republics as well as the leaders of the Autonomous Soviet Socialist Republics.

It goes without saying that Abkhazia was no exception. Between the day of Stalin's interment by the Kremlin wall and the dismantling of the USSR, many first secretaries were replaced. And every "First Secretary" left their mark on life in Abkhazia.

But among them was one in particular—Mikhail Bgazhba, Mikhail Temurovich.

Bgazhba was active during Khrushchev's rule and his activity was partly determined by the spirit of the times. But if other leaders, one way or another, strove with scrupulous party-disciplined pedantry to at least approximately model an image consistent with that of a leader at that time, Bgazhba did not even attempt it. He lived according to his own rules, which were completely incomprehensible to many others.

Like Khrushchev, he was not entirely free from many of the constraints on his nature that were characteristic of the steely Stalin period, but at the same time, thanks as it were to certain unfathomable laws of nature, he was conscious of his own—quite exotically piquant—leader's image. In doing so, *he* won the successful and harmonious cooperation of the period itself on the basis of equal rights and partnership. Such a partnership could only have been achieved by an exceptional and uniquely talented individual.

Indeed sometimes, as if by predestination, a particular segment of time and a certain individual are specifically designated to encounter each other. Just such an encounter occurred between Abkhazia in the second half of the century and Bgazhba. Mikhail Bgazhba. Mikhail Temurovich.

Mikhail Temurovich—he was always addressed as such. And only under this name, his own and his father's, both run together "Mikhaltemurovich," is he remembered even today by those who knew him personally, of whom only few survive, or by those who have more acquaintances in the next world than in this one.

The Russian suffix "-ich" was generally accepted in the ruling institutions of Abkhazia, just as it was right throughout the Soviet bureaucratic realm. Lads of nineteen or twenty in the Communist Youth League organizations addressed one another only as David Nikiforovich, Vladimir Durmishkhanovich, or Gheorghy Vladimirovich . . . It goes without saying that these days it raises a sadly ironic smile when one recalls how lads with lapel badges bearing Lenin's portrait learned to call one another dutifully by name and patronymic in the Russian style with the termination "-ich," to tie their ties correctly, and to shave . . . And, on top of that, learned from experienced party and managerial staff the skills of bringing out toasts to good effect in a dashing and business-like manner. They "won their spurs," so to speak. All this and much else besides was essential to gain possession of the "big, cosy" armchairs of office. They were drilled like commandos, they were supposed to take the future hostage, swiftly and without blunders.

In the USSR at the end of the 1960s, in the period when the idyll of communist capitalism flourished, a new generation appeared on the horizon and began to mature quickly, a generation torn by mutually exclusive aspirations, a generation of dreamers and pragmatists: lyrical romantics and devotees of comfort ...

And quite strangely, especially at this time, was the name of one man in Abkhazia, a personal name, a patronymic, and a surname—Mikhail Temurovich Bgazhba.

His name ended with the patronymic "-ich," but everyone I heard pronouncing the name "Mikhail Temurovich" released these two words with a special melodiousness and for some reason their faces lit up.

For those who knew him well, this "Mikhaltemurovich" always sounded like a single word. And more than just a name.

And so, I shall attempt in this book to call him "Mikhaltemurovich," as if it was a single name, the only one of its kind, and to repeat it with the intonation of his friends and associates, rather than using what is customary for Georgians, namely, "Baturo Mikhail," "Mikho", "Mikha," or just "Misha," although I know that this "-ich" grates on the ear in Georgian pronunciation and eventually drained away its political full tide along with its communist homeland ... Despite all this, I shall try.

It looks like it is coming off for me. Just listen, for does my "Mikhaltemurovich" sound different from the official, bureaucratic "Mikhail Temurovich?"

Of course, it sounds different. You just have to listen and then ...

The entire country was populated by his friends. He would even say of someone he did not know: "He's my friend."

For over ten years, he was the First Secretary of the Abkhazian Regional Committee, then he worked continuously in scientific research institutes, he was a geneticist (And no, I am not writing his obituary).

With one of his friends, he would talk about Alfred Nobel as if Nobel were his blood relative (I shall discuss this later. For now, I shall just say that he was enraptured by Nobel, but most of all by his prize).

With the Japanese billionaire Tadao Kasio, as indefatigable as he was, he signed absolutely amazing deals (of this more anon).

In Pitsunda, he searched for the grave of Aristotle . . . (Let's talk about this another time).

And so on and so forth . . .

By his own rapid steps and the speedy pace of his own life, he outdid the already accelerated rhythm of the twentieth century.

He was a man of the cosmos rather than a man of comfort. And he was much else besides . . .

Gagarin's cry "Lift off!" and Armstrong's first steps on the moon, along with all humanity, Americans or Russians, Nigerians or dwellers of Asia Minor, world evolution or revolution, all this was part of him.

And probably part of him first and foremost because, when an epoch which had forgotten about the phenomenon of humanity was searching for a man in other galaxies, it found him on Earth and treated him carefully (No, this is not a toast in his honour).

And by the way, he knew Gagarin personally and Armstrong, too. He "drank brotherhood" with both of them, with wine from a drinking horn.

The President's Cat | 25

So while (and this is also, by the way, today, when, for my fellow countrymen who have dispersed around the planet in search of work, an American visa means much more than all old and new American poetry put together), the years of my youth come back to me, the days when my friends and I searched for and immersed ourselves in reading verse by American poets (and others, too) that were on the verge of being censored.

America was sending us signals from afar! She was sending signals to my generation, America with her Vietnam, Hiroshima, and Nagasaki, which became, after the 1945 atomic bombing, more American than Japanese and also with her Cuban crisis, her music, hamburgers, President Kennedy...

We found our America in Sukhumi Port in the form of jeans purchased from foreign sailors, chewing gum, records by the "Chicago" rock group, Elvis Presley, the "stars and stripes," bearded Hemingway with his boxers and hunters, Coca Cola, Voice of America, when overseas ships called at our port just for a few hours, sometimes with their hatches tightly battened down.

And we waited for America, to spite communist propaganda.

One of America's first steps in communist Abkhazia was the advent of a Pepsi Cola factory. The company built it in Gulripshi district. The city of Sukhumi wanted to extend hospitality to the Americans, so that the company produce would come out under its aegis and in its name. I remember how angry Gulripshi folk were at Sukhumi residents, this was a shameless injustice (not merely an "injustice" but a "shameless injustice").

And it was then that Mikhail Temurovich declared:

"Pepsi Cola belongs to the people of Gulripshi, just like the psychiatric hospital built there. If Pepsi Cola is ours, the hospital ought to be registered under the name of Sukhumi, too."

At this point the Sukhumi folk fell silent. And so, the American Pepsi factory remained part of Gulripshi.

And then he added:

"By the way, Pepsi is the taste of America."

And so, America's taste came to Abkhazia.

Mikhail Temurovich visited the US several times himself.

On one occasion, when he had only just come back, he told us sadly:

"America, guys, is a highly developed Soviet Union and nothing more."

Then he added, even more sadly:

"Don't wait for America . . . I didn't understand anything about it over there, even where it's located . . . So now and then it seems to me, my dear fellows, that America is sometimes really in America."

I recall that moment with absolute photographic clarity. We were sitting at the table, the students and he, a man of my father's age. In his hand was a glass of Isabella wine. The Isabella grapes had been picked and pressed in his home village, the small Abkhazian village of Gup in Ochamchire district.

Yes, he was born in Gup, but nevertheless Mikhail Temurovich was a "Sukhuminite" from head to toe. It was this city, as he himself declared, that witnessed the supreme mystery or, as he added, the "Sukhumnisation" of his soul.

And he and his "Sukhuminised" soul were the subject of thousands of incidents related by Sukhumi Abkhazians,

Georgians, Armenians, Greeks, Russians, Ukrainians, Estonians, Germans . . . Need I go on?

They were told to me in Sukhumi, Tbilisi, Moscow, Istanbul, Sochi, St. Petersburg, Nalchik, Athens . . . I shall not enumerate further.

One of my respondents said: "Everyone has his own relationship with God, everyone in the Bible reads his Bible. And how unfortunate that you did not know Mikhail Temurovich well. Had you known him well, you would have known his Bible."

And I began to search for his Bible.

And I realised that I would not have comprehended his Bible, had I not known his Koran, his Buddhism, his songs of Krishna, his own psalms . . .

And a second respondent said: "You are scribbling something there, but why won't you say a word about Mikhail Temurovich? Aren't you from Sukhumi? Everyone should know about him. I have no idea at all what is going on. We offer the world so many good things: satsivi sauce, adjika paste, khachapuri and elargi cheese bread, chacha schnaps, white and red wine and the world knows nothing about it. The world knows nothing either about Mikhail Temurovich, or Kukur-chai, or Vianor Pandzhovich, or the "Amra" restaurant, or the "Brekhalovka" . . . It knows nothing about us. All in all, I don't understand what is going on. Are you not a native of Sukhumi, or what? Doesn't this surprise you? After all you know who he was. Mikhail Temurovich . . . He was . . ."

And then he lapsed into thought and fell silent

Who was he—Mikhail Temurovich?

Dozens, hundreds of people recalled him in conversation with me.

By the time the one-hundred thirtieth or so person had sought me out and struck up a conversation, I was finally convinced that Mikhail Temurovich had eventually become the principal hero of Sukhumi folklore, the principal character of Sukhumi mythology . . . I close my eyes and I can see him even now, in a coffee bar or in some restaurant or in a café, sitting in a circle of friends . . . Behind him the smooth marine surface of Sukhumi port, covered by white ships . . . It is summer, a sunny day. One would think it to be hot, but here it is cool; there is a breeze from the Black Sea . . .

And so, I decided to write a book about Mikhail Temurovich: "The Cat of President John Fitzgerald Kennedy" ("The President's Cat"). Only do not imagine that this book is actually about Kennedy and his cat . . .

And so, I am beginning to write and you, I hope, to read.

You may have heard one well-nigh fabulous story, which nevertheless really happened. Once upon a time a certain nation, which had been expelled to foreign climes, preserved its literacy by entrusting every family with the task of baking bread in the shape of a letter of their script. And they were reared on this "alphabet." Children grew up on it, for them the world began with their own native tongue, with their own letters. With this "alphabet" they buried the dead and celebrated weddings. Whether in joy or sorrow, the people of this nation would come together, and every family would bring bread baked in the shape of a letter, and in this way their literacy was always present on the table along with their local wine . . .

A script known as Mikhaltemurovich (alphabet or code) has spread around the world (mainly among the natives of

The President's Cat | 29

Sukhumi). Some know only one of its letters, others two or three, but nobody knows it right through.

And this book is an attempt to recall, investigate, and recreate this literacy . . .

And so, I have set to work on this book, having been transformed myself into the act of writing. I describe things as I recall them, things I have discussed with many people. Or I describe them as these numerous people remember them: the man himself, his travels and adventures, his friends, his city. Generally for us, the people, everything happens the way we remember it and not as it was in reality.

And therefore, I humbly ask you to read only what is written in this book rather than what is not written herein.

For just such a method of reading exists when you read what is not written, not written but inferred, sometimes by the author, sometimes by the reader, sometimes by both of them together, as if by agreement.

In this book nothing can be inferred . . . except what is written in it.

I am writing every chapter as it was told to me. They told it in different ways, each in his or her own fashion. After all, our hero himself enjoyed a variety of styles. So, for instance, he would sometimes propose a toast as a prayer, like an "Our Father," and sometimes in Sukhumi slang. It all depended on the general mood, both his own and his friends'.

Nowhere do I quote the personal or family names of my authors or co-authors, if only because it could overload the book. And I want it to be pleasant, like the smell of the sea, like the song of a bird, light as a convivial table. or champagne bubbles, or a joke told by Mikhail Temurovich, multi-coloured and floral as a summer beach and to excite the blood like the laughter of a beautiful woman.

I do not know what will result, a woman of a book or a toast of a book, or a prayer of a book, or just a memoir of a book. Let's take it a bit at a time and we'll see.

Most important is that we should not lose the light of days gone by.

And that the text should not be weighed down too heavily.

And that we negotiate all the reefs.

And do not end up on a sandbank.

And may there always be a favourable wind to assist us.

And may our ship, Lord, have seven feet of water under our keel for the whole voyage.

I can already sense now that some episodes will clearly be brief, well, quite itsy-bitsy, like Japanese verse, whether a haiku, or a hoku, tanku, or tonku. I have forgotten what they are called, and there is no time to look it up in a dictionary. How many lines are there in these verses: four or six in each? I cannot remember this either, perhaps three?

But then, small chapters also have a right to exist. As he used to say himself: "That's essential, too, baba!"*

If no decent book results, we shall decide like Solomon the Wise and you will have to forgive me for the book's non-publishing, and I shall remit you of the same sin.

For this book is *our* book, our joint book. True, the fate of the book largely depends not only on how it is written, but no less on how it is read.

We are co-authors.

---

\* Affectionate form of address from an older man to a younger one.

The President's Cat | 31

And we shall be jointly responsible for it.

And the book will be our meeting place.

And we are engaged in a conversation.

Sometimes we will converse as if we have just met by chance, traveling in a train and telling each other about the most varied incidents in our lives, both our own life and other people's lives. How lovely trains are! The knocking of the wheels, towns giving way to villages through the window, villages giving way to towns, day turning to night, and a long, long journey still ahead of us. We are served a cup of tea and a biscuit. We drink tea and talk and talk and talk. And we, for our part, can peep into the windows of the houses close to the railway track, observe the people. We can see them, but they cannot see us. They see only the train. And we even feel somehow embarrassed that they cannot see us, while we can peep into their windows. But what can you do about it. That's what trains are like.

But sometimes we talk as if we are travelling in a car. Countryside gives way to town, town to country, day to night. There is a long, long road ahead of us. And we can see passers-by on the street, and they can see us. They can see us and our car. How nice cars are! We do not feel embarrassed, we can see people, and they can see us. That's what cars are like, a miracle of democracy and equality.

Sometimes we will talk as if we have met by chance on an ocean liner and are telling each other things. It's a good thing to sail on a ship! We sail and sail and seem to stay in the same place, as if in a different time dimension. How nice our huge ship is! Just sea all around. Neither towns nor villages, nor houses, nor people . . . A ship is a mysterious form of transport, seemingly created according to designs by dwellers of other planets. It exists—and appears not to. Ships are seen only in port or from close up. On the seas or oceans, the ship is a Flying Dutchman. Every ship is a Flying Dutchman. A ship is unknowable, like someone deceased or not yet born. You do not see it (if it is not in a port, as I have only just said), but you know that it exists in some square, let's say in square B177, of eternity and infinity ... And you sense its closeness ... Moreover, you can always sense it, anytime you wish to.

Sometimes we will talk as if we have met on an airplane ...

But that's enough for an introduction!

For *this* introduction, which says almost nothing ...

And so, to business! Now to business! Major encounters await us!

We are counting down:

Seven!

Six!

Five!

Four!

Three!

Two!

One!

Lift off!!!

(I get the impression that this countdown has not come across sounding as cheerful, bold, and self-assured as it was supposed to be, as it was with our first emissary into space. But I suspect that even he at that moment was overcome by no lesser doubts. So, onwards we go!).

# 2

Joseph Stalin was succeeded by Nikita Khrushchev.

The new leader of the communist part of the globe soon threw down the gauntlet to world imperialism and announced the full-scale construction of communism in the USSR. But full-scale construction, especially the full-scale construction of communism, requires a hundred eyes for supervision and a hundred ears for the same purpose, for people everywhere remain people and in the Soviet Union as well.

Like a true son of his era, Khrushchev presented a face that was not merely his own personally but also partly that of Joseph Stalin and always considered the harsh demands of the moment. First and foremost, he formed a country-wide body, the USSR Party and State Inspectorate, which was charged with carrying out regular checks on the citizens and country. This body was staffed by comrades with an "unblemished record," repeatedly checked by the KGB and as reliable as if chiselled out of granite.

And so, one fine day, a group of the above-mentioned comrades arrived completely unexpectedly in Sukhumi from Moscow and turned up at the party's District Headquarters straight from the airport.

When thirty people poured into Mikhail Temurovich's office, he immediately followed the reciprocal greetings by inviting his unscheduled guests to dinner. In response, he received a cold and quite soul-chilling refusal: "We have already dined on the plane, we haven't got time, we have to conduct a comprehensive inspection of the Autonomous Republic, our time is limited, we only have a month."

After this information, Mikhail Temurovich very cordially asked about their boss: "How is Gennady Mikhailovich?"

They gave a quick answer: "Comrade Figurin is very well, but we haven't got time to chat, we have to inspect your Autonomous Republic, and we only have a month to do it."

Mikhail Temurovich pondered for a moment. The uninvited guests had confronted him with the necessity of taking an urgent decision.

"Yes, but . . . I mean, how is this going to work out?" The expression on his face, benevolently serene and affectionate, as befits a hospitable host, gave way to one of boundless amazement. "I mean, Nikita Sergeyevich and I came to an agreement . . . Comrade Khrushchev and I came to an agreement that we wouldn't be inspected this year. He talked to me personally . . . He probably forgot to mention this conversation to Comrade Figurin. Dear old Nikita Sergeyevich! He has so much to do that he could have forgotten, that's hardly surprising. People have forgotten about Germany. And now America has squeezed the life out of us . . . However, there is no point in speculating. Let's ring Nikita Sergeyevich right now." His face resumed its expression of benevolently serene affection.

Beside Mikhail Temurovich's armchair, on a table slightly lower than his writing desk, there were about twelve telephones. One of them was red in colour and gleamed like a Christmas tree decoration, a picture of the Kremlin glittered on the silver metal in the middle of its dial. The boss treated this red phone with particular respect.

The red phone differed from the others in one additional respect—it wasn't connected to anything, its cord disappeared somewhere under the table, but nobody could see where . . . It was this phone which Mikhail Temurovich picked up and "telephoned" on.

He waited two minutes for the receiver to be lifted at the other end. During these two minutes the visitors did not seem to breathe at all and sat there wide-eyed. From beyond the closed window, one could hear the singing of the birds on the branches of the mushmula and firs, just as if they were singing right in the room and sitting right on the red telephone.

Finally, Khrushchev "took up" the receiver, doubtless a receiver from the same kind of red phone, and responded to the call personally and directly, himself, with his own hand.

Mikhail Temurovich's face was glowing almost brighter than the telephone itself:

"Greetings, Nikita Sergeyevich . . ."

". . ."

"And yourself . . . Well, I hope . . ."

". . ."

"Not bad, not bad . . . And how is Nina Petrovna?"

". . ."

"Ah, so you're pining for us? Yes, I'll be coming soon. I will."

". . ."

"And me. Me as well."

". . ."

"O-o-oh."

". . ."

"Soon . . ."

". . ."

"Yes, soon . . ."

". . ."

## 36 | *Guram Odisharia*

"And when will you visit us?"

". . ."

"I've got such a special red wine for you . . . A real high-flier . . ."

". . ."

"A high-flier and not just the wine, but even . . ."

". . ."

"From Gudauta, of course. The red wine there is . . ."

". . ."

"That's such good news, Nikita Sergeyevich. I'm quite embarrassed . . ."

". . ."

"Yes . . ."

". . ."

"Yes, of course, Nikita Sergeye . . ."

". . ."

"Never mind, never mind . . ."

". . ."

"Yes, yes, they're here . . ."

". . ."

"Very nice fellows . . . From the Party and Economic Inspectorate. You're really on the ball, Nikita Sergeyevich . . . As you and I were saying about Comrade Figurin . . . Yes, yes, Gennady Maximovich . . . I also asked you . . . Yes . . ."

". . ."

"How, how?"

". . ."

"Yes, yes . . ."

". . ."

"Yes, yes . . ."

Dead silence reigned in Mikhail Temurovich's office. Khrushchev had already been "speaking" almost three minutes.

"I'll pass it on, Nikita Sergeyevich . . ."

"  . . ."

"Yes . . ."

"  . . ."

"So, it's Ajara . . ."

"  . . ."

"So, they can carry out their inspection in Ajara? Ajara?"

"  . . ."

"Yes . . ."

"  . . ."

"I'll pass it on . . ."

"  . . ."

"In other words, they can travel today. To Ajara . . ."

"  . . ."

"So they can go to Ajara today?"

"  . . ."

"Nikita Sergeyevich . . . Well, leave them with me for one day at least . . . They are guests after all . . . Besides, I've got this wine . . . But that's embarrassing. Just for a day, Nikita Sergeyevich . . ."

"  . . ."

Another lengthy silence reigned in the office, a respectful pause. Nikita Sergeyevich spoke for a further two minutes. Nothing could be heard but the twittering of the birds, and again it was as if they were not twittering outside the window, but here in the room, perched on the telephones.

"My dear . . ."

"  . . ."

"What a treasure you are . . ."

"  . . ."

"I would count it an honour . . ."

"..."

"Regards to the family, Nikita Sergeyevich, to Nina Petrovna and young Sergei..."

"..."

"Thank you, thank you..."

"..."

"Thank you. Bye for now..."

"..."

"And from me as well..."

The red telephone receiver returned to its place.

Mikhail Temurovich slowly turned to the visitors. His face bore a pensively mournful expression like Don Quixote. He spoke softly:

"Well, you heard it, esteemed sirs," he said, pointing upwards with his finger. "To cut a long story short, you have to inspect Ajara... It was very nice to meet you... What a pity that... But you'll be back to see us too sometime... Well now, I'm not letting you go so easily. For special guests we have a good supply of magnificent dark red wine, a renowned red from Kaldakhvara. It's not as heavy as some red wines, you can drink it and drink it. In short, it goes down like chocolate... And we *are* colleagues after all..."

As the First Secretary of the Regional Party Committee, Mikhail Temurovich was also the Chairman of the Abkhazian Party and Economic Inspectorate Committee.

The colleagues rose pensively to their feet. One of them, evidently the group leader, simpered:

"We've already eaten, on the plane. We haven't got time. We must conduct a comprehensive inspection of the Ajaran Autonomous Soviet Republic. We don't have much time, only a month..."

When the inspectors from the Party and Economic Inspectorate had left the room, Mikhail Temurovich turned to the Regional Party Secretary, Pyotr Krasinsky, who happened to be on the spot.

"Well, Pyotr Petrovich, Pyotr Petrovich. You see how interesting life can be . . ."

Although an unusual amount of snow had fallen in Ajara that year, it was remembered by Ajarans not as the year of the great snowfall, but as the year when the USSR Party and Economic Inspectorate came calling, the group which appeared like a bolt from the blue, descended on Ajara and then cleared off altogether.

# 3

I learnt about it from a brochure.

It was issued by the local publishing house Abkhazian Collective Farm Library as part of a popular science series.

The subject in question was the buffalo.

Only not the buffalo which advanced science studies, but the one which he alone had seen and knew. And yet it was a scholarly paper and . . . his song, his psalm, his hymn to a being more ancient than Adam.

The brochure included a foreword from the editors, and for several minutes this foreword took me back half a century.

Let's just sample it:

"The Communist Party of the Soviet Union and the Government of the Soviet Union have set the following objective: to achieve, over the next few years, a sharp rise in the output of cropping and livestock produce with a view to satisfying fully the growing demands of the population in food products and light industry. Inspired by the resolutions of the USSR Communist Party's Twentieth Congress, collective farmers, and the staff of mechanized tractor stations and state farms in the Abkhazian Autonomous Soviet Socialist Republic are continually releasing new potential with a view to bringing about a steep rise in various branches of agriculture to ensure fulfilment of the sixth five-year plan ahead of schedule.

One of the least progressive branches of stock-raising in the Abkhazian ASSR is buffalo farming. However, in Abkhazian conditions the buffalo is a valuable and, in several cases, irreplaceable animal. In view of this, attention needs to be paid to some issues bound up with prospects of developing this species."

But the real story of his buffalo was not at all like the one in this foreword. Just as he himself was not like his era or any particular era at all. Like him, his buffalo wandered in three time frames—past, present, and future—and besides roamed in other places, in an unknown dimension that was not subject to reason.

We are informed at the very beginning that nobody knows what nations first domesticated the buffalo, although it is nevertheless well known that the buffalo is depicted in Babylonian stone and pictures of it have been found in other parts of Mesopotamia.

The buffalo was most likely domesticated about five thousand five hundred or five thousand six hundred years ago (As always, he used figures to great effect, freely juggling them).

Some scientists who have scrupulously studied the structure of the buffalo' horns and skull bones, consider that its birthplace was India. Others have concluded, on the basis of many years' research into their hooves, that they originated in Mesopotamia.

However, its original habitat possibly was the island of Celebes, where even today there is a multitude of wild buffalo called Anoa.

Or maybe it was in fact Mindoro, one of the Philippine Islands (there is a Mindoro buffalo).

Generally speaking, the buffalo can be subdivided into two broad categories: African and Asian. African people are familiar with the red short-horn buffalo. But in the environs of Lake Chad, the black buffalo is more common.

There are also many wild buffalo in India, Burma, and Ceylon. The Asian buffalo is like the Asian night: tranquil, graceful, and slow.

Although African buffalo are no less graceful.

Way back before Christ, the Chinese had domesticated a brindled red buffalo.

In Japan, the buffalo are mainly short-horn. Those of Southern Europe differ from them considerably, except for Caucasian buffalo, which stand out as distinct from the latter.

And among the Caucasian buffalo, the Abkhazian variety can be singled out.

The Abkhazian buffalo is unusually sensitive. There is a popular belief that it can die from being hit by a peach stone. And nobody knows what fatal link exists between a little peach stone and a huge buffalo. Nor has anybody seen a buffalo perish from a peach stone.

Our buffalo is productive and powerful, on a special cart it can pull a load of up to two tons.

(All the same, don't throw peach stones at buffalo.)

Its legs are thick, its muscles are strong, its hooves are broad and cloven. It calmly overcomes hills and unhurriedly copes with downhill slopes, like a man rendered wise by experience.

It can serve a person for twenty to twenty-two years.

In a single year, a buffalo yields between one thousand and one thousand four hundred litres of milk, almost twice as much as a cow. Its milk is very rich in fat. Anyone who has sampled matsoni yogurt from its milk even just once will never forget its taste.

There is nothing more pleasant during a hangover.

And buffalo milk is a wonderful remedy for a sore throat; among the ordinary people it is used to fight colds.

And what about its meat . . . Let's listen to what the *big man* himself writes about it: "A kebab of smoked buffalo meat roasted on a spit is generally acknowledged to be a superb dish."

And when seasoned with adjika hot sauce, buffalo meat acquires an extraordinary taste!

I forgot to mention that buffalo matsoni yogurt is so thick that you can cut it with a knife (he once read me this brochure himself, accompanied with verbal commentary).

A buffalo's hide is rougher than a bull's and its horns are stronger. In 1956, buffalo ploughed up to 66.2 percent of Abkhazia's cultivated land (if he idealised something, he really idealised it!).

But just one or two farms won't help—buffalo farms must be established everywhere. After all there are magnificent conditions for this in Gup, and in Kindgi, and in Adzubzha, and in Kulanurkhva, and in Achandara, and in Aatsi . . .

Buffalo really like marshland; they will lie down in the green water and rub their bellies and hips against the bottom—and with such pleasure . . . Then into the marsh . . . And they will find their way to islands beyond the reach of humans or any other animal. And there they graze on the succulent grass. Or just feed in the marsh on young reeds, rushes, and swamp grass.

Unlike bulls and cows, buffalo consume dry maize stalks completely, right down to the root. They are very useful animals and very economical to keep. We should be breeding them!

If you stroke a buffalo, you may get the impression that this is not to its taste at all. But anyone familiar with its habits is well aware that buffalo are terribly fond of being caressed (especially around the neck area).

And buffalo also adore rain—it feeds the marshes.

And in Abkhazia, it rains a lot.

# 4

I once had a cat called Malka. Every time I looked around, my aquarium seemed to contain fewer fish; the fish were disappearing. I guessed that it was the work of Malka's paws, but I needed to catch her in the act.

One day I headed for the door, treading loudly, as if intending to leave the apartment. I banged the door, clicked the lock, and hid right there by the wardrobe. Then, quiet as a mouse, on tiptoe, I sneaked towards the living room. I saw that Malka, thinking that I had gone out, had her paw in the aquarium—it was "fishing time."

Mikhail Temurovich reminded me of a cat. He was affectionate in his own way and cunning in his own way. Only he was like the very best cuddly, affectionate cat, combined with the best traits of the very best dog.

# 5

In Bgazhba's day, when he was the First Secretary, I was chair of the collective farm in the village of Tsebelda, Gulripshi District. Let me tell you about one incident. It was the time of maize harvesting, and the entire village was out in the fields. We were snapping off the maize heads, the plan was hanging over us, and we had to fulfil it. I found myself continually "on the wheels," up and down the hills, around the fields. The weather was good, sunny, with no hindrance at all from rain.

To cut a long story short, I was treated to some chacha schnaps by one of the teams and returned to the office very drunk. On the road, I almost crashed into a tree with my Willys jeep. My driver was even more drunk than I was, and I had taken the wheel myself, while he, of course, was sleeping on the back seat.

The office building was old, and we were all accommodated in one room, while the other room stored hay. I had a bookkeeper, quiet but wily, and a shady operator who continually dreamt of taking my job. He claimed to be educated and boasted about it. He had some sort of document implying he had graduated from some sort of college. And that was why he blathered on about me not having completed higher education. In short, he had his eyes set on my job.

Look, I told that bookkeeper: "I'm drunk out of my skull. I'll just go and have a nap there in the hay, and, to whoever asks for me, say I'm out in the fields and then I might go to the District HQ on business."

"Yes," he said. "Of course, whatever you say."

I collapsed in the hay and fell asleep. When I awoke, it was already evening. I got up and went into my room. My

The President's Cat | 47

bookkeeper was sitting there writing something and clicking the beads of his abacus. Didn't anyone inquire after me, I asked. Yes, they did—"Bgazhba came by and asked for you." And he just said it without raising his head . . . "So, what happened?" I gasped. "I couldn't lie to him . . ." "And?" I asked. "He's there in the next room," I told him. "Then what?" "He went in and saw you snoring in the hay. In a nutshell, he left instructions that you were to present yourself tomorrow morning at Regional HQ. And he also said that you had plainly been drinking chacha, even the hay reeked of it. 'He must be a hefty drinker,' that's what he said."

Well, I was done for—what have you done to me, damn you! Twitch and twitch I might, but there was no way I was going to kill him. I had only ever met Bgazhba once, at a banquet. What possessed him, a man occupying such a lofty post, to call on my crummy collective farm? I was more afraid of District Committee and District Executive Committee personnel and hardly imagined that Mikhail Bgazhba himself would favour us with a visit! No, never! But as a rule, he was good at such stunts, unexpectedly descending on you like a sudden snowfall and, in this case, on such a nonentity. If the situation interested him, that was that.

To cut a long story short, the next morning I arrived, knees trembling, at Regional HQ, for Bgazhba had summoned me. I was sure that my career was over, that I would certainly be stripped of my post, no question about it: a collective farm chairman snoozing in the hay after guzzling vodka during harvest time, during the day, in bright sunshine or, to be more precise, right at midday. He walked in and, if you could have seen me then—I could barely put two words together. Bgazhba asked me about this and that, then talked about the plan, then about the weather, then about khashi soup and so-bering up. But about yesterday's incident—not a word! And I kept waiting and waiting, any second now he's going to let me have it or right this minute . . . But, as if nothing were the matter, he talked about completely different matters. And in the end: "Well, off you go and get on with your job."

"Mikhail Temurovich, is that all you have to say to me?" I bleated, having got as far as the doorway.

"Yes, there's just one other thing. I didn't like the look of your bookkeeper. He's not a good man, it seemed to me. You should transfer him somewhere. Have a think about it."

I flew out of the Regional HQ like an arrow, back to the collective farm. As soon as I got there, I immediately let him have it: "We can't work together, chum."

He did not argue but got up quietly and quietly left.

# 6

They say Fidel Castro never came to Sukhumi. What are they talking about? Of course he came. But only a few people know about it, almost nobody in fact.

It is no secret that Fidel visited Pitsunda, but what about Sukhumi?

It happened like this. I was working then as part of Bgazhba's security team. Hardly anyone noticed us, such was the way we worked our routine. Not like now, when whole teams of bodyguards look after some barely known bureaucrat. The times were different. They were good times.

Khrushchev had brought Castro to Pitsunda. One day they were invited to Lykhny. The toastmaster, of course, was Bgazhba. Mzhavanadze was also there. They were drinking red Lykhny wine. Temurovich handed a drinking horn of pure Alaverdi wine to Fidel Castro. I can't remember what the toast was. Castro was already pretty soused and flatly refused to drink out of a horn. Khrushchev, who was already legless, was pleading: "Give it to me. These Cubans don't know how to drink." And gallantly tried to "drink to brotherhood," arms interlocked, with the First Secretary of the Gudauta district Party Committee, Dmitry Khvartskia. But even Khrushchev was unable to drink the horn to the very end and spilled half of it on Khvartskia. Dmitry Andreyevich was clad in a white tussore suit, and the wine turned all his apparel red. He looked as if he had been wounded, soaked in blood. Khrushchev was wearing a Ukrainian style shirt and white trousers. He was also looking bloodied. Red wine was dripping from both. Khrushchev's security team took him away to his holiday home at Pitsunda. And Khvartskia went home as did Mzhavanadze, he drained the same horn and left.

But Castro stayed on.

It was one o'clock in the morning.

Bgazhba was pestering Castro: "You haven't seen Sukhumi. Let's go. You'll see what sort of city it is. It's like Havana. We also have examples of colonial architecture. We can view everything in an hour since you're leaving the day after tomorrow. It could be several years before you come to Abkhazia again. Let's go. You'll see what a great city Sukhumi is!"

He won Castro over and talked the Central Committee security team into it, and that wasn't easy.

We made our way to Sukhumi covertly, like guerrillas. We had three vehicles: Fidel's security team, Temurovich's security team, an interpreter, and Mikhail Temurovich's deputies.

It was 2:30 a.m., and we were still strolling along the Sukhumi embankment. The city was asleep, no one on the streets. But we, the security team, were on the ball, all eyes and ears.

From the port we walked as far as the drama theatre.

"Well, what do you think of it? Is it a nice town—Sukhumi?"

"It truly is, extraordinary," Fidel replied, tugging at his beard.

Suddenly, by the fountain close to the theatre, with its gryphons and other monsters, the midnight silence was broken by a chorus of frogs. The fountain had been switched off and was not making any noise, and, therefore, the croaking of the frogs soared to the very heavens. I was amazed. I had never heard frogs there before. The city facilities management services must have done a poor job, or else there would hardly be croaking in the city centre, would there? The fountain had not been looked after.

Fidel could not conceal his surprise: surely they weren't frogs, or did it just appear so?

Of course, Bgazhba was not expecting an encounter with frogs either, but he kept his wits about him: "They are our pride and joy, our sacral frogs, and therefore they live near the sights of the city." Then he spoke at length about the rare breed of frog found only in Abkhazia: "They are our aboriginals. This kind of frog is called a 'guest frog.'"

The Cuban, who was a great connoisseur of delicacies from frog meat, instantly believed Mikhail Temurovich: "What fantastic frogs you have!"

Incidentally, several years later, when Bgazhba was no longer First Secretary, he put out a scientific work about frogs, a small book. If I am not mistaken, here, too, he mentions in passing this aboriginal "guest frog."

So, when they say that Fidel Castro did not come to Sukhumi, don't believe them. Fidel *did* come to Sukhumi; I swear on the soul of my mother. He was there, and only a few people know about it. Of these people, I am the only one still living. Though that's not quite so, there is Fidel and I. So, if anyone asks Fidel if he has been to Sukhumi, I am sure he will reply that he has. If he can't remember, ask him about the frogs in front of the theatre, the frogs in the gryphon fountain, the "guest frogs." And you will see he is sure to recall that evening.

# 7

"One of my mates had a German shepherd dog, which was getting on in years.

One day my mate brought home a puppy, also a German shepherd.

He set up a separate kennel in the back yard and made it a member of his household, too.

The old dog took offence at this, seemingly her masters no longer needed her. So she left home.

She became a bazaar dog. She got fed there and she served the bazaar in her own way.

But if she saw any of the members of her own former family, she would lick them all over and, without retreating a step, escort them all the way home but, in spite of the entire family spilling out into the street, stroking her and urging her into the yard, she would go back to the bazaar again.

She considered herself mortally offended.

She loved the family very much, but, great as this love may have been, she could not forgive their offence.

Here's to the pride of that dog! Everyone should drink this glass to the dregs! And do so standing up!"

# 8

"So we were sitting in the fortress completely surrounded by the enemy and waiting for the enemy to charge at us. We shook hands with one another for the last time and squeezed the weapons in our hands harder.

The enemy did not show.

And when the bread and water, courage and patience had run out, we left the fortress, cast away our weapons, and surrendered.

But it turned out that the enemy had long departed, and we were sitting and feasting on the banks of a radiant, pure river in the shade of century-old trees. Feasting and bringing out toasts, including toasts in our own honour.

And we began to tremble and weep ... And we wept and we trembled, and we did not thank the Lord."

## 9

"On the first day, bathing in the sea should be continued for two to three minutes and, on subsequent days, gradually increased to ten and even to fifteen minutes. It is possible to bathe once a day, only people with a very sound health may bathe twice a day, but at an interval of three to four hours."

("Doctor's advice", 1937)

## 10

I used to work for the Gulripshi district newspaper. I once published a small piece about an eagle caught in the mountains of Abkhazia. I wrote that its wingspan was two metres and eighty centimetres. My article was reprinted by the regional newspaper. Except that the regional paper published that the eagle's wingspan was three metres and eighty centimetres. Within two weeks, one of the Tbilisi newspapers reported: "In Abkhazia an eagle has been captured with a wingspan of four metres and eighty centimetres."

Vianor Pachulia sent this information on to Moscow, to the journal "Around the World." The piece was published. Except that this time, and now for the final time, the eagle's wingspan had "attained" seven metres and eighty centimetres.

Foreign specialists flew into Sukhumi on the trail of the information from "Around the World." They asked to be shown this wonder, the No. 1 eagle in the whole world.

The foreign specialists were met by Vianor Pandzhovich and Mikhail Temurovich.

"Unfortunately, the eagle has flown away," announced Mikhail Temurovich with a sorrowful mien.

And, just as profoundly saddened, Vianor Pandzhovich confirmed his words.

Then Pandzhovich told the foreign visitors:

"However, we have reliable data about a "snow man." The "snow man" dwelt in the environs of Lake Ritsa, and his burial place is somewhere there."

The specialists and Vianor Pandzhovich spent a month searching for the grave of the "snow man" but without success.

# 11

"A stroke of genius!" said Mikhail Temurovich with a guffaw. "If he did it on purpose, he's simply a genius!"

This was said about a little-known poet, after he had read a word of welcome from the stage of a Sukhumi theatre at an evening jubilee celebration for a widely renowned writer. With a cheerful energetic stride, he approached the microphone, took from his pocket a sheet of paper folded four times, unfolded it, and proclaimed at full volume with artistic pathos:

"Two piglets, four turkeys, ten chickens . . ." Everyone, including the hero of the day, froze for an instance. Then the hall erupted in guffaws.

It turned out that that poet had been entrusted not only with the address of welcome, but also with the organisation of the festive banquet, and, weary from the daily run-around, he had mistaken a grocery list for the text of his welcome speech.

## 12

"Oh, my Europe, aged and eternally young, wise, and cultured! You know nothing about my satsivi and adjika sauces, my mineral waters and wines, elargi and khachapuri cheese breads. You know nothing about our toasts and our Academy of Conviviality.

I see you often, almost every day, while for you . . . It is as if through a glass darkly I see you, but as for you seeing me—nothing at all!

Just ask for once, how am I getting on here, what distresses me, what delights me . . . Tell me, what have I done wrong, what have I done right . . ."

## 13

A homeless puppy started to frequent our common yard. Because he was black, we named him Pele. He was an affectionate dog, continually fussing around somebody, big or small, and trying to lick everybody's hands.

Then one day he was hit by a car.

He died like a child, his whole body trembling and breathing rapidly.

At that moment, Mikhail Temurovich appeared from somewhere. He knelt in front of the pup, stroked its head, caressed it, and said something to it. Pele died in his arms.

Mikhail Temurovich got up and left us without saying a word.

When I attended Mikhail Temurovich's funeral, I saw that his body was shod in rather worn out shoes, and my heart skipped a beat. The day Pele died he was wearing the very same shoes.

## 14

We invited the well-known journalist Kuznetsov to the "Merkheuli" restaurant. On seeing the huge wine vessels half-buried in the ground by the restaurant entrance, he turned to Mikhail Temurovich and said:

"When I was here a year ago, I think they were a bit smaller."

"They've grown," responded Mikhail Temurovich. "They're made of clay, so they gradually expand if you keep them in the ground."

"How is that?" asked Kuznetsov, who was amazed.

"Well, they just expand," said the restaurant owner, backing Mikhail Temurovich up. "Come back next year and you'll see."

# 15

In his book "Songbirds of Abkhazia," he wrote: "The Abkhazian thrush sings eighteen distinct melodies. In other regions, a bird like this can sing only five to seven."

In the same book, he attributed the traits of some parrot to the Abkhazian thrush.

This information caused a great flurry among ornithologists. A host of letters from them arrived in Abkhazia, some of them even reaching Sukhumi.

But he attempted to justify himself: "The shortcomings of my book are all Kapanadze's fault, he didn't proofread it properly."

# The President's Cat

He opened both the blinds on one window. Then on the other window, too. The office was pervaded by the warm cool of the winter sea.

It was January 1962. Or, more precisely, January 13. By then, He was already on friendly terms with the number 13. Earlier it had somehow set him on edge.

A day earlier, he had left the city in quite a different state, pacified and content. But on the thirteenth, the sun had come out early in the morning and the white, white snow sparkled even more brightly. The blue sky gleamed still bluer because of the snow, the snow was even more blinding, even the sun's rays were excessively, simply quite cosmetically, pink, also because of the sea, the snow, and the sun itself.

Incidentally, it is because of this blue and their rich green and pink colours that seaside towns resemble beautiful women. And not just beautiful women, but women in general, especially when these and other colours are supplemented by that of freshly fallen snow.

I don't just like snow-covered seaside towns—I love them. In these towns, the briefest moments blend with one another, the whole world shrinks and becomes so endearing, and people look stranger than strange, intoxicated by their populous loneliness.

The President's Cat | 63

As a rule, if the pronoun "I" is mentioned in the chapters of this book which are entitled "The President's Cat," you can be sure that this "I" refers to me, the author. The "I" in all the other chapters (that is, the numbered ones) refers to quite a variety of people. I have merely jotted down incidents from their lives (and I mean merely), while the incidents with the President's Cat I narrate myself (in my own name!). Not surprisingly, therefore, writing about what happened to others was easy, but writing about the President's Cat was difficult. And how many years now have I kept tormenting myself. Several times I abandoned those chapters about the Cat, but a certain alter ego that has settled within me in recent years gives me no peace, awakes me every time long before daybreak and commands: "Write, write . . ." I already seriously suspect, is it not he, that someone—he? But, you know, I am somehow not entirely sure about this . . .

And so, it was the morning of January 13, 1962, the eve of the Old New Year.

While I was talking about this and that, he had already opened the third window of the office. He was alone in the room and, therefore, waved his hand as a sign of greeting to the sea, which was shining like a dolphin's spine, and shifted his gaze to the fluffy white blobs amidst the greenery of the trees in the seaside park.

Before him lay the most blessed and the, at the same time (and primarily for this reason), biggest and smallest city in the world. Eternally palpitating and pensively quiet. I think a city is only yours when you no longer rush away from it to some other place. You live there and walk around it with a sort of pampered disposition, with a sensation that your home is unshakeable. It is through the absence of such sensations in other parts of the Earth that a man's eye and heart distinguish his hometown.

The city is a place for observation and scrutiny via countless rapid alien glances. Especially in summer. And a resort town more than anywhere. It is full, even in winter, of mischievous ghostly glances of the most varied kind, streaming, gleaming . . . Except for one difference, summer glances are relaxed if watchful, while winter glances are calmer and more unfettered, as it were.

In fact, he did not see, but knew, that a little way off, down by the launch jetty, on the tables of the coffee bar, old men had set out chess pieces on boards and were probably already playing. He could even visualise them, the pensive biblical elders of the town, with voices muffled by snow, and he felt the desire to be there with them. An unendurable desire. But he ought to have been in his office, he was after all the No. 1 man in Abkhazia. Besides, a meeting was soon to take place. A conference with the No. 1, that is, with him. An important meeting.

And that morning, as he had done quite often of late, he thought of the possibility of the impossible, of what was impossible according to all laws and rules and could nevertheless occur, happen, be fulfilled . . . After all, it is impossible now to travel in time, but tomorrow it may suddenly be possible, and to go back into the past, to many centuries ago . . . Only quite recently it was impossible for mankind to fly up into the sky, to walk on the moon, but it has nevertheless become possible.

He looked at the world map on the office wall, glanced fleetingly at the rivers and countries well known to him and checked if the cities were in their right place or not. The names of the rivers meandered along the whole length of their courses, while the mountain peaks, owing to the lack of space, were only numbered. "It's good to be a river," he smiled. "And I don't want to be a city at all. When you are a river, you are called by your full name and you flow your own sweet way, spreading out over the earth. You journey on, calmly observing your banks."

And barely had he taken a second look at the seashore and the town, that he noticed an unfamiliar little bird sitting on the windowsill, greenish yellow and miniscule. He remembered, it is that bird, the one that will not be able to fly if it puts on even a single extra gram. Before he could give any thought to this, the bird disappeared.

What sprang to mind was the verse by Morev, the eternally popular Kostya Morev. This Morev had come to Sukhumi from some seaside town. He knew by heart, it could be said, the whole canon of Russian poetry (and not just Russian). He would stroll along the embankment and, more often than not, recite Pushkin's "hooligan" verses. Those who regularly frequented the embankment laughed and shoved money into Kostya's pocket for wine and vodka. And because people liked his creative work, he delivered a mountain of entirely new verse with lightning speed. Thus, for example, when Nikita Khrushchev declared: "We will catch up with and overtake the United States of America in the production of milk and meat," the next morning, by the launch jetty, Kostya declaimed at the top of his voice by the colonnade:

> In milk production we have matched America and quick,
> But in meat we just can't make it since our bull has sprained
> his dick.

On the following morning, mentioned in the special bulletin sent to Mikhail Temurovich every day from the KGB, this "poem" by Kostya also lay on the table. Mikhail Temurovich laughed long and, like the entire embankment, immediately learnt it by heart. The same evening, he told the KGB chief: "Don't take Morev seriously, he's insane. If he wasn't insane, he would hardly have done something like that. You must be aware that his mind has been affected by an unhappy love affair and now he lives like a tramp around the Black Sea coast . . ." The KGB chief did not know the details of his background and was amazed how Mikhail Temurovich knew so much, and even felt a little sorry for poor Kostya.

I was still a boy back then, but even now I remember Kostya Morev well and the poetic fireworks he set off on the Sukhumi promenade.

On this morning, Mikhail Temurovich was brought the usual daily bulletin from the Ministry of Internal Affairs. More precisely, the report was already waiting for him on the table. Overnight, an eighteen-year-old lad had been stabbed to death with a knife on the promenade. His body was found under the eucalyptus growing by the Blue Library, not far from the mouth of the Besletka River.

The bulletin said that it was snowing when the young man was killed. It was snowing, and at that moment he was killed! It was snowing, and they killed a man! They killed him with a foul blow (or someone killed him alone), stabbing him several times, in the chest, in the belly, in the leg . . .

The eucalyptus was highly visible from the office. But the library was not. The huge snow-covered eucalyptus looked more like balloons.

The President's Cat | 67

Then he rang the Minister of Internal Affairs: "Why don't you divulge who was killed, release his name?" The Minister said: "We'll let you know soon. We still haven't identified him."

He strode up and down the room several times. The way people begin to walk up and down before a journey, when they are setting off for somewhere far away. They may be just walking around a room, but, in reality, they are already on their way—a long, long way from home.

He rang a friend, the one with whom he had been invited out yesterday by a certain family. The night before, he had drunk too much brandy. In the morning, he was awakened by the sound of breathing. His eyes instantly squinted in fear: a German shepherd was standing over him and sniffing his hand, touching it with a moist nose. Then it licked his face. He gathered his courage and opened his eyes. How the dog had ended up in the room he did not know, did not remember. He had been home alone these past few days. He then managed with a struggle to grasp the notion that he was very fond of dogs—and German shepherds more than any. The dog realised this and began to lick him more vigorously.

He got up and took some salami out of the fridge. The dog sniffed it but did not touch it. He complimented it on being such an ecologically educated animal.

But the friend informed him: "The host gave you the dog. Surely you remember?" But he said: "I must take it back; we can't live together. It won't eat salami . . ."

After conferring, he indicated with a gesture that the City Chief Executive, Dmitry Khvartskia, should stay behind. When they were eye to eye with each other, he asked: "Why don't you hand over the flat?" "Who to?" It was as if Khvartskia did not understand. "So you don't know? To *that* woman."

"Which woman?" "Grechko's mistress." Dmitry Khvartskia unhurriedly opened a new pack of cigarettes. And smiled like a child opening a box of chocolates. Dmitry Khvartskia lit up, looked him in the eye and calmly said:

"Look, Mikhail Temurovich, let's come to an agreement. Here are the keys. Go to the city council building, sit in my place, and issue an order yourself for a flat for that whore."

Again he smiled.

"Dima, look at it from my angle. What am I to do? He telephoned the marshal himself. After all, he is the army's commander-in-chief..."

And then, for some reason, he added:

"If I ever write my memoirs, I'll write them in the style of a military dispatch, with short sentences..."

And he shrugged his shoulders.

"Sometimes I appear to be living in a diary, my own and someone else's and written entirely in short sentences... And our dialogue will be recorded there."

And he laughed.

When he had let Dmitry Khvartskia go, his secretary brought in a fresh piece of information: the man killed on the promenade was a football player in the Sukhumi Dynamo club. He remembered him, number ten. That footballer had played in the forward line, number ten. He was quite often on the booze in the "Ritsa" restaurant. And that night he was sitting with his mate; they had been squabbling over something with visitors from Gagra and Gali. It was the latter that the investigation suspected of the murder.

Snow was falling ,and a man had been killed.

And suddenly he leapt up from his armchair: "Why, yes, it was Valera, Zinaida's boy."

The President's Cat | 69

He called for a car. He turned down a Volga and demanded a Chaika limousine. This Chaika spun him round the city for a whole hour. He looked at the snow-covered streets and at the pedestrians. He went up on the cable-car and visited Mayak, a new suburb. Light snow fell from time to time.

He stopped the car on Pushkin Street, not far from the medical centre. It was there that Zinaida generally sold seeds from morning to evening, and she lived nearby. He got out of the car and crossed the footpath and the yard. Zinaida lived in a tiny house along with her daughter and Valera.

Before he entered the house, his nose was assaulted by the smell of fried fish. Zinaida was cooking barabulka on a primus stove.

"Mikhail Temurovich!" she greeted him joyfully.

Zinaida still knew nothing about the death of her son.

"Zinaida Nikolayevna . . . Well, how are you? I hadn't seen you on the street and wondered if you were unwell."

Even though they had been friends almost since childhood, they always addressed each other by name and patronymic.

"I don't feel altogether well, Mikhail Temurovich. You know what it's like. The rheumatism is killing me."

"That's because you don't move around much, Nikolayevna. It'll be the death of you.

How many times have I told you, you need to do more walking?"

He realised he would not be able to tell her about her son.

Zinaida had somehow begun to resemble the photo from her own passport. Even in this guise he liked her.

He sat for half an hour at her place and ate some fried barabulka. He noticed that the longer he stayed with her, the more the wrinkles disappeared from her face.

On saying goodbye, Zinaida complained to him that her cat had gone missing.

"Well, let it go missing, only pray that it's still alive. In ancient Egypt, when a cat was dying, its owners would shave their eyebrows," he smiled.

And Zinaida smiled, too.

In the late evening, he sat in the restaurant of the "Abkhazia" Hotel, in a booth with friends. That day, more than any time, he needed both friends and a restaurant. From time to time, he opened the booth door slightly and looked out into the hall. He also needed these unfamiliar people, who were enjoying themselves here. Perhaps even more than his friends and the restaurant crowd itself.

The Birdman Lukich appeared in the broad restaurant window as he passed along the street. He felt like asking someone to bring Lukich into the restaurant but thought better of it.

A self-satisfied laugh resounded in the hall. He found out that it was some petty bureaucrat. His voice sounded as if he alone had created that part of the world which was known as the "Abkhazia" restaurant.

"There are flat bottomed boats which skim easily across shallow water or go where a ship cannot sail," he thought. "And how many flat-bottomed people there are in the world . . ."

And he was reminded again of the lad killed during the night.

Without warning an unknown tipsy couple entered their booth. The woman resembled a queen from a pack of cards and the man was like a jack. The Queen and the Jack apologised and wanted to withdraw immediately; they had gone through the wrong door. He wouldn't let them: "You are guests of our city, and we are pining for guests. Nobody has called on us

The woman was giggling, the man fidgeted in his chair with a tipsy meekness.

He proposed a toast which was appropriate for the moment.

"Let's drink to the harmony that descends when the woman is beautiful, and the man is drunk!"

Everyone drank in silence to "the harmony."

Soon, the Queen began tenderly buzzing in the Jack's ear: "You're a non-believer, you say. You don't believe. You don't pray." And the Jack responded: "Three times today I have shared greetings with good people. Surely that's equivalent to a prayer?"

The next toast was to these three good encounters.

Then he explained to the Queen and Jack: "If you are the Queen and the Jack, then I am the Ace."

"You must be the manager of a food store," they responded.

"Almost right," chortled the revellers.

One of the drunken guests in the banquet hall was almost chewing the microphone: "Hurray for good old Ochamchire! Nowhere in the world it's superior!"

Offering the Queen a banana, he announced to those at the table: "There is nothing in this world sexier and more frightening than a fruit. Why otherwise would the military refer to grenades as lemons, apricots, and grapefruit?"

"What about bananas?" someone asked.

"Humankind will soon invent something resembling a banana," he assured the company. "And for pineapples, too."

Someone opened the door slightly and shut it with lightning speed.

"Aha, they got scared. They recognised us," he said.

"Are they so scared of a food-store manager?" asked the Queen and the Jack in unison. "What did you imagine? We're in the Caucasus," came a guffaw from the table.

And he rose and made the following toast:

"When life comes to an end, one door closes, but another one immediately opens, the next door, and we look in there in fear: what awaits us beyond that door? When the door closes, there is one sound, when it opens, there's a different sound. The door escorts those departing with one voice and greets newcomers with another. Let us drink to "the Door," to doors! The doors that close and open."

Late at night, when they were leaving the restaurant, he remembered some African tree and, restraining the departing Queen and Jack by the sleeve, loudly told the guests and hosts:

"The leaves of these trees are eaten by elephants and giraffes, but when the amount of foliage is catastrophically reduced and the trees are on the verge of extinction, their leaves become poisonous, and then the elephants and giraffes can't eat them. After a certain time, when the trees have regained their balance, their leaves multiply and again become suitable as food."

His words bestrewed the snow-covered streets of the town like peacock feathers . . .

And the guests and hosts walked on with such radiant faces, as if they had only just emerged from the tender waves of an August sea.

# 16

Tadao Kasio was a Japanese billionaire.

Mikhail Temurovich made his acquaintance in Moscow, in the hall of the Cosmos Hotel at an international symposium during one of the recesses.

Tadao and his assistant were drinking Ceylon tea between bites of a tula cinnamon bun.

Mikhail Temurovich joined the "cosmic" tea party. As a rule, he was not very fond of tea and, moreover, had maintained all his life that tea and tobacco had done more harm to Abkhazia than anything else and had sucked all the juices out of the land. He blamed Russia for the cultivation of tea in Abkhazia and Turkey for the tobacco. Tea had deprived our women of health and tobacco had done the same for the men, he said.

As for himself he liked only bilberry tea.

"Do you like Ceylon tea?" he asked Tadao Kasio through an interpreter.

Mikhail already knew who Tadao Kasio was, a billionaire who had been successful in the tea business.

Tadao and his assistant smiled simultaneously and nodded to their new drinking companion.

"What you have . . . O.K.," answered Tadao or something like that.

"It's obvious you haven't drunk anything better," said Mikhail Temurovich, or something like that, and took a minute to bring a waxed paper packet out of his pocket.

In this packet of his was tea.

"Where is this tea from?" asked Tadao Kasio.

"It's tea from Abkhazia," replied Mikhail Temurovich.

Tadao Kasio had no idea what Abkhazia was and even less an idea where it was located.

"Abkhazian tea," Mikhail Temurovich repeated. "We call it Ushguli tea."

Tadao knew nothing about Ushguli, either.

"Ushguli is our Fujiyama," Mikhail Temurovich explained to him. "It's in the Caucasus!"

Something was gradually dawning on Tadao Kasio's brain, like the rays of sunlight at daybreak on Fujiyama.

"We, unlike you, have several Fujiyamas," Mikhail Temurovich explained more specifically.

Tadao Kasio's faculties of reasoning finally lit up.

Then he was offered "Ushguli tea." Tadao Kasio politely agreed to try it as did his assistant.

The Ushguli tea stood out for its unusual aroma. As he drank, Tadao Kasio was contemplating some point in the far distance. Mikhail Temurovich could not understand whether Kasio liked the Ushguli tea or not.

"It was the favourite drink of our Caucasian samurai. We have recreated it, preserved it . . ."

The Japanese billionaire kept gazing at a far-distant spot, while unhurriedly drinking the Ushguli tea.

"Only our water and our air can endow this tea with its perfect taste and aroma," said Mikhail Temurovich.

It did not occur to him to ask what Tadao Kasio thought of the Ushguli tea.

He invited him to Abkhazia.

And on that they parted.

Ten days later he received a telegram from Kasio: "July 9 arrive Sukhumi. Tadao Kasio."

"Sosik, he's flying in!" He burst into the laboratory of the Bebeisiri Academy, waving the telegram. "What a maniac! In two days he'll be here, Sosik, my dear scholar! We urgently need some Ushguli tea."

At the mention of "Ushguli tea" Soso Kapanadze realised who was coming and turned pale.

"Never fear, Sosik. We've got bilberry and dried mandarin petals and tea! Away with Shevardnadze's husks! Long live Ushguli tea!"

But the pallor did not depart from Soso Kapanadze's face.

And yet a few minutes later, side by side with Mikhail Temurovich, he was rooting through glass-fronted cabinets, gathering up jars, getting some crockery ready.

"He's coming, Iosif Spiridonovich, he's coming. And I didn't think he would . . . What a maniac . . . How was I supposed to know? The things life throws up!" Mikhail Temurovich kept reiterating.

By evening, the Ushguli tea was ready, created from a recipe by Mikhail Temurovich: 30 percent dried mandarin petals,

10 percent desiccated blue bilberries (the main component of "Ushguli tea," brought from Svanetia), and the remaining 60 percent—scrupulously selected Georgian tea.

The next morning, the staff poured the miniscule tea seedlings onto the Bebeisiri Academy's testing trays. They were seedlings of ordinary Georgian tea, which were destined to become Ushguli tea after Tadao Kasio crossed the academy's threshold.

"They'll guess, Mikhail Temurovich, they'll guess that it's Georgian tea and nothing more," Soso Kapanadze agonised.

"It's Ushguli tea. The main thing is to get it into your head that it's Ushguli tea, and everything will be fine . . . Then he will also believe that it's Ushguli. He's a man of the Japanese tradition. He cannot think otherwise."

Tadao Kasio, his assistants, and tea tasters flew in at Babushera airport. Mikhail Temurovich met the visitors accompanied by a suite of four Volga saloon cars.

Following reciprocal greetings, they all took off in the direction of Achigvara, towards Bebeisiri Lake.

Mikhail Temurovich and Tadao Kasio sat in the back seat of a Volga. Beside the driver was an interpreter. Through the window, Tadao Kasio viewed the mountains of Abkhazia and looked for the Abkhazian Fujiyama.

"We haven't got the time, Tadao-san, or else we would show you some icy peaks," said Mikhail Temurovich, second-guessing what Tadao Kasio was thinking of.

The Japanese billionaire really did not have time.

"My grandmother was a highlander, a Svan—that's a local group of people," he explained to his guest. "That's where they first developed Ushguli tea. It was in the first half of the second century before records began. Ushguli tea is a warrior drink,

The President's Cat | 77

which enhances human courage and increases male strength seven-fold."

Within half an hour they were already on the shores of Bebeisiri Lake. The hosts, natives of Gali region, had laid a remarkable table for forty guests, adorned with dishes of the purest, highest culinary art, right on the Korofa Peninsula.

"What does Korofa mean?" the interpreter asked.

"It means 'love' in the Mingrelian language. That's what Mikhail Temurovich christened the Peninsula," answered Soso Kapanadze.

"He also discovered it," Mikhail Temurovich added.

"And he discovered it," Soso Kapanadze echoed.

"Well, now let's try the tea," said Tadao Kasio. "We fly out tomorrow at daybreak."

"First, we must relax at the table, all together, and then have tea! That's the local tradition," said Mikhail Temurovich.

"Well, if that's the case . . ." Tadao Kasio smiled and shrugged his shoulders.

Elargi, satsivi, khachapuri, a kid boiled in milk, gebzhalia spicy sauce . . . Tadao Kasio was totally bewildered.

"Try this first, Tadao-san, then this, and, after that, the dish on the Japanese tray."

Mikhail Temurovich strove to assist his newly acquired friend.

Right from the start, Tadao Kasio refused to drink wine. "But it's our tradition, honoured down through the centuries, and traditions are sacred," retorted a whole chorus of diners. Of course, Mikhail Temurovich played the solo part.

The billionaire laid down his Japanese weapons, but with an imperceptible gesture he forbade his tea tasters to drink. That day he drank almost seven glasses himself.

When the toastmaster, Mikhail Temurovich—well, who else could be the toastmaster?

As a rule, in this book and in that life, there and then, if a table was laid anywhere, he, Mikhail Temurovich, and only he, served as toastmaster.

In short, when the toastmaster proposed the first toast, to the guests and hosts, Tadao Kasio asked what was happening.

"Tradition!" How many times did that word resound that day?

"You have a tradition of drinking tea. It is our tradition to pour wine," Mikhail Temurovich tried to convince his opponent with the gravest argument.

"With a cup of tea, you are more inclined to keep silent, but we make toasts when we pour wine," he added after a while. "Your silence and our talk are equally conducive to rapprochement and mutual understanding between people."

The spontaneous applause drowned out the voices of all the songbirds and non-singing birds in the environs of Bebeisiri Lake.

The next toast was to friendship between the Japanese and Soviet people. As he remarked, these nations had been friendly since time immemorial, since the sixth to seventh centuries BCE, although there were other hypotheses according to which this friendship dated back to the twelfth to fourteenth centuries BCE. Then he sorrowfully relayed the misunderstandings during Second World War and added that while they were a test of our friendship and our mutual affection, nevertheless, they withstood all the trials without wavering in the least.

"And I fought, too, back then," said Tadao Kasio.

"I also fought, only on the western front," said Mikhail Temurovich.

"I, too, fought on the western front."

"How could that be?" Mikhail Temurovich was taken aback.

"Our west is your east." A smiling Tadao Kasio set his mind at ease.

"You weren't a kamikaze by any chance?" asked Mikhail Temurovich.

"If I had been a kamikaze, I wouldn't be sitting at this table," said Tadao Kasio, laughing.

The others laughed, too.

"Kamikadze is a Georgian surname," said Mikhail Temurovich. "In the town of Gali there are twelve Kamikadze families."

"Kamikaze means 'divine wind,'" said Tadao Kasio.

"And exactly the same in Mingrelian," said Mikhail Temurovich, "only in a different order: wind divine, like that. In Abkhazian, kamikaze sounds different . . ."

While he was trying to remember what "kamikaze" sounded like in Abkhazian, a nice coincidence was revealed. Tadao Kasio and Mikhail Temurovich were born on the same day of the same year, on December 7, 1917, only in different corners of the world, one in the village of Ueda in Japan, the other in the rural settlement of Gup in Abkhazia.

"But I have a different day and a different year registered in my passport. They got them mixed up. The revolution was starting, Tadao-san. Confusion, disorder. A lot of folks were bewildered. Indeed, some have remained like that to this day, bewildered. And so, they registered my birth as 1915 in the document," declared Mikhail Temurovich.

The seventh toast he proposed in honour of songbirds and mute fish. The birds and fish of the Black Sea and the birds and fish of the Sea of Japan.

And after several toasts he added: "Your sake is similar to our Khokka wine, as complex and diffuse as Asian verse."

"Yes, but what about Omar Khayam?" asked Tadao Kasio in the tone of an examiner.

"Omar Khayam's verse is also quite diffuse, but only in the original. In translation, it is abridged, especially in Japanese translation," responded Mikhail Temurovich, at no loss as to what to say. "Have you read Omar Khayam in Persian, Tadao-san?"

Tadao-san had not read Omar Khayam in Persian. It should be noted that he did not even know the Persian language.

"A pity . . . I'll give you the opportunity now to hear it in the original."

And he read Omar Khayam's verse to his guest, the other guests, the hosts, the birds, and the fish, to Lake Bebeisiri and the Black Sea, the mountains, the clouds . . . He read Omar Khayam to all of them in a language which had not only remained unknown up until that day but had not even existed.

"Sake bears itself like a falling star in the night: it flashes past and disappears, while wine bears itself like a long sunny day. Sake holds one long kugir,* while in wine they are numerous and brief."

Tadao-san listened to him in amazement. With eyes that had widened to European proportions.

And then something from the age of Adam.

---

\* In Zen Buddhism *kugir* signifies a pause or intermission in a musical or poetic work.

The President's Cat | 81

"In our laboratory, there are soil samples from all five continents. I brought them myself. All soils consist of the same elements. There are samples of water and blood from inhabitants of all five continents. We studied them. I entrusted my academicians with this work. I directed this project personally with Academician Soso Kapanadze (The guests looked at Soso with great respect and so did the hosts). It was confirmed once again that we all have the same blood. We are all brothers, only here's the rub: we still don't realise it."

Then he recalled an incident from Japanese life, from the same age as Adam's.

"One warlord was fighting another. They were sitting on hillsides facing each other. In the valley, their samurai were killing one another. Then the first warlord rode his horse in a mad gallop towards the other hill, charged up towards the other warlord, and brandished his sabre. The other warded off his attack with a fan-shaped shield and recited some verse, a haiku, which he had composed on the spur of the moment. After this, the first warlord, also in a gallop, rode down to his samurai, commanded them to stop fighting, and returned home with them. Tadao-san, don´t you remember that haiku?"

Tadao-san could not remember that haiku. He did not know about this incident, nor had he heard anything resembling it. Perhaps he had heard about it at some time, but he could not remember. Neither his assistants nor the tea tasters knew the haiku.

At that moment, Mikhail Temurovich read the verse in a mysterious voice (he almost recited it in Japanese, but remembered in time that Tadao Kasio was Japanese and thought better of it):

East and West alike,
Poverty ubiquitous,
Cooled by the same wind.

While he read the verse, Japanese music was already playing on the Korofa Peninsula.

Tadao-san's eyes became flooded with tears . . . And the eyes of his assistants also. The tea tasters held out, probably because they had drunk only tea.

"One of my distant ancestors was Sulkhan Sala Orbeliani, a writer of genius," said Mikhail Temurovich. "He wrote a book called *The Wisdom of Imagination*."

Tadao-san was once again overwhelmed by tears.

Perhaps because he had not read *The Wisdom of Imagination*.

After the banquet, they all moved into the shade of the pine trees and lay down on blue and white striped chaise-lounges.

The "tea tasters" of the Bebeisiri Academy were enchanting blondes of twenty to twenty-five years brought out from Sukhumi. They had skin as white as Chinese ceramics and blue eyes. They were wearing black tights and miniskirts. Tadao Kasio surveyed the fair-haired "tea tasters" with a look full of incomprehensible sadness.

"Excellent!" the voice of one of the Japanese tea tasters resounded at length.

"Excellent!" Mikhail Temurovich's "tea tasters" repeated (only bashfully), with voices more like the twittering of birds.

Then Tadao Kasio viewed the nursery of the Ushguli tea seedlings.

Evening was already setting in; the sun was descending towards the sea.

The mighty son of the "Land of the Rising Sun" looked pensively at the setting sun: the sun was creeping away towards Japan.

"I need one million seedlings of Ushguli tea," said Tadao Kasio.

"We'll start sending them off in a year and five months," Mikhail Temurovich promised.

Soso Kapanadze imperceptibly nudged Mikhail Temurovich: "Think what you're saying."

"We have to breed Ushguli tea whether we like it or not, for us nothing is impossible," Mikhail Temurovich whispered to him.

Soso wanted to nudge Mikhail Temurovich again for the very same reason, but Mikhail Temurovich's words forced him to reconsider; he could, after all, manage this task, too.

Then, Tadao Kasio's assistants took some leaves of snow-white paper from their briefcases and spread them in front of Mikhail Temurovich on the blue-painted garden table. Mikhail Temurovich pondered and pondered, and finally signed the paper.

The next morning, Tadao Kasio and his assistants and tea tasters flew out.

Two weeks later, Tadao Kasio transferred fifty thousand US dollars to the account of the Bebeisiri Academy. Upon receipt of the Ushguli tea seedlings over the next one year and five months, three million US dollars were due to be transferred.

But the war broke out. The area was occupied by combatants. Plus, by those resembling combatants. And by those resembling those resembling combatants. Over a mere few months, the mini-tractors ("Moles") belonging to the Bebeisiri Academy disappeared. As did the laboratory and an electronic microscope worth twenty-seven thousand US dollars donated to Mikhail Temurovich by the director of some institute of genetics (no one understood the mind of this director, but for some reason he melted at the sight of Mikhail Temurovich).

The war took it all away.

Absolutely everything.

The war took it all away in the hands of its people.

There were a lot of them.

Nobody could stop them.

Not even Mikhail Temurovich.

# 17

He was sitting in the "Dioscuri" restaurant, in the company of Sukhumi old-timers.

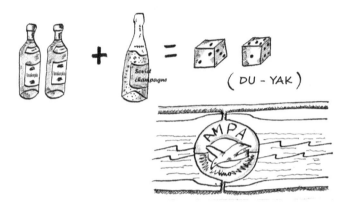

Holding in his hand a crystal flute filled with a sparkling beverage named "Du-yak," he raised it above the heads of his table companions and proposed a toast.

At the same time, he was admiring the sea.

For the benefit of those not up with the play, I shall explain: Du-yak denotes not only the position of the pieces in backgammon (2:1), but it is also the name of a beverage comprising one part champagne and two parts white wine. This beverage was as a rule quickly prepared in Sukhumi restaurants and widely consumed at feasts, a bottle of champagne (let's say, "Soviet champagne") and two bottles of white wine (say, "Anakopia") were poured into a decanter. Sometimes sliced peaches, pears, or apples were added, also tossed in there were ice and a few small sprigs from a large bunch of grapes, three or four berries and this improved the Du-yak" even further.

There was also "Se-yak" (3:1)—one part champagne and three of white wine, as well as "Yagan"—one bottle each of champagne and white wine, "Dubara" two bottles each, and so on and so forth. You know, backgammon played during a banquet recalls the most Asiatic virtual game imaginable. I am describing this to make some "remnants of the past" more comprehensible to the younger reader.

I am sure that this invention is no less important than any scientific invention or run-of-the-mill geographical discovery, even more so so, because it is dictated, prompted by the Black Sea, beautiful women, an immemorial sense of male solidarity and mutual support, and the very nature of this city—half fabulous, half real.

And so, he was admiring the sea.

He raised the crystal flute of Du-yak high and proposed a toast.

And he proposed a toast in honour of the open horse-drawn carriage, which, sometime at the beginning of the twentieth century, had been hired one summer for a whole day by Sukhumi fans of convivial dining, who had gone round all the town's restaurants and taverns, singing to the sound of the zurna pipe, concertina, and drum . . .

And he lauded the colt harnessed to the phaeton, whom the revellers at one restaurant had lubricated with a hefty crock, the size of a good pot, of chilled French champagne, turning him into a fellow reveller. Tipsy from the champagne and the song, the colt made a dash for the most magnificent young white mare at one of the small Sukhumi markets.

And he proposed a toast in honour of the aroused colt, who, regardless of being harnessed to a carriage, somehow contrived to tup a magnificent mare, clambered up on her according to all the rules and began rhythmically rocking the carriage, which had been forced up on its back wheels. And rocked, and rocked, and rocked the seated passengers, who had no understanding whatsoever of the drunk musicians and revellers, who nevertheless continued to sing their songs to the glorious sound of concertina and drums, spreading their arms wide, as if dancing and as if wishing to embrace the entire world.

And he praised that colt, that mare, and that town. That town and that rhythm, that magnificently magical, fabulously divine rhythm, a creative rhythm, the source and the inception of all life which beats in every one of us, in every animate being, and in the very essence of stars, galaxies, mega-galaxies in general . . . Like a mysterious and eternal music.

## 18

"I have a kind of strange desire to sleep," said the dying woman with a smile of embarrassment.

Mikhail Temurovich's eyes were moist.

Then he straightened the pillow and whispered in her ear:

"Believe me, this life has worn me out even more. If only I were in your place now, how relaxed I would be!"

# 19

I once happened to be in Guria together with Mikhail Temurovich. The hosts had worked themselves to a standstill, they could not do enough to please us. Before the start of every dining session, young maidens would bring spring water in jugs, and the host would request: "Dear guests, let us grace our hands!" (not "Let us wash," but "Let us grace" our hands).

In one corner of the yard, Mikhail Temurovich saw a spring. He excused himself to his hosts, removed his footwear, and dipped his feet in the spring water; it was like being born anew, he said.

When we were returning home, already in the gathering twilight, right by the bridge across the Supsa, our way was blocked by a truck. It had closed access to the bridge, so we stopped. Some robbers leapt off the back of the truck, armed with what seemed to be almost flintlocks, forced us out of our cars, even fired a couple of times into the air, and took us captive.

We were frightened, truly frightened.

Then they lifted us onto the long bed of the truck. There we were greeted by a table already laid and the harmonious laughter of the hosts hiding by the table: now the feast of the real lions was due to begin!

The Gurians parked the vehicle right at the edge of the surf, next to the village of Shekvetili. It was a moon-lit night. At the height of the banquet, I got down from the truck to do number one. On turning around, I encountered a picture which has imprinted itself for ever on my memory: the sea, the moon, and the folk feasting in the back of a truck.

Mikhail Temurovich was ecstatic: "Long live creative hospitality!" He even sang "My poor head, you have no good fortune in your life," an aria from the opera "Daisi," Twilight, by Zakaria Paliushveli, which he loved.

As a rule, he did not drink a lot. Generally, his cheeks would turn red after a couple of glasses. He used to say: "If there is even just one pretty woman sitting at the table, I tend to drink more, she endows me with strength."

Subsequently, I visited Mingrelia together with Mikhail Temurovich. During one of the banquets for one hundred guests, the lights suddenly went out, then a door opened, and, one after another, nine goat kids appeared with flickering candles affixed to their horns. When the kids stopped in the centre between the tables of diners—the tables were set up in the shape of the Greek letter pi for the convenience of the serving staff—a light blazed on and lined up before us were roast kids with sprigs of greenery in their mouths on wheeled stands. They were bound together by a cord and, invisibly to others, the cord was being pulled by someone sitting at the head of the table. Then the kids were distributed table by table.

Sitting beside me at that banquet was a man from Ochamchire. At the end of the banquet, he rolled up his shirt sleeve and showed his right arm. On it was tattooed "Vazha +." The remaining words had been erased.

"It once read: "Vazha + Zurab + Shota + Otari = Brothers." Vazha—that's me, the others were my friends. They caused a lot of bother in their own lives and in mine. They turned out to be unworthy of our brotherhood. They messed up, and I erased their names with acid. A few years later, I nevertheless restored the name "Shota", but once more he messed up, and I erased his name again."

# 20

On the road to Ritsa, not far from the Blue Lake, there is a waterfall. A foaming torrent drops noisily from a high cliff, and it is totally white, white as milk.

One day, Mikhail Temurovich was taking a delegation of Chinese comrades to Lake Ritsa, showing them the wonders of Abkhazian scenery, and stopped on the way by that waterfall. The Chinese were in raptures from all they had seen, and they asked Mikhail Temurovich why the waterfall was so white.

"Don't imagine it's water," he replied. "This waterfall is totally milk. Up there in the mountains, high up, there's a dairy farm of 3,567 cows. They get milked every morning and this is how the milk is transported to the dairy factory on the seashore, since there's no road link to the farm. Our method is super-innovative, and the results are remarkable: we have noticeably reduced the price of milk, a litre of milk costs us just one kopeck."

He then asked the astounded Chinese: "How many millions of you are there?" The Chinese replied: "Almost a billion."

Then Mikhail Temurovich said:

"Let's form a union, you Chinese and we Abkhazians. Then there will be not almost a billion, but exactly a billion of us."

## 21

At the beginning of the 1980s, I was working in the Sukhumi district.

One day, he came and said: "I need a section of land. I want to build a house." We helped him out. In Gvandra, on the seashore, he built a miniscule house. It was there that we usually met. As well as at the Dzidzlan restaurant, which was also in Gvandra. That was what Mikhail Temurovich had named it. Dzidzlan means "water maiden" or "mermaid" in Abkhazian. Beside the Dzidzlan, we had a traditional Abkhazian meal.

We used to travel to the North Caucasus on business, we were trading in agricultural produce. In return for mandarins, they provided us with meat, cheese, and seedlings. Mikhail Temurovich would also often travel with us. He had friends everywhere and he helped us.

At the table, he introduced us to the hosts as academicians, professors, and high-ranking managers.

Once in Nalchik, he was asked: "In Abkhazia you have people of so many nationalities, how do you manage to get on with one another?" He answered: "We have a wine called "Abkhazian Bouquet." We called it that because we live like a bouquet of flowers. It's a bouquet in which every flower has a unique scent."

During one visit to Russia, we became acquainted with a certain exotic lady. She was a member of the communist party of Cuba. Mikhail Temurovich requested: "Let an old gent have this woman, she's more suited to me. You carry on with the young ones."

A toast to women was always special for him. Afterwards, he invariably kissed women on their left hand, the left hand being closer to the heart.

## 22

At an isolated table in the "Amra" café, Mikhail Temurovich was sitting with a young fair-haired woman, drinking brandy. The woman was drinking, too.

Mikhail Temurovich was showing the woman his pocket watch.

"Look, Irina, look at my watch. It's made of wood. You see how poor I am. I haven't even got a regular watch . . . Only this wooden one. Ho Chi Minh gave it to me in Vietnam. Don't you feel sorry for me, Tanya, being so poor? No, no, you have a heart of stone, like all beautiful women."

The woman laughed resonantly. Then Mikhail Temurovich said something to her in an incomprehensible language. He spoke for several minutes.

The woman asked what language he was speaking as she could not understand anything. Korean, he answered, one of the Korean dialects. "But how do you come to know this dialect. I even wonder if you know the Korean language at all." It was all Mikhail Temurovich.

The woman continued to laugh.

Mikhail Temurovich laughed, too.

Then the woman suddenly burst into tears, weeping her heart out. Seemingly, she was recalling something from the past, something that tore at her heart.

Mikhail Temurovich comforted her: "Look at the beauty all around, how wonderful and amazing this world is . . . And you're weeping, darling . . . Don't cry. You mustn't."

In profile, Mikhail Temurovich was like a Roman emperor on a gold coin.

## 23

I was working in the Merkheuli restaurant as an assistant cook. How can I forget the way we received Khrushchev! The only thing is which of his visits to recall?

He was mad about satsivi sauce. The way you make satsivi, you could make nails edible, he used to say.

Vodka he drank like water.

He got over hangovers with the aid of ekala, our local sarsaparilla, which grows wild in our mountains, prepared with nuts. He would eat this snack and, within ten minutes, feel in shape again. We seasoned the ekala with wine vinegar. and that helped a lot. He used to ask: "Why don't you have ekala plantations?"

Mikhail Temurovich replied: "Ekala is a native plant. It grows only here. It can be found in other places, but there it loses its anti-hangover properties."

"Then establish plantations here. Our Soviet ekala will cure humanity of hangovers!" said Khrushchev in an impassioned voice.

In return, Mikhail Temurovich demanded special conditions for the republic: "Then cut our plan for tobacco and tea."

Khrushchev agreed and entrusted his assistant with the task of writing down this request and shelving the Abkhazian plan for tea, tobacco, and any other culture, if necessary, as long as ekala plantations were established, it would promote the propagation of our ideology.

# 24

The sea looked as if somewhere not far away the Lord himself was taking a stroll.

A radiant, scintillating sea at 6 o'clock in the morning.

And the sky was radiant, too. It was a morning sky of 6 o'clock and one minute.

And on the sea a sole, single man was drifting.

"Come out, come out," he called out to that man in a merry and jocular voice. "It's my turn now, I have to go in the sea . . . Come out, come out!"

While he was calling him ashore like this, the clock struck exactly 6 o'clock two minutes.

Then 6 o'clock three minutes.

Then 6 o'clock four minutes.

Then 6 o'clock five minutes.

6:06.

6:07.

6:08.

6:09.

10 . . .

12 . . .

24 . . .

## 25

At one session, I happened to sit beside Mikhail Temurovich. At that time, I recall, he was the director of an experimental station. The Secretary of the Sukhumi District Committee, Astiko Gvaramia, was in a total rage, attacking the Executive Committee chairman: why hadn't he ordered the mandarin boxes in good time and in the necessary quantity. "There aren't enough, you see, and the crop is spoiling." "But what am I supposed to do," said the other. "I passed on the number of boxes to my deputy Bgazhba, so what's it got to do with me?"

The Secretary of the District Committee was shouting out of control: "Who the hell is Bgazhba? You sure found the right person to ask."

He did not know that Mikhail Temurovich was in the hall, did not see him.

When Bgazhba was the First Secretary in Abkhazia, the Secretary of the District Committee was working in the Communist Youth Organization and trembled with fear at the very mention of his name.

I glanced at Mikhail Temurovich. He was smiling, a strange smile, I cannot even explain it. One thing was clear: There was no offence visible on his face. He was smiling as if to say: "I foresaw this, too, it was all meant to happen just like that, it could not have been otherwise. In a word, this life of ours is not all that interesting . . ."

# 26

What great affection we felt for each other that night, sitting in the "Amra", the café "Amra" rather than a restaurant.

And we talked and drank.

The broad-mouthed decanters were swiftly emptied and refilled.

They were filled with light white wine and peaches, pears and apples were sliced into this wine, sometimes cherries were tossed in, a little Avadkhara or Borzhomi was added—for fun—but, rather more often wine, sometimes champagne, sometimes red wine, sometimes additional white wine and then champagne again . . .

In short, that evening we dragged that wine by the tail like a Caucasian sheepdog pup, played with it, lovingly tormented it, stroked its head, tickled its tummy, caressed it, tugged at its legs ruffling its long thick hair.

And the wine moaned with pleasure! It squealed for joy with us, sometimes barking and sometimes even wetting the table.

But then everything was moaning, squealing, and yelping as it journeyed through our veins.

And a stellar-lunar breeze was blowing, and that breeze ruffled the long fair hair of our women and the black hair as well.

And our women were becoming semi-transparent—because of the starlight and the moonlight and also because of the sea breeze . . .

And we loved everyone and one another . . . And with such love . . .

## 27

He was once the toastmaster at a table where the majority were women. He had twice drunk to the health of that camel which, despite being a camel, was nevertheless suffering from thirst.

And he had twice passed the right to prolong the toast, in Alaverdi wine, to the women, first to one, then to another. He was about to propose this toast for the third time, but the women, roaring with laughter, gave in: "Don't drink the toast, everything's clear to us as it is."

Then he proposed a toast to the bee.

"Among the many species of bees there is one that is special, the Abkhazian bee. It has the longest proboscis in the world, selects nectar from the deepest flowers. With its proboscis it reaches areas which other bees cannot get to."

The women guffawed without restraint: "We wish we could see what kind of bee this is."

And he promised: "I'll make sure I show you as soon as we rise from the table. We'll go out to the wood over there. The Abkhazian bee lives there, in the depths of the wood. Only we'll have to go a long way in, my princesses . . ."

# 28

At one meeting he flew into a rage:

"We are trying too hard. There is absolutely no reason to get carried away when extending our hospitality. We need to discriminate between people and then respond accordingly. A Central Committee instructor recently came out from Moscow. I invited him to a friend's house in Novy Afon. All night he made merry, enjoyed himself, was entertained with singing and dancing. But when he got back to Moscow, he informed on my friend to the Central Committee: 'Where did he get the resources to occupy a whole floor in a two-storeyed house?' We partied on the ground floor of my friend's house; he did not go upstairs. He couldn't even imagine that my friend owned the top floor, too. Had he known, you can imagine what he would have written in his denunciation."

## 29

During one banquet, a local journalist voiced a request for the residents of Besleti village.

"Mikhail Temurovich, there's no bridge across the river in this village, and, to get to the other side, you have to take a detour and it's a long way. Perhaps some means can be found to build a bridge in the village."

For some reason, Mikhail Temurovich, he was then the First Secretary, paid no attention to what the journalist said.

The journalist repeated his request on behalf of the village residents.

Even then he paid no attention.

The journalist would not back down.

When he raised it for the fifth time, but already *demanding* that a bridge be built, Mikhail Temurovich said, as if he had only just noticed him:

"I can see that you are doing a good job, suffering on behalf of the people. How can we not fulfil your request. Only, out of respect for you, we will build not one bridge, but two: one for crossing over to the other bank and another for coming back."

# 30

We were sitting at the buffet of the "Abkhazia" Hotel—Mikhail Temurovich, Vianor Pachulia, and I. We were in a wonderful mood. Mikhail Temurovich had ordered everything necessary, including a bottle of brandy—Vianor Pachulia was a diabetic and avoided wine in favour of brandy.

Vianor Pandzhovich asked the waiter: "How many stars does your brandy have?" "Three stars," was the reply. Vianor: "But we want five stars." Waiter: "We only have three stars." The small threatening conflict was settled by Mikhail Temurovich.

"What is it, Vinor, don't you know that all brandies come out of the same barrel regardless of their number of stars?"

He always addressed Vianor like that: Vinor. No doubt because, thus modified, his friend's name recalled a beloved beverage—wine.

Vianor Pandzhovich was his faithful friend and keeper of secrets, especially regarding women.

He said of Pandzhovich:

"When I was the First Secretary, he would meet me an evening by the exit of the Regional Committee building and tell me in detail about what had happened in the city over the day. In the morning, he would also meet me at the threshold and let me know what had happened in Sukhumi overnight. So Vinor was my unofficial Minister of Information."

And so, we were sitting at the buffet of the "Abkhazia" and swigging brandy.

Strolling past not far away and greeting us was KGB agent Walter, who had been assigned to the "Abkhazia" Hotel. This was known to everyone. And he himself did not conceal it.

Mikhail Temurovich spoke with irony, as he quite often did.

"Not a single city in the Soviet Union is organised like Sukhumi. Only Marxists live here. We have the KGB on Engels Street and the synagogue on Marx Street. Strictly speaking, the KGB ought to be on Marx Street and the synagogue on Engels . . . But maybe it's better the way it is, a better fit. Those devils have thought it out well."

# 31

In 1929, Maxim Gorky visited Abkhazia once again. At that time, Mikhail Temurovich was fourteen years old. To cut a long story short, according to Mikhail Temurovich, his childhood mates on the Sukhumi waterfront pinched a white military-style jacket from Gorky. Gorky was admiring the view of the sea and the waterfront and forgot about his jacket. It was then that the Sukhumi youngsters made off with it.

Mikhail Temurovich was not present during the theft, but he was there when the jacket was returned.

The same evening, Nestor Lakoba, at that time the First Secretary of Abkhazia, invited Gorky with his friend to a restaurant. At the height of the banquet, a local waif entered the restaurant and handed Lakoba a bundle wrapped in paper. The latter unwrapped it. Inside was Gorky's jacket. Gorky was pleased that the jacket had been returned to him. He put it on, thrust his hand into a pocket and discovered a note there. He read it and laughed loudly:

"Nestor, well, you are a figure of authority!"

Then did he read the note out loud: "Dear Nestor, we did not know that this sucker was your guest. We are returning the military jacket. The five roubles we have given to the lad who delivered it."

## 32

Sometimes I wonder whether that time was all a dream. Prewar Sukhumi? Kukur-chai and his teahouse? Kukur-chai would also compose verse:

> "Don't smoke, you silly children, try
> And drink your tea with Kukur-chai"
> or
> "Fail to drink at Kukur-chai's,
> And no success will greet your eyes"
>
> "Come along and hurry up!
> Grab yourself a steaming cup"
>
> "Give our steaming tea a go,
> And you'll be merry as Makhno"

And when he was asked if it was true that Makhno was such a jolly man, he replied: "How should I know? I needed Makhno for the rhyme." And then there was Gabo, the port worker who had a headband with "No. 2" inscribed on it. When he was asked who No. 1 was, he became frightfully angry for some reason. At the "Brekhalovka" restaurant, Professor Alaniya once complained: "I have three daughters—well, my wife just couldn't give me a boy—while this spastic Gabo has four strapping lads." Gabo, who was standing close by, stands up and makes the professor an offer: "You just let me at your wife, and you'll see. She's sure to give you a boy." "I'll kill that no-hoper!" roared Professor Alaniya and rushed at Gabo. Mad Gabo and the professor ran as far as the "Dioscuri," while the Sukhumi residents rocked with laughter.

That's what the city of Sukhumi was like.

The President's Cat | 105

And Svoboda, in his peakless sailor's cap and striped vest, would most commonly pop up by the "Sukhumi" Cinema with a guitar in his hands. "We must save the children of the world!" he used to shout—and what!

And Maradona. The most mobile of all Sukhumi's fools. You saw him everywhere. One minute by the grand clock, then strolling in the vicinity of the Red Bridge, then at the bazaar, then in Mayak district. He went round half naked winter and summer alike. His sun-tanned neck was adorned with a necklace of stones on a string. Not long ago, I found out by chance that Maradona had died at the beginning of 2007. The news tore my heart as if I had lost a friend or close relative I was out visiting. We duly honoured Maradona's memory.

In the early morning, adults and children alike gathered by the Dioscuri and played football. One of the teams was called the Red Peppers and the other the Hurricanes. They would laugh and joke.

One time we were drinking coffee in the "Penguin" along with Mikhail Temurovich and with us was his friend, the photographer Khionidi, and the press photographers Tarasov, Dgebuadze, and Melikian. How many photos were taken that day!

Not one of them remains in my possession.

Then we were joined by Colonel Satsivi, the celebrated traffic inspector. I had better restrain myself and not name him. He was called Colonel Satsivi because every week he dispatched a five-litre thermos flask of satsivi sauce to some big shot in Moscow. It turns out that this big shot was mad about the sauce. And so, in an instant, an ordinary traffic cop was transformed into a colonel or, more precisely, into Colonel Satsivi. The satsivi was prepared for him by a woman from Eshera.

On the steps leading down from the Penguin to the sea, someone had smashed a bottle of champagne. After a while, a rat crept out from somewhere and began to lap up the spilled wine. Mikhail Temurovich asked the press photographers to snap that champagne connoisseur.

Four cameras clicked instantaneously. I do not have these photos either.

"Come on, let's drink," Colonel Satsivi proposed and put three bottles of champagne on the table.

Mikhail Temurovich proposed the first toast—to women:

"Here's to women! A woman is like the earth: sometimes burning like Africa, sometimes cold as the Antarctic, sometimes like an alpine meadow, or a river of the plains, or a mountain peak, a sea, an ocean, a continent, a wind . . . Here's to every precious cell of her body!"

I wonder where the photos taken that evening are.

Audible not far away was the sound of women's laughter and an offended youthful voice: "What do you think I am, Vasya, some Macedonian sucker?"

The beam of a searchlight alternated between the sea and the sky.

"And now let's pay a glorious tribute to wine itself, a beverage over ten thousand years old, which sagely regulates the relations between man and woman," said Mikhail Temurovich, proposing the final toast.

# 33

If someone is hit by a "stray bullet," you might as well consider him doomed. There is a woman behind it. The bullet has been tested first on pigs, then on corpses, and only after that has mass production been instituted.

## 34

Mid-November 1992. Sukhumi was being bombed periodically. I was travelling to the village of Pshali. Residents there are relatives of my son's wife, our Armenian kin.

I remained in Pshali for three days. Returning to Sukhumi, I met Mikhail Temurovich by the door of my house. He hugged me and said: "I'm hungry, Sosik."

We went inside. No water, no electricity. I laid out the produce given to me by my Armenian relatives, including a three-litre container of unboiled milk. I boiled half a litre of the milk on the Primus and set the table. We had polenta with cheese, fried chicken, and small churek loaves baked in the fireplace. We ate. Then we talked about various things. Including the pumpkin "Atlantis", which was ripening in my cellar. We visited Atlantis. It was alive and well.

ATLANTIS — TITANIC

"Atlantis must not on any account be allowed to dry out. We must get a harvest from it," he said, stroking the sides of the pumpkin.

Even though he was very weak, he still sat down at the piano and played Beethoven's "Moonlight Sonata." Then a popular aria from the opera "Thais."

I saw him off about 11 o'clock at night. I divided up the produce from Pshali and accompanied him as far as his house.

The breeze carried the scent of mandarins from somewhere. We greeted it like a friend we had not seen for ages, we stood there for a long time and breathed in the mandarin scent.

On parting he hugged me again. "What happiness to meet a friend and chat with him. Tomorrow I'll be waiting at home after three. We'll also discuss some key questions of biology."

## 35

"Look at this map, Sosik, just look! How different the countries are! Look! Look at the shape of that country. And this one. Cuba is almost the same size as America. What sort of hemisphere is this? Here there is one thing and there quite another. Or the colours of the countries, the way they change, red, yellow, brown, grey, green . . . Like some kind of traffic lights: 'Go! Stop! Go away! Come! Here! There!' Doesn't this planet scare you?"

# The President's Cat

He emerged right by the shore, removed his mask and the tube of his breathing apparatus for underwater swimming, and called out to Soso Kapanadze, who was sitting under a pine tree.

"Sosik, that was how I also found the seventeenth one, of course. Seventeen in all, no more and no less. In the same way, of course, like that."

Soso Kapanadze noted in an exercise book the location of the seventeenth underwater spring of Bebeisiri Lake.

They were studying Bebeisiri Lake, or rather the Bebeisiri Lakes, Major and Minor. And before that, the same summer, they had been investigating the migration of stones at sea, so-called "Turkish stones," which had over the years—in a manner of speaking, of course, that is—in this same way, drifted towards Sukhumi, by way of Sarpi and Batumi. They were studying "Russian pebbles," which "travelled" from Novorossiysk to Batumi. From time to time, he lay down on his back and, closing his eyes, listened to the sound of the waves and the cautious rustle of the stones.

"Advancing like the army of Alexander the Great, Sosik."

Bebeisiri Lake is located in Gali district, not far from the sea. River Okumi flows into it, as do the Mokhokha and Namgvale Gullies, and it is connected to the sea by Wolf Gully. The lake is situated between the Black Sea and the Trans-Caucasian railway. The Bebeisiri Lakes together occupy an area of two square kilometres, their depth varies from three to five metres.

He rubbed himself with a shaggy towel and turned towards the sun:

"Seventeen is not a bad number. All numbers are good if they have a seven in them. For instance, the seventh of November."

And he laughed . . . Then he looked at Soso Kapanadze's map.

"Look, look, Soso, I was right when I said that Bebeisiri was like a woman's bosom. Your map is like an anatomy textbook. You see the Korofa Peninsula, the way it cuts into this bosom! Well, look, look, just look how, eh? It's a magical place, Sos! Korofa is like a penis and at the same time it resembles a human brain, as if viewed from the spine. Bloody hell! A male brain and a penis have the same shape!"

He himself had named the Peninsula Korofa ("love" in the Mingrelian language). The local names of the gullies were established together with Vianor Pachulia.

On the Korofa Peninsula there was a scientific research centre, where he worked with Mikhail Alanidze and Soso Kapanadze until August 14, 1992.

They wrote of Bebeisiri:

"The water temperature of the lake in winter varies from +6 to –3 degrees and, in summer, from +27 to 33. The absolute minimum air temperature is +11 and the maximum is 41. The lake water varies from reddish to darker brown and its transparency in summer ranges between 50 and 150 centimetres. There are up to 170 days of cloud cover a year and up to 193 sunny days and the average annual rainfall is 2,200–2,700 mm.

Rain falls mainly in winter and spring. Summer is largely dry, with no wind, but a light sea breeze in the mornings.

In the gorge, where the lake is located and in the surrounding countryside the trees include: white beech, lime, black beech, chestnut, oak, bladdernut, hazel, maritime fir, pear, apple, cherry plum, and blackthorn. And the following introduced trees: acanthus, actinidia, camellia, fortunella, poncirus, eucalyptus, juglans, phyllotaxis, pteleocarpa, lotos, d. sineusis, aleuzites, and the camphor tree. And the following water plants: water chestnut, water rose, lotus, wind-grass, and the lemna and wolffia duckweeds. Wolffia is an ethereal oil plant, eaten by fish, the silver carp, and the white amur. Wolffia is found both on the water surface and on the bottom. Its movement from top to bottom and bottom to top is determined by temperature variations. When the water temperature falls below 10 degrees, wolffia ceases its synthesis of ether oils. Its specific gravity rises correspondingly, and the plant drops to the bottom of the lake. When the temperature rises above 10 degrees, proportionately, the synthesis of ether oils increases, and it emerges on the surface of the water.

The lake is inhabited by fish: sheat-fish, common carp, big-head carp, white amur, an exotic carp (introduced by M. Alavadze), tapelas, herring, trout (introduced by M. Bgazhba), common bream, common rudd, pike, and others. It should be noted that saltwater pike often invaded the lake from the sea and destroyed the local fish. To prevent this invasion, the bay of the lake closest to the sea was fenced off with synthetic fibre netting (at M. Bgazhba's initiative).

He often said and wrote that the process of urbanisation had reduced the area of Abkhazia's forests, that every year up to eighty-one thousand tons of earth were swept away, especially from the environs of the village of Upper Eshera, and that it was essential to introduce and acclimatise new cultures, but not to the detriment of Abkhazia's native green cover. According to him, the greatest harm had been inflicted by two industrial cultures—tea and tobacco. Tea had been imposed by Soviet authorities and tobacco by Turkey.

He worked to set up a hybrid citrus gene fund. This collection included 188 varieties, among them an orange that was a clone of the Thompson navel and christened anew in the Soviet Union as JVS (Joseph Vissarionovich Stalin). Mikhail Alanidze was very fond of Stalin and therefore launched the JVS over and above the prescriptions of the five-year plan.

The idea of establishing the Academy of Colchis Regional Genetics came into his head back in 1949, when he arrived in Sukhumi as a graduate of the Timiryazev Academy, together with a group under the well-known ophthalmologist Filatov, to study the pilocarpus. The pilocarpus is related to citrus fruit and resembles boxwood, an evergreen plant. In Brazil, there are impenetrable forests of pilocarpus and pilocarpine. The costly medicine prepared from it, which was considered effective against the serious eye disease glaucoma, was shipped from there to the Soviet Union.

The Filatov Group, which, apart from Bgazhba, included Khomezurashvili, Khasaya, Miminoshvili and the German scientist Hartmann, also studied the aloe in Sukhumi. Soon, conservatories were built in Sukhumi for the pilocarpus and the aloe.

It was then that one morning he made the acquaintance of Soso Kapanadze, who was selflessly pottering about in the laboratory. For a whole day they talked and argued about genetics and towards evening he told him: "From this day on we are brothers."

The group left Sukhumi with a new experimental medicine, aloe in ampoules.

Vavilov was a world-renowned geneticist, as was Lysenko. At first, Stalin tried to provide both with ideal conditions for work. Lysenko obtained shoots from potato peelings and promised to increase the potato crop several times over. "Bravo, Lysenko!" Stalin greeted this discovery. Half-starved Russia needed a lot of potatoes. Vavilov maintained that Lysenko was playing with chimeras and that we should not deviate from the road outlined by nature. Lysenko believed in vegetative reproduction and Vavilov in natural reproduction. Lysenko's route was a short one, Vavilov's a long one.

Just before World War II, Vavilov was arrested and imprisoned in Saratov, where he caught a cold and died of pneumonia. Stalin was already trying on his own to make sense of genetics, as he later attempted with linguistics.

Soso Kapanadze considered himself a true follower of Vavilov's cause, in fact, a disciple of Vavilov, but he shared some of Lysenko's views. From 1965, Mikhail Temurovich and Soso Kapanadze worked together, whether in the Sukhumi branch of the Institute of Sub-Tropical Cultures, at the institute´s experimental station, in Gvandra, Gulripshi, or Achigvara. And in Sukhumi of course, too.

"You won't survive without me," he told Soso Kapanadze.

And indeed, that was the case.

One day, Academician Lapin offered Soso Kapanadze work in the research centre of the Sukhumi ape nursery. Mikhail Temurovich was furious: "What do you want with those stinking apes? Can't you see how much work we have!"

Right from the beginning, they worked on breeding frost-resistant varieties of citrus fruit, on problems of global warming, on forecasting future floods and they studied the nature of the hydrogen sulphide accumulated on the bottom of the Black Sea. To conduct research and experiments, they set up a unique tower in the sea at a depth of thirty metres and a second one on the shore, in a forest.

They developed a strange plant, a trifoliate lemon, frost-resistant and fit to eat.

Of the feijoa he said: "An amazing fruit, child of the wind. Everywhere it follows the wind, is born by the wind, flies with the wind. That's how it has survived. This is something other fruits should be taught."

They declared that all products could be obtained via photosynthesis, and they obtained them. At the Okhurei greenhouse enterprise a viscous liquid was obtained containing substances necessary for stock feeds. It was used to fatten geese.

Along with Kapanadze, he developed industrial varieties of tea Indust-4 and Indust-5. Together, they also obtained the "Achigvara" nutrient solution for growing Indust-4 and Indust-5. Ten days before the beginning of the harvest they had the tea watered.

In 1991, fifty tons of tea were harvested from the experimental plot.

He worked on ways of accelerating the growth and development of tropical and subtropical cultures. He even shot a documentary film of the acceleration.

All in all, at one time or another, he and his friends brought to Abkhazia: the December peach (from America), the wild strawberry tree, the honey tree (from China), the Rodop lemon (from Bulgaria), the Volkameriana lemon (from Italy),

The President's Cat | 117

and the Tajima Natsumikani and Yamaguchi lemons (from Japan).

At a symposium in America, he stole the seeds of a giant pumpkin, simply put them in his pocket and brought them to Sukhumi. The pumpkin had been bred by Mexicans who named it the "Atlantis." Some of the pumpkins weighed up to four hundred fifty kilograms.

In one of his papers, he wrote: "In a journey of one thousand kilometres, a car destroys as much oxygen as a human being in the course of an entire lifetime. In the Sukhumi Cytogenetics Laboratory, we discovered benzoids in the peel of citrus fruits. We sent appropriate material about it to V. Vigorov in Sverdlovsk. We more or less established that one litre of benzoid replaces three litres of benzene, which, because of combustion, has become the enemy of absolutely everything on earth. You are quite aware that people also commit suicide by shutting themselves in a garage and starting the car. Death results from the exhaust fumes. In towns and particularly in cities, between 5 and 12 percent of the population die from exhaust fumes."

## 36

In the spring of 1962, Abkhazia was visited by the First Secretary of the Communist Party Central Committee of some Central Asian union republic. Mikhail Temurovich drove the guest in his Chaika limousine as far as Gagra. Then he mounted a banquet in the "Eshera"—the "Eshera" restaurant in Eshera.

On returning to Sukhumi, they spotted a donkey grazing peacefully on the slopes of Mount Eshera. "Well, well, you have donkeys, too!" said the delighted visitor, but then asked: "Mikhail Temurovich, do you use them anywhere?"

"Of course," replied the host. "We have alpine villages which vehicles can't reach and that's where donkeys help us out. Only we don't have many of them, not enough." At this point Mikhail Temurovich's voice trembled, and a tear rolled down his cheek.

"Well, let's solve this problem." His tipsy guest had no less sympathy for Mikhail Temurovich.

Several weeks later, some Central Asian donkeys were delivered to Sukhumi, in five railways wagons. The distinguished guest had kept his word.

When Mikhail Temurovich was informed that some donkeys had been sent from Central Asia, he took a long time to recollect who such an eccentric gift was intended for. Eventually, he managed with some difficulty to recall Eshera, the Eshera restaurant, the visitor from Central Asia and the solitary donkey peacefully grazing on the hillside.

What was to be done? Where could so many donkeys be employed? So, they were set free on Mount Eshera. They ate the grass, brayed on cue around mid-day, at the time determined by nature, and lived their own lives. And when the grass was finished, they gradually climbed higher and higher up the mountains towards the forest. Then winter came and the donkeys were eaten by wolves—all of them, no doubt, or else someone would have heard their braying.

# 37

From the roof of the Abkhazia hotel or, to be precise, from the rooftop restaurant, the sea looked black. Although it was still not quite as black as the ancient Greek chroniclers and historians described it.

He particularly lauded that white-bearded old man who sat winter and summer in a faded raincoat on Peace Avenue in the public gardens in front of the confectioner's and fed the pigeons.

The pigeons were friendly towards the old man, sat on his head and shoulders, cooed, hobbled around him with their waddling gait, fluttered from place to place.

In the city, it was said that during World War II the old man had served in a concentration camp, he was a collaborator.

In the city, it was said that after the war he had fled to Sukhumi, hiding from those seeking revenge.

They did tend to talk a bit in the city.

But Mikhail Temurovich used to say that pigeons were the souls of those who perished in that camp and the old man was redeeming his sins. All the same, the pigeons had long since forgiven him.

# 38

"If a man is unhappy in one place, he is bound to be happy in another. Ali Beir wrote about this as far back as the ninth century. It is the law of symmetry," so declared Mikhail Temurovich at the table one day.

Then he raised his glass in a prayer for the soul of the diver Kolya, who had committed suicide. He had drunk two bottles of vodka all on his own, taken a boat far out to sea and sunk into the water for the last time.

It turned out, he said, that he was already calling it quits with life even back then, when he was drinking coffee with us, when he was greeting us, when he was getting a light from our cigarettes, when he was making love, when he was sleeping . . . "And I hope we don't have among us, sitting at this table, a man like Kolya, this minute taking leave of his life, of his own free will?" It saddened him to think this.

"But if Kolya was unhappy here, he is bound to be happy in another life," he added, consoling some of those present.

## 39

Rain over the city, rain over the sea, streams of rain over everyone and everything.

New Year's Eve.

(And rain also over the "Dioscuri" Restaurant, it goes without saying.)

It had been ten minutes since he went out of the Dioscuri onto the street, but then suddenly he returned, took a glass full of brandy, and declared while standing there:

"I went out for just ten minutes, but do you know what toast I managed to overhear? It'll appeal to you. There, in the booth, right nearby. Some shady type is glorifying sparrows. I'll try to convey his words as I heard them: 'To cut a long story short, it's blowing a gale outside, Vasya . . . I'm going up some steps and there are sparrows there, jumping about on the steps. I remembered about the swallows, but where are the swallows, I ask. There aren't any. It's clear why: it's winter, they've flown off to the resorts, to a good life, those, those f*ckers, those rascals . . . To cut a long story short, the sparrows are still with us. They are not flying away. They're jumping about on the steps, cleaning out their feeding troughs, chirping away. You see what's happening, what worthy sparrows they are, how intuitive, Vasya . . . I'll go with them just as well to reconnoitre, Vasya . . . And the swallows? What do we have in common with those airborne muddlers, eh? To cut a long story short, long live the sparrows! They're our little brothers and sisters! Oh, how tough they are! Won't leave the city for anything, won't abandon us!'"

We also rise. And drink to those sparrows which are fussing around on the steps of the Dioscuri in the cold

The President's Cat | 123

Novorossiysk wind, in the rain and to those sparrows which flutter, fuss, chirp, and hop about in the Sukhumi streets and squares, in the port and railway station, in gardens, markets and stadiums, hills and fields, on bare twigs and in dry grass . . .

At the same time, we drink to the sparrows of other towns and villages, other countries, capitalist, socialist, it does not matter, but especially to Chinese sparrows, which were meant to be wiped out, but survived the genocide, to them, unbroken physically and spiritually. We declare our solidarity with them, and we are ashamed of ourselves. We blush for a great country like China, covering itself with indelible shame in this battle for the complete extermination of little sparrows. In the Dioscuri, we send, by the "aerial" route, a copy of a final, harsh, strict note of warning from a branch of the United Nations Organisation and each of us pledges himself to it with his signature and a glass of brandy. Then we voice a wish for a long life to the sparrows of other planets. Our toast becomes inter-planetary, inter-galactic.

And indeed, if there is life anywhere else, there are undoubtedly sparrows there. For it is impossible to imagine a world without sparrows. And we believe that, whatever happens, a sparrow will always remain a sparrow, just as faithful as our Sukhumi sparrow, always faithful to its home nest, like this miniscule mini-Sukhuminite, this magician, equal in size to the most joyous and the saddest organ of the human organism, the heart.

## 40

When Yuri Gabisonia was promoted and made one of the most important people in Abkhazia, many were amazed.

It was said that Mikhail Temurovich had a hand in it.

"Indeed, my hand is involved," he laughed. "And do you know what Yuri's nickname was at school? No? They called him Mendeleyev. And why? Do you know? No? That's just the point! He was just the sort of man that was simply essential to our Young Communist League.

You should have heard the dossier against him our KGB spooks presented me with. When Yuri was in sixth grade, his grandfather died. The family entrusted him with enlarging a photo of his grandfather. They gave him a small photo and the money. The rascal went and bought himself a bicycle with the money. It turns out the bicycle was his life's dream. He bought one of the famous Kharkov brands, second-hand, but still a Kharkov. Then at school he took a portrait of Mendeleyev from the chemistry office and touched it up, so it looked, well, very much like his grandfather.

At school they rang the alarm, began to look for the portrait and the thief, but couldn't find them. And Yuri had an alibi you couldn't beat: his grandfather had died, and he hadn't been at school. Our old maid of a chemistry teacher got more excited than anyone, the whole responsibility for what had happened, not just the ideological and material responsibility, which goes without saying, but also the moral responsibility, fell on her.

Everything was going well enough, but . . . A delegation from the school appeared at the funeral and suddenly one of its members recognised the portrait of the great chemist nestled among the flowers and the wreaths and exclaimed loudly: 'It's Mendeleyev!' and fainted. You will have guessed, of course, that it was the chemistry teacher.

While they were bringing her round, Yuri fled into a maize field and hid in a barn.

Well, then it began, what ought to have been expected: the Mendeleyev affair was examined at a meeting of the village council. The Chairman of the District Council banged his fist on the table.

'Gabisonia, how dare you steal the portrait of a Politburo member, you counter-revolutionary, you so and so!' Then he asked specifically which comrade's portrait the culprit had stolen. 'Mendeleyev' came the answer. All the more so, said he. 'How dare you steal the portrait of Comrade Mendeleyev, you wretched Trotskyist!' The Secretary of the village council explained to the chairman in a whisper that Mendeleyev was long dead, that he had been a scientist and was, moreover, never a member of the Politburo. This enraged the chairman: who had dared to hang the portrait of some dead geezer among the members of the Politburo? What sort of opportunist was this? He was then told that Mendeleyev's portrait had hung in the chemistry office among those of other well-known chemists. By now the chairman needed a straitjacket: nobody save Politburo members ought to be hung on the wall, the hand of imperialist agents could be detected, he would report it all to the District Committee that very day!

In a word, he became Mendeleyev. That's how Gabisonia's nickname stuck.

In the Young Communist League we had never had a Mendeleyev, and that is why I helped. A man like that must not be lost to the cause. Personnel like that—inventive, blessed with initiative—are simply essential to the Young Communist League."

## 41

I was his son-in-law for thirty-two years. He had two daughters—Natasha and Tanya. Natasha was the elder, and she was my wife. Natakha, that's what he called her. Like her father, Natasha loved animals. He used to say: "Natakha has my blood. At one time we kept four dogs at home, a Doberman pinscher, two Rottweilers and a Dwarf Pinscher. We also had snakes and frogs."

He did not spoil the girls; they went to school by foot and to their institute as well. "My car is a state car," he would say. "To serve me, but you have your own row to hoe."

My mother-in-law, Katerina Antonovna Vasina, worked at the Ministry of Agriculture, a calm, unassuming woman and a good specialist. I recall once when we were seeing Mikhail Temurovich off on a trip abroad, he lifted his bag and asked my mother-in-law in a surprised voice:

"Katya, what have you put in there? Why is it so heavy?"

In the bag were three irons.

"Well, you like pressing things, so you can take the irons with you. They'll come in handy."

The point was that the night before we had had visitors from Moscow, and the more Mikhail Temurovich drank, the more he stroked the hair and shoulder of an exceptionally beautiful woman sitting beside him. To the calls of his wife to desist he replied:

"Katya, you have no idea how much I like pressing the flesh."

Sometimes he recalled World War II, most commonly that period when his unit took part in the liberation of Tchaikovsky's home in Klin. We took many fascists prisoner, he would say. He never said "killed," but rather "took prisoner."

He never spoke ill of anyone; he would even call someone he did not know "my friend." His favourite words were "maniac" and "devil" ("Ah, those devils won't leave me in peace" or "What maniacs, they don't like each other!"). He would flare up, get angry, he might cast a bitter word in my direction, but in just five minutes his feeling of offence evaporated, and he would strive to make peace with me:

"Come on, young fellow, let's play the piano. I'm talking to you, Mobili. What, can't you hear me?"

To make his peace with me, he always played "Suliko." He could scarcely play more than ten tunes, but he sang well. He couldn't read music at all, but put it on the piano, sometimes even turning the pages, as if to say: "Look, I'm playing music from the script."

When I married Natasha, he came to my father's house in Kutaisi. He was delighted to see that we had a big library. "I knew your father well; God rest his soul." He said he was a remarkable man. I'm sure he didn't know my father, but that was what he was like—he had to say something nice about everyone.

In Sukhumi we lived together on Frunze Street. We had a big round table, he did not like new furniture. We did not live lavishly and were surrounded by plants and animals. He had several souvenirs from abroad, those were the only things he really treasured.

He did not like to observe birthdays. In our family, we marked only the birthday of my son, Tengo. Incidentally, his friend Professor Soso Kapanadze did not like to observe his own birthday, either.

In the house, we had a large ancient plate with a portrait of Alexander II on it. He said that Katerina Antonovna had links with the Tsar's family. At the beginning of the war that plate was broken by looters. When I arrived in Tbilisi, I brought the fragments of the plate with me, put them together, glued them and now it's in my new apartment. In memory of Mikhail Temurovich and life back then in general. The plate is the only thing I have from Sukhumi.

During the war, the looters confronted him with demands to open the door to them. They brandished a rifle butt at the old man. He was very traumatised. I knew he would not survive the war. His nephew had been put before a firing squad threatening to shoot him. They did not, but within one minute the thirty-year-old man's hair turned white. His neighbour's house was looted with the aid of a crane. His songbirds and parrots died from the racket of the rocket launchers and machine guns. He had frogs of a rare breed. He fed them with bread. They swelled up, became like toads and they also died. No, he would not have been able to survive the war.

He had a portable Japanese tape recorder. In addition to human voices, he would record everything living, frogs croaking, cows mooing, snakes hissing, flies buzzing, parrots shrieking, snakes hissing, cats meowing, dogs barking . . .

Sometimes our dogs wet on the parquet. My mother-in-law got angry and indignant, but his reaction was: "Well, so what?"

In Gvandra, he had a small holiday home of two rooms. He did not let us family members in there. It's my laboratory, my academy, only my friends ought to call here, he used to say. He raised bantams there. But only once did he bring anything from Gvandra, a pair of old hens. We boiled them all day, but they remained tough. A couple of times he brought eggs from these hens. That is all there was. Wherever he worked, he never even brought home a single mandarin.

In Gvandra, he had songbirds.

On feijoas he bestowed lavish praise; they enhanced male strength. However, this plant is something of a wheeler-dealer, heading whichever way the wind blows, but if it does not behave like that, the wind will break its back. Just look at its name, it is a manifestly sexual plant.

In general, he spoke well, but he was a bad listener. Of all the restaurants he knew, he singled out and liked the Eshera and the Merkheuli. He usually said: "Today we have a serious matter we must discuss and therefore we are going to the Merkheuli." Or to the Eshera.

Often, it was I who made his breakfast. For decades the menu remained unchanged: a soft-boiled egg, a glass of matsoni yogurt, apple puree, and a piece of cheese. In fact, he did not eat dinner, only breakfast and supper. He ate like a bird. Nor did he drink much. Some think he drank a lot. No, he never drank to excess. A banquet for him was a means of socialising. A banquet for him was a theatre, an airport, a rocket base. He could not imagine life without socialising. He loved veal, tkemali sauce prepared by my mother, and meat patties. As well as kharcho soup, which was amazingly prepared by our neighbour, Rosa Tsumaya. But, as I have already said, he ate little, pecked like a bird. He talked about one bird which weighed fourteen grams. If it put on even a single gram, it could not take wing. As for drinks, he was most fond of Vartsikhe brandy from Georgia or Armenian brandy.

He preferred not to wear his shirts tucked in. He also liked jackets as well as white socks. From April till the end of November, he slept on the balcony, on a couch. Instead of a mattress, he lay on a cape, and he covered himself with another cape.

There was a vine of Isabella grapes climbing up in his direction on the balcony. It thickly entwined the balcony, but usually yielded just five to six bunches. In autumn, he would pick them and say:

"Well, I've finally cashed in on the harvest."

We had an all-season air conditioner, in summer we used it to cool the air in the rooms with it, while in winter we heated with it. In winter, when Mikhail Temurovich came home, he would be sure to leave the balcony door open, there could not be enough fresh air for him.

"Look at him," my mother-in-law would say. "He wants to heat the whole of Sukhumi."

During the war, he remained in Sukhumi together with my son Tengo. At the beginning of the war, I was also in Sukhumi. Then I left. And now I feel that his soul took offence at me for this and not just at me.

## 42

"Let's suppose you're wearing a white suit and you're walking along the edge of a bog, hurrying to a wedding. Suddenly you see someone drowning in the bog. You stop and begin to give advice in a loud voice. Or, more precisely, you yell at him to get his arms and legs moving to reach the bank somehow, grab hold of a tree root, or some water weed . . . What do you think, would you help him like that?"

"No doubt we'd help."

"You won't help. If you really, with all your heart, wanted to rescue him, then be so kind as to step into the bog in your white suit, put your arms around him and press him to your chest, that's the only way you'll be able to drag him out."

# 43

Tsakva Shakirovna Khonelia was the director of the biggest fashion studio in Abkhazia, called "Fashion House" and located in a four-storey building on October Street in Sukhumi. Her Fashion House had an artistic council of which Mikhail Temurovich and Soso Kapanadze were members. Indeed, without Mikhail Temurovich's support, there would have been no Fashion House.

Tsakva Khonelia was a fine-looking woman, and Mikhail Temurovich introduced her to Khrushchev as follows:

"Nikita Sergeyevich, may I introduce Tsakva Shakirovna Khonelia, who is a direct descendent of Empress Tamar."

The same day he introduced Khrushchev to Soso Kapanadze:

"Nikita Khrushchev, may I introduce the greatest scholar of our era, Soso Kapanadze. We were suckled at the same breast."

Sometime later, a seriously indignant Soso Kapanadze whispered in his friend's ear:

"Mikhail Temurovich, you are four years older than me, so how can we have been suckled at the same breast? Or Tsakva Shakirovna, in what way is she related to Empress Tamar? . . . What if Khrushchev finds out?"

"Oh Sosik, Sosik, you're a good scholar of course, but you've no idea how to give a foal an enema. Khrushchev believes in symbols more than anything else: the Caucasus, babies suckled at the same breast, Empress Tamar . . . He needs legends. See for yourself."

The whole evening Khrushchev treated Tsakva Shakirovna as if she really were Empress Tamar risen from the dead. And his glance often focussed on her golden koshi slippers.

The evening before, Mikhail Temurovich had given Tsakva Shakirovna the koshi, which were embroidered with golden patterns and so they were the sole indisputable proof of a direct link of kinship between Tsakva Shakirovna and Empress Tamar. Indeed, only substantive proof was to be presented to the General Secretary.

# 44

He once read bureau members an extract from the testimony of some witness on a criminal matter.

"In the middle of the night I was woken by a voice. In the yard I was met by two tall men. They were wearing silver clothing. 'Who are you?' I asked. 'We're from another planet,' they replied. Good and well, I thought, cheering up. It could have been humans, burglars, I thought. My fear vanished. I sighed with relief."

His voice trembled as he read, and tears glistened in his eyes.

## 45

In Gagra, at the place where the world's shortest river, the Reprua, flows into the sea, he stood like the Statue of Liberty, raising high a horn filled with red wine and turned to the setting sun.

He was clad only in his underpants. Behind his back, by a table laid right on the sand, men and women like him sat with their sun-bronzed legs crossed, having just emerged from the sea and listened to him with smiles on their faces.

But he, as if ignoring anyone around him, was addressing just the sun alone:

"Send me all the homeless and despairing, all the defence-less and persecuted! Awaiting them with a torch in my hand, I stand by golden gates, with bated breath, trying to restrain my heartbeat!"

They listened to him attentively but did not understand much.

# 46

One day, the staff of the Plant Breeding Institute met him at Babushera airport on his return from a work trip.

"A dreadful thing has happened, Mikhail Temurovich, dreadful! Gabunia has raped Margarita in your office, on your divan, right under Lenin's portrait."

"On my divan? I'll teach him, that Gabunia, to wave his instrument around just any old where," said Mikhail Temurovich.

But then he asked:

"Gabunia is about twenty years younger than Margarita. Do you really think that Margarita allowed him to rape her?"

"Yes, we had doubts, too, but Margarita has raised such a commotion: she says he must marry her. Besides that she sat down right on the roadway by the river Macharka and blocked the traffic. She 'Won't get up till Gabunia marries me.'"

On reaching the Institute he summoned Margarita and Gabunia separately.

Just two days later, Margarita left on a paid vacation at a resort in the Carpathians. He sent her on her way with the words: "You've suffered such stress; you must have a holiday!" And to Gabunia he awarded a bonus. "I'm perfectly well aware who was actually raped in this situation and who is entitled to compensation."

## 47

The French scholar Jean Meslier wrote in one of his books that Aristotle spent the last years of his life in Colchis. This view was shared by the Georgian scholar Namoradze. He provided more detail: Aristotle lived on the bank of the river Phasis, died in Pitsunda, and is buried there.

Mikhail Temurovich summoned two scholars, Medzhit Khvartskia and Shota Misabishvili, and commissioned them to organise an expedition. They were to set off for Pitsunda and find Aristotle's grave, whatever it took.

The First Secretary's assignment was only partially fulfilled. An expedition was organised to excavate Pitsunda for several months. But it did not find a trace of Aristotle's grave. The archaeologists indeed found ancient burial grounds, but the location of the tomb of the great philosopher remains unknown.

"If only we had found it . . . Aristotle's grave is a lot more significant than hundreds of currently hale and hearty scholars, a lot more important than dozens of present-day cities, and a lot more essential than thousands of various banquets, even if their toastmaster is me."

# 48

In the fourteenth century, the monk Bonaventura made himself wings from white silk. He soaked them in a substance unknown to us and took off from the top of the cathedral. He was arrested and burnt at the stake, poor Bonaventura. And his wings were also committed to the flames.

The wings snapped in the flame with a frightening crack and soared to a height of several metres, then to a height of several hundred metres, and finally disappeared altogether.

The folk crowded into Rome's main square fled in fear with loud wailing. But the wings continued their flight somewhere in the unreachable expanses of space. In Zhoekvara Park in Gagra, he toast-mastered for a table laid under a big oak. There were about twenty people there and the toastmaster proposed a toast to Bonaventura's wings.

"Mankind needs wings, absolutely, needed them in the fourteenth century and will need them in the twenty-second century," he said.

And he concluded:

"Here's to the wings that were burnt and to those that will be burnt. And, it goes without saying, let us drink to those wings which are being burnt today, right now, this minute."

## 49

"Vianor, do you know what I remember most of all from the book you wrote about Gagra?" he asked Vianor Pachulia. "That in the times of the Prince of Oldenburg, in 1908, all the donkeys were numbered? Yet where did you dig this up: two donkeys are being removed from the list, no. 8 and no. 11, of which one went missing and the other was dashed against rocks, after falling from a cliff? Still, what does the written word mean? I am now experiencing what was written at that time—feeling sorry for the donkey that fell off the cliff, no. 11, but no less sorry for no. 8. If I write a book someday, I will no doubt number the chapters. I prefer numbered chapters to chapters with titles. Moreover, the chapters themselves must not be long, nor must the book itself be too large. And I will definitely mention those donkeys in it."

# 50

I once saw him in court. There was a gypsy on trial. He was "rooting" for him.

A gypsy named Kukuna had stolen a Baku air-conditioner from a warehouse. The most active person in the court room was Kukuna's mother, Fonda. For some reason she addressed all the militiamen who were almost the same age as her Kukuna as "uncle."

"Uncle, will all this be over soon?"

Kukuna got three years.

As soon as the judge had announced the sentence, he was targeted by a hail of glasses, bottles, and files. Some of the gypsies had already taken their shoes off, and they also were aimed at the judge. Fonda hitched up her five skirts and exposed her bare buttocks to the judge. Then she shouted to Kukuna:

"Kukuna, son, you will drink brandy again as you used to, and these pederast judges can suck my cunt."

"God is not a sucker," cried the gypsies.

"Sukhumi is a sucker-free city," said Mikhail Temurovich with a smile.

## 51

Some important ministers once came on a visit from Moscow. There were three of them, and all three were important. For comparatively less significant ministers do exist, who are ministers, yet not "very important" ones.

The important ministers were accompanied by some Englishmen who were very well known back in their own country.

He invited the guests to the "Amra." In the banquet hall a table was set for forty diners. Of course, the city mayor was also present, the most distinguished Dmitry Khvartskia.

During the banquet, Mikhail Temurovich raised a horn of wine in honour of Sukhumi.

"Present among us today is the mayor of the city of Sukhumi, Dmitry Andreyevich Khvartskia. He will confirm that, literally within the last few days, archaeologists of world significance here in Sukhumi, where the Chalbash River meets the sea, have discovered some clay tablets whose contents have established that 3,517 years ago Sukhumi already existed as a city under its present name."

Dmitry Khvartskia seemed frozen on the spot, at that time no excavations were being carried out anywhere and thus, accordingly, no tablets had been discovered.

Several toasts later, he announced that Sukhumi and Babylon were built together, that is, at the same time.

And a further couple of toasts later he said:

"It has finally been established that the construction of Sukhumi preceded that of Babylon by twenty-three years and nine months."

The English kept shouting "Bravo!" for him.

The President's Cat | 143

And the Moscow ministers all responded with "For he's a jolly good fellow."

At the end of the banquet, he invited the guests to celebrate Sukhumi's five thousandth jubilee.

"We shall be celebrating it in two years' time. The mayor extends to you all an early invitation."

Dmitry Khvartskia sat there without raising his head.

The following day he received a telephone call:

"Dmitry Andreyevich, I suspect that yesterday I went a bit far, but I beg you as a brother: Don't take offence. Generally speaking, if you look at the issue, ancient history is a very appropriate subject for a banquet. And besides you can see for yourself, Dima, how fascinating this life of ours can be."

## 52

There was a special intensity that day in the way the rain tested the drainage capacity of the city streets and the storm-water system of the squares and paths and the waterfront. There were already puddles and big enough for cars to get stuck in them and engines to be cut off. The rain forced men and women to take their shoes off. Laughing, they ran through water up to their knees to the nearest shops and to their own homes.

All day on the rooftops, the city drummed like the sensation caused by the smell of jasmine: tile, slate, iron, concrete, making merry like a madman.

We were sitting in the cable-car restaurant on Sukhumi Hill. From the veranda, the city looked like a toy town. Except that from that height the sea appeared slightly choppy. The more we drank, the choppier it seemed to us.

The cool moisture from outside gradually filled the room.

The rain was viridian in colour, it enshrouded the city and the sea in a mist, swept away the boundaries between the green of the plants, the white of the houses, and the blue of the sea. It frolicked, mixed the colours up, changed them about.

And Lukich was with us, the birdman. The same Lukich who had a hundred songbirds living in his house.

Then Kukuna stepped straight out of the rain into the restaurant, the gypsy Kukuna. He was wearing a long brown raincoat, he left wet footprints on the floor.

The wet trail ended next to our table.

"Well, here's one more friend dropping in on us," said Mikhail Temurovich. "Sit down, Kukuna."

Kukuna sat down. But first he took of his raincoat, which was sodden and heavy, and hung it on a hook by the door.

The aroma of sparkling champagne hovered over the table.

I will not say who the toastmaster was, you can guess yourselves.

Lukich had a cage containing two little red-breasted birds he had caught that morning in the woods by the cable-car.

The cage was standing in the middle of the table. The little, red-breasted birds were jumping about in the cage like rubber balls and occasionally even whistling.

"No, your father should not have fought in the war," Mikhail Temurovich was telling Kukuna. "It's hardly a gypsy's business, war, is it? A gypsy's homeland is the entire world. What's a gypsy doing in political dog pounds? Never go to war, Kukuna, whatever happens, don't go to war! It's none of your business! Will you give me your word?"

Kukuna gave his word not only to him, but to all of us, that he would not go near a war, that his homeland was the whole world—trading in clutter, sinka,* chewing gum!

Kukuna's face was smiling and tearful at the same time, besides, that day he was in a strange condition. First, he waved aloft some white tea towels over the table and held them there

---

\* Sinka, in Russian, is blue power for dying linen.

for several minutes, then with a glance moved two full bottles of brandy sitting on the shelf together, so that they made contact with a dull clink. In doing so, he almost broke our hearts, what if the bottles had broken!

Joined like Siamese twins, the bottles began to look like naval binoculars. Those same binoculars, thanks to which we penetrated that day, with our inner eye, the most distant corners of the world.

When Kukuna, with a single hand movement, set alight the Greek curtains five metres away from us, we delicately let it be understood that that was quite enough and gently asked him to dowse the flame, which he did.

Then we asked the young waitress to bring the largest fluted glass, poured champagne into it, and forced Kukuna as a latecomer to knock back a "penalty" draught to somehow subdue his black mischief.

"It's the rain that's responsible. When it rains, Kukuna gets into a particular mood. When it rains, all these pranks of his come out." Mikhail Temurovich looked at his friend with pride and proposed a toast to the rain.

And he proposed a toast to all the rains of the world, to the rains which have been, are and will be. He glorified heavy deluging rains and showers light as a fan, prolonged rain and brief showers, rains over huge areas and rains irrigating no more than a handful of earth, night rains and daytime rains, warm rains and cold rains, historic rains, rains of future generations, high and low rainfall, blue, red, green, white, yellow, dark rains, jolly and sad rains, maritime and ocean rains, and desert rains, rains with large drops and small drops, forest, mountain-top and meadow rains, town and village rains, the rains of Australia, Africa, America, Asia, Europe . . . Loud rain and soft rain, angry rain and songful rain, rustling rain and whistling rain, the rains of those in love, children's rain, women's rain, men's rain, old folks' rain . . . Migrant rain and profoundly settled rain, aboriginal rains, guests' rain and hosts' rain, rains of desire, rains imbued with the smoke of shacks, the "symphonic" rains of maritime cities, rains that pour down on Fujiyama and the pyramids, on the cities of the Incas, on New York, on the expanses of Russia and the conglomerations of the Caucasus mountains, palace rains and hovel rains, flowing rain and showy rain . . .

And then he informed us that:

"When the rain doesn't fall for a long time and drought destroys the crops, the men from one of the tribes in Argentina, who call themselves Jaguars, organise a big ritual contest. The Jaguar people fight one another with huge clubs. According to their beliefs, the greater the amount of blood that flows, the sooner and the more liberally, the rain will fall. It will come and water the fields and those fields will feed humankind. The Jaguars consider themselves the saviours of the world."

We all rose and drank to the Jaguar people, we all emptied our glasses, not leaving a drop of wine. Then we opened the bottles of brandy.

Someone asked if the Jaguars kill one another in this contest. "No," was the reply. "They only wound, and their wounds are considered divine. But the main point is that, following their contests, the rain really does fall."

The little, red-breasted birds whistled.

Evening was descending, and, from time to time, the restaurant doors "yawned" lazily. Sometimes people came in, sometimes people went out. More people came in.

One of those entering said that the rain had covered almost all the city streets with torrents of water and most of the cars were at a standstill, with their engines having conked out.

The garages would be raking in the money tomorrow, said Kukuna.

When the rain stopped late in the evening, Lukich was persuaded to let the red-breasted songsters out.

## 53

The day spent with friends concluded in a remarkable way.
But the evening still fell short by the following margins:

A couple of glasses of "Stolichnaya" vodka,
A flirtation with a female stranger on vacation close
to the Chipileta River,
As well as a mournful French melody.

## 54

The issues examined at the Central Committee in Moscow, the Mecca of the Communist Party of the Soviet Union, had to be studied at all costs within a few days in all party organisations without exception, even in the smallest ones, be they as few as three men strong.

In this way, Moscow made its way into every city, town, and village; in this way, it was expanded over one-sixth of planet earth and covered the entire land of the Soviets.

The USSR was Moscow.

Moscow was the USSR.

The Central Committee passed grandiose resolutions on the most significant and, at the same time, the most grand-scale issues. For instance, resolutions about agriculture, residential construction, the strengthening of internal party discipline, work with young people, improving active measures in the struggle against capitalist ideology and so forth.

The Central Committee also passed secret and top-secret resolutions. Sometimes it was even possible to scrutinize the secret resolutions within party organisations. And this was done to create an aura of self-importance and secrecy among the members of the country's sole party, in contrast to the other non-party inhabitants of this country. For exclusivity and mystery demand a respectful attitude, mixed with fear and caution. In short, the most important thing was concern for the welfare of the people. This was something the party was only too well aware of, and it methodically strove to improve and maintain the chosen course.

As for the top top-secret resolutions, they were made known only to the top-rank leaders of the Union and

The President's Cat | 151

Autonomous Republics. By this very fact, the party underlined their exclusivity and mystery—of the top-rank leaders, in contrast to other selected initiates. Among the people, the former enjoyed a respect that could be multiplied by ten.

The Number One was always the Number One. And these days as well. Who would disagree?

This formula goes back to antediluvian times.

There were also secret decisions, which were supposed to be known only to the First Secretaries of the Central Committees of the Union republics or only to members of the Central Committee Bureaus.

Imagine, a secret decision known to nobody—nobody!—except to the First Secretary of the USSR's Communist Party Central Committee. He made such decisions himself as a rule—as the First Secretary.

So, the Central Committee's First Secretary enjoyed the status almost of a demigod, at the peak of the communist pyramid.

Even though Moscow examined multifarious and diversely significant issues, it never addressed comparatively insignificant questions. Such as, for example, the theft of a goat.

Moscow would not sort it out, but Sukhumi did.

It sorted it out within its "Bureau," the Bureau of the Regional Committee of the Communist Party. The Bureau was a Central Committee but smaller, a local incarnation of it.

"Oh, the Bureau, it's like . . . There could be times when you would enter it like a man and come out a pile of manure or, on the contrary, go in like a pile of manure and come out a man . . . That's what the Bureau is like." This phrase was often reiterated by members of the Bureau, or candidates for Bureau membership, or those Young Communist League members who dreamt of Bureau membership.

And now à propos the above issue: the theft of the goat.

In one of the villages of Ochamchire region, a man stole a goat from a neighbour. Both were party members. So the victim of the crime, a communist peasant, complained to the regional authorities about the offender, who was also a communist and a peasant. The Party Regional Committee took a routine decision without lengthy deliberation: it expelled the goat thief from the party and, besides that, obliged him, as stated in the resolution, to buy the victim an "analogous goat," that is, a goat of the same age and weight as the one that had been stolen.

This case reached Mikhail Temurovich. Not one of the Ochamchire residents was known to him, neither the victim of the crime, nor the thief. Mikhail Temurovich took an interest in the case. "Very interesting!" was his comment.

And he had the "interesting" question placed on the agenda for discussion by the Party Regional Committee Bureau. The question of the goat's kidnapping was formulated as follows: "The case of a party discipline violation within a party organisation in Ochamchire district."

The Second Secretary of the Party Regional Committee, Damian Gogokhia, attempted to convince Mikhail Temurovich to change his decision, but nothing came of it. Although it should also be noted that, now and again, Mikhail Temurovich did give an ear to Damian Gogokhia's advice. The communists of the older generation, who delved deeply into every case, used to say: "Gogokhia operates like a communist, but as for Bgazhba, you can't understand anything."

At the Bureau meeting, the First Secretary of the Ochamchire Party Regional Committee gave a brief account of the matter under discussion and several times stressed the fact that the Ochamchire Party Regional Committee had taken an objective and principled decision with respect to a party organisation member who had brought shame to the name "communist" and had, therefore, been punished, expelled from the party, and, on top of that, as having shamed the party, been obliged to purchase the humiliated communist an analogous livestock item, or goat, equal in weight and age to the one that had been stolen, with the aim of indemnifying the moral and material damage. Apart from that, he pointed out, indemnification of the material damage in the given specific instance was fully possible, but, as for indemnifying the moral damage, that was impossible even to imagine.

"At what time was the goat stolen?" Mikhail Temurovich asked the Secretary of the Party District Committee.

"Around 5 or 6 o'clock in the evening."

"As far as I know, the victim of the crime wasn't home then."

"Yes, Mikhail Temurovich, he wasn't home."

"And then what?"

"Yes, Mikhail Temurovich."

"But then, do you know, perhaps, whether the man you expelled from the party had a guest?"

"Yes, the evidence mentions a guest."

"And then?"

"Yes, Mikhail Temurovich."

"In the evidence . . . Well, then, was he not supposed to accord due honour his guest? A guest is a gift from God, after all. Besides, it was most likely a guest that couldn't be hosted with just a single roast chicken and some mealy porridge. It was a very highly esteemed guest for this family . . . So, he had to slaughter a goat, a quadruped rather than a biped. Not a biped, but a quadruped, isn't that obvious? It wasn't a khachapuri guest, it was a man deserving of a goat on the table . . ."

" . . ."

"He didn't have a goat, and his neighbour wasn't home, so he went and slaughtered his neighbour's goat and paid his guest the respect due to him, continuing the tradition of our forefathers, the tradition of hospitality. And what did the Ochamchire Party Regional Committee do? Expelled this man from the party! And for what? For paying due respect to his guest. What is going on here? We all live in the same republic as one family. If I don't have a goat today and a guest calls, I will host him with my neighbour's goat on the table. And if my neighbour has a guest tomorrow, we'll slaughter my goat for his guest. Isn't that how it works, comrades?"

Bewildered, the Bureau members began to nod their heads in unison, with smiles of embarrassment.

"It's a poor state of affairs you have here in Ochamchire; you are forgetting our forefathers' most sacred tradition, hospitality, and you offend a true communist, a peasant, a man who is perpetuating this tradition. It's a lack of vision, myopia. Surely that's not what our party teaches us? Maybe some other party does, but not ours. Our party is not known for that kind of attitude. Doesn't Lenin write about it . . .? Vladimir Ilyich?"

At this point he couldn't for the life of him recall what Lenin had written in defence of goat stealing and the traditions of hospitality.

"Damian Vladimirovich, surely this kind of thing doesn't go on in Gali when a host has to honour a guest? And besides, I know the Mingrelians, they would carry a neighbour's goat on that same neighbour's horse to get everything done as it should be as quickly as possible, so the guest wouldn't weary of waiting for the banquet to start. Isn't that so, Damian Vladimirovich?"

Damian Vladimirovich hung his head.

Silently, without a single word, the Bureau agreed with the First Secretary.

"I move a motion to withdraw the penalty imposed by the Ochamchire Party District Committee on a communist who was defending the honour of his village and entertaining a guest in a worthy manner and to reinstate him within the ranks of the party. These days, comrades, we have a shortage of people like him. We must support them, otherwise what are we to tell the future generation tomorrow? For they must perpetuate the finest traditions of our forefathers!"

The Bureau silently agreed to the motion.

"And in addition, the district party leadership must purchase a goat for his neighbour, and I mean his neighbour, not the "victim of the crime," as you put it. I trust no one is opposed, comrades? And it goes without saying that it must come from the district budget."

There were no votes against and no abstentions.

## 55

"Our Father, Who art in Heaven, hallowed be Thy name. Thy kingdom come on earth as it is in Heaven.

Give us this day our daily bread and forgive us our trespasses, as we forgive those who trespass against us!

And besides: save us and keep us, our Father, me, my family, my city, my country!

Help us and keep us!

And if Thou art not needful of this and wishest not for this and desirest it not in the meantime, Father, then help and keep someone else, other families, other cities, some other country!"

# 56

Here's to the Caucasus mountains! First and foremost because they are special, and no other mountains are like them.

If you stand in the very centre of other mountain ranges and hail them: "Greetings! How are you?" the echo of those other mountains will resound: "Greee-eee-eee . . . How are-how are . . ."

But stand in the middle of the Caucasus mountains and shout: "Greetings, mountains! How are you?"

And then listen closely!

And you will hear:

"Greetings-greetings . . . Not bad, thank you-not bad, thank you . . . And how are you, my friend? Is everyone well in your family? Greetings to all of them-greetings to all . . . Regards to all . . ."

# The President's Cat

Science is still today searching for the secret behind constructing the framework of the living organism. As for the question of how the first living cell arose, now there are various answers.

As a result of the union between tissues a new—transitional—form appears.

These are somatic forms, the same chimeras. The vegetative form is primary: if photosynthesis does not take place, there will be no life on earth. Nor on any other planet. Animal forms arose later.

In Abkhazia, Iosif Kapanadze and Mikhail Bgazhba worked on the problem of constructing the framework of a living organism. And the historian Vianor Pachulia encouraged them and was entrusted with their secrets.

Citruses are considered classic plants. They used them for their first experiments.

And they did discover this secret, the secret of constructing the framework of an organism. Two components create a unifying tissue. The organism begins with a single cell, which then splits into two and engenders an initiating tetrad. The cells create a framework and take the form of a pyramid. The first cell of the pyramid engenders pith in the case of plants and bone marrow in the case of animals. Other cells are formed later. Pith in plants, bone tissue in animals. In animals, bones are followed by flesh and muscles.

A trifoliate was implanted with a lemon. The cells of both plants combined, merged into one. In this way, a transitional fruit was obtained from crossing an orange and a lemon.

Mikhail Temurovich also worked on accelerating the maturation periods and increasing the fertility of plants. He would dress in a white coat and nothing else. He forgot about everything in the world except his plants. He had to see everything for himself, check everything, scrutinise it for the umpteenth time. Together with Soso Kapanadze he locked himself in the laboratory for long hours.

They submitted their work for discussion at geneticists' conferences in various countries.

On one occasion, it was in the 1980s, Mikhail Temurovich arrived at an international conference in America two days late. Before reading a paper about his scientific research to an audience of one thousand five hundred, he apologised to everyone for his lateness:

"I made a detour to Germany on the way. There I visited Halle. We also have a city with a similar name called Gali, and, therefore, I was interested in Halle. In Halle there is a sculpture, a monument to a donkey. My fellow academic friends have calculated that, with the aid of the wheel, billions of tons of freight have been carted, but donkeys have carried an amount that is twelve times greater, no more and no less. As a matter of fact, incidentally, the wheel was invented by the Caucasians along with the Sumerians. So much for my introduction. Now let's talk about our new discovery."

The conference attendants laughed whole-heartedly and, thereafter, listened to his new concepts with redoubled attention.

He was a good speaker. According to Soso Kapanadze, when he was still a student of the Timiryazev Institute, it was through his talent for oratory that he entranced Stalin.

From one conference he came back to Abkhazia with the well-known German scientist Bergan of Jena University. He collected hybrids of plants and had a huge collection of them. Of all those in Abkhazia who were aware of his status, nobody could even have dreamed that Mikhail Temurovich would succeed in bringing him here. But he did. They arrived together by car, via Sochi.

"Bergan and I have some serious issues which we have to discuss," said Mikhail Temurovich, but, first, invited him to Merkheuli, then to Amra on the following day, and to Eshera on the third day. Bergan told Mikhail Temurovich and Soso Kapanadze that he was delighted by them and their discovery.

In Merkheuli, they talked about the framework of the organism, in Amra about global warming, and in Eshera about Washington grapefruit plantations. I should mention at this point that the Washington grapefruit has the potency of two ordinary oranges, i.e. it is twice as beneficial in health terms. And in Abkhazia it is possible to harvest one hundred twenty tonnes of Washington grapefruit per hectare as compared to thirty-seven tonnes of oranges.

Bergan arrived in Abkhazia two years before the war. And a year before the war, Mikhail Temurovich visited the headquarters of the Nobel Prize committee in Stockholm. He also visited the Swedish Academy of Science and Royal Society. Their discovery should have been, if not worthy of international acknowledgement, then, at any rate, an object of international attention. For this, it was necessary to submit their achievements for the Nobel Prize. Only the Nobel, only his prize! That is what Mikhail Temurovich decided. The Sukhumi staff had everything ready for it: balsamed cells, a collection of hybrids (the most meritorious of them a hybrid of trifoliate and lemon), various preparations, publications. A description and several recommendations had to be attached to the application; a special commission was supposed to come and look at the plantations.

Perhaps they would be awarded the prize for achievements in the field of peace and progress established by the king of dynamite, and the award would come in the interval between the ninetieth and one-hundredth year of the prize's existence.

Along with their friends, they dreamt of the Nobel Prize. Moreover:

In Moscow, he periodically met with Levan Gugushvili, student of the legendary Demikhov. Demikhov and Gugushvili had worked on the transplantation of animal organs. Wandering around in their laboratory were two-headed dogs and dogs with paws and hearts grafted from other dogs. Mikhail Temurovich was interested in their activities, but he could not have sacrificed the lives of animals for the sake of experiments.

At home he had a snake, which lived there for the whole of two years. Then he released it into the forest. And he prohibited killing snakes in general. He loved to water plants himself, every day, both at home and at work. As soon as he appeared at work, the pigeons were the first to greet him and followed him at his heels. He always had chunks of bread or buns in his pocket for the various birds and pigeons. Soso Kapanadze nicknamed him "Mindia," after the hero of Vazha Pshavela's epic poem. Before leaving a restaurant, he would sometimes ask the waiter to wrap up food leftovers in paper and use them to feed stray dogs and cats. He once picked up a pup on the street, reared it, asked for a kennel to be made for it in the basement of the institute's central building, and kept it there.

From time to time, he would visit Zinaida Nikolayevna. They would sit till late at night and talk and drink tea, sometimes coffee. The murderers, or murderer, of Zinaida's son were never caught. The suspects from Gagra and Gali were found not guilty and released. Zinaida Nikolayevna was cared for by her daughter and Valery's friend Roma. Roma lived in the neighbourhood. To the woman's spiritual anguish, physical sufferings were added, she grew weak, her arms and legs no longer responded, and rheumatism overcame her. He took on her expensive medicines, some he obtained from the Pharmacy Authority, others he brought in from abroad, but even these medicines did not help. On one occasion, he brought her a great big ginger tomcat and said that, when he was in America, John Fitzgerald Kennedy himself had given him this cat. It was a "therapeutic cat," bred from all the therapeutic cat breeds in the world. He had a huge "bio field." He healed everything, particularly the heart and the blood vessels, nerves, joints, liver, and stomach. He regulated blood pressure, absolutely everything. "Just make sure you have him beside you all the time, and you will see what a champ he is; he likes fish just like you. And another thing, you must make sure that he has his fur stroked as often as possible. The Kennedys wouldn't keep just an ordinary cat in the family, would they? It's the President's own cat, specially bred for him. You can call him Johnny sometimes, or John Fitzgerald, or by his full name, John Fitzgerald Kennedy."

He used to treat his own lungs, but not many knew about this. Only a few people. Among them was Soso Kapanadze. In

1968, he was diagnosed with lung cancer. He treated himself with folk remedies and drank the medicine Colchicum, which was delivered to him from Kiev. Colchicum contains the poison colchicine.

One day, he came to the institute with a young blonde in black tights and a miniskirt. "Sosik, sign her up as a lab assistant. She's no more stupid than your assistants, and, besides, I'm sure she'll be a great help to us in winning the Nobel Prize." Soso dug his heels in: "No way!" Then he found the non-existent lab assistant a vacancy as water reticulation inspector: "Science demands sacrifices, and you, Sosik, haven't realised that yet."

He was friendly with children. He once gave money to eleven boys playing football in the institute's yard to buy eleven footballs: "Your ball is quite tatty."

On summer mornings, he used to go to the seaside with friends. There, on a closed beach, he had his own personally allocated space, with an umbrella and a cubicle for changing. It was there that he was once informed, while basking in the shade, that his youngest daughter had got married and run away from home. When he found out the name of his son-in-law, he flew into a rage like a Shakespearean hero: "Those damned Mingrelians! They're determined to assimilate me; just look how they've upset my equilibrium. They're putting the brakes on my research." He rejected the company of Vianor Pachulia and others: "Only Sosik will come with me, he is well familiar with my neuroses." Within half an hour their Volga was speeding up to the place where the young couple were "hiding." Having first kissed his daughter, he embraced his son-in-law and kissed him on both cheeks: "Well, children, where would you like to spend your honeymoon?"

## 164 | *Guram Odisharia*

"Vinor," he said to Vianor Pachulia. "No doubt we were once some sort of plants, then animals. So yesterday, when you rubbed me down with bear fat, I was a bear all night. In fact, I feel as if I was once a buffalo."

He believed that in Gvandra neither winter nor summer were the same as in other parts of the earth. "In the Gvandra winter, I cover myself with the Gvandra summer and sleep like that," he would say. "And in the Gvandra summer, I drink the Gvandra winter like chilled champagne, a little at a time and leisurely. Here, even the egg I fry with a friend has a quantum yellow colour and light and the vibrations of the sea as well."

"However unwell I may be, at the sight of a pretty woman, I draw myself up to my full height. It just takes a single glance from her to cure me."

On other occasions, on the seashore, in the woods, or in the meadows, he would lie down on his back and gaze for ages at the sky. "They cure me," he used to say. "The earth and the sky." The earth fortified his back and the sky his heart.

At any moment, he could recall his childhood. At any moment, he could recall the living and the dead. He spoke of them as if they had only just been standing beside him. He did not see a great difference between the living and the dead. He could be both in town and in the country at the same time. In short, he could be at the same time in the city, the country, in two countries, on two planets, in two dimensions."

Among his sayings were:

- "A man is shaped by his enemies. Glory and love to them. But what if I don't have any?"
- "A man's word ought to be tested the way they tested gold in old films, with your teeth."

The President's Cat | 165

- "The world can be accommodated in a single room, the ocean in a single drop. We are born journeying. We journey between spaces. That's why I love ships, cars, and trains. In my own car, I always sit in the front beside the driver. Broadly speaking, it is more common for a man to be born, and rarely does he die, but not many people know that."
- "I see God when I rove amidst human interrelationships."
- "Our entire life is a conspiracy against the newborn. Look how we strive to deceive them in our world. With rattles, gaily coloured toys, whistles, bright coloured balls. How we decorate Christmas trees for them. How we dress them up on their birthdays, how we indoctrinate them with our lying."
- "The most important things are the heart and the soul, for a kind face and a foul-tempered face are still both the same face."
- "The greatest thing is that which does not exist, but which we still nevertheless have in our possession."

And then the expressions he used:

- "There are people who see no further than two metres, and people whose gaze extends a thousand kilometres."
- "Some parties actually degrade music."
- "There are rains which soak the city like a bun."
- "Lying in my heart is the mist of the Black Sea, both young and old at the same time, but always so joyful."

And the stories that went around about him:

- "So, Mikhail Temurovich says to me: 'You've killed a fly. What factory can now recreate that fly? May you have a boil on your backside for every fly you kill, so you don't dare to kill a cockroach, or a snake, or a lizard, or a bear . . .'"
- "He once told me: 'Well, what misfortune! Yesterday I came across some odd people on the street. There were three of them. I greeted them, and they didn't answer. I wanted them to become 'mine,' at least to a small extent, but they didn't need that. For them I was alien.'"

- "I wished: God help me to find a foreign India to discover my America!"
- "I phoned him, and he addressed me before I spoke up. 'Greetings, Dmitry Andreyevich!' 'How did you recognise me?' 'I recognise penniless people by their silence,' he laughed."
- "At one banquet, someone spoke about our common acquaintance, AirTrust. Mikhail Temurovich flared up: 'There's no need ever to talk like that about someone, whoever he or she may be, especially if they are not among us at the moment!'"
- "While in Gagra, he told us: 'Gagra is so beautiful that it's impossible even to think of science; the city gets in the way.'"
- "I recalled how in a geography class at school the teacher wrote Columbus's name as 'Christ Opher Columbus.' Since that time, Columbus for me has been not Christopher, but Christ Opher."
- "In a restaurant, he told one drunk and disorderly debaucher: 'What are you doing, pursuing the curse of my wife? Why are you poisoning this evening for me?' The furious drunkard turned to face him, but on recognising him, dropped his hands and left the restaurant."

We were sitting in Gvandra in the yard of his house. The sea was rolling and topped by a light ripple, the noise of a train resounded from somewhere, the sun in the sky was alternately covered by clouds and peeping out anew, the kettle was boiling in the kitchen, an old man passing along the street was coughing, and we were drinking wine from Achandara. He was telling us all sorts of things:

That

it is possible that love is a religion and that possibly it will be replaced by party spirit. He cited the example of the English king Henry VIII marrying Anne Boleyn, although he soon cooled towards her. Anne was imprisoned and then beheaded.

The President's Cat | 167

That

the sexiest item of clothing is the "zip," because it caused a revolution not only in clothing but also in sex.

That

the tale of Scheherazade is the queen of tales.

That

mankind is the strangest species of life on earth and the hardiest of all the remaining ten million species.

That

Venice alone is sufficient reason for Italy to stand proud.

That

besides America, the author of the greatest mistake in the world, Christ Opher Columbus, introduced Europe to tomatoes, potatoes, and bananas.

And that we were sitting in Gvandra at a table laid by Columbus and supplementing the banquet with wine from Achandara as well as Indian tea, African coffee, walnuts, Czech beer, and cake baked at the Sukhumi confectionary factory.

And on this day, as happened quite often, probably all the time, our guests were the entire world, and we had the entire world for company.

## 57

I was a pupil in the seventh class at Tamysh secondary school. The history teacher took us, the four top scholars, to Leningrad to show us historic places, museums, and the "Aurora."

I shall never forget that New Year.

In Leningrad, we unexpectedly came across Bgazhba. He and my teacher had been classmates. Bgazhba was very glad to meet us. "I will be expecting you this evening in the hotel restaurant," he told the teacher. "And you must bring the children. Don't you dare let me down!" He said goodbye, kissed us all on both cheeks and hurried off.

A few hours later we were at the fashionable Astoria restaurant. He also had guests from Hungary and Romania.

Slightly inebriated, he introduced our teacher to his guests as the Abkhazian Minister for Education and announced us as winners of a "Wunderkind" competition in Paris, a competition of planetary significance, he said.

For us it was like a bolt from the blue, but what could we do?

Having released this information, Bgazhba immediately informed his astounded but delighted guests that the children knew chemistry, physics, mathematics, and history at doctorate level, and, apart from that, were fluent in Abkhazian, Mingrelian, Russian, Georgian, Armenian, Turkish, Greek, ancient Hebrew, old Spanish, ancient Japanese, Thai, Macedonian as well as the language of one Asian tribe, Urdu.

Our food got stuck in our throats. The teacher very nearly fled.

"Just look what interesting children they are. They will have an exotic life, a holiday rather than a life," he said.

The guests gave us souvenirs and hugged us: Was it true that we were just ordinary children?

Then the weather forecast on the television screen caught Mikhail Temurovich's eye. They were announcing that there had been a big snowfall on the Black Sea coast and traffic had been partly disrupted.

He immediately asked for a telephone. It was brought directly to the table. He phoned an urgent telegram to Sukhumi, to the Party Regional Committee, and the Council of Ministers.

I remember its contents to this day:

"I have heard that snow is falling in Abkhazia. Generally speaking, snow is a remarkable phenomenon, but a lengthy and heavy snowfall is not. In this regard, I am placing an obligation on the Party District Committees and the District Executive Committees, the state and collective farms, and the entire population of Abkhazia to make an effort to ensure that songbirds survive the winter safely and to provide them with food. Their death would be an irredeemable loss for Abkhazia. I will be arriving in two days and be checking on the spot what measures you have taken. Mikhail Bgazhba."

## 58

"Here's to the wretched of the earth. May God help them and guide their hand.

There is a fire-service plane which can suck up dozens of tons of water in a minute or two from a lake or other large reservoir, holding it in its belly of a tank, and then pouring it all on a fire.

This plane is used to put out forest fires.

When it takes up its supply of water, the plane itself almost "sits" on the water, a very powerful four-engine plane, I have seen it with my own eyes.

In August of last year, a big fire broke out in the forests of Canada. Which way ever they tried to extinguish it, whatever means they used, the forests kept blazing for a whole week.

That plane was 'working' in Canada at the time.

During its regular water 'gulping,' it also 'gulped' up a diver and several minutes later spat the poor wretch out along with the water, straight onto the raging flames.

On behalf of this Canadian diver, let us drink to all those who run out of luck."

# 59

In the eucalyptus thickets where the Besletka flows into the Black Sea, under the oleander bushes, he found a stray ginger cat. He took it in his arms, pressed it to his breast and stroked and kissed it.

The cat squinted with its green eyes, meowed loudly and untiringly, rubbed its head against his chest, and licked his face with its sandpaper tongue. It carried on as if they were old friends.

"Look how much he resembles you," said Soso.

And Vianor piped up, too: "This is the first time I've heard a cat meow in such an astounding way."

But he said: "There's nothing astounding about it. Take a good look and you'll see that fate has sent us an extraordinary cat, that's what."

He brought the extraordinary cat home and shampooed it.

A few days later, he gifted it to his childhood friend Zinaida Nikolayevna, who was one of my neighbours.

Zinaida Nikolayevna's joints were so sore that she did not rise from her bed for half a year or more.

"Zinaida Nikolayevna, I have brought you a therapeutic cat of a specially bred variety.

It was given to me by the President of the United States of America, by John Fitzgerald Kennedy himself. You can call it John Fitzgerald Kennedy or simply the President's Cat."

Later, Zinaida Nikolayevna actually pronounced its name: John Fitzgerald Kennedy, or less frequently, the President's Cat. She believed in it with extraordinary conviction. It is simply impossible to convey how strongly she believed in it.

"Make sure you don't forget about the President's Cat; you see how cuddly he is."

And Zinaida Nikolayevna would not part with the President's Cat.

A month later, she went out with the cat, first into the yard, then onto the street, and, in no time, they were strolling together in Pioneer Park.

John Fitzgerald Kennedy's cat! How impressive it sounded!

# 60

"And now let us discuss those birds, those mammals, those insects which did not make it into Noah's Ark.

Among them also was a buffalo, but it was saved by the fact that it had bellowed out Noah's name:

'N-oo-aa, N-oo-aa!'

The ark was full and about to cast off at any minute when the buffalo's 'N-oo-aa' was heard.

And Noah took the buffalo into the ark.

But the others became victims of the flood. Perhaps because they did not know how to roar, cheep, or buzz, how to attract Noah's attention.

Let us remember them, unfortunate then but happy today, like those who were never born."

## 61

"When I was studying at the Timiryazev Institute in Moscow, I had a Russian friend, Vasily Kuzmich. He was a scientist studying the North Pole and, therefore, he would often traverse the icy polar expanses on various expeditions.

You probably know that in those latitudes dog teams are generally used for transport.

Every team has its leader. To become one, a dog must repeatedly fight off others, sometimes in battles of life and death.

During one expedition, Vasily Kuzmich's team was led by a dog named Buran. Buran was a young dog with shaggy black fur and a broad white chest. Vasily liked Buran more than the other dogs. The dog may not have been able to speak, but they understood each other regardless. The closer the expedition got to the Pole, the fiercer the frosts raged. Every night one or two dogs became their victims. In the morning, a frozen dead dog would be released from its harness and replaced with a live one. The body was just left there, and the team continued on its way.

The leader, it went without saying, remained at the head of the team, and, behind him, the other dogs were tied to the chain in pairs. And at night the dogs slept in the same order: first, the leader lay in the harness, and, tied in pairs, the others lay resting behind him.

But the frosts continued to intensify, and the number of fallen dogs increased.

One day, when the frost had become completely intolerable, Vasily Kuzmich became alarmed that Buran, too, might freeze. He unchained him, took him into the tent, and forcibly

The President's Cat | 175

kept him there on a rope. And lay down himself and fell asleep, dead tired from the cold and the footslogging.

When he awoke, the first thing that caught his eye was the gnawed remnant of the rope, which Buran had chewed through in the night before he escaped.

Vasily Kuzmich ran outside and saw Buran again lying back in his place, at the head of the team, in the leader's place. He had hidden his face behind his paws and, deeply offended, did not even look in his direction. And the other dogs were also lying in their places, in pairs, in the snow.

Vasily Kuzmich burst into tears, realising he was guilty before Buran, for if the team leader had spent the night in the tent, his dogs would not have acknowledged him the following day, would not have obeyed him, followed in his path, pulled their chains liked guitar strings, and the sledge would not have budged.

The dogs would not have forgiven Buran for a night spent in a human's tent, they would have chosen a different leader.

So, let's drink to the health of a leader among men resembling Buran, albeit to a small extent. Believe me, this is a toast for one or two, at the most three, people. No more."

## 62

"I was once appointed the head of a delegation of thirty people. We were due to hold meetings in Mozambique. It was an important visit. The Soviet Union was looking for allies in Africa. Sometimes it even found them. Except that it cost a lot of money.

An important member of the Central Committee entrusted me with this task.

'Go to Mozambique, Mikhail Temurovich, take these people there and bring back good news.'

We set off from Odessa, by sea, and sailed across the Black, Aegean, and Red Seas, into the Indian Ocean. Then we reached Mozambique itself via the Mozambique Channel and anchored at the port of Maputo.

I was very interested in one tribe there, the Tuku. When we had finished the official meetings, I asked our hosts to take me and show me the areas where the Tuku lived, even if just for an hour.

Well, they showed me.

While the entire delegation was attending a concert of folk ensembles, I was taken on a small ship to the mouth of the river Savi, where the Tuku tribe lives. Also with us was an Italian priest, a missionary named Antonio, Father Antonio.

The Tuku tribe live off fishing. They have an interesting ritual: first, three men take a boat into the channel, sail towards Madagascar, catch a fish, just one fish, release it into a large vessel filled with sea water, and return to shore. This species of fish is called the baramba. A mature baramba weighs between three and seven kilograms.

Then the Tuku release the caught baramba into a special pool and spend a week feeding it with a select diet.

After a week, the same three men take the well-fed and satiated baramba back in the same vessel filled with water and let it go.

Before setting it free they say to it: 'Tell your family, your kin, your friends, and all your neighbours, absolutely everyone, that you had a good time here on shore, say that tomorrow at sunrise we will sail here with many boats, gather them all up, and bestow on them the same great honour as you received.'

The following day at sunrise, they sail there with thirty boats, to this same place and, indeed, catch so many baramba that they can barely carry them away.

The catch suffices for a long time, and, after a certain period, the whole process is repeated: those three special men again sail into the ocean. For one and only one baramba . . .

Father Antonio and I talked with the fishermen, and they treated us to baramba. They roasted the fish on a fire. They explained that the first baramba caught would believe what they said, and then the others would listen to it and believe it, too. 'And we believe that our relations will continue in the same way, that our god and the god of the baramba are friends.'

After the meal they prayed by the fire.

'Ialo!' one of them exclaimed (which in their language means 'one').

'Ialo!' the others repeated.

'Oili' exclaimed the first man (which in their language means 'two').

'Oili!' the others repeated.

And then again: 'Ialo! Ialo!' from some of the worshippers and the response, 'Oili! Oili!' They prayed like this for about ten minutes.

'This is our main prayer,' they told us.

'No, the main prayer is 'Our Father,'' said Father Antonio and then spent a whole hour teaching them the Latin text of the Lord's Prayer. To my surprise they quickly learned it by heart.

It was already night when our ship left the area. Father Antonio and I were standing on deck. Suddenly we heard strange voices, looked out at the ocean, and beheld two Tuku running across the surface of the sea, their legs splashing in the water. I swear on my mother's grave that they were splashing across the water.

'Father, we have forgotten the end of the prayer 'Forgive us our trespasses . . .' but what comes next? How are we supposed to end the prayer?' The Tuku were running the length of the boat across the water.

'Don't bother, you don't need it . . . Pray the way you prayed before, in your own style, your own main prayer!' exclaimed the overjoyed, agitated, and shaken Father Antonio.

And now let us glorify true believers! The Lord loves them. Ialo!

Oili!"

# 63

Egeos Marmarilos was a descendant of the Argonauts. When the turbidly swirling waves of history, adorned with Greek ornaments, had rolled back, when the glory of Dioskuria had sunk into the sea forever, and the erection of the city of Sukhumi had commenced in its place, a long distant forefather of Egeos Marmarilos was cast up on a sandy shore, washed by foaming surf, all alone, without shelter, and imbued through and through with the smell of anchovies.

But he did not lose his head, he taught the local dwellers some secrets of construction and took up the profession of surveyor.

Whether that was true or not, every third scion of his family line was bound to become a surveyor.

Egeos was a surveyor. The shores of the Black Sea and the mountains and valleys had been measured or remeasured by his kinsmen so many times that the total length spanned by their pairs of compasses probably covered the distance from here to the edge of the universe several times over.

Egeos Marmarilos's real name was Dmitrios Chionidis. His nephew Nikos Chionidis was well known in the city as a photographer. It was thanks to them that the Chionidis name became, so to speak, widely renowned in Sukhumi in a visual sense. Thousands of photos taken in his photo studio bore the lettering "Photo Chionidis" in Russian in the lower right corner.

But it was Mikhail Temurovich who dubbed this family Egeos Marmarilos. The majority knew Dmitrios Chionidis only under this name, Egeos Marmarilos, which combined the two Mediterranean seas' proud and beautiful names floating freely aloft like naval flags in the wind: the Aegean and the Sea of Marmara, seas which have caressed the feet of Greece since the world began and not just the feet, but her entire ancient body. Egeos Marmarilos liked being Egeos Marmarilos, but his historic homeland, which he, nevertheless and despite great difficulties, succeeded in visiting at the end of the 1970s, he found he did not like. He travelled there as a guest, saw his relatives, and, once again with great difficulty, on account of the Soviet Union's very strict border regulations, returned to Sukhumi.

"It's quite a different country," said Egeos Marmarilos with a wave of his hand on meeting his friends. "Different people, different customs. Just imagine, if you haven't made arrangements beforehand, even a relative won't receive you as a guest. They are eternally short of time; they may not even bother to pour you a glass of wine. But I'm a Sukhumi old-timer, and it was beyond my comprehension. Imagine me calling on someone in Sukhumi and not being received because 'my time is all scheduled for today' or not being invited to the table."

Egeos Marmarilos was also a carpenter. For several years, he worked in the carpentry workshop of the Gulripshi field station. The director of this station, also for several years, was Mikhail Temurovich. It was there that they got to know each other.

It happened like this: Egeos Marmarilos and another carpenter, Otar Kiziria, were making a coffin for a deceased staff member who was already retired by then. They worked unhurriedly, stripping, planing, and varnishing, pottering around for nearly three days. Then they drank some vodka for the repose of the deceased's soul, so his memory would shine bright, and, at this point, they slightly overdid it, drinking a bottle of

Stolichnaya each for their mate. It was already night when they carried the coffin to the home of the deceased. On the way, they had to cross a small stream, the Chipilpeta, which is not far from the railway station. On the shaky bridge over the Chipilpeta, Egeos Marmarilos tripped, the carpenters dropped the coffin into the stream, and, swollen after rainfall, the Chipilpeta carried the coffin out to sea! The two tradesmen chased after it along the bank but were unable to catch up with it.

When they told Mikhail Temurovich, he had a good laugh, then made the bookkeeper issue everyone a bonus equivalent to a month's pay: "Let's shame them, so they don't lose any more coffins."

For the forty-day wake, Egeos Marmarilos and Otar Kiziria made a gravestone to assuage their guilt over the coffin borne away by the stream. They worked zealously, abstained from drink, made a beautiful inscription on the stone, and then covered this inscription with a gold dye. They worked as behoves penitent Christians.

Except that they got confused and placed the stone on someone else's grave.

Once again, Mikhail Temurovich laughed with all his heart, and once more a bonus was awarded to everyone: "Let's hope this time that we have really shamed them, and that now they will place the stone where it's needed." And added: "You see, in this case, alcohol had nothing to do with it, they were sober."

After this, Mikhail Temurovich became even better acquainted with Egeos Marmarilos. First, they had a chat on the banks of the Chipilpeta and then, in the carpentry workshop, they drank a bottle of Isabella grape wine each along with Professor Soso Kapanadze and finally became true friends.

Once they went hunting. Except that Mikhail Temurovich did not hunt, did not even take along a firearm, he merely strolled in the forest.

The others were not very keen hunters, either, because their hunting dogs had become enamoured of each other. They travelled out in a couple of Fiats. One dog went in the boot of one car, the other in the boot of the other. As usual, when they drew near to the hunting site, they would release both. The dogs instantly went for each other and gave themselves over to attempts at lovemaking, confining any chasing exclusively to each other. And it continued like this all day, they were not up to hunting.

But no, they still caught a hare, killed by Gadzho, the old footballer. When they brought the hare to a restaurant and handed it over to be roasted, the chef found a piece of paper in its back passage. On it was written: "I was killed by Gadzho. The hare."

It turned out that the hare had been bought that morning at the market by Egeos Marmarilos, who had shoved the piece of paper where necessary with his own hand. The rest happened as if of its own accord: Egeos Marmarilos "planted" the hare in some bushes and led Gadzho to those bushes sometime later.

What a commotion! Gadzho threw himself upon Egeos Marmarilos, wanted to kill him, but the others took his firearm away and, several toasts later, even reconciled them.

Later, Egeos Marmarilos again took up the profession of surveyor, but he did not break his friendship with Mikhail Temurovich.

"I ask you to treat him with favour and affection, he is my friend," Mikhail Temurovich would proudly introduce Egeos Marmarilos, slapping him on the shoulder. "He once dropped

The President's Cat | 183

a coffin in the river and put an old man's tombstone on an old woman's grave. An amazing man! One of his forefathers built Dioskurias, and this man was just like him: he handed Dioskurias over to the sea purely on account of a mistake, he built it on the very edge of the shore, almost in the sea. Well, the sea did not squander its chance: how could it fail to appropriate a thing of such beauty!"

## 64

He devoted a scientific work to the goat.

And this work, like several other works of his, was published as a separate volume by the Abkhazia Collective Farm Library.

In this work, he singled out the Abkhazian goat.

Several centuries back, the Georgian geographer Vakhushti Bagrationi had written about a type of Abkhazian goat, which had horns a metre long and a beard reaching the ground.

Mikhail Temurovich singled out several of the Abkhazian goat's qualities.

He wrote that a good goat could yield over eight hundred litres of milk a year.

That this goat's milk was rich in calcium and had healing properties.

That the goat's fat was a unique remedy against colds, it needed to be melted and rubbed on the chest and throat (or possibly the neck) of the patient.

That the goat's skin was used in the manufacture of carpets, and, if one square decimetre of sheepskin cost 14 kopecks, then goatskin (of the same dimensions) was valued at 30 to 62.50 kopecks.

That if the goat liked grass (and, most important, it should like it), it can eat over eight kilogrammes a day.

That the goat liked young, pure grass and climbed up into the hills in search of it, up the steepest cliffs, and, for this ability, it was very highly valued. Because no herbivorous domestic animal was so undemanding in terms of care. You herded it out in the morning, and it would find its eight kilogrammes of grass on its own in areas completely inaccessible to other animals and, when it got dark, it would return home of its own accord. Although it still needed a goat herd because it was liable to become absorbed in its highland-searching and get lost.

That the Karl Marx Collective Farm in the village of Eshera was staffed by herdsmen of various nationalities, who displayed an excellent standard of work.

That the author of this research saw with his own eyes how these herdsmen helped the goats during kidding, the way they looked after them for two or three days in a closed barn, and, if a goat had twins, they would feed them extra milk.

That he himself also observed how they strove to protect the goats from bad weather during heavy rain and storms, how they herded them into pens or sometimes into mountain caves.

That the goats were very fond of salt because salt helped them to digest their food, and, even if it did not help, they would enjoy it all the same.

That the meat of this goat was magnificent, especially when boiled in milk (best of all, of course, in goat's milk, although the result was remarkably good with cow's milk).

That greater attention should be paid to goats and their numbers multiplied.

That in Abkhazia there were so many hills that goat farms should be established everywhere.

That in the hills of Abkhazia the area suitable for breeding goats came to no more and no less than 89.500 hectares.

That the names of these mountain locations were: Dauchi, Lamkats, Soipsara, Kuniashta, Akharva, Tsekeztou, Khodzhal, Anara, Jisp, Berchiga, Avadkhara, Kuabchara, Gvandra, Tsadim, Guagua, Aibga, South Uren, and so on and so forth.

That if anyone managed to "smooth out" the hills of Abkhazia, it would be revealed that Abkhazia's territory was equal to that of France (Whereas, no, this is not written in this book, but he did say it once to a French journalist when she asked how big Abkhazia was).

# 65

Coffee for two: "We put two teaspoons of high quality freshly ground coffee into a traditional Turkish coffee pot or cezve, pour in two cups of water, add two teaspoons of sugar (or more, or no sugar at all, depending on local preference), and place the cezve on red-hot sand (heated on a special electric plate). When it begins to boil, we remove the froth. Or don't bother to remove it. We bring it to a boil. Then the coffee is poured into cups. It may be served with a glass of cold water, depending on personal taste."

## 66

He was climbing unhurriedly up Sukhumi Hill, he was already seventy by then. Not that he found walking too difficult, but all the same, at seventy years of age an uphill climb is no joke.

He was met on the way by Kukuna:

"Mikhail Temurovich, till what age does a man remain still a man? You were talking about it yesterday in the 'Nart,' and I wondered about it."

"Kukuna, leave me in peace. Don't force me to stop."

And he continued on his way.

"No, but until what age?"

"Don't stop me, leave me alone, Kukuna . . ."

"But really . . ."

"Do you see that woman up there? The one ahead of us? You see her? If she disappears from view, if I lose sight of that woman, how am I to get up this hill? Aren't you human or something? Don't stop me . . . I'm on a towrope behind that woman, Kukuna, on a towrope!"

Above them, thirty paces away, by the music college, walked a tall brunette, her hips gracefully swaying. From behind, her figure was like a violin. And an Italian violin at that. She was probably so similar to a violin because at that moment she was passing the music college.

## 67

"In the region of the Gagra weather station, especially near the hotels, there are too many cats. We require that cat owners place collars on them. Cats without collars will be exterminated." (Act no. 306, dated 5/21/1909)

# The President's Cat

Two years before the war, a genetics institute had been set up in Bebeisiri at *his* initiative. And "Institute of Genetics" was inscribed on the gate at the entrance. *He him*self named it the Colchis Institute of Genetics. And to the scientists incorporated under its roof, *he* passionately wanted to demonstrate the genetic unity tying together all the Caucasian nations and Caucasian nature in general.

*He* briefly formulated *his* plan for Bebeisiri's development to *his* friend as follows:

1. Lake Bebeisiri must yield up to fifteen tonnes of fish a year.
2. The old irrigation system, which will water three hundred hectares of land, must be restored.
3. Sacrophyte must be extracted from the lake (to the tune of twenty-five tonnes per year) and reprocessed into peat compost.
4. Five hundred heads of cattle must be bred, two hundred heads of buffalo, five thousand geese, five thousand ducks, and three thousand turkeys.
5. The river Samgle must be deepened, and another fifty hectares of irrigated plantations established there.
6. Tourist and health complexes must be set up.
7. A testing and exhibition nursery of international significance for sub-topical cultures must be established.

In 1991, construction began on an open canal to link the Okumi River with the Great Bebeisiri Lake by the Mokhokha

Gully. Concrete and asbestos paving and steel pipes were transported there. Machinery was acquired: an excavator, four passenger launches, and eight wooden cargo boats.

After the canal was put through directly from the bridge across the Okumi, providing access to the Great Lake, launches were meant to cover the run as far as Sukhumi, which would have shortened the trip from Achigvara to Sukhumi by eighteen kilometres.

The Elita Centre for Scientific and Industrial Research was opened.

The nursery was already stocking and propagating: Jesus citrus, jambir, Lapin trifoliate orange and Ichang lemon. As well as kollman, raski, sevedzhi, 511, and kumquat. These varieties produce a large quantity of starchy seeds which birds feed on. The people of Bebeisiri were in absolute agreement with the Chinese position that with these seeds it is possible to rear a huge quantity of birds.

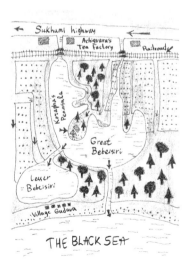

In 1990, a cytology laboratory was opened, and a reactor established which processed thermal waters. The scientific research complex, situated on the Korofa Peninsula, occupied an area of 3.4 hectares.

They also worked on the hybridisation of subtropical persimmon, feijoa, mulberry, avocado, pecan, and bamboo.

They worked on breeding buffalo and wild pigs. Before the war, they had seventy-five buffalo, including eleven white ones.

Several centuries earlier, cuttings of local varieties of hazelnuts, walnuts, pears, and apples were exported from the area of modern Abkhazia to the countries of the Mediterranean. Mikhail Temurovich maintained that similar exports could take place in the future, but in Abkhazia it was essential to diversify the range of fruits. For instance, French marron chestnuts and early varieties of Japanese persimmon should be propagated. Apart from that, the less productive walnuts from Saken needed to be replaced by those from Pskhu. And besides, if the churches and monasteries of Jerusalem, France or Bulgaria were built earlier with timber exported from the Kodori and Bzyb river basins, then in Abkhazia we must build new churches from the same timber.

The first such church was due to be built on the grounds of the Bebeisiri Academy.

Also set for construction on the grounds of the Bebeisiri Academy, according to Mikhail Temurovich's plan, was a brothel of a completely new type: undergraduates and master's students of the academy from various countries should not have to waste their time looking for women on Black Sea beaches. Women were essential, sex promoted learning, helped a man to think. The number of staff at the brothel was set at fifty women. And the number of master's students was intended to be thirty. Over a period of five years at the Bebeisiri Academy, they were to study reproductive genetics and taxonomy.

And on top of that, in order not to miss an opportunity, an Abkhazian Disneyland was to be built here. In short, people in Bebeisiri would study, relax, pray, and entertain themselves; they would get to know one another and become friends. People from all over the world. In Bebeisiri!

All this would be financed from the income of the Bebeisiri Academy, its business activities, and the tuition fees of foreign students. But also possibly from the Nobel Prize (which was, by all means, possible), the sum of which should come to approximately or exactly one million four hundred thousand dollars.

The Bebeisiri Academy was founded in 1991. In November 1992, Bebeisiri was due to host an international symposium which would examine topical world issues in biology.

But on August 14, 1992, the war broke out in Abkhazia.

As for the issues proposed for examination at the symposium, they were as follows:

- Global warming and biological means of stopping it
- Integration of cells in the course of transplantation and the advent of the initial tetrad
- The advent and development of callus and its cellular differentiation
- The results of remote hybridisation in the mandarin subfamily

## 68

"Here's to women! All women! Dark-eyed, grey-eyed, brown-eyed, and blue-eyed. Blondes, brunettes, redheads! Here's to them!

Hot as ovens, relaxing as an August sea, cool as an April breeze, cold as snow, as silver—here's to them in all their most varied diversity, to all of them!

Summer and winter women. Nighttime, daytime, and morning women! Women rivers! Women mountain peaks! Women oceans! Women winds!

Cheers to women—cheers to wings!

Women pyramids!

Women icebergs!

Women who listen to the world with a breast swollen with desire and drink in the world with bewitching eyes and mouths.

Long may their light shine!

Women who are ever hurrying somewhere and seemingly betraying us and, at the same time, apparently being faithful to us and loving us.

Women whose caresses and smiles and entrancing curves have been working their magic for thousands of years and for whom bishops have drunk wine from their shoes while kneeling before them.

Yes, here's to women whom we shall never meet and yet love and those women whom we see every day and yet love. Have loved and shall love.

Women of Fujiyama, women of the Sahara, women of the Ganges, women of the steppes, women of the seas and oceans, of the prairies and mountains, women of the Bible, women of all the earth's continents, women of space.

Here's to the Taj Mahals, temples, verses, and melodies dedicated to them.

Here's to their colours—green, red, yellow, white, black!

Their embankments, their streets, their beaches, their rooms, their telephones, their bathrooms, their addresses, their beds—here's to them! Their perfumes, their breath, their aroma!

The centuries in which they lived and the centuries in which they will be born anew.

Here's to women who have been lucky in love and those women who have not been lucky in love!

Here's to their bodies, their dresses, their cosmetics, their hips, their legs, necks, lips, breasts, their life, their bashfulness, their bewilderment, their groans, their tightly bound hips . . .

Those moments when you are dying, and dying, and dying inside them—and are yet still alive, and you are coming and coming to a climax inside them—and you begin anew . . .

You are dying and you are climaxing, and you revive, and you begin again, and come to climax, and die and revive . . .

Those moments, those moments—here's to them.

Here's to women! All women! Who . . . Whom . . . Who . . ."

Thus, *he* concluded the toast, and within our hearts a joyous light suddenly began to play, to throb.

## 69

But did *he* drink a lot? I never saw *him* really drunk; *he* got more enjoyment from socialising. *He* would chat and joke. And I never saw *him* bored.

I was a neighbour of *his* and I know a lot about *him*. One day *he* met me in the yard and had a man with *him*, but *he* did not refer to him by name and kept calling him "doctor." "This is my friend," *he* repeated from time to time.

But the "doctor" was pretty much soused. At first, I thought he was a doctor of science, but he turned out to be a medical doctor.

I invited them back to the apartment, and they duly came.

"This is my friend the doctor. He's the sort of man before whom, if he takes someone by the horns, the Lord God Himself would retreat."

The blushing "doctor" laughed whole-heartedly; he was a good guy evidently.

"Not so long ago, he strove hard to snatch my friend Vinor Pachulia from the claws of life but couldn't manage it."

Birds and singing whales

Then *he* proposed a toast to wine: "Nobody blesses wine, but that's unacceptable, so here's to wine as well and all other beverages, brandy, vodka, liqueurs, absolutely all beverages. First and foremost to Isabella, it is a wine with a woman's name, and it truly caresses you from the inside, but also, unlike a woman, it is never unfaithful to you. Isabella is also called "Odessa." So, this lady-wine is Isabella from Odessa."

It was cold outside. *He* remembered how *he* had drunk martinis along with friends in a restaurant not far from Montmartre. How *he* had tried frog meat for the first time and initially thought it was chicken. But when *he* saw the way the bones bent, *he* guessed precisely what *he* had been eating. And *he* asked for a second helping and sampled wine snails, too. *He* also recalled friends arranging a motorbike ride around the streets of Paris and waving to some hippies.

Then *he* read us some verse in French.

It turned out that the "doctor" knew French.

"That's not French. That's some other language . . ."

"A-a-ah, doctor, you thought I was reading the poem in modern French. No, *mon cher*, it was Old French. You don't know that language," *he* said, giving me a wink.

"And in any case, after a bottle of Isabella, who knows what language you are going to speak?" *he* immediately added and gave me another wink.

Then *he* poured the wine and said:

"What can be better? Sitting here now, eating the same food, drinking the same wine . . . Those who sit at the same table and drink the same wine and propose the same toasts in the right order, they are a race apart, special people. You cannot imagine how wonderful this is, no, and no one can imagine what it means."

Then *he* raised us to our feet, and we walked to *his* apartment. We did not want to at first, but *he* insisted and took us to *his* place. There *he* had us listen to the hissing of snakes recorded on a cassette. It was the voices of snakes in love, he explained: "I brought this recording from India. Snakes' love is legendary, they are faithful to each other until death."

Finally, on behalf of enamoured snakes, *he* drank to all those anywhere who are in love.

No, *he* did not drink much, but rather joked, and talked, and talked . . . And I never saw *him* bored.

# 70

The Secretary of the Gali District Young Communist League had raped a YCL girl in a thicket on a hill slope not far from the Merkheuli restaurant in the village of Merkheuli in Gulripshi District.

The Gali Bureau of the Party District Committee relieved the secretary of his duties and expelled him from the party.

Mikhail Temurovich demanded that the YCL District Committee Secretary's case be investigated at a session of the Party Regional Committee.

Well, they investigated him.

A detailed and specific inquiry into the event was presented to the Bureau by the Secretary of the Gagra YCL District Committee, a young woman.

The information made frequent mention of the Merkheuli restaurant, in which the young YCL members enjoyed themselves with the girls who had come to Abkhazia for a holiday. Also "figuring," so to speak, in the inquiry were the forest and the adjacent hills.

"Have you thoroughly investigated the so-called scene of the rape?" Mikhail Temurovich asked the Secretary of the Gagra YCL District Committee.

"Of course, Mikhail Temurovich."

"In other words, as you say, this so-called rape occurred on the slope of a hill."

"What do you mean by 'so-called rape', Mikhail Temurovich? A forced sexual act really took place there."

"I don't believe it, it's impossible to believe, no ... If only because you haven't studied the incline of the slope. You haven't studied the incline ... Its slope, the length of the slope ..."

"It's just a slope, naturally with an incline . . . What else were we supposed to examine there?"

"Well, what do you mean? You simply astonish me! You are young with a future, simply a very nice girl. The future belongs to you. I have no doubt that promotion awaits you, advancement, so to speak—and you didn't check the incline of the slope?"

"But why were we supposed to check it?"

"Well, for example: how many degrees was the incline of the slope? You should have established how many degrees the gradient of the incline. There are after all appropriate instruments."

"But why, Mikhail Temurovich, why is this necessary?"

"What do you mean, why? You astonish me. Once again you've astonished me. Well, listen good and proper. If the incline of the slope is over forty-five degrees, it is simply impossible to execute a sexual act there. In other words, in such a situation a representative of the male sex will not be able to rape a representative of the female sex. He will slip down. Any representative of the male sex will slip down, simply slide down, even if he is the Secretary of the YCL District Committee. On top of that he would end up in a very pitiful position . . . forty-five degrees! Remember this, for it may be of use to you in the future. So, in that situation it was impossible to commit that deed, examination of which you have compelled us to spend so much time on, dear comrade. I have an excellent knowledge of the Merkheuli environs, I have traversed everything there on my own two feet. I know that hill and forest particularly well."

Then *he* addressed the members of the Bureau:

"Comrades, I still harbour some small doubts as to whether the 'Merkheuli man of the moment' acted correctly, but he still

The President's Cat | 201

doesn't deserve expulsion from the party. And our comrades from Gali have dealt with him too severely. Therefore, I move that he be reinstated in the ranks of the party and sent to the Senior Party School, where we hope he will adopt a superior party ethic and learn how a real communist ought to behave with women."

And indeed, by the end of the week, following that session of the Bureau, the former leader of the Gali YCL organization had flown off for studies in Moscow.

## 71

It was December 1962.

Most likely December.\

I recall it was cold.

It was cold outside, not indoors.

Mikhail Temurovich and my father were sitting at a table, and I was sitting beside them. I was a small boy back then.

Mikhail Temurovich and my father were drinking brandy. And chatting. Somewhere over there, above the Caribbean Sea, aeroplanes were taking off from the decks of aircraft carriers, scouring and lacerating the sky. Somewhere cruisers and ships armed with missiles were bisecting a watery surface ridged by waves. In Pitsunda, a room was being made ready for the author of the Caribbean crisis, Nikita Khrushchev. He was due for a holiday on the shores of the Black Sea. John Kennedy was sitting in seclusion in the smallest room of the White House examining a shot of Cuba taken from a surveillance plane in which Soviet missile installations were ubiquitously visible. Kennedy did not reply to telephone calls and did not let anyone into the room, not even Jacqueline. Standing at the threshold and unhurriedly trying to open the door, which was locked like a safe, was the Third World War. And four Soviet submarines were speeding through ocean depths to the Caribbean Sea. All four of them were packed with torpedoes bearing atomic warheads. The Americans were observing them both from space and from ships at sea, not allowing them to surface. When their accumulators went flat, the lame boats would be forced to come to the surface to recharge—submarines back then were not yet atomic—and, there, the others were waiting for them.

Somewhere in Africa some boys were pursuing an antelope wounded by a spear. In Australia, a Spanish emigrant was playing an Andalusian melody on a guitar. In Thailand, in the Rose Garden close to Bangkok, a woman was transplanting orchids in coconuts shells. In Greece, on the island of Rhodes, a blue wind was blowing. Over Fujiyama, a new day was dawning.

But in Sukhumi we were suffused on all four sides by cold pink December twilights . . .

Smiling, Mikhail Temurovich looked out of the window at the moon. The moon resembled the bottom of a glass filled with brandy. It was still, as it were, beaming. Mikhail Temurovich and my father drank coffee. And talked.

Then Mikhail Temurovich got up, went over to the bookshelf, took several brochures from it, and began to read.

They were brochures which had been written by *him*.

*He* read them out as if they were poetry.

*He* read about the pecan and the Canadian date, about the Japanese fan palm, the tulip tree, the laurel, about the Chinese mushmula, the Avandista Oriental persimmon, the Chayote Mexican cucumber, the Unshyu mandarin, about those flowers, those bushes and trees whose homeland was somewhere far away, but which had long taken root in Abkhazia and felt comfortable here.

*He* would raise *his* voice and draw out the vowels as if singing when *he* read:

about the peaches of Eshera and Adzyubzha,

about Abkhazian apples,

about the red apples of Tsebelda,

about Sukhumi Duchess pears,

about Merkheuli pears,

about the peach with the name "May rose" and the apples with the same name,

and about one further peach, the "Victory," and about grapes.

*He* read about Sarajishvili, the industrialist from Tsarist times, who used barrels made from Abkhazian oak for his brandy. This oak gave the Sarajishvili brandy a special taste and aroma. Particularly oaks from the forest glades of Bespakhuba.

*He* said that good wine and brandy were also made from the grapes of Avasarkhva. In 1888, Sarajishvili ordered an apparatus for distilling brandy spirit from Switzerland, and his brandy business began operating still the same year.

*He* read that Sarajishvili had used grape varieties from Adzyubzha, Atara, Gup, Babushera, and Eshera:

Ajipsha

Isabella

Atiruzha

*He* read about Michurin, who dreamt of expanding the geography of citruses northward from the Caucasus.

*He* read about the alder and the Isabella grapevine, that the alder fixes nitrogen, enriching the soil, but does not absorb nitrogen itself, while Isabella feeds on it. That the alder and Isabella help each other. That alder and Isabella, which winds around it, form a wonderful pairing. That this was an example of symbiosis. The same sort of symbiosis as the one between maize and beans.

"Here's to symbiosis! Of the alder and the Isabella, maize, and beans," *he* said and took a drink of brandy.

My father also raised his glass to his lips.

Then *he* read about the Abkhazian bee and honey. About the Greek military commander (I won't mention his name) who tried to subdue Abkhazia (in the fourth century BCE, it seems), but, in the middle of Abkhazia, sampled the local honey along with his soldiers, and their intentions clouded over, and they could no longer even stay on their feet. And so, he was compelled to leave this region with his army mentally deranged. Thus, the Abkhazian bee saved its homeland. The Abkhazian bee stands out from all other bees for its extremely long proboscis with which it can gather nectar from the very depths of any flower.

*He* read about the most elderly Abkhazians, old men of 103, 111 and 127 years.

And then *he* talked about the theory of the possibility of the impossible. *He* was no longer reading but talking. It was *his* own theory, one which *he* had still not completely formulated. *He* was still only preparing to write about it. *He* put it like this: "I will attempt to write it in the rhythm of drinking toasts. No, not write it, but compose it," *he* corrected himself.

Meanwhile, the starlit and moonlit night had acquired the colour of Isabella wine and was even murmuring.

Somewhere over the Caribbean Sea fighter plans were roaring, on the island of Rhodes a blue wind was blowing, and over Fujiyama the day had dawned.

## 72

We were drinking tea in Kukur-chai's teahouse, Mikhail Temurovich, myself, and Kukur-chai himself.

Mikhail Temurovich was recalling how once in their childhood, *he* and Kukur-chai had crept one night into the tent of a circus visiting Sukhumi and ended up in a lion's cage which had been left open for some reason, face to face with the half-asleep beast.

"For five minutes, probably, we stared at it, transfixed, unable to take our eyes off it. And the lion stared back at us. Seemingly, the lion did not even have a clue as to how a different, a wild lion would act in his place. Eventually, the circus staff threw the lion some meat, dragged us out of the cage, and chucked us out of the circus, rewarding us with a few clipped ears."

I was drinking tea and eating khachapuri cheese bread. Mikhail Temurovich and Kukur-chai just drank tea and fed the khachapuri to stray puppies.

# 73

*He* once attempted to breed waterfowl in Abkhazia. *He* involved the staff of the Ministry of Education in this enterprise. *He* sent them to Russia to bring back duck and goose eggs of various breeds.

Three weeks later, there was a telegram from them: they were returning without any eggs.

"Yes," *he* sighed. "Some have eggs and some just have balls."

## 74

"An idea uttered aloud is no longer an idea," *he* read out in a loud voice and put the book aside on the sand.

Vianor Pachulia and Soso Kapanadze were lying on chaise-lounges, each under his own sunshade and listening as they contemplated the marine horizon.

The breeze ruffled *his* scrupulously coiffured hair, and *he* covered *his* head with a straw hat.

The sea was murmuring. The waves often broke on the shore, and the pebbles rustled.

"Oh, how mischievous the sea is these days," *he* thought.

"Oh, how mischievous the sea is these days," thought Vianor Pachulia and Soso Kapanadze.

Not far away the amaranth was blooming.

# 75

"Vianor, listen, I'll tell you a new joke. A man was asked: 'What kind of sex do you prefer, group or individual?' He replied: 'Group sex, of course.' 'Why?' 'Because with group sex you can take it easy now and then.'"

## 76

"Consider the birds of the heavens: they plough not, neither do they sow, nor do they gather the harvest, nor bake bread, and yet the Heavenly Father feeds them. Consider humanity: it continually wages wars and bears malice, and people destroy one another; yet despite this the Heavenly Father loves each one of us, although sometimes His heart aches on account of all this, and the tears well up in His eyes. Here's to these tears!"

## 77

"And now let us rise and drink to the first of us to depart this world!"

"To the first of us to depart!"

"To the first of us to reach the other side!"

"To the first of us to ascend to Heaven!"

There were seven of them sitting at the table.

They all rose and, without saying a word, drank to the first of them.

## 78

The chairman of the Achadara collective farm, Guram Sichinava, got a phone call from the Regional Party Committee: "Tomorrow, towards noon, in the Sukhumi district, on the grounds of your farm, to be precise, Mikhail Temurovich will be taking a stroll with *his* guests. *He* is interested in the state of the Gumista riverbanks. You know yourself how to receive *him*."

The chairman of the collective farm drove all the collective farm members out into the citrus plantations, gardens, vineyards, and fields. The "hottest work pace" was set on the banks of the Gumista.

At noon the following day, like yachts in full sail, a Chaika and a black Volga slipped through along the main street of the village, approached the riverbank, and stopped. Joyful labour was in full swing all around, everyone from tiny tot to pensioner was working with a sort of feverish joy digging the ground, cutting trees, preparing the soil for tobacco planting. Everything was the way it ought to have been for the accelerated construction of communism.

Nobody got out of the Chaika or the Volga. The cars stood there for a while as if hesitating. Then they slipped away as graciously as they had arrived.

After an hour, Guram Sichinava received another phone call from the Regional Party Committee: "You seem to be lacking in experience. Mikhail Temurovich just wanted to entertain *his* guests in the bosom of nature on the banks of the Gumista, in a peaceful setting, and what a farce you staged!"

The next afternoon not a living soul was to be found on the bank of the Gumista within a radius of several kilometres,

The President's Cat | 213

the area seemed completely uninhabited and virginally intact.

And once again the Chaika and the Volga zoomed in. Except this time their doors opened wide and from them emerged Mikhail Temurovich, *his* dear guests, and some even dearer gorgeous blondes as well.

## 79

"If only I could find the shards of a jug from the times of Alexander the Great," *he* announced once, lost in a daydream.

"What jug?" I asked.

"The one he broke before his wars in the desert sands. Don't you remember? When their water had run out, and only a single jug of water was left, they brought it to Alexander, and he broke it before his troops' very eyes and spilled the water. 'I must remain thirsty like all my men.' I think he was sitting on his horse at the time."

"But why do you need the shards from that jug, Mikhail Temurovich?"

"I would build a museum for them. In Greece, perhaps . . . no . . . In India? No, in front of the UN building. No . . . Somewhere here, in the Caucasus. And just as well, I would build a museum for those stones with which Mary Magdalene was supposed to have been pelted, but Christ forbade it. You must remember, surely? And a museum of the first wheel. Actually, I would build three separate museums: for the shards of that jug, for those stones, and for that wheel."

# 80

*He* used to call me Birdman. *He* would say: "Where have you been, Lukich, Birdman?" I had about four hundred birds. Some of them were at home on Lakoba Street, some out in the country at a mate's place. Some were songbirds, others were seabirds, river birds, or birds of the mountains or fields.

I became close friends with Mikhail Temurovich after *he* acquired a pet parrot.

My aunts, old maids, collected some money and sent me to Leningrad for some furniture. And there I met a man who was trying to sell a talking parrot. He valued it at two thousand roubles. I thought for a long time about what I should buy: the talking parrot or the furniture? In the end, I decided to buy the parrot—well, I did not have a talking parrot. At the airport, my parrot was x-rayed, to check if it had a diamond in its stomach.

When I took a parrot to the aunties instead of a "three-piece suite" or a wall unit, they raised a dreadful uproar and cry. But that was nothing. The main unpleasantness was still ahead: at midnight my parrot suddenly bawled out in the voice of a drunkard:

"Thief, thief, there's a thief in the room, f*ck him."

Then it shrieked in a woman's voice: "Leonid Ilyich, think of the people for f*ck's sake!"

The aunts needed a straitjacket.

It was the period when Brezhnev was in power.

The KGB found out about my parrot and called me up to inquire: "Who had taught it to swear?"

Well, things were going really badly for me, and Mikhail Temurovich rescued me, *he* had acquaintances everywhere. *He* told them: "Malkhaz is my friend."

*He* often came to my place after that and talked to the parrot. *He* would listen to it and roar with laughter. *He* would bring Vianor Pachulia along. We often sat at the table to the sound of the parrot's monologue and the songbirds' chorus.

Those really were banquets.

"Ah, how happy they are, those devils, those birds!" *he* said. "For them, boundaries do not exist, they peck grapes here and there, in everwhich country they leave their droppings, God alone knows."

# 81

From Gagra, we scaled Mount Mamzishkha and lit a campfire. It was 12 o'clock at night. The sea glittered under the light of the moon. There were twelve of us, mostly of mature age.

*He* tried to convince us that Colchis was a Latin word and meant "shell." *He* kept repeating the words concha, conche, and conchi, meaning "shell":

"The whole Caucasus is like a shell, a peculiar seashell. If one looks at the Great Caucasian Range from Apsheron or Taman, you will see the spine of a shell, while the Colchis lowland is like the entrance to a shell, which joins it with the Black Sea and then with all seas and oceans, with the entire planet.

In the centre of this ensemble is Bozhy Mys, Cape Divine, the very Katskhi Pillar by which the gods descended to earth. The pillar stands on Gora Lubvi, Love Mountain." It was *he* who named it so.

There were three places on earth where Zeus communed with us humans: the first was Parnassus, the second Corax, the third the Katskhi Pillar.

Once upon a time, people lived alongside the gods in the heavens. But we wanted equality with them, and they cast us down to earth. In particular, they concealed from us the secret of multiplying or breeding, being the same thing, and would not give us fire.

They were Caucasians: Prometheus, Amiran, and Ardzakan. Prometheus stole the fire from the gods, Amiran and Ardzakan—the secret of multiplying. Today everyone knows about Prometheus, but few know about Amiran and Ardzakan. It was beyond the powers of one man to steal the secret of multiplying from the gods by himself. It required two selfless knights.

Zeus ordered all three to be chained to an inaccessible rock in the Caucasus Mountains or, and this amounts to the same thing, to a huge shell, and there they are to this day.

And towards the end, I will let you listen to the voices of Amiran and Ardzakan. They are real men, of course, but still even they groan sometimes."

*He* asked the ranger to light some specially gathered logs of beech and hornbeam. The beech first. The crackling could be heard in the silence. When the beech had turned to ash, a large piece of hornbeam was placed carefully in the fire. The hornbeam bean to crackle in a quite different voice.

"The beech in the fire groans with the voice of Ardzakan and the hornbeam with the voice of Amiran," *he* said.

*He* had a small tape recorder with *him* and recorded the voices of the burning trees on that tape recorder that night.

# 82

Once at a convention, a woman doctor sharply criticised Mikhail Temurovich for only building restaurants and giving no attention to hospitals.

She was a tall Russian woman, a blonde.

As a rule, Mikhail Temurovich dealt with women very cautiously.

*He* affectionately addressed his angry opponent.

"I do that because restaurants have healthy food and drink, and, above all, people can relax there, enjoy themselves, dance, sing. They are a wonderful means of socialising, and what is even more important or the most important fact, people who frequent restaurants are almost never ill. And what's bad about that, my dear?"

"Mikhail Temurovich, are you not afraid that, when you are no longer First Secretary, you will be remembered solely as a restaurant builder?"

"I will take pride in it, my charming one."

## 83

The caretaker of the Soviet Union's National Research Institute for Subtropical Cultures, a middle-aged woman living in the neighbourhood, was detained at the institute's mandarin plantation and brought to Mikhail Temurovich's office, accused of stealing mandarins.

Mikhail Temurovich sat the woman down in *his* own armchair and told the security staff:

"Remember, a woman never steals, she only takes what she fancies."

Then *he* thanked them for their vigilance and asked to be left alone with the woman.

"Forgive me, Mikhail Temurovich. I wanted to send some mandarins to relatives in Russia for New Year, and, on my pension, you can't buy anything; there's barely enough to feed yourself."

Mikhail Temurovich took down the addresses of the woman's relatives and sent them boxes of mandarins in her name.

It turned out she had eleven relatives in Russia.

# 84

*He* stopped the Chaika in which he was travelling with Khrushchev from Pitsunda to Sukhumi, near a place known as Tyoshchin Yazyk, Mother in Law's Tongue, where a magnificent view opens up. Khrushchev was astounded by the sight of the partly denuded slopes of Mount Eshera.

"I thought it was all rampant greenery down here."

"Tea and tobacco have ruined us, Nikita Sergeyevich. Colonial cultures, they have sucked up all the ground's juices. It has lost its cohesion, become like dust. But maize is a different matter: it consolidates the soil, ties it together, enriches it. Perhaps you could axe our plan for tea and tobacco?"

Khrushchev ordered his assistant to write Mikhail Temurovich's request down on a pad.

Then *he* pointed to the distant Eshera forests and told Khrushchev:

"We have a particular long-snouted breed of pigs. When the piglets are two-months-old, the local population releases them into the forest, where they feed on fruit, nuts, chestnuts, acorns, and roots. Thanks to their long snouts, they can easily dig them out of the ground, however deep they may be. It's a unique breed, Nikita Sergeyevich. They have the tastiest meat, better than wild boar."

"Are they an economical breed?" asked Khrushchev.

"It works out at one kopeck per pig. Not per kilogram, per pig. One kopeck or the cost of a single hunter's cartridge. When the long snouts reach maturity our hunters shoot them. End of story."

Khrushchev told his assistant to write this down on his pad, too.

They spent some more time enjoying their conversation at Tyoshchin Yazyk and then continued their journey.

## 85

Our Kutaisi hosts had set up a table for us in the open air. It was August. We were sitting only in shorts and shirts, our feet in the Rioni River, up to our knees in water.

Mikhail Temurovich had only just arrived back from Vietnam. In the centre of the table, *he* placed a drinking vessel of bamboo brought back from there and announced:

"Let's pass it round in a circle, and whoever drinks the last drop has to sing."

We all sang in turn.

Mikhail Temurovich sang twice. First the children's song "Firefly" and then "Variada."

Then *he* had us all listening to the songs of singing cats. "I recorded them on my portable tape recorder in the Pacific Ocean."

Then we listened to the voices of frogs. First Californian frogs, then frogs from Adzyubzha, as *he himself* explained.

Towards the end, we listened to the songbirds of Abkhazia, particularly the thrushes.

It was August. The Rioni gave us the benefit of its cool.

The tender night inconspicuously descended.

## 86

"A woman once had a dream about an unfamiliar, deserted town. She was walking through it completely alone. Suddenly some footsteps resounded behind her; a tall, handsome man was following her. Whenever the woman turned, he did the same. Eventually, her way was blocked by a blank wall.

In her confusion the woman turned and shouted at the man:

'Leave me in peace. What do you want from me? What is it?'

Freezing to the spot, the man shrugged his shoulders:

'How should I know, Ma'am? It's your dream.'"

# 87

"'The blow was inflicted by a heavy, blunt object, possibly with the head.' That is what the investigator wrote down in the witness report," *he* read to us.

## 88

*He* liked people of all professions, particularly shepherds and winemakers.

To a man named Tsurtsumia, whose acquaintance *he* had only just made at the table, *he* said: "My nanny was of your family, also a Tsurtsumia." And *he* tried to convince a man named Kvaratskhelia that *his* godfather was a Kvaratskhelia as well.

*He* had one million three hundred nannies.

And one million three hundred godfathers.

And as for *his* friends, you could not count them.

We were sitting at the table in the home of a peasant farmer in Achandara. It was winter. Having drunk up a horn of wine, which had been passed round in a circle, the guests and hosts struck up a song together. We had not sung half of it before there was an unexpected sharp bang on the window. The window opened so violently that both casements hit the wall, and the head of a buffalo with eyes wide open thrust itself into the room. He was breathing loudly, and steam poured from his nostrils. The host dashed into another room, leapt out with a hunting rifle, and pointed it at the buffalo: "I'm going to shoot that son of a swine. How dare he frighten my guests!"

It turned out the buffalo was a music lover, he only had to hear singing somewhere and he would make a beeline for it, would stand next to the singers and listen.

Mikhail Temurovich shielded the buffalo with *his* own body and shouted to the host: "Kill him by all means, but you'll have to kill me first."

*He* hugged the buffalo, kissed its eyes, and gave a signal to continue the singing.

And we sang on for almost another seven hours. We made toasts, drank, and immediately resumed singing. The buffalo stood right by us all that time.

And the whole episode was repeated: Not far from the Dzidzlan restaurant they were preparing to saw down a one-hundred-year-old tree as they wanted to widen the road. Mikhail Temurovich was travelling past at the time. *He* stopped the car and rushed towards the tree fellers: "Chop the tree down by all means, but you'll have to chop me down first."

That tree is standing to this day.

## 89

Tadao Kasio died in Tokyo during the Abkhazian War.

The President's Cat | 229

# 90

"My esteemed Guram!

I have read your book about M. T. Bgazhba. Who knows, maybe this book will have a lot of readers. We'll see, God will provide. When I visited *him* a few days before *his* death, *he* told me (I talked to you about this back in the winter of 2003): 'Sosik, when I die, you must tell the people about me, you must prolong my life after my death.'

That is what *he* told me. And *he* even said so when *he* was about to die. And so it turned out (You have written about it. I specially met with you and talked to you about everything then, so that you would write at least something about Mikhail Temurovich).

But now I am thinking: shouldn't I write a book about *him* as well? I did write an article (or articles, to be more precise), but few people read these articles. They were on the scholarly side. But *he* wanted a lot of people to know about them. Maybe it would be possible to write a play and stage a performance of it? Let's put on a play. After all, you have friends who are theatre directors! A play would be better than a book, but even that would be beyond me. Couldn't you carry the job through? A play would be altogether a different matter. Quite different. And if we could film it, that would be even better. A lot better.

It's good that you gave me the book to read before it was published. I have several comments, and maybe you will consider them.

First of all, the book should have said more about the relations between Vianor Pachulia and Mikhail Temurovich and between Mikhail Alavidze and Mikhail Temurovich. They were the best of friends. Just like Mikhail Temurovich and me.

Don't take offence. You must let me know if you can't find any facts (or stories) about *him*. You need to make a better job of searching. You also needed to find out about *his* other friends. True, it appears I am the only one still breathing, but even so, it would be preferable to find more stories about incidents in *his* life.

*He* demanded that the word "brothel" be replaced by the word "korofa" (meaning "love" in the Mingrelian language). You have brothel written somewhere. It must be changed. *He* insisted on it, after all.

You write that *he* travelled a lot. But *he* didn't like just rambling for its own sake, for *he* also got things done. *He* brought white buffalo sperm from Cambodia, and it was to *his* credit (it should be added) that we had eleven white buffalo in Bebeisiri.

I had a friend in Japan, a well-known citrus expert named Tiozaburo Tanaka. He once sent me a strange animal from Thailand with the following letter:

Dear Iosif, this animal is the result of me crossing species. It breeds only with pedigree dogs, and it results in the finest, most beautiful puppies. They live two or three times longer than ordinary dogs.

Try tying it up with your classical dog.

In love with Joseph, Tiozaburo Tanaka.

Joseph was amazing, he was unlike a dog, or a cat, or a marmot. He bore more resemblance to a rat. That's what Mikhail Temurovich named him, "Rat," and commandeered living quarters for him in the cellar. Then *he* crossed "Rat" with a dwarf pinscher. She had four pups. One of the four survived. Mikhail Temurovich sold Rat's pup in Rome. With this money, we bought a speedboat. This fact could have been written up as a minor episode. And just for your general information, a mule (or, the offspring of a horse and a donkey) lives for thirty-six years, i.e. much longer than its parents.

And here is another fact or episode: our laboratory was often visited by two graduate students, Ahmed and Muhammed, from the University of Alexandria (we are talking about the years 1968–1971). Ahmed's surname was Rokba. He took pride in being a scion of the Mamelukes.

Ahmed told Mikhail Temurovich: 'You, too, are a Mameluke. Your name means 'son of a prince.' I'm sure that your great great-grandfather was sold at the Istanbul market like my distant forefather.'

Mikhail Temurovich was delighted to hear this: 'You see, Sosik, I'm a Mameluke as well. A Mameluke!'

When *he* came to my place, *he* always had some treat for my cat. And Malka was simply crazy about *him*, snuggled up to *him*, crept beneath *his* clothes. One time she was so persistent that *he* was compelled to take her home with *him*. She spent the night at *his* place. In the early morning at 5 o'clock, Mikhail Temurovich rang me: 'Your Malka has killed my Siberian cats' (*he* had two of them). The following day we sat till evening discussing the question: why had Malka killed the Siberian cats? We arrived at the following conclusions:

1. Malka was a local cat, and the Siberian cats were not, and, therefore, Malka did not accept them.
2. Malka was jealous.
3. Malka had taken out her competitors.

There was a traditional inn in Sukhumi (behind the railway station) whose proprietor turned out to be serving dog meat to his guests. Mikhail Temurovich, Vianor Pachulia, Misha Alavidze, and I sometimes visited this inn for the spicy Georgian soup known as khashi. He also used to stock smoked meat. His khashi was of the very best and the meat also. The proprietor himself was the chef. His mistress had been unfaithful to him. He took another mistress, but the old one blabbed that he was serving dog meat. Mikhail Temurovich took me to the trial: 'Let's go see what kind of man he has turned out to be, listen to what he has to say, look him in the eye.' The inn keeper did not deny his guilt: 'Dog meat is regarded as a delicacy throughout Asia, and we should get used to it.' Then he announced: 'I didn't feed dog meat to everyone, but just to 'dogs'' (that is, militiamen). He got six or eight years; I can no longer recall. That's how it turned out.

*He* once told me when *he* had only just got back from Germany: 'Over there, I met a friend of Bergan (the great geneticist), and he begged me to get him some citrus oil made by Kapanadze. Sos, why are you so keen to conceal open secrets? That's not right. Didn't we work on that oil together, you and I?'

We really did work on citrus oil, which we obtained from the flowers of the citrange. What sort of citrange? A cross between a Washington navel orange and a trifoliate. Our oil cured cancer (the cancer is destroyed by nectar from flowers and ethereal oil).

We saw out the testing period before commencing mass production of the oil, but where is the basic hybrid of this citrange now? Some pigs burst into the testing area and gobbled up the new citrange, which was due to bloom in 1993–1994 (Perhaps you will make use of this fact?).

By the way, *he* also wrote a hilariously funny story entitled 'Guarapaa Rpisar' and translated Gogol's *Dead Souls* into Abkhazian.

Mikhail Temurovich had a double-barrelled gun, but *he* had never once fired it. *He* regarded the extinction of any living being (including plants) as equivalent to the murder of a human.

An old cat once wandered into our institute. She had been frightened by dogs and scrambled up a tree. Before going home in the evening, Mikhail Temurovich instructed the janitor: 'Once everyone's gone, tie up the dogs. The cat's been sitting up in the tree all day. Give her food and water, and then she can go where she likes' (maybe this fact will also be worthy of your attention).

My grandfather had some pedigree pigs, quite huge animals. Two of them, I can remember to this day: one was called Khio and the other Nio. They were so big that my grandmother would pile sacks of maize on them and drive them to the mill. One day, Khio and Nio found a dead bull in the woods near the mill. While grandmother and I were waiting our turn for the grindstone, they ate up that bull and only the bones and horns remained (and the hooves as well, it seems). Why have I described this? Ah yes, when Mikhail Temurovich and I became friends, I invited *him* to my village, showed *him* the surrounding countryside (mountains, forests, valleys, and rivers) and the place where our pigs had gobbled up the bull. Mikhail Temurovich said a pig was more like a human being than anything else, in blood composition, anatomy, psychology, intelligence, appetite, and conscience. All in all, we had a good time that day, we had fun. I have passed this information on to you, I don't think you will find it of value, but nevertheless . . .

And so, my esteemed Guram, on this note I conclude my letter, Guram. If you have any questions, telephone me (you know my number). I wish you success."

## 91

Following his death, God showed one man the path of life he had traversed and his footprints on it.

"But whose footprints are those following mine?" asked the man.

"Mine, I have followed you all your life," said God.

"Where times were difficult for me only one set of footprints is visible. Why did you desert me at those times?" asked the man in an offended tone.

"When times were difficult for you, I took you up in my arms, my dear crackpot. So those are not your footprints but mine," said God with a smile.

# The President's Cat

On the day the war began, the morning was magnificent. Magnificent and slightly austere. Like a church. And the sea breeze, gentle as a dove, wafted around all the wide-open windows of Sukhumi. Except that, for some reason, it was like a winged dove. On this occasion. It was August 14. August 14, 1992.

Some people were drinking tea. Some were on their way to work. Some were dozing in the seaside park, in the shade of the magnolias. Some were enjoying frolicking in the sea. Some were . . .

And nobody could understand how the war had crept up on them, insinuated itself into the city, how the rumbling and bellowing had started.

Some people, even years later, understood nothing about the war.

First, a military helicopter began circling above the city. It was a Russian "Crocodile." Then a tank crashed through. Bursts of machine-gun fire resounded. Suddenly an armoured car, a comically small one, burst into flames.

Then a woman phoned the fire station: "Come quickly, there's a tank burning in front of my house!" She was talking about that same armoured car.

Meanwhile, another woman was trying to calm her frightened neighbours from Lakoba Street: "Don't be afraid, folks.

No tanks will enter our street. After all, our street has one-way traffic!"

But quickly and completely the war not only enveloped the one-way streets but also ploughed over the whole city.

At the end of the third month of war, Mikhail Temurovich told *his* friend Soso Kapanadze: "I was wounded a few times during the Second World War, and I've seen a lot in my time, but I have never felt such a sensation . . . It's as if I've landed on a different planet. What's happening to me . . . Help me, Sosik."

One day during the war, a strange kind of rain fell. It enhanced and adorned the sea at the foot of the city with golden raiment. It fell for just three minutes. In that golden light, images of female fingers descending from the sky kept appearing and disappearing. The sea frothed quietly like champagne. And then the picture was hidden by the smoke of war.

Those women for whom it sufficed to be paid a couple of compliments to elevate their beauty from the ordinary to the divine while kissing their hands, they all vanished somewhere. All it took was a couple of compliments and, as it turned out, a single war.

*He* saw one of them dragging a huge eucalyptus branch shattered by a shell; in a city left without electricity it was cold.

When *he* lit a candle, the darkness in the room became even more oppressive.

Everything which had earlier pulled the city up from earth to sky, filling its whole space with life, had fallen back to earth like shreds of balloons shot down by bullets and attempted to penetrate its very depths, to turn it into ashes without leaving a single trace.

The front line passed by near Gvandra. The "front," as it is called. Sometimes *he* unwittingly imagined *his* little house gradually losing its comfort and warmth, restraining its breathing, and whimpering like a dog abandoned by its master, and *he* felt sharp pangs in *his* heart, pangs of a different kind, unlike those caused by physical pain.

Once *he* dreamt of those places and a rose-coloured night above them whispering its own stories, like a huge watermelon cut in half. And the golden stars in the fluffy glow of its beams were like the seeds of the watermelon. *He* himself was standing in the waters of the Black Sea with a glass in his hand, and the glass was full of dark red wine. *He* was slightly drunk and made a toast. The people standing in the water like *him* listened with bated breath. The next morning, *he* could not remember what toast *he* had proposed.

And *he* had another dream: *he* had led a horse to a river and the horse dipped its head in the river so deeply that even its neck was not visible . . . *He* woke up bathed in perspiration.

The city had lost its aroma, its colour. And the sea its ability to think aloud.

The warm mischievous evenings had vanished as did the red-topped Sukhumi taxis.

The beams of light in the eyes of stray dogs and cats had been extinguished.

In the silence, the lonely moon could no longer gather its strength.

The light-bearing women of the city had been driven out.

Somewhere on Bebeisiri Lake, along the Korofa Peninsula, the wind was blowing away the white sheets of documents prepared for dispatch of the Nobel Prize presentation.

And the looted Bebeisiri Academy stood like an orphan.

The looted towns and villages lay like orphans.

The rains washed and washed but could not wash away the blackness from Sukhumi, and the snow failed to cover it.

The tree standing in front of *his* office had been burnt to ashes. The fire ran along the dry grass and, in a matter of seconds, leapt up onto a palm, climbing higher and higher, spreading, intensifying.

The faces of the people were blackened like on a spoilt photo negative. Yes, so it was.

Oddly dressed people appeared on the streets, both among the civil population and the military. Some wore leather coats from the 1950s, others wore the military uniforms of some unknown countries, and others still had attire from looted theatre costume wardrobes.

The theatre-city was waiting for a hero. The theatre-city was waiting for a traitor.

Maradona went on a spree for several days holding a theatre trophy and wearing Roman tunic, and helmet. Although later as the slaughter intensified, even the carnival of lost its colour.

It seemed to the people that they were trying to regulate traffic on the crossroads of history. They were committing strange acts, brandishing flags and machine guns. Some were already marking out a place for the construction of their own pyramids, erecting pedestals of monuments to themselves.

From time to time, the rounded sounds of church bells rang out over the city and then it looked even more pitiful.

The present was rapidly turning into the past and so was the future.

The President's Cat | 239

But suddenly, the past to which *he* had long bidden farewell arose before *him*, the year when *his* father was shot. And that year faced *him* at such close range that *he* no longer saw it. *He* did not see it but was entirely imbued by it.

In his own city, not a single window welcomed *him*. Not a single door was expecting *him*. Looking out of these windows from time to time were desperate people who had been deprived of all their bright colourful days suddenly and forever.

The sea cast up the body of a dolphin which had been blown up in an explosion.

The city was abandoned by its songbirds and seagulls.

Only the sparrows and pigeons turned out to be capable of enduring the war.

In one school, drunken soldiers practiced shooting, taking aim at dogs, cats, and pigeons. And seagulls as well. And, from time to time, at one another.

The peace of the city was bombed by a city war, silence terminated by din.

From the entrance of a neighbouring building, they brought out the dismembered bodies of those who had been taking refuge there from the bombardment of a BM-21 rocket launcher.

Bodies lay about the streets, corpses. Graves became bottomless; they lost all sense of depth.

The sea, as it were, turned its back on it. The sea turned its back on the entire city.

On the street, *he* bumped into a soldier who looked like a priest and a bandit at the same time.

The war, in its own way, was now curing *him* of *his* incurable love of life.

Unfamiliar, alien people were wandering around. People whose hearts turned to ice much more quickly than water in a winter frost.

People reverted once again to a time which paid homage to the "Destroyer" and tried to destroy the "Saviour." A time which attempted to equate God and the devil.

The voice of weapon-tuning is a male voice. There is no such thing as a female weapon. The whole town was banging and clanging with male voices. Rattling and clattering.

Not a single female body said: "Tomorrow the sun will rise."

Hearts were overfilled with penetrating masts, bloody red sails, faded voices.

*He* observed the innumerable gathering of purified souls manifesting themselves. And of life itself, which was quite different. This time it was not as an instructor in hypocrisy, but as an instructor in insanity.

Everything happened quickly. So quickly that sometimes *he* did not manage to spot anything.

And sometimes even *his* own name, which had once been on the lips of women, men, children, or old folk, suddenly began to resound simultaneously on all the corners, on all the streets of the city: "Mi-kha-il Te-mu-ro-vich!"

*His* neighbour, who had suddenly been transformed into a soldier, had killed his friend, another "suddenly transformed into a soldier." He was drunk. They had argued about something. With a single Kalashnikov bullet he had shot through both his helmet of World War II vintage and his self-confidence. Convinced that he had killed him, he head-butted out a window and jumped from the fifth floor, leaving the occupants of the room idly astounded, and fragments of broken glass covered him like the feathers of a bird that has been shot down. The bullet was stuck in the dead man's forehead like an illuminated third eye. That night, Mikhail Temurovich beheld death with this third eye, which was aflame like a poppy. And it did not turn out to be so frightening, *he* thought later.

This "later" subsequently became *his* eternity.

Tears poured forth by the silver porch ...

"Look, Sosik, the old times are back: a lamp, a candle ... Look, look ...

God is a very long way away from us, Sosik, a very long way. What is needed is something different, something greater than religion. Greater than love. Or else God will not be able to prepare us for acceptance into the waves of his dimension.

In Sukhumi no verse was being written. In Sukhumi people were dying. They were dying in Sukhumi, and, at the same time, they were dying everywhere and all the time, sometimes even in eternity itself they were dying. They were dying in Gagra and in Tkvarcheli, in Ochamchire and in Gudauta, in Gulripshi and in Gali ...

All cities are like one city, and all days are like a single day, and all women are like a single woman.

All wars are like a single war.

All lives are like a single life.

All deaths are like a single death.

Before I was afraid of death, now I am afraid of life, Sosik.

We are God's children, born before our birth, dead before our death, Sosik."

During that period, *he* visited Zinaida Nikolayevna only three times. Zinaida Nikolayevna and the meowing heir of the Kennedy cat. *He* tried to read the future in her face, but from the face of a once beautiful woman came ill tidings. *He* looked at her and thought: 'When they grow old, women become like men and men become like women.'

During one visit, Zinaida Nikolayevna boiled *him* some "humanitarian aid" rice.

Fortunately, that day the electricity was on for a few hours, and she switched on all the bulbs of the chandelier (despite warnings from the military) and with gleeful schadenfreude declared to someone unseen: "There you are, everyone!" That night not only did the portrait of her murdered son glow, but the faded roses in the vase came to life again.

When *he* called on her for the last time, there were several women neighbours in her room. Zinaida Nikolayevna was lying on the bed and groaning intermittently. There was a pungent smell of cardiac drops. *He* was told that that morning they had found out that Valera had been killed by Roma. Roma was a childhood friend, a neighbour, the Roma from whom Zinaida Nikolayevna had cut off a lock of hair on the day of Valera's funeral and declared him to be her adopted son in place of Valera. It was a month since anyone had seen him in the city. He was said to have fled.

Mikhail Temurovich recalled that winter morning when *he* had found out about Valera's murder. The city kept searching for the murderer thereafter, but all in vain.

*He* looked around for the President's Cat. In one corner of the room, *he* thought *he* saw a ginger-coloured patch, the President's Cat was curled up in a ball there. *He* took him in *his* arms and placed him beside Zinaida Nikolayevna. Then *he* stroked the woman's head, kissed her hands and forehead, and left the room. That was their last meeting.

On the street, a wretched looking solder had killed a dog with his machine gun. *He* did not even stop, did not even tell the soldier not to kill dogs and cats, a dead dog and cat can take their revenge. Unlike the way *he* had earlier shouted at soldiers firing from a large-calibre machine gun at a statue of Lenin: "Don't shoot at statues. Remove them from their pedestals and take them away, especially Lenin, he was a dreadful man. Don't fire at his statues, in particular, or at any others, they may take revenge."

The city's buildings began to resemble apples, pears, apricots, and chocolates taken to the bedside of a dying man. Final gifts: sad, tenderly consoling, like angelically tender marks of omission at the end of an unfinished sentence . . .

One day, during a bombing raid, *he* saw a man leap out of an outside toilet and dash for the safety of a tunnel with his trousers around his ankles and his backside still dirty . . .

*He* also saw some drinkers caught in a bombing raid hiding under the table and one of them had not even let go of his full horn of wine. The spectre of a hand holding the horn crept out from under the festive table devoid of revellers and twitched like the hand of the Statue of Liberty.

The Sukhumi "maniacs" and "devils" had vanished somewhere.

Once during the war, *he* lit up a cigarette, *he* had trouble coming to terms with loneliness. Like a mist, cigarette smoke enshrouded the room, the apartment, the city trees, and the sea. And nevertheless, *he* experienced for the first time something like gratitude for the soul of Columbus, for tobacco.

*He* would take a book by a philosopher from the shelf, then one by a poet, then some travel writing. *He* went through the motions of reading, but *his* heart was not in it. *He* turned over the pages and looked at them as *he* had once looked at the bed of the Black Sea or Lake Bebeisiri, through the mask of a skin diver, but . . .

"Kalimera!" *he* greeted what was probably the last Greek left in Sukhumi, Egeos Marmarilos. Egeos Marmarilos had grown all wrinkled in recent times, all dried up and begun to resemble an ancient Greek ornament.

"The sea is cursed," said Egeos Marmarilos. "All wars and misunderstandings are bound up with the seas. The more beautiful a country is, the greater the number of wars fought over it and for it. Better for me to be an eternal tourist. I would keep wandering and have no nationality or homeland."

"Not an eternal tourist, but an eternal wanderer," Mikhail Temurovich attempted to correct him.

"An eternal tourist!" Egeos Marmarilos obstinately repeated.

Even though *he* regularly watered the flowers in the room, they had dried up.

The parrot died; his heart ruptured from the shooting.

A few times, *he* was visited by Dmitry Khvartskia and his wife Nina. They brought *him* food.

Everyone except *his* grandson Tengiz abandoned *him*.

In fact *he* remained alone.

*His* food *he* shared with stray dogs and cats.

At the end of 1992, *he* was visited by Soso Kapanadze. Soso was still pottering around the Botanical Gardens; he was caring for the trees and flowers. In the Botanical Gardens stood the old building of the Institute of Tea and Tropical Cultures, which was built back in the nineteenth century. In November 1992, an artillery shell landed in one of its walls and stuck there. For three or four days they waited: "It'll explode any day now, today for sure!" but it did not explode. Nobody dared to pull it out. Then they completely forgot about it.

That day *he* talked with Soso Kapanadze about the origin of life and the structure of the cell. They even argued. Unexpectedly in the middle of the conversation, *he* recalled *his* childhood:

"A circus once came to Sukhumi. It brought a small merry-go-round. An old lame horse was forced to make this merry-go-round revolve. It seemed to me that this horse was making the whole earth revolve."

*His* neighbour's house was burgled. They could not break down the iron door, and there was nobody home. They moved in a hoist from somewhere and crawled in through a window. In broad daylight. They did not know how to control the hoist and initially raised it two storeys too high.

"They are a whole two octaves too high," *he* bitterly joked at the looters.

But they did not get the joke, they were not musicians.

That was possibly *his* last joke. On the first day of 1993, *he* told Soso Kapanadze who had come to visit *him*:

"I won't be able to see it through. After Christmas, on the eve of Christ's Baptism, I will close my eyes forever. But you will have to deliver a word of farewell. You must tell everyone what kind of a man I was."

At that time, Kapanadze did not know what the term "Christ's Baptism" meant. He found out later, asked around, looked it up in books.

In the room it was cold. Snow lay over the city. A lot of snow had fallen that year. Some said it was on account of the rocket launchers, others said it was because of the war.

Soso talked to *him*, rubbing his hands together the whole time as he sat in the room with his jacket over his shoulders. *He* was cold too, as was *his* city. There was not enough food. A lot of garbage had accumulated in the kitchen.

"Bury me in Mikhailov Cemetery beside my mother. I don't want to go into the Pantheon. Marble frightens me, I prefer ordinary cemetery grass. You know what I mean! I have pined so much for the countryside, Sosik, for the smell of my old wooden home.

After my death I will give you pointers from time to time, to look after the trees and the cats and dogs. Listen to your heart, and you will recognise me immediately.

There are seven years till the end of the century. Seven is a lucky number."

That may have been *his* last smile.

Just before the Baptism of Christ, *his* apartment filled up with plants and animals. Tramping round the rooms with their heavy tread were black and white buffalo, Babylonian buffalo, Mesopotamian, Japanese, and Caucasian buffalo. Bees were flying, goats bleating, bulls mooing, flowers, shrubs, and trees blooming.

On one tree a cloud had dissolved.

The room was flooded by the Black Sea. And the rivers: the Gumista, the Korodi, the Bzyb . . . The Chipileta also made a claim.

The gigantic pumpkin Atlantis expanded at will.

And, as well as that, there were the greetings of chimeras: unfamiliar plants of the future, unfamiliar animals of the future . . .

"Death is a great feast, a huge table with numerous people in attendance. Slowly, inconspicuously, you become intoxicated. Surely you are not dying? No, you are merely an ordinary man in his cups. Is it from the wine that you are intoxicated or from the years you have lived? They smile at you: what, are you tipsy, brother? That is how they joke with you. A great feast...

Oh, how hard the hangover will be, Sosik!"

Somewhere in Africa, boys are pursuing an antelope wounded by a spear. In Australia, a Spanish émigré is playing an Andalusian melody on a guitar. In Thailand in a rose garden close to Bangkok, a woman is planting orchids in coconut shells. In Greece on the island of Rhodes, a blue wind is blowing. Over Fujiyama it is getting light.

Moving uphill and down the dales are world armies which watch from the sky above like coffee grounds, coffee ground soldiers, fortune-told soldiers. Toy soldiers from toy countries running across toy hills and toy valleys.

A breeze caresses the Taj Mahal... And the snow of Canada shows the reflection of a rosy sky. Somewhere the last man on the planet is wandering...

On the seventh day after Christmas Eve, *he* distinctly heard the last bird trembling in his cage say to the Lord: "Surely this planet was not created just for humans?"

It was like a reproach. To be more precise, it *was* a reproach.

*He* talked for the last time just with the bird. And then *he* said not a word more, the bird died.

But there is more, the guardian angels of the house and all the houses that had been abandoned or burnt gathered in *his* apartment on the seventh day after the Baptism of Christ.

It's a lucky number, seven.

And all the other days and all the other nights, all the tender words and all the beloved faces, all the actions, kisses, embraces, toasts, sounds, memories, hopes, everything blended on this day and in this night.

The last thing *he* heard was the voice of that dead bird saying: "Open your eyes."

*He* opened *his* eyes and beheld God.

And *he* was astounded—*he* had not expected that God would be like that.

In the morning, *he* was found dead. *He* was lying on the floor next to the bed, covered by a felt cape, clutching the edges of the cape with both hands. *He* was smiling. In *his* trouser pocket they found three packets of some kind of seeds.

Unfamiliar

Unknown

Seeds

Maybe

From a flower

Maybe

From a tree.

During the war, the Gumista River divided the warring parties. One of Mikhail Temurovich's favourite restaurants, Eshera, remained open to Abkhazians and another, Merkheuli, remained open to Georgians.

Not far from Eshera stood an Abkhazian rocket launcher bombarding the Georgian positions. The Georgian rocket launcher next to Merkheuli was firing at Eshera Hill.

During the war even Mikhail Temurovich's favourite restaurants declared war on one another and, instead of select wines and exquisite delicacies, dispatched explosive shells at one another.

During a war everything changes. Restaurants, too. They become deserted, plundered, solitary, orphaned, silent in desperation and longing.

They cannot withstand war.

And Mikhail Temurovich did not withstand it.

And on the day of the funeral, the Eshera and Merkheuli rocket launchers howled and roared.

On the day of the funeral, the small procession moving towards Mikhailov Cemetery included Zinaida Nikolayevna. In her arms was the President's Cat's grandson. He was also ginger, like his distant great ancestor. He was also called John Fitzgerald Kennedy. And of course, he was also a healer.

o

The day of *his* funeral was sunny. At night, the moon shone.

The moon that night was not the usual moon, and, therefore, the meowing of all the Sukhumi ginger cats kept lapping it up till dawn.

The moon resembled the President's Cat.

The President's Cat | 251

# The Shore of Night

## A Novel

*Daur Nachkebia*

*Me—not me.*
N. N.

Adgur A. began a journal at the end of August in 1992 and kept it up until his death in the outskirts of Sukhumi in the summer of 1993.

The standard school notebook is dark blue in color and consists of ninety-six pages. The first few pages have been torn out ("I was too hasty in ripping them out and now I regret it. The text was amateurish and clumsy, but painstakingly contrived. The student was sweating, fishing words out of his meager, still-fresh dictionary. The words hardly recognized themselves on the page: The schoolboy was not especially literate; he got confused. But the words revealed the author with an impossible and deliberate accuracy. Without knowing it, or vaguely, guessing at it in panicky terror, he exposed himself unguardedly, peeling off his loneliness. However, as the notebook is a graph pad, numbers are also text, deceptively mute and stubbornly straightforward . . .") The notebook is filled with writing in ball-point pen and breaks off mid-sentence; the black of the letters fades with each successive word. All those efforts led to nothing: The impatient, irritated trace of the depleted cartridge has nearly pierced the paper.

The notebook was not destined personally for me, nor was it bequeathed to anyone in general: Adgur A. did not stoop to saccharine flirtation with fate (". . . I'm writing to nowhere— there are few things to be found among human affairs that are

The Shore of Night | 255

more unselfish and truthful. Expectation of an echo is weakness, if not cowardice and self-pity"). But the person who had been with him on the day of his death had heard of me once or twice and remembered me. We met in Sukhumi by chance, got to know each other, and he gave me the notebook. We got to talking and he recounted to me the circumstances of Adgur A.'s death, if one can call death a desertion. But all in good time.

The day was relatively quiet, no skirmishes or firefights. True, the howitzers were firing, but below the spot where they were sitting—into the ford and the nearby suspension bridge. Yes, the sniper who was holed up in the forest above them, behind the clearing and closer to Shroma, harried them, preventing them from raising their heads. They paid little attention to this and, solely out of boredom, after each shot, they performed a feint: They would hold up a rag of a suitably aggravating color. As it happened, suddenly, for no reason, a bullet would whistle past. The Shroma shooter had evidently lost his nerve after his first miss and was now firing into every shadow. No sooner than the bullet had flown by than an answering choice smattering of abuse was released in Abkhazian, Russian, and Georgian. Occasionally, the silent, swarthy Zaven would unleash his humble Armenian contribution. In the first two languages—Abkhazian and Georgian—swears sound particularly savory and varied, though at first glance, in terms of swearing, it is difficult for the newly scripted Abkhazian to keep pace with the experienced Russian. In Georgian, due to a lack of familiarity, it is scant, barren, full of boring repetitions.

They wonder who it might be tracking them down with a predatory eye: some Gogi with a university diploma—

because how could a simple Gogi, especially a Kakhetian or a Rachinian, manage the scope—or one of those Baltic Shrews from the White Stockings, some fair-haired, white-skinned filly? Most people in truth tend to prefer the idea that what's pointing and shooting at them isn't something gruff and hairy, but something soft, tender, and resilient. They dream aloud about how sooner or later they'll happen upon that sniper lying on the ground and rip off her white stockings, no matter how much she kicks her long legs and . . . The swears also change accordingly.

Adgur A. took an active part in all this, even suggested his own word, either in Latvian or Estonian. It was also an abusive word, which he had heard from a fellow student at the Literary Institute. Their northern swear word was found by everyone to sound rather bland.

During a lull, Adgur A. suddenly got up, climbed over the low embankment that had been serving them as natural cover, took off his helmet, which he had worn throughout the war without ever removing (and for which many made fun of him, though Adgur A. had always appreciated the joke and never took offense), and threw it away with all his might. Tossed it up, to put it more accurately. The helmet traveled in a steadily ascending though not exactly sharp arc, reached the apex, and, poisonously flashing in the rays of the sun that had recently and languidly passed noon, rolled down along the same invisible but already descending curve to the ground, where it landed noisily and whipped up the dust.

(The guy had put it differently; I thought of that later. He simply said: Adgur A. took off his helmet and threw it away. No one saw how it had flashed, what the form or formula was of the curve it drew through the air, how it whipped up the

The Shore of Night | 257

dust when it fell or if it had at all. Perhaps it had fallen into the withered grass with a sound . . . Of course, there had to have been a sound, there couldn't not be—it's an immutable characteristic of the earth's airy sheath, otherwise called the atmosphere.

But the arc and the radiance, which no one noticed, the sound that must have been produced but which went unheard by anyone, not reaching anyone's ears through the somnolent haze—why should these things be included in the text? And the aforementioned sun, as though it had not been scorching since morning—because it was summer, an unbearably hot summer—and only then peeked out to descend to the helmet and give it the opportunity to glitter in its rays—why should the sun be included? I don't know. This whole passage seems to me like it was sucked out of my finger. I can imagine how Adgur A. would have cringed.)

Adgur A. hurled, dropped, tossed, threw, or in some other fashion got rid of the helmet, however one might like, and, after a few seconds (it's tempting to say "wearisome") fell, followed by the subdued pop of a gunshot from afar. The bullet hit him in the head and killed him instantly. He fell, and the helmet continued to draw its simple geometry through the air.

Why he did this was a mystery to everyone. They speculated, proposing different things, but they never came to an understanding. In hindsight, an explanation was found, a word that he allegedly said the other day which seemed to betray his intention. But at the time, it didn't penetrate, and they missed it. And in general, his entire state of being in recent days had consisted of sudden blackouts, when he would freeze out of nowhere, as if encased in ice, his eyes unblinkingly staring at some random point, how silent he was, tongue-tied. All of these peculiarities, which had never before presented themselves, indicated some kind of internal problems.

For some, Adgur A. remained exactly as he had been forever; the deviations from the norm, accurately noticed by the adherents of the previous version, went unseen. It's likely that Adgur A. was exhausted, that he needed a break. At least for a week. Then maybe everything would have worked out. He couldn't take it—he wasn't made of steel, after all.

Still others blamed everything on grass: Adgur A. was a glutton for it and often smoked it until he lost his pulse.

But that he climbed onto the embankment and laid himself bare to the bullet on his own recognizance, everyone admitted.

*Not far from us, down the ravine and above the river, lay the ruins of a thousand-year-old fortress. It—or, more precisely, what's left of it—sprawled across a hill overgrown with ancient oak trees, stout and mighty. What pitiful ruins! Only the robust—the tongue begs to say "sick"—imagination of some museum devotee of antiquities, an admirer of legacies, could construct something majestic and patriotic from these ruins.*

*Everything that's been defeated by time is pitiful. It's even funny. After all, it was all too often erected in opposition to time, in the eternal hope that it would remain an indestructible island in the all-corrosive current. I wandered through the remnants of the fortress and felt nothing but disappointment; there was no trepidation or elation. My heart remained indifferent, beating evenly. Foliage has overtaken these stones which man once hewed*

*The Shore of Night* | 259

*and piled up in order to force himself and his fear into a wall
of them. Occasionally, a thread of sunlight will break through
to the ground and then what they really are becomes clearer:
a corpse. I wandered through a stone corpse. And the tender
grass, ghostly pale, lifeless . . .*

*Sleep didn't come. The fortress flew into my mind with
its supposed associations: the continuity of time, the heroic
past, mandates of the forefathers . . . The fortress was trying
to rise from the dust. Except that I didn't allow it; just as it
was beginning to crest and surge towards its dubious former
grandeur, I cast it back into ruin.*

*Things not created by the human hand increasingly began
to occupy me. I felt a more penetrating kinship with them:
night, the stars, the forest . . . Night, with its black-as-pitch
darkness and its night sounds, enigmatic and terrible, some
of which made the blood run cold in my veins. The forest lived
its life without inviting me to participate. It rejected me. Or,
if not that, then it certainly pushed me away as though I were
alien, dangerous. I felt it with all my organs, all my skin:
I am a stranger.*

*If the forest in which I spent my time and even tried to sleep,
trusting in it, didn't recognize me, then the stars shining in the
unreachable icy heights even more so. I wasn't necessary to them.
For them, whether I existed as a man or as a slug was all the
same. My presence or absence in the substellar world neither
enriched nor diminished their cold glimmer.*

*(By no means am I presenting this shopworn truth as though I'm the first to discover it, nor am I mindlessly repeating an adage. I'm not speaking in someone else's voice. I felt the frigidity and indifference of the stars, and of the skies in general, as I never had before and, perhaps, as no one had before me. What it revealed to me was magnificent: uncared-for by the stars, unneeded by the skies, I was free and alone.)*

*She then said: "What a night!" In all likelihood, she said this sincerely. But for me it sounded rehearsed rather than experienced in the moment. It seemed to me as if she were yielding to my expectations. Except I wasn't expecting anything; quite the opposite. I was afraid she would say something like that and I didn't want it. Perhaps the night itself was demanding that we praise it? Have we not grown exhausted of this withered word?!*

*But her "what a night!" sounded now different to me, not commonplace and crass. Someday, as I'm breathing my last, I'll also say something like this, without any cowardly glance at literature, and I'll fade into what might perhaps be the final summer of the war.*

*The night flowed on and it resembled that one with her. We had then gone out to the river. It did not flow as noisily as during the day, and it gleamed in the light of the moon. All the elements of a cheesy romance were there: the night, a river, the moon . . . Or like this, perhaps: A river, the moon, the night —the night could easily embrace both the river and the moon. Or could it not? After all, the night was here while the moon was over there, outside it.*

*The river. I listened, trying to tune in to its soothing sounds, which entered my soul with silken steps and filled it with a moist languor. But sleep didn't come. Then I imagined I was flowing with the river in its cold, stone bed. The half-asleep human wail, called life, is vanishingly short in comparison with the long flow of the river through the hills, among the boulders, rearing up on their hind legs like prehistoric beasts. Perhaps, in an especially hot summer, it became shallow—just the right size for some dog to lap it all up—or even disappeared completely into the sand along with its noise, mutely hiding between the stones while the dry white-stone bed snaked from the mountains to the sea, gazing dumbly and greedily into the rainless sky.*

*From here I heard only the noise of the flowing water, but when I imagined myself flowing along with it, the noise disappeared. Then, the cold of the water and the hardness of the stones that formed its bed appeared. I was huge, the entire length of the river. I laid in its bed and the water flowed through me, cold to the point of chills at the source and then, closer to my feet, becoming warmer. It flowed and flowed, endlessly, uninterrupted, while hills rose up at my sides.*

*If only to flow so eternally . . . !*

*Sleep didn't come. Fragments of things I had read, or mostly things B.N. had told me over a cup of coffee at Amra[1],* chaotically clamored into my mind: about the stars, galaxies, the Big Bang... Some kind of bird was crying at the top of its lungs (A Bittern, maybe?). Or it was the typical sound of some creature unknown to me, who produced it easily and without any anguish. Naturally, like another person's fart. Those nearby, wearily laid down in the boundless unconsciousness of sleep, farted in an original way, far beyond the prophetic claims of Dali. (We sleep almost in the open air, in a fairly spacious cave-like depression in the slope rising sharply up above us. The cold of ancient stones is in the air here; long ago, primitive man, whose gaze, like ours, helplessly affixed itself on the starry sky, found shelter here.) The stars winked, the glittering emissions of universal gasses. Now, as a matter of course, they blinked off and on to the delight of idiots like me.

I turned onto my left side, sticking my ass out into space—something warm and alive in the frigid, deathly inertia of infinity—and with great pleasure released a rich-juicy-adjika fart. A real fart's fart!

That was an exaggeration. On account of my thinness, only that special volatility of the mixture of stew, condensed milk, and adjika—our typical meal besides bread—could so loudly express my relationship to the world. Such volatility was clearly not enough, as the mixture was diluted with water—the thirst that came afterward was unbearably torturous. But in the silence of the night, my oratory fart rang out quite boisterously, and I was satisfied.

*And farther away, beyond Sukhumi, near Kelasur,
a Georgian howitzer farted and banged on—better to say
"fart-banged on," as it more accurately conveys the immensity
of the event—but, due to its uninspired thickheadedness, not
through cosmic space and instead at our position. The shell
farted even louder as it completed its explosion somewhere in
Lower Eshera.*

*Having farted, I embraced both the lower world as I lay in
a deep sleep and the incessantly glittering higher realm with
the exhaust of gasses spiraling from my stomach, expressing my
stubborn disagreement with the world order, with the seductive
deception of the starry crust of night and the unbearable beauty
of the nocturnal forest. Relieved, with an ebbing melancholy,
I tuned in to dreams. I wanted nothing more than to forget myself
for a while. To forget everything and everyone, just like the dead
who instantaneously and forever forget their unnecessary 'self,'
under the weight of which they warped for so long—for the entire
duration of their earthly life. Perhaps by the morning I, having
hidden in the womb of the night until dawn, will rise up from
sleep, new and unprecedented. Perhaps the world, frantically
rushing past this bulbous fruit, will have spent all its murderous
ardor and I could then find it not far away, grazing peacefully in
the pasture.*

*Under the sway of this multifarious and complex fart, I fell
asleep . . .*

*I'm writing under a tree. Morning has just broken. We're all
in for it, waiting for shift change. We rattled off our ten allotted
days from bell to bell; now it's somebody else's turn to break
a sweat. As for me, as soon as we get back to school where we're
billeted, I'll take a couple days off and go to my uncle in the
village. Away from all this, where the gunfire and the explosions
aren't audible, hopefully the fear that squeezes my heart with its
frosty hands will go quiet, weakening, unclenching its fingers,
and my soul will look at everything with ease.*

*I took a step back from need, both big and small; then, again,
the ballpoint pen with the black cartridge, its color more visibly,
more mercilessly desecrates the virgin whiteness of the sheet. Does
there need to be a disclaimer here? That the notebook is in a cage,
and that it's already as if . . . I don't know—I'm messing around
on the paper. It's an abyss covered with a fig leaf of a notebook,
and beneath the pages—nothing. I'd like to pierce it and have
a look.*

*Some of the pages have been used for needs . . . it's obvious
which ones. Another, seemingly profane hypostasis of paper.*

*I'm writing while sitting on a huge boulder. Above me the
leaves murmur like the hustle and bustle of a hectic morning.
Sometimes the bright light of the sun pierces the space between
the branches, playing on the pages of the notebook and then
disappearing, hopping about blindly like a bunny.*

*The tree isn't a distraction, although in the days that we've
spent here I have more than once stood beneath it, craning my*

The Shore of Night | 265

*neck up to see how decisively it cuts into the sky. I could stand that way for hours, cutting with the tree into the cool blueness of the firmament. In the forest, at least in the part of it that I've managed to examine, this tree is the most powerful, with an unbending posture of straight lines. Other trees, one way or another, have made concessions to the sky, compromises. The majority of them hold their heads at an uncertain, self-deprecating angle, their trunks lumpy, pointedly hideous. As a rule, they don't hide their coarseness, their flaws, the way they've been beaten down by fate. On the contrary, they display these things shamelessly, with an incomprehensibly malicious stubbornness, as if this could help them ward off trouble. We're monstrosities—have pity on us!*

*But this one aimed itself at the sky. The others constantly rustle their leaves, whispering to themselves, babbling, chattering their teeth, but this one is silent. If it speaks, it'll be under the threat of a hurricane or some other elemental force as powerful as it is itself. And I'm sure: it'll speak with a voice unlike any other, and its words will not be fussy.*

*I'm writing in a hurry. Since I fell asleep last night, I'm describing approximately. But, even if I had more time, what could I add to this? After all, the instant you're plunged into sleep and sink to the bottom and the light still visible to you above the surface of sleep, because you're still really awake, suddenly goes out is the moment the cage door slams shut. I can't find an exact word to describe this transitional instant. I could write for a long time about the plunge into unconsciousness stretched out in length or, rather, in depth.*

*The issue is clearly not in the word, but in the fact that the person sleeping is unable to recall this infinitesimal moment. Either they're sleeping or they're not sleeping—almost like that ancient "dead or alive . . ."—and in the passage from one to the other it's as if, no matter what, the person disappears. Since childhood this has tormented me. I kept trying to remember that narrow—now probably impossible—border that I crossed each night between sleep and wakefulness. I didn't succeed. Every night I lost myself and every morning I miraculously found myself anew. I got to the point where falling asleep really became a torture, practically impossible, and I didn't understand the carelessness and lightheartedness with which adults did it. If the moment of transition into sleep was so elusive, then the moment of transition to death would just as easily slip away. I didn't agree with this.*

*But—they're calling . . . I'll remember that tree for a long time. It won't leave my mind.*

Beslan put the notebook in his duffle and forgot about it. Or, more likely, he forgot about it until he needed to dig into the bag for something or other and then noticed it—dark blue, lurking warily and expectantly in the depths. He immediately recognized it and, having recognized it, was disconcerted by that same, first disconcertment. He couldn't refuse, despite feeling that spiritual discomfort at his unexpected and rather unpleasant role as the heir to another person's secrets, as he and Adgur A. had had little contact for that last year and a half before the war. They'd only seen each other in fits and starts, according to the law of Brownian motion, and their friendship had gradually faded away. It had been a friendship born, so to speak, from circumstance, from the lack of anything to do. Not a friendship so much as 'friendly terms.'

A residue from their relationship had remained with Beslan, although there had been no ambiguities, disagreements, or secret jealousies or grievances between them. Something, however, had greatly estranged them. After a year of close, almost daily communication it became clear to both of them. Suddenly, they had both felt ashamed and quietly separated. And when Beslan learned of Adgur A.'s death, the bitterness of their aborted friendship intensified, as if Beslan had secretly hoped that not all was yet lost and that that person to whom he had once related so many of his cherished thoughts might finally become close to him. Now, though he feared he might find something that would open his eyes to the true nature of their relationship and that this nature would be cold, indifferent and apathetic to him or, on the contrary, that it would turn out they had separated due to some misunderstanding, some petty disagreement, Beslan began reading the notebook.

It was hardly necessary for him to read it, nobody was forcing him, and it wasn't as if Adgur A. himself had bequeathed him his writings. Take the notebook and give it to one of his relatives. Beslan knew a few of them. They were all similar in their unsociability and incomprehensible secretiveness, but were known as kind and sympathetic people.

He made a decision: since the writings had been done during the war, then there could hardly be anything in them relating to their friendship and, therefore, there was no need to fear that something petty or shameful would be revealed in them. There had been no one closer to Adgur A. than Beslan, and Beslan knew it.

Everything—if measured rationally, without quibbles, without flirting with the past and assessing it with the benefit of hindsight—led to the fact that he had to read Adgur A.'s notes. If they had been written for anyone, then first and foremost they'd been written for him.

Before the war, Beslan had rented an apartment from an elderly mixed couple: the husband was a Mingrelian who had immigrated from western Georgia in the mid-'40s. The wife, Babets, was an Abkhazian. Paul (the almost-quantum and almost-German name of the old man) had at one time held a high-ranking and profitable position with a winery. With the money from leftover, unaccounted-for bottles of sparkling wine he'd built a house on a hill not far from the train station. The eldest son had followed in his father's wine-making footsteps, occupying a less important post than his father but a more profitable one, keeping account of bottles of sparkling black wine with which he built a white stone mansion in Achara, near Sukhumi. Regarding the daughter, an unusually beautiful woman over forty, smiley Mingrelian cunning had combined in a surprising manner with hard-headed Abkhazian stubbornness. Both had already started families and lived away. The youngest—the spoiled, troubled favorite of his father and mother—was still unmarried and lived with his parents. He was known to be among the Sukhumi gangsters.

Beslan's small room was located on the first floor on the northern side, so the sun rarely reached him in the off-season on its way from summer to winter and back.

The Shore of Night | 269

These old folks received Beslan like a loved one. They didn't know what to do and for a long time didn't believe he was alive, that he was the same Beslan who had rented a room from them for several years. Babets, apparently missing her native dialect, started babbling. She was a tough, stupid old crone, with centuries-old prejudices which had not, however, prevented her from marrying a foreigner. In Abkhazian, after each word gasping and groaning, she cursed the Georgians for all she was worth.

The old men were extremely impressed by the machine gun, the kit, and Beslan's shaggy appearance. They began assuring each other that none of their sons were fighting against the Abkhazians: "God forbid!" They'd all gone to Georgia, however, for fear that they might be confused for someone else, and would return "as soon as the misunderstanding is cleared up and everything goes back to how it was before." They said that they'd gotten flak for renting a room to an Abkhaz—a neighbor had denounced them. The police searched the house, turning everything topsy turvy, and hit the old man with the butt of a rifle. Throughout the story, Babets kept sobbing: "Sons of bitches! Sons of bitches!" The old man also sobbed. He was not a sensitive person, even rude, but the occasion forced it from him.

They thought Beslan was going to remain with them and when they found out that he was moving, they grew genuinely upset. In him, after all, they would have had protection from raiders and looters. Then they suggested that he commandeer the neighbor's house, the owner of which had fought—that "Son of a bitch!"—and would now never see Abkhazia.

The old folks had managed to save almost all of Beslan's junk: Clothes, books, his record player and records. He moved these things to the apartment of a distant relative, an eccentric old woman. Magbulia, as she was called, died at the end of the war a lonely, childless widow. Her husband had disappeared into Stalin's camps. She survived and remained faithful to him, as she was to Salin, and believed in her soul that she and her husband had been guilty despite the fact that they had both been rehabilitated during the years of the Thaw. She regarded rehabilitation as a personal offense. "I wouldn't have done a thing!" said the Old Bolshevik, considering it an unprecedented shame that the country had sunk to such depths of pathetic self-flagellation. She predicted hell for Khrushchev, forgetting in her vindictive irascibility about her own militant denial of God and His judgment in the afterlife.

Beslan didn't forget about Magbulia—besides his relatives, she had no one—and once a week he visited or called, while his mother trudged out of the village every month with bags of supplies in tow.

The old woman, terribly mistrustful, who didn't have faith in anything on earth besides the Party, believed that all these signs of attention were to ensure that the apartment would go to them after her death and with Bolshevik bluntness, unceremoniously, she laid out her suspicions. Beslan's mother, who already disliked Magbulia for her haughtiness and obstinate character but patiently carried out her familial duty (let's call it a mix of a compassionate heart and the eternal concern for what people might say), had, after this, stopped visiting and the crone understood that she'd made a mistake. She asked Beslan to tell his mother that she regretted her words.

It was a two-room apartment in the city center opposite the Botanical Garden. When she died, she asked her neighbors to give him the keys.

The old, hardened communist had lived like an ascetic in an unimaginable, abnormal purity: Everything was as if licked clean, scoured away. Beslan's mother cleared out the apartment, although he could have done it himself. There was nothing to clear out, just three months' worth of dust to wipe away. She removed all the woman's things, as she was a superstitious person and feared that the misfortunes that had harried Magbulia all her life might pass on to her son. Beslan suspected his mother had burned everything.

At first, Beslan felt uneasy. It seemed to him as if the spirit of the old crone, as vile and anemic as she herself had been, still inhabited the apartment, sometimes materializing in the vague shadows that attentively watched him from every corner.

Desolation, ruins, robberies . . . Sukhumi was flooded by looters, but its own: following the advance units that liberated the city, they descended on it as if on an enemy objective and plundered it. Only an ashamed few hid themselves in camouflage. The majority wore civilian clothes, with machine guns at the ready. Some went on foot, some in shabby cars, loitering and ambling through the streets in search of easy spoils: unoccupied dwellings, hidden valuables, cars in still-locked garages . . .

Looters and bandits, loudly calling themselves the troops of the State Council of the Republic of Georgia, robbed and killed Abkhazians mostly but, for good measure, nabbed a few Russians, Armenians, and Greeks as sympathizers. In recent days, another wave washed over the city from the north and Georgians, their houses, and their apartments were already being targeted. But they could not be sated. The stomachs of the marauders turned out to be bottomless, and they robbed everyone indiscriminately.

After the armed looters, the peaceful, partially armed population came onto the scene to pick up the scraps. The madness of insatiable greed, the illness of seizure and robbery took possession of many. They carted off everything they could get their hands on: tables, chairs, lamps, pillows and pillowcases, sheets... Convoys of wheelbarrows piled with these "trophies" wound through the streets. Some would load their ill-gotten gains directly onto their own backs. On fences, gates, and doors there appeared the triumphant word: "Occupied!" But this "Occupied!" wasn't throwing its weight around in proud solitude. In the majority of cases, the name and surname of the occupier was scrawled beneath it, oftentimes including the name of the battalion in which he'd allegedly served.

Beslan didn't go out so as not to witness the shamelessness that was unfolding, this second mass hysteria (the first having been the war itself). He was shocked by what was happening. He hadn't expected it. He was afraid of being unable to keep himself in check, which could lead to disaster: either he'd be overwhelmed, or he'd shoot one of the looters. He had already been on the brink of doing so once when, in the middle of the night, several armed thugs broke into the house of a neighbor, an elderly Russian woman whose Georgian husband had left for Tbilisi.

She managed to scream before they covered her mouth with a towel, tying it in a tight knot at the back of her skull. The war and its constant danger had instilled in Beslan the habit of sleeping lightly, sensitively, as if with his ears pricked. Any rustle could wake him. (That was probably why he never felt completely rested in the mornings.) Instantly, he awoke, jumped up, and grabbed his machine gun. It was quiet, but this quiet didn't fool him: He knew for a certainty that someone had called for help. What he hadn't been able to determine was from whence the call had originated. He decided to look in on his closest neighbor first, and then to the others.

Her door was slightly open, and it was already well after midnight. Entering the apartment, in the dim light of a kerosene lamp, he saw her tied tightly to a chair, her eyes bulging with fear and the veins in her neck swollen as she continued to scream inside herself. But some of her sounds still made it through. They reminded Beslan of the death rattles of a slaughtered pig.

The looters were busy in the rooms. They tried not to make noise, but they couldn't help it. Beslan didn't point the machine gun at them. That would've looked too cinematic and, moreover, it would've given the impression that he was afraid of them. Instead, he held it muzzle down, keeping his finger on the trigger just in case. Noticing him, everyone turned around at once and froze in surprise. "Hey, man, what are you doing?! Everyone here is on our side," one of them said as he finally came to his senses. He spoke with the type of voice Beslan hated more than anything in life: brashly contemptuous, self-confident, affecting thuggish criminal slang.

His heart clamored: trash like this had to be dealt with immediately, right here at the register, and then let come what may.

By strength of will, Beslan restrained himself, though his hand raised the machine gun on its own, the muzzle now staring them down like a gaping, hungry hole.

He couldn't do otherwise, though he knew that if he didn't kill them now, tomorrow they would shoot him themselves from around a corner in retaliation or send others to his apartment. But he couldn't do it.

He lowered the gun and said: "I won't let you loot here, you better leave."

"C'mon, man, quit bullshitting. A Georgian lived here— and a bad one. We did our research."

"I won't allow it."

It was impossible for him to budge, or they'd steam-roll him.

He could say: "She's my neighbor," or "my relative," or "you can kill me . . ." but all these unconvincing words would mean to them was that Beslan had lost his nerve. And then things would go poorly for him.

They were unkempt and had the look of people who had fought, each with his machine gun. No fear or embarrassment, to say nothing of shame—and that was the most infuriating thing of all.

They went into the next room and began arguing about something until an authoritative voice that seemed familiar to Beslan interrupted. They left the room then, silently walking past him with all the dignity they could muster in such a po-sition, and left the apartment, closing the door behind them with mocking delicacy. Beslan ran into the room, untied the poor woman, pale from the terror she had experienced, and gave her some water.

It was clear that one of the looters knew Beslan, and that was what had saved him.

He couldn't recall such people from his time in the war. There hadn't been any on the front lines, in any case. From un-der what rock had they now crawled?

During the day and more often at night when the city plunged into impenetrable darkness, as there was no elec-tricity, battles—in the local sense of the word—took place between various groups of looters. People were wounded, even killed.

Beslan only went out to buy bread and other groceries from the nearest kiosk, lying down to read Hawking and killing time. Nearby in the corner stood the machine gun, its burnished barrel gleaming fiercely. Out of habit, Beslan sometimes took it in his hands to feel the unpleasant familiarity of its cold weight. He put the Kalashnikov, not yet warmed up by the heat of his body, back into its corner. The fear of being caught off guard had sunk deep into him, though he didn't know what or who could so catch him these days. The weapon gave him peace of mind. Beslan was tied to it. During that year of the war, the Kalashnikov had become for him a living creature with its own special visage and temperament, not fully within the bounds of his understanding and therefore frightening. It gradually took power over him. Sometimes Beslan thought he could hear an ingratiating whisper suggesting that it, the Kalashnikov, could solve everything that seemed insoluble at first glance. That whisper was almost a declaration of love: it was nearby, it would never abandon Beslan.

The Kalashnikov and Makarov slipped themselves in to fill the void that appeared in Beslan's life after the war. No matter where he was, he never forgot that waiting for him at home, with full magazines, was that gleaming Kalashnikov, his faithful friend. How very many troubles it had hauled him out of whole and unharmed, and what a feeling of strength, even power, it birthed in him during such moments! And that Makarov at his belt. it was comforting to feel its reliable weightiness, its foreign—even a bit otherworldly—and at the same time companionable touch.

But this attachment began to weigh heavily on Beslan. It irritated him how the machine gun skulked expectantly and demandingly in the corner, at the head of the bed. Laying low until the time was ripe. Until when? What ripeness? After all, the war was already over.

Hawking jogged his memory. There were times when Beslan, from the depths of a trench and under the chilling gaze of the winter stars, would tell the guys about the universe, about galaxies, about what would happen to the world throughout the immense sediment of time. They listened eagerly, though not without irony, from time to time getting in a harmless joke. And then everyone, as if on cue, would start to smile. No one wanted to reveal just how much Beslan's story had touched him: they were busy with important endeavors and the firmament, with all its arcane arithmetic, could wait.

Why are things set up such that no one can know for sure when they'll die? It's hardly necessary for someone to know the day and hour of their death, but it's certainly possible for some sign to suddenly appear to them when that fatal boundary is approaching. But there are none.

Natela's mother prayed frantically to God, in whom she had not believed before but in whom now, after unbearable pain and in anticipation of her approaching end, she had come to believe. She believed not just as an insurance policy but because something within her had suddenly opened, so he might let her know when he was coming to pick her up. And she died in her sleep. In her sleep! It's difficult to imagine a greater mockery on the part of the heavenly overseer: he took her, and in response to her desperate pleas, he sent his bony men in white quietly, imperceptibly, to come for her at night. In the morning, she was dead, eyes glassy with horror—meaning she had had time to look at her uninvited guests!—as she laid in the bed.

Natela missed her mother's passing. Unable to cope with the fatigue of so many sleepless days and nights, she nodded off. Sleep fell upon her dark and heavy and she didn't see how her mother died! Her mother didn't manage to share her last words—the fundamental, wise words that make a daughter's life easier. Natela waited, hoping that her mother had already prepared her farewell in that twilight before the long, endlessly long night, that she'd thought it through to the final letter and was simply waiting for the inspiration of approaching death and that, having gotten it, she would give some kind of sign—a call, gesture, or glance—and, beckoning to her daughter, would whisper the cherished words in just the right voice, many times rehearsed in the depths of her mind.

Or perhaps she didn't have those words. Perhaps they don't exist at all and the coming of death is as mundane as the coming of dawn. How many times has it happened that we've woken up to be met with a brisk morning . . . Do we stay awake? The morning will come anyway. And will she, Natela, also die, not having said, not having found . . . ?

Why, then, did her mother so badly wish to know the hour of her death?

She was terribly afraid of sleeping through the hour of her death and weaned herself off sleep. The pain didn't allow her to forget, anyway. And Natela, still a child, stupid, understood that her mother tortured herself in this way for her sake.

But when the pain and exhaustion finally wore off, when she, depleted in her battle against sleep, gave in, death came . . . It "overtook" her, as people usually say, implying that life for each of us is an eternal flight from death. This flight also indicates an eternal look backward: is death holding the scythe close by or far away? Will I soon feel its frosty breath against the back of my head? Will it soon grab me by the scruff of my neck and drag me off into the distant darkness? This flight produces in each of us a latent, chimeric hope: What if somehow I really do manage to sneak away? As a result, we have an eerie picture of how death mercilessly pursues someone, the way a hunter pursues prey, unrelenting until the point it catches up with its target, and the person flees, never stopping or looking back. This flight is not, however, a "running from" but a "running towards." Many of us, not realizing it ourselves, run joyously towards this meeting, with feverish impatience, dreaming up along the way hundreds of methods to speed up the arrival of this long-awaited rendezvous.

Natela grappled with this riddle all her life. Sometimes it would seem that the solution was nearby. One had only to think it through to the end, straining with one's last efforts, and the secret—whether monstrous or beautiful—would be revealed. Her heart intimated that it was terrible, that living afterward wouldn't be worth it, that it would be impossible to live without a heart made of dried meat, a cool liquid flowing within one's veins instead of blood . . . When her mother died, Natela couldn't return to herself for a long time because she had never managed to hear the words that she had so needed from her mother. She had been deceived, perhaps deceived even more cruelly than had been her mother, who had so hoped for mercy from on high. In an instant, life became empty and meaningless. Natela suddenly found herself in the midst of a terrible, unimaginable loneliness. She hadn't managed to get what she wanted. Fate, however, is cunning and through her mother's silence, she believed she had been told everything she needed. She was beginning to understand this now, approaching her maternal years herself . . .

The death of her mother became for Natela that event which later determined the structure of her soul and thoughts for the remainder of her life. Even war slashed through her heart with a knife that was duller, less cold. If anything were to once again rouse her, it would probably be her own death or, more precisely, the approach of it. It has been said it is our own death that seems not to exist: We cannot know it because, when it exists, we ourselves no longer do.

Once a week, Beslan went to meet a bus from the village on which his mother sent cheese, corn flour, various greens from the garden—a week's provisions. The driver , an overfed hog who, according to rumors, had spent the entire war in a remote mountain village, looked at him mockingly. "I finished university," his rough face implied, "but it was pointless." Beslan cared little about this or, more precisely, not at all. He still divided people according to the principle established during the war: either someone fought or didn't fight, and he looked down upon those who hadn't fought with a perhaps unfair amount of contempt. But the weekly reminder that he was sitting idle in Sukhumi while his parents there worked themselves to the bone, to their last drop of sweat, as a rule, aroused in him a terrible feeling of annoyance at himself. He cursed Sundays, and the bus, and the monstrous sack that arrived with the same regularity as the bus itself returning to whence it came.

Sometimes his mother would even come. She would sell turkey, chicken, cheese, and nuts at the market, leave the money with him, and head home, finally timidly asking him not to forget about them and to visit.

Beslan did not visit. He remained in Sukhumi. He didn't know himself why he didn't get out of the city, unoccupied as he was, without work, half-starved. He rarely returned to his native village—only if a relative died whose funeral he didn't have the courage to miss. Perhaps he was afraid to return to the place where had spent more than a year fighting, where he had seen death and blood, where he had been wounded.

But he could neither return to the familiar, lived-in world. Beslan was waiting. Everything was too hot to cool off without having given rise to anything significant. He couldn't believe in this. His heart told him that he couldn't let the experience pass by without a trace and so he lived in patient expectation that something unprecedented and grandiose was about to happen, and that everything would then return to normal—not a pre-war normal, but something real.

He could not return to the shabby university, to the damp, dimly lit laboratory, to the retirement-age instruments to once again wear holes into his trousers with phantasmatic scientific work. He was finished with physics. It had become odious to him and now lay like a corpse in his past.

Beslan hadn't thought of such an outcome before. He had already abandoned his ambitious dreams of becoming a great physicist, but the thought of moving to a place where science could be practiced safely sometimes occurred to him. He could even become a Doctor of Science. Beslan felt that he had the strength for such a thing and, if was lucky, he might even come across a significant discovery.

The war and Adgur A.'s writings, however, changed something in him. Something shifted. His life divided itself into before and after and everything that had been with him or inside him before seemed unreal to him, a formula into which had

The Shore of Night | 281

crept some error. He saw his purpose differently, from a different angle. There was no intended goal sent to human existence from an unknown place, he thought, but instead a chain of atoms and matter—in sum, a person and their brain. And just as there is no memory of the time before birth—our 'I' at the other end of the scale rests on the moment of conception which touches us little and fails to drop us into despair and melancholy—so there is no continuation of this 'I' after death which does not, however, prevent us from mournfully lamenting that. But only the living person laments. This discord in their feelings can be explained by the presence of a reference point on the scale: their birthday. This is the fundamental day and only death with its drop of tar spoils the sweetness of existence. However, plunging into sleep each night, we lament nothing and even peacefully endure this compulsory departure. That means that death really is possible and really will come, despite all our stubborn unbelief, and when it does appear, menacing and decisive, we will endure it.

Beslan didn't erase the old, incorrect formula because a new purpose had been revealed to him. The old formula was no good; it was impossible to continue living according to it.

And what he had experienced once as a student in a university dormitory he already questioned, though he didn't forget about the feeling that had suddenly gripped him, that he was irreducibly included in existence. To talk about a feeling, that is about something extended in time, is not exactly correct. It was a flash, no longer than a crack of lightning, and everything was illuminated: 'I' turned out to be a fiction that didn't belong to anyone. He didn't cry out like Falter surveying the foundations on which the world stands, but there arrived a quiet sadness: there was no meaning around him.

Then the years downed out that flash with their array and he rarely recalled it. Somewhere in his soul it smoldered as the answer to all his questions. That event had no organizing influence on his life. It continued just as it had always done. If he'd been Hindu or Tibetan, cradled in the arms of a powerful tradition, perhaps he might have nurtured what happened to him into some kind of teaching and spent the rest of his days as a guru in the lotus position.

Invar Tamshugovich, head of the laboratory and Beslan's scientific advisor (as he had already begun writing his dissertation prior to the war, was bald, short, and potbellied. He called Beslan back to him. Beslan met with him at the Brekhalovka promenade [2]—at the coffee shop Akop's Place or at Adunei, a mixture of cafe, eatery, and gambling house where he usually sat after work, playing chess.

His first seven moves—advancing the second-to-last pawns and withdrawing his bishops to their vacated squares—remained unchanged, no matter what color he played, and would probably remain unchanged to the end of his days. And he made these moves quickly, almost blindly, not paying attention to his opponent's choices. The other player could do whatever he wanted—moving his knight not in a G formation but in a pas—and Invar Tamshugovich would only notice the disorder after the seventh move when he suddenly became serious, falling silent and tensing up, causing his somewhat loose figure to take on the dense, rounded shape of a cannonball. The real fight had now begun, the former having only been the boring but obligatory opening volley, the harbinger of an exciting battle.

It couldn't be more hopeless. It was time to put the king on his side to concede the loss, which would have been both

The Shore of Night | 283

more courageous and more worthy, but Invar Tamshugovich never gave up and instead stubbornly led the game to the end, rushing around the board with his doomed pieces. On receiving a checkmate, he remained for some time at a loss, looking incredulously at his partner—apparently waiting for him to confess to a cruel joke—and then at the board, where the king was frozen in the disastrous outcome.

Beslan found his earnest bewilderment amusing. Either he completely forgot about all his past losses, unable to glean any lesson from them, or he had such a high opinion of his skills at chess that he perceived each loss as a trick. After all, every move he made was correct, if not the best! Why, then, did they all add up to the wrong outcome?

Invar Tamshugovich was a weak player and, like any weak player who had not comprehended all the difficulties of chess, he thought that he simply had not to "zone out," in which case everything would be fine. And his stubbornness in the face of an obviously losing position was explained by his hope in his opponent's own "zoning out."

On weekdays Beslan went to the public library. Three stone steps down into the dimly lit borrowers' hall, smell of dampness and book mold, where there stood shelves of books. Between the rows, iron hooks protruded from the ceiling onto which one could hang a lightbulb on a long black cord. Readers, hanging the bulb from hook to hook and squeezing into the narrow spaces between the shelves, looked for the books they needed.

An underwater world of books and glowing watersnakes.

The wooden staircase led upward, to the reading room.

He would spend two, sometimes three hours in the library, but no more. He got tired. It happened that even the shortest commentary (and he devoted all his time to reading commentaries on the famous and even less-famous names mentioned in the books, carefully calculating the number of years they had lived) would exhaust him. This was the case for those who had lived too short a life, meager in their years, or, conversely, for those whose lives had been distinguished by abundance and enviable longevity. In those instances, Beslan's imagination worked double- or even triple-time. It turned on at full power and from a few paltry words he erected a majestic edifice out of someone else's life in which the very last brick held meaning.

He was interested less in the famous little fellows who had lived some measly twenty-five, thirty years—some mathematician, poet, or musician (and among them were many such young and early deaths)—than in those who had added to their fame a long series of years (or else had managed to become famous over their long lives). Some old timer— a wretched old fart and grouch—who had been crowned with laurels, wheezing over to the award of the well-deserved obituary that claimed he'd "departed too soon." This despite the fact that he was a general, maimed by countless battles, despite the fact that his whole life had been out there. But could it be that such a man really hadn't known those suffocating moments, glitches in the soldier's mental mechanism developed over the years, when he would take a guilty look—guilty because there could be nothing but oblivion inside his own soul—inside himself, and suddenly wish for a different path, a different fate? Perhaps not even a general, but anyone else who rarely but nonetheless still occasionally doubted his own past and who, despite the honor, glory, love, and envy of those around him, did not walk smugly along a path that he had not chosen for himself.

The Shore of Night | 285

Beslan envied the dead. Envy was not the correct word. To take not just take someone else's place but to live someone else's life with someone else's body and someone else's heart—to this he would not have agreed. And it was not the dead—that is, those who had physically died long ago and since rotted—that he envied. He envied the strong, well-knit backbone of their lives. He envied the purposefulness of their fates (if one believes the biographies), its clear, unambiguous gait that was later cast in the same clear, unambiguous words. The life lived had taken its own course and it had flowed in a worthy, meaningful fashion, not always without panache. The course had been intended specifically for that life. It could be surveyed from source to mouth. The end seemed to Beslan fortunate, even if perhaps the liver of this life had died in terrible agony—physical or mental—because it was complete: everything complete is beyond doubt. Then that life laid itself into these few lines, dry and impersonal, which Besland read over and over again in order to catch between the words the real smell and taste of another person's fate.

The scent and taste couldn't be captured; they slipped away. But he didn't want to know more than the vague outline of the biography. Otherwise, he could have taken other books, with more detailed and verbose descriptions: "This famous so-and-so was born on such-and-such date of such-and-such year in such-and-such a city-village-country . . ." Rather, from the gray and insipid phrases, he needed to restore the life of the so-and-so. The fewer words there were to describe that life, the more aggressively he worked to restore it.

Exhausted by the hopeless struggle with the lives of others, Beslan left the library and walked to the promenade to get some air in the midst of people. Even better than forgetting oneself in books was forgetting oneself in communication; that is, in the utterance of general, understandable worlds, thereby temporarily muffling the persistent "I" within oneself. But the promenade, the coffee shop Akop's Place, formed the final, twilight chapter of his life's journey for the day. Before that, he had wandered aimlessly around the city for several hours, stumbling into unimaginable nooks and crannies, the existence of which he had never previously suspected. In these abandoned outskirts of the city, overrun with weeds and burrs, where the condemned and dilapidated houses stared through the empty eye sockets of their windows and human voices or the rumble of cars rarely disturbed the ear, peace found Beslan. His head turned off. His soul fell silent. The neglect in these places gratified his soul. It, too, dreamed of the same: to be forgotten, for no one's recollections to stick to it, tearing it out of oblivion again and again.

> *We're lying side by side after night watch. After midnight, we were alerted. We got out onto the road and moved in single file to the Upper Bridge. You couldn't imagine a stupider scene: from the other shore, the road is clear as day, the moon is shining, and the enemy—without even a "night light"—can detect and lay mines. We're silent. Talking and smoking are prohibited. Having arrived at the spot, we took up a position right next to the river and didn't close our eyes until morning. Well, maybe someone did—especially the Kid—but not me.*
>
> *Kid is a nickname, as is customary among us. We're gray-haired, but everyone is Murki, Musiki, Astiki, Akhrikhi . . .*

*Before the war, television announcements for funerals usually
first included the legal name, as seen on the passport, and then,
in shy parentheses, a diminutive, usually the nickname by which
the deceased was known during his lifetime. The country also has
two names: Apsny—local, native; and Abkhazia—foreign.*

*The Kid's name is Daur, but hardly anyone ever remembers
his real name: The Kid's the Kid. The nickname clearly doesn't
fit him: He's a tall guy with a hulking, bullish neck. We have one
Coward on our team who is, of course, a recklessly brave man.*

*But Daur didn't acquire that nickname solely out of the spirit
of contradiction, I don't think. He really resembles a teddy bear.*

*The Kid, when not busy with something, immediately falls
asleep. In any position: sitting, standing, lying down. Whatever
is going on around him is no bother. They say he even once fell
asleep during a battle—he ran out of ammunition—but that's
probably a joke.*

*The Kid proudly talks about his family's ability to fall
asleep at any time of day and in any place. All the men in his
lineage, finding themselves unoccupied, alone with themselves,
immediately would fall asleep, confirming that popular opinion
from the beginning of time, from, apparently, one of the first
old timers who managed to maintain a sense of memory and
clarity of mind: Life is like a dream. That's why they lived an
indecently long time—by giving themselves over to sleep beyond
all measure, they conserved the necessary strength for reality,
so deafening and depleting.*

*This explanation provided by the Kid doesn't suit us. Rather, we claim, they were hardboiled and thick-skinned, like those buffalo with which they plowed their fields. There was little in life that seriously touched them or made them care except for this plowing and barns full of corn. Their minds were primitively snoozing in their impenetrable skulls, limiting them to the internalization of two or three crude, everyday rules.*

*The Kid doesn't get offended by this. He just closes his eyes and goes to sleep.*

*Night. Stars. The river is murmuring. The sky over Sukhumi is bright; the city is shining. Anxiety spills throughout the silence. Every sound has meaning, and we listen to find out what it is. We wonder why they drove us here in the middle of the night . . . Rumors spread that a breakthrough was expected in this direction. But that side of the shore is empty. There is a large field there, and by the time the Georgians pass through it, we'll have had time to prepare and can give them hell.*

*We're sitting in a trench, cramped, hearing the breath of our neighbors, pressing our machine guns to our chests. We're closer to each other now than ever. We're united in a common destiny. Many of us are experiencing fear, but some of us are good at hiding it. Generally, it's impossible to overcome fear. They drive it deep inside themselves, covering its mouth so it doesn't scream. Those who succeed are considered brave. There are also those in whom the ardor of what's happening awakens a genuine joy. What others consider a curse, they receive playfully. Constant*

*The Shore of Night* | 289

*tension and the sharpness of sensation inspire them. But they, too, eventually grow exhausted and become grey, grouchy, dissatisfied types. If they survive . . .*

*Lately, the feeling that dominates my heart is that this is all made up, it's unreal, that we've found ourselves the victims of mass suggestion, that someone's evil will has shackled us to some unknown end. In the middle of the night, when one should be sleeping peacefully in bed—and it would be nice to do so with a woman, drowning in her sweet warmth—several dozen people, mostly men, huddle in a ditch, this long depression in the ground, holding in their hands devices capable of causing such injury to a living body, after which it will stop walking, talking, thinking—that is, living. In the distance, in the same way, in another ditch, huddle together those who intend to make us—living, talking, thinking creatures—into cold, motionless corpses. Why is this necessary? Why do we do it so diligently, and already for more than a month, spending a huge amount of lead and human bodies? We, sitting in this trench, know. And they, in another trench, also know, in their own way. But why did they come to kill us?*

*And when you imagine this portrait, seeing it as if from the outside, you're overtaken by a feeling of unconquerable ecumenical stupidity.*

*It's funny. And terrifying. Before M., it wasn't so scary, though I don't count myself among the crazy, brave men. It's not that I'm afraid of death. I love death, much more than children or music. I don't surrender to my instincts. At least, I try not to follow them blindly; I'm their sworn enemy, including the stupidest of them all—the instinct to self-preservation. But M.! Perhaps I'm also drawn to her because of a damned instinct the hidden purpose of which is the continuation of the human race? But I don't want to continue on in anyone (and before I never experienced the desire to spill my seed into someone's womb in order to replicate myself). The purpose of a seed is to sprout. But I'm not just a seed. I would like to believe that despite the fact that today I'm reduced to my body. My life is worth nothing. It's even in the red, to borrow the words of Alkhas, who's no stranger to thieves' cant.*

*I yearn for her. I'm missing something. A hole has formed in me, as if a piece of meat were torn out by a huge splinter, and this spot keeps aching. Everything hurts. My former indifference to my fate is gone. Not entirely true, but this great, dark hopeless indifference has diminished in agility. Before, it carried me briskly, recklessly. And now I want to rein it in—because of M.*

*Despite the threat of a Georgian breakthrough, the night passed peacefully. At dawn we moved back, but along a different path through the forest. It took longer, and we were tired. Now, we're resting. Some people are playing backgammon, others cards. The Kid's asleep.*

He was an old man's old man. An ordinary old timer, with a short and daring Komsomol past and long, downright boring years of a neat Party existence with its monthly dues and the corresponding "PAID" stamp in his party card. With his brains withered from such a life, he now tried to determine the cause of what he believed was a great atrocity: the death of the USSR. Why be clever about it, talking about the collapse with an undisguised but deeply buried hope that in these breakaway parts the USSR and its great spirit could one way or another be preserved? The trace of its scent could, for some time, still be detected in the outskirts of the empire, but the empire itself has disappeared and disappeared completely. Its death was not an accident. There was malice involved and unheard-of deceit. Such a giant as the USSR could not be brought down with a frontal blow. They approached it snake-like, covertly and conspiratorially.

In the old files of *Pravda* he searched for confirmation that it was an enemy conspiracy that killed the USSR.

The old KGB officer, as he confessed to Beslan in a candid moment, knew from experience that any agent of imperialism—both sent or recruited within the country—speaking publicly or in the press unwittingly lets slip his true intentions, goals, and objectives. That is, he exposes himself. When you speak a lot for a long time, sometimes a word slips through that while for a simpleton will seem ordinary and unremarkable among other words, for the expert will stand out as characteristic of spies.

Over the later years of the cold confrontation between the two systems, word signs, from the '20s to the '50s and then even later, which unmistakably exposed the enemies of the people lengthened into whole turns, into intricate phrases, behind which a secret agent could be given out. Yes, and he even wanted—in a subconscious effort to legitimize

292 | *Daur Nachkebia*

himself—to, if not fully reveal himself, at least hint to the unknown ears listening to him who he really was, nourishing in his soul a hidden hope for sympathy. Living with such a burden—not being oneself is akin to not being at all—is difficult, at times unbearable.

From this vantage point, having surveyed the pre-crisis editions of *Pravda* (the old man dismissed *Izvestia* as an inferior product) with his weak eyes behind his thick glasses, he came to a shocking conclusion: Some members of the Poltiburo—he did not name names, apparently still in the habit of keeping state secrets—had been engaged in efforts to undermine the country from within. Whether they were stooges of the bourgeoisie or acted out of their own thoughtlessness, some kind of cloudiness of logic, the old man couldn't determine for himself. The latter—this cloudiness and the organizational determination that stemmed from it—is not impossible, if one keeps in mind the old age and senility of the majority of the highest-ranking Party bosses.

The old man didn't touch on the General Secretary, who reshaped the map of the world at the end of the millennium in an unexpected and fraught way, because he didn't find latent destructive intentions in a single word of his—and he pontificated, as is known, beyond all measure. "He wanted good things, but they didn't give them to him," the old man concluded. It's clear who didn't give them: a power-hungry corrupt trinity—a Slavic one to boot—who secretly conspired in the forested twilight to cut down the pillars on which the Soviet Empire was built with a view to eternity.

At the mention of this trio, the old man—he and Beslan were standing not far from the library, in the rays of the still-burning autumn sun—farted, really farted. To call his fart juicy

The Shore of Night | 293

would have been an inappropriate exaggeration, a sin against the truth of life. It was as meager and on its last legs as the old man himself, but it was hardly accidental. Precisely at the mention of this troika! A goal, partly malicious, was visible here: the old man was hinting that he equated the fruits of their conspiracy with an ordinary fart—a product of the same quality!

Beslan fell on deaf ears, but the man continued imperturbably—not to fart, but to dismantle the triumvirate.

*That feeling that everyone experiences when taking a pen to a clean sheet of paper—a virgin sheet, as some other writer might say—has been chewed over and then chewed over again. It's like fear. Almost a mystical horror. It's as if the whiteness of the paper—its innocence, as another might say—is terrifying. It seems like the black letters, lining up in some inevitable row, make a path through the wilderness, uncovering a hitherto unknown world. The letters, like pincers, cling to the leaf and gnaw a hole in it, a black hole where the meaning goes, goes, falls, is absorbed ... (According to B.N.'s stories, it's quite possible that over time the world itself will fall into one of these black holes, patiently lying in wait for it, and the lid will slam shut.) The letter I write devours a part of me, the word grabs a piece of my soul, and the page swallows it whole ... Writing is an empty undertaking, an enterprise obviously doomed to failure. An unprofitable business. Life decreases, time decreases, but there are more and more letters and words.*

*But is it worth tormenting yourself with these fears? Is it worth reinforcing the impossibility of writing with such invented obstacles, all these pathetic attempts of a person to grasp by some loophole the edge of eternity with their tiny "I" and, if possible, to scratch a little groove on its stone body? I want to sit down and let it out somehow so that it's ... eternal, on a tablet. Not for the consolation of pathetic vanity, as someone bogged down by the hustle and bustle might think, and not because that fabled self-expression compels it, but rather, as written above, to provide an anchor, a stake: "Here was I!", "I was here!", "Was I here ...", "I was here ...", "I was here?!", "I was here ... !" —in any variation you like.*

*Maybe self-expression is enough. I ran overboard, because my pillar should be the only one of its kind, not to be confused with anything else, a transposition of myself into a solid stone something—into a word. Again, the same self-expression. What is an "I"? Bones, meat, skin, and between all of them a soul. And so I go, my "I" goes, this sum of bones, meat, skin, and the mythical soul, propels itself forward, harboring in the depths of the heart an irksome dream of expressing itself with little letters, fussily scurrying across the white paper. But I'm already expressed through everything I see, and which sees me; not the gaze of a random passerby but something with thoughtfulness, out of necessity, with a calculated and far-reaching intent: Everything around me needs me, just as I need everything around me. I'm already included in the text, whether I wish to be or not.*

The Shore of Night | 295

And therefore, after all, this is all the effort of pathetic human vanity to become more and louder through text and letters.

The circle is closed. Self-expression is self-will, almost pride. "I'm already written in" —but that's not the case! It's not enough, or I don't agree with it, and I undertake to alter, erase, make additions . . . No one can tell me whether I'm ruining the original text or making it better, more intelligible.

A word has appeared that may turn out to be the cornerstone: Intelligibility. More intelligible for whom? This is also a question from a series without answer. Anyone who understands every word, such as those I've written, is not in need of additional explanations. There arises an itchy, dizzying suspicion: He, to Whom everything is already clear, wrote me in; He is the real Author. The rest are just pitiful plagiarists. I want to make the text into which I've been written intelligible to myself. I need to understand what's written there, and if it's actually about me, if there's any substitution—accidental or intentional—in order to find my text myself as the fulfillment of a life debt, which I have no desire to do—and in trying to understand, maybe I'm just not choosing the best approach. Or is it just an ordinary itch in the fingers and then hand to pen, pen to paper, and off we go? I don't know. These notes of mine are also useless, a pouring from one emptiness into another emptiness of words that have long since lost their meaning. I'm sick and tired of it! But the nightly refusal and the firm word to myself have *evaporated completely by morning, and the urge to write tingles freshly in my fingers by then. It's akin to physiology.*

*This notebook will most likely be lost. I'm unlikely to survive this war, and moreover there's no particular need for that. Nobody will ever read it. It'll be trampled into the mud by someone's feet or burned for warmth. It's quite possible that another winter will catch us in the midst of this cheerful activity of mutual murder. And then a whole notebook will do just fine.*

*But there is a hope, to which I will never admit, that, I think, looms distantly before each writer, which is that the texts, once written, immediately become known to the appropriate authority. What kind of authority is not difficult to guess. The boring Wet Blanket, eternal seeker of morality, who will say, didactically raising their pointer finger: This is heavenly! I will not specify which heavens or about who in the Heavenly Abode assigned each their corner. All of this is from the realm of terribly intimate things, those scrupulously guarded things that more often than not alienates people from each other instead of bringing them together. Everyone carries within themselves some secret knowledge, as it were, about their last and final location, where they will be loved and protected. That's why they allow themselves loneliness; they don't need others. They have somewhere to go or, rather, somewhere to be exiled to against their will, and they try to reconcile to it in advance. (God is loneliness.)*

*Basically, leaving all this sophistry by the roadside, let's go directly to the point: the moment when a bullet with all its murderous scope will hit me in the head and create a bloody mess, unimaginable chaos, Egyptian darkness, erasing all records at once. That the bullet will kill me by no less than having made a hole in my skull inspired me from the first day of the war. I am wearing, alone in my entire battalion, a second skull made of iron: a helmet. When the bullet completes its work, then what I wrote will still be preserved.*

*I know someday I'll take the helmet off and throw it away. It won't be a gesture. I'll just have had enough of wearing this heavy thing. You could call it a joke.*

*(Until I wrote it, I didn't know. The theme of the helmet continued on its own accord and descended into vulgar theatricality: in the midst of battle, the hero removes his life-saving helmet and throws it away. The helmet was just a thing, that is, a joke—supposedly it could save something, and our character for a long time abused this ponderous joke: Look, one iron hemisphere is enough to . . . 'An amazing invention,' he spluttered, 'By comparison the wheel is a clumsy projection onto the page of an unlucky draftsman.' Hooray for the head-protecting object! Hooray for the iron hemisphere, this product of human genius achieved through creative torment and long struggle! Hooray, hooray! We are saved: our heads are intact, our brains are intact, although what on earth do we even need them for?*

*But if you believe, even for a minute, that everything follows a rigid plan and no ad-lib will accidentally creep into this plan, then the helmet flying along a theatrical arc didn't fit into the text by some whim of my imagination, but prophetically. And now I, as an honest young man, am obliged in the middle of battle to . . . And further on in the text.*

*Of course, this will all have a meaning and the final gesture—a gesture nonetheless!—will explain a lot. All the various movements that I've managed to make in my life, following what was predestined, will be fixed in this final tension of the hand and its swing, and the helmet will fly along the pattern of this wave until earth's gravity takes it— the pattern—and begins to bend it to the ground, lower and lower, and—bang!—it doesn't balk at the point of impact.*

*Wow, I'll put my back into this swing!)*

The reading room was in the charge of a girl with sad eyes and unusually beautiful fingers. For some reason, Beslan got it into his head that she wouldn't mind talking to him, but past bitter experience stopped her.

He suspected that her body was as young as her fingers, that it was fragrant, and he imagined God knows what, carried away by his thoughts into soft, moist, sweet things. Her fragrance partly came from the perfume she wore, and all the time Beslan's breath caught in his throat, his head began to spin, and visions of paradise appeared. Her voice wasn't tired, hopeless, and capricious, in its overtones there was a certain chill, but even so its youth was still perceptible. That face with traces of a deep inner life, so unusual for those down-to-earth individuals whom he had known until now (and Natela he did not include among these), with undoubtable signs of strong character and quiet self-respect, sapped from him all his courage, and the two or three words they exchanged while he checked out the book did not go well.

Before his self-obliterating dive into the text, Beslan felt her warm, comforting, and reliable presence, and he felt good—and then only reading, those first words coming sluggishly, their sound alone slipping into the brain while their meaning was delayed; a few lines, noisily and meaninglessly bogged down in the gray matter, disappearing beyond the horizon of memory so that the next can follow in full semantic attire, and he floated along with the text, further and further from himself—only reading erected a wall between them. She moved away, and disappeared.

There was no one in the tiny reading room except for the somewhat deaf old man who had been reading Pravda files for the past seven or eight years with extraordinary diligence. Sometimes during a session, students would run in, leafing through their textbooks in a panicked hurry, hastily copying something down, and then running away just as noisily and fussily. Silence would reign in the hall again. The old man sometimes disrupted it with his dissatisfied muttering, sometimes with angry bubbling sounds hoarsely escaping from his elderly throat.

Sometimes she was called to coffee, but she usually refused. In any case, while Beslan was there she had never said yes and gone down to her colleagues, one hefty, ugly elderly lady, heavily rouged and with the shifty eyes of an inveterate gossip, and a timid village girl who had recently become a city-dweller, reeking of cheap soap and stupidity.

Those first days, confused by her refusal, they continued to call her several more times with notes of bewilderment and looming resentment in their voices. Then, having guessed what was the matter, out of decency and so as not to offend if suddenly she were to decide to reconsider her refusal, they invited her only once more and, having received the expected rejection, which spurred on their curiosity and envy, they restlessly drank their coffee.

He handed over the books silently, without looking at her. She also looked—shyly, as it seemed to Beslan—somewhere down at his feet. Then he went down the stairs: "Goodbye!"

"Goodbye, young man!"

Beslan left, and he always had the feeling that there, upstairs in the empty reading room, among the unnecessary books and magazines, he'd left behind someone unrecognized but dear to him.

*We went down to the river. Everything necessary for a tacky romance was there: night, moon, river. But they, in their supposed necessity, were only enlivened by our feeling: She ... I don't know, although she spoke incessantly, drowning out the sounds of the night with her flowing voice, and I seemed to listen, her words didn't convey her mood, which is probably why I didn't remember them. I felt one desire, a rising bulge in my groin. But my literary tempering did not fail. I would be the last realist writer if I began to describe that night in its other details. My pen is not so sharp as to dare to do such a thing. This scene lies beyond the boundaries of literature and I'm still hopelessly stuck in it. It's only possible to get rid of—literature, that is—by throwing away the pen, that is, the ballpoint pen with which I am now defiling the innocence of a white sheet. The struggle for viability! Omnipresent law. I'm fighting for a place in the spotlight.*

*It was all stupid, out of place, because I felt strongly that this was neither the first time nor the last. I already knew what she would say and how she would say it. The Night, the moon, the river catching with their nets. M. was at one with them—she had caught me. She didn't fish like a woman, she actually fished without realizing it, just as anyone fishes, through words and thoughts, imposing her soul on another.*

*Was M. beautiful? Yes. Khaki transformed her. She became much more alluring. I can't vouch for the correctness of my perception. I was blinded by desire . . .*

*I didn't expect to meet her here. Everything has changed. The habit of long acquaintance still dulls our vigilance, and we continue to see in the old way. But, looking closely at even the most impenetrable faces, it's impossible not to notice that they are no longer the same, that a newness has broken into each one, erasing the old one without a trace. Probably only for a while, for the duration of the dislocation. As soon as the joint is reinserted to its usual place or remains in its new position, with the pain almost subsiding, most would return to their former selves.*

*But I didn't really believe in her rutnr; she was too distant from her past self. In Amra, I saw a frivolous and attractive*

*girl—a girl, though she was already approaching thirty. It
seemed, at least to me, that she had not yet lost the hope of getting
married even though when her face broke into a smile, her eyes
remained sad. Another confirmation of how stupid I was in my
assessments, following along with the tacky majority.*

*Her face smiled, but her eyes jumped from place to place,
calculating and exhausted.*

*She never came to Amra alone. Some men, most likely
unmarried, silent ones with some subtext in their own minds,
accompanied her. There are such types. Not bad, in general,
once you get to know them, but terrible bores precisely because
of their stubborn taciturn quality. They sit with that typical
Swiss neutrality on their faces and it's unclear whether they're
listening or thinking about something on their own. They usually
have the habits of middling thieves. In their rare words, at least
one is sure to derive from camp jargon. They stoop a little, even
the short ones. Their gestures are exacting. They always say
one meaningful thing in different ways: We respect ourselves,
honestly is paramount to us, we don't touch anyone and we don't
allow ourselves to be touched. They fascinated me, in a way. They
knew to keep a mark. That is, they treated themselves and those
around them—and life in general—with a certain seriousness.
They were solid types, self-sufficient, they felt their "I" firmly.
It was never scattered across their imaginings of other people's
lives. And I asked myself: Is she like that too? Do they really
have a similar kind of soul? She and these pompous turkeys, full*

*to bursting with the consciousness of their own importance? It detracted from the image of her I had created in my heart.*

*Yet there was nonetheless something elusive about her. It was difficult to decipher her. She spoke, almost jabbering, and they remained silent. Her entire manner betrayed such a cheeky girl . . . Again, such worn-out words! I'm trying to recall in my memory the way it was then. The ready-made words are right there, tucked beneath my arm, and they brazenly insert themselves into the text. But the real ones, which would bring it as close as possible to its essence, hide, reluctant to reveal themselves, and have to be dragged out into the light by force. And one can believe that there are such words, precise, tenaciously grasping the subject. The things themselves carry their names. You just need to be able to deduct them. That's equally unattainable, and everything written by people is only approximate. This blind affixing of words to objects . . . Maybe you'll wind up in the top ten by accident! They don't make it into the top ten, things keep getting deleted, and one is left instead with lots of orphaned words for which the thing they describe has long since died.*

*I fired off the first word that came to mind and made her an ordinary Sukhumi girl—moderately flirtatious, moderately charming, moderately stupid. But sadly, I wonder if it was really accidental, that first word. Isn't this a case of the first throw when you hit the target without aiming? All objects, of course, even people, have a harmful, disgusting habit of hiding behind false names. Even if you burn their real names into them, they'll still* deny it and try to cover it up. M. seemed cheeky. One could find a similar word, but that wouldn't fit either because she wasn't who she said she was. If she had continued in the same vein, maybe she would've grown into it. But the war ...

Bread with cheese, tea, lemon that I squeeze into a glass. That's my breakfast, lunch, and dinner. True, I could fry an egg for lunch, depending on my mood and if I'm not feeling lazy. Then I head out. Here, a question arises before me in all its enormity, each time shudderingly acute: Where to go? I stand, not knowing where to move my body, fatigued by stopping and rest, and at the same time my tired soul, invisibly merged with this still young but already worn-out flesh. And in this indecisive moment, I am a creature who has completely given over to chance. The habit has probably endured since the war. Space itself absorbs me, sucks me in like the funnel of a whirlpool, determining my future route. I pretend to make a choice, resisting the forceful pressure for several minutes. In this city of three streets and one square there's nowhere in particular to go. Head to the promenade to drink coffee and chat about nothing: What are the Georgians up to? How will the Russians behave? Can we rely on them? Will they betray us again? Into this flaccid, boring conversation some crestfallen gladhander will without fail insert a remark about the weather, saying, "What a blessing! We live in such a paradise but we don't appreciate it!" The rest—some silently, others with exclamations—will agree.

The Shore of Night | 305

"Global warming is underway. Soon we'll turn from the subtropics into the tropics."

"Will bananas grow here?"

"Sure they will!" The expert says, importantly.

We have a special weakness for the banana. In recent years, it has rapidly entered our everyday life and now this exotic fruit, with its striking yellowness and respectable size, decorates tables at both holidays and funerals. What especially attracts us, however, is that, according to rumors (we don't yet know for sure), it grows in the wild, right in the forest on a tree. All the work required is to pick it, remove the fatty, soft peel, and stuff it in your mouth, and then you're full for the whole day. Rainbows and butterflies for toothless old people: You can munch the tender flesh of a banana with your bare gums.

Citrus fruits, which require constant care and a considerable amount of fertilizer, are capricious, often sour. They're far inferior when compared with the banana.

We await the dawn of these blessed tropics with bated breath.

So, whether to head straight to Akop's Place or down the Prospect to the library—this is the crossroads at which I find myself each morning. No, I don't stand in place and toss a coin in my mind to decide left or right. I don't linger in the entryway longer than I need to in order to display my free will. My legs themselves carry me towards the center, and in this time between home and center, my future route is slowly taking shape in my brain, with each of my cautious, uncertain steps along the street (and mostly along the street, not along the sidewalk; there aren't many cards and the sidewalk is dirty, the slabs out of place, such that when you step a thin plume of dirt hits your foot). So, I find myself in the center, under the clock, or, apparently more correctly, the Clock. The ordinary clock above the former City Soviet, now the City Hall, has long since left the category of ordinary clock and become a Clock. The location is to blame. From afar, through the branches of the camphor trees that line the street, I see it and, using the face as a guide, I slowly approach. What time now appears there?

The fact of the matter is that it usually functions correctly but then suddenly begins to measure out who knows how much time. I suspect that at other moments it rearranges itself in the silent darkness of night, secretly, without being caught by anyone, and then in the morning presents itself to the disoriented townspeople. For several days, the Clock will tell time in a new way, its own way. The city authorities, who apparently view themselves as being in charge of time, too, notice this disorder and send someone up the stairs to make an example of the Clock, who then forcibly resets it to the supposedly correct, respectable time. The Clock ticks for several days in accordance with the wishes of the people, who stare at it from below with an incomprehensible mixture of anxiety and hope. Anyone who wished, equipped in advance with a personal watch for insurance (which proves without further ado that time is a human invention; if it were otherwise, and time had its own self-sufficient meaning, people would not need time-measuring "handcuffs"), could look and make sure that his own time corresponds to the main time and that he, too, along with everyone else is now—O, tender hand of fate! O, constancy! O, joy!—included in this order.

But one unpredictable night, the Clock malfunctions and the next morning, to the chagrin and secret fear of the

The Shore of Night | 307

townspeople, it begins to spout complete and utter nonsense, displaying some alien time which it alone understands.

*Everything that's happening around me has rattled my previous ideas to such an extent that I cannot write. What I am still writing is like when the head has been cut off and the body is still convulsing: the run of life continues although the finale is already behind it. It's the same with me.*

*At first, the words seemed to resist the chaos into which we have all been drawn. There was order on the paper. The letters were in the right places. They combined to form words. And words have meaning. It also seemed to me that part of me was passing into words, that they said more about me than all the photographic images and all the autobiographies I could create in my life. I not only passed into words, but I remained in them. Even if the paper on which I've written burns, if my words are reduced to dust they, once written down, are included in the text. I don't know which text, but without faith in that it's nearly impossible to write.*

*I couldn't manage without this word, no matter how much I might wish to: Faith. As I say it, I am almost blushing with embarrassment, like I've been caught in an act of petty theft. But when you're on the precipice of something that has never been with you, when the path leading into darkness (and, from the time of night and sleep, here is another narrow, nomadic definition of that very thing from which there is no return,*

*as recognized by everyone and confirmed by the irrefutable*
*experience of the cemetery) is one-way and you're taken by*
*surprise, then for lack of better options you resort to such*
*substitutions.*

*Now I see that the word is powerless. Life cannot be created*
*from it, nor can it be incarnated in this word. The word is*
*a shadow.*

*B.N. argued almost the opposite, saying that the original*
*Word is immaterial, is that from which all that is visible,*
*tangible, olfactory, and mortal sprung.*

The city was alien. I tried timidly, shyly to get used to it, to create a complete image of it within my soul, after which it would feel closer to me. For this I needed a guide, and Adgur A. unwittingly took on this role. He was on friendly terms with the city, as he had been born and raised in Sukhumi.

I would have preferred a slightly different guide. If only he were not so lean, wiry, if he had more volume, like soft, rounded shapes that looked like a slightly modified infinity sign. And if he had squinted differently—not myopically, just to see, but conspiratorially, slyly, with a meaning known only to the two of us.

But the two, with their similar data points, who worked with me dreamed only of graduate school. They were distant relatives of Invar Tamshugovich. Ugly and rabidly devoted to science, old maids were rapidly maturing within them. Such a future was already written in the entire narrow width of their foreheads. They themselves understood this and had partly resigned themselves to it, though they harbored some secret hopes for a Ph.D.

Our society honors people who have pursued higher education with a special servility, and if they also have graduate degrees, then people simply shit bricks. This opened up roundabout paths for the poor spinsters to a legal but purely arranged marriage. Over time, society could slip them some philanderer who had been on a spree and who, by the age of forty, had suffered gonorrhea more than once and had finally, at the insistence of his relatives, decided to give up bachelorhood.

Only on particularly stressful days did they, with their very vapidness, awaken desire in me. If it became unbearable, I ran to the bathroom. Having furiously rubbed one out and expelled my all-consuming melancholy, I returned devastated, with the bitter sense of yet another weakness. With my cleared vision, the spinsters became what they really were: unattractive individuals of indeterminate gender.

Adgur A. was the author of several short stories overloaded with subtextual meaning. Not short stories, but rather parables. The lively life in them was distilled into short, dry lines, in contrast to his recordings which were pretentious and verbose. He worked slowly, hard, and was always dissatisfied with himself, the typical example of a writer rendered barren by the immeasurable demands he placed on himself. They were published in a local literary magazine and went unnoticed, which Adgur A. did not lament.

In one of his stories, the hero lives in anticipation of meeting a certain person. A certain person informed the hero that in such and such a place this person would be waiting for him and that he should under no circumstances be late. The hero is worried, attempting to anticipate this meeting, wondering what this certain person will say to him. Without much effort, the reader could guess that the "certain person" is death and the hero is simply waiting for the hour of his demise, has spent his entire life waiting for this. And now the long-awaited meeting takes place that the hero has been dreaming about throughout the course of two incomplete pages. Who does he see, with a sinking heart? Himself. Standing in front of him is his doppelganger.

In another, a boy repeatedly asks his grandfather to tell him the story of how he killed a wolf in his youth. The boy feels sorry for it. He hopes his grandfather doesn't kill it. Since the grandfather tells the story in different words each time, the boy hopes that in one of the retellings, the grandfather will miss the wolf and it will remain whole. But the grandfather's story always ends the same way: the wolf is shot and its blood stains the melting snow. Then they leave the *amatsurta* [3] and go to the *akuaskia* [4], where they must sleep. During this time, the boy feels how his grandfather's hand gradually turns into a wolf's paw: its nails lengthen and sharpen, it grows over with fur, and the paw holds the boy's hand tenderly, with love. The boy doesn't dare raise his head to look at his grandfather. He knows that he will see his burning wolfish eyes, eclipsing the stars with their brilliance. The boy clings to him.

In a third, there is a mountain pass. A woodsman and his life live far from the village. The woodsman, at the insistence of his wife, who nags him because they live like rubes who don't know what's happening in the big, wide world, finally decides to install the antenna for a radio receiver he bought long ago. Because the house is situated in a ravine, he has to raise the antenna higher. A few days later, armed people show up. It turns out that there's been a war on in the big, wide world for a long

The Shore of Night | 311

time. The soldiers accuse the woodsman and his wife of espionage and shoot them.

The others were in a similar vein.

Adgur A. served, as he put it in an old-fashioned way, nearby in a publishing house. It only took him two minutes to get to Amra. I had to trudge over from the New district for about twenty minutes on a stuffy trolleybus that was always sweaty and crowded.

There came a time when no one cared about anything and discipline in the laboratory—and not only there, but far beyond its confines—hobbled to a halt. I could be absent for days at a time and no one would notice a thing, except for those poor spinsters. But even if someone among the bosses had noticed, no administrative penalty would have followed. Then, work in our laboratory boiled over. The spinsters didn't leave their instruments for a moment. They literally tortured them, taking various readings and drawing unimaginable lines from them. If even one substance in nature behaved in this manner, the world would not exist at all, or else it would be completely different and, still, it's hard to say whether there would be a place in it for those poor spinsters.

Then, Adgur A. went to Moscow to enter the Literary Institute. He enrolled and we saw each other again a year later, the day after I turned twenty-five. I felt that something irrevocable had changed in my life.

*For once, we have some quiet! It will be like this for about a week. We and the Georgians play a game of silence though not, it's true, always consistently. Sometimes, it happens that the burst of an automatic or machine gun, even the roar of*

*a howitzer, breaks the snow-covered silence. (And the snow
fell to its heart's content this winter.) But it's all good-natured,
sleepy, exhausted. Rumor has it that this is the time before the
offensive—ours, of course. The Georgians are firmly seated on the
left bank of the Gumista and, it appears, aren't thinking about
any kind of breakthrough. They want to starve us out.*

*If indeed an offensive is to be launched on our part, then
there's more than enough reason to rest. I persuaded the
commander, despite his resistance, meaningfully hinting at
unforeseen circumstances, to let me go for a day or two.*

*The night turned out just right. A slice of the moon got stuck
in the branches of a pear tree, bare in the face of the coming
winter. The snow is laying a blanket of white, drowning out all
rustles and sounds with its cottony body. In the cold sky the stars
shine, needle-sharp and abluted. The sounds and smells are the
familiar ones of childhood.*

*How impatiently I waited for summer, when the boring
school year would end and my father would take me to the village
to visit my grandma and granddad for three brilliant months!
They're already dead. Only my uncle and his family remain.
My uncle, who has three sons (my cousins, all three of whom are
fighting), is an unbelievably kind person and loves me in a special
way. It's possible he's not as worried about his sons as he is about
me. To be honest, that bothers me a little. But I won't give myself
away with a single word: to offend someone like my uncle is an
unforgivable sin. My visits to them are an extraordinary joy for*

The Shore of Night | 313

*him. First, he asks about his brother, my father, and his sister-in-law, my mother, who stayed in the outskirts of occupied Sukhumi. I know nothing about their fate.*

*That one tree often comes to mind, suddenly piercing my heart with a sweet, unearthly light. Especially at night, when everything seems hopeless, meaningless, and you're abandoned alone in the starry abyss. My favorite thing to do before going to bed, since I was a child, is to imagine something. Let's say, for example, that I'm swimming in the sea, or flying. Most often, however, I find myself at a great height. I mentally climb a tower using a ladder, higher and higher, climbing until my heart skips a beat and goosebumps are prickling along my spine. And, always, I want to jump. For some reason, I'm sure that I won't fall but will fly. Even the piercing sensation of the endless power of the sea, its wet, maternal womb, forgotten but recalled every time I plunge into its waters, its embrace, menacing and indulgent at the same time, cannot compare with the bliss of flight. And this is familiar to me. I've dreamed more than once that I was flying. But that's a story for another time—right now I'm talking about that tree.*

*Before I fall asleep, as I lie in fear of loneliness and meaninglessness, I suddenly remember that tree. Without much effort, I recover the feeling of its physicality and the enormity that I experienced on first meeting it. But my imagination goes farther. I become the tree, living its long life through the rain, the snow, in the summer, in autumn . . . And I understand how petty, disgusting, and shameful my life is in comparison with the dauntless life of the tree.*

*I dreamt of my long-dead grandmother. We find ourselves in some marvelous garden. The dream is black and red: the garden is all black, and the flowers growing in it are unusually large, red as red can be, indescribably beautiful! Grandma leads me by the hand through the garden and says in her soft, kind voice: "Don't be afraid, Nan [5]. See how good death is, Adgur!"*

*Grandmother, in her old age, went a little off the rails, fearing that there wouldn't be enough space for her in the next world and she would be cast back. She didn't want that. She was hoping to meet her relatives and loved ones, and there were many more of them there than remained here. Her fear was based on a simple logic: So many people had gone there! In her memories alone, there were so many . . . The immense dimensions of that world amazed grandma, whose mind had so weakened. She was sure that sooner or later the other world, expanding due to the arrival of new residents, would overtake this world and absorb it into itself. Just try figuring out who was alive and who was dead then . . .*

*I woke with a miraculous sense of peace that I haven't known for a long time. Maybe ever.*

*You need a miracle to happen to you. No miracle has happened for me yet, except in my dreams. How, then, can I believe in God? What if dreams are proof?*

The Shore of Night | 315

He didn't write her name, only M., which could mean: Manana, Maria, Miziia, Margarita, Mary, Marina, Maya, Milana, Madina, Maka, Marianna, Mayana, Miranda . . .

The singular thread is M. Using that, I have to unravel the entire tangle and find M., the one for whom, apparently, Adgur A. possessed some feelings. But where to find her? Maybe she died, like Adgur A. Maybe she left Abkhazia after the war. Maybe she's disabled, legless and armless, sitting at home unable to make peace with fate, angry at the whole world, or, on the other hand, resigned and radiating goodwill and warmth.

I could track her down to see with my own eyes or, at the very last, find out where she is and what happened to her. If she was a nurse, and most likely she was, then I could contact those who served in the medical battalion and probably get all the information I needed about any nurse whose name began with "M."

But I didn't do this, relying instead on fate. I said to myself: perhaps it was not by chance that Adgur A.'s writings came to me—after all, they could have been burned, gotten lost, fallen into other hands, but instead here they are, with me— and perhaps, after reading them, it was not by chance that the thought occurred to me (not even a thought, but a clear, strong feeling) that I should become a kind of continuation of Adgur A. or, rather, that, while remaining myself, I ought to— I must, in no other way—continue him. It was both my desire and my duty . . . I can't find the exact words to convey what I felt then. It was as if in a dark room—where you couldn't see your hand in front of your face!—the light was suddenly turned on, and not an ordinary 60 or 100 watt lightbulb, but all 500 watts. Your eyes hurt, but everything becomes so real and comprehensible! I had to, while remaining myself, somehow continue him, find a place for him and his unlived life. That is, if all this was not in vain but rather operating according to some twist of fate unknown to me. That meant I would find M. without much work. The mechanism is already wound up, so we'd meet anyway. We'd meet, get to know each other, with some sixth sense we would each guess that what had happened was what should have happened and that we knew about it in advance. No, we wouldn't just pass each other by. At least, I definitely wouldn't. I would recognize M., and in her eyes would be the memory of Adgur A.

In the previous paragraph lies an assumption that emerged from the smoke of the letter. After all, words pull thoughts along with them, running ahead, and, putting your faith in them, you can agree or, more accurately, get up to all sorts of nonsense—like that M. wouldn't pass by, or that she wouldn't recognize me by some sixth sense, which isn't even possible or necessary. A filmic image appeared before my eyes. A man and a woman walk towards each other, each noticing the other. Looking at each other and slowing down, they approach each other and gaze into each other's eyes, saying: "Is that you? It is you!" I say, "It's you, M., the one Adgur A. wrote about!" She says, "It's you, B.N., the one Adgur A. spoke about!" Then we hold hands and silently stare into each other's eyes for a long time. All questions are resolved. The search is complete. Life is sealed.

But it wouldn't be like that. It couldn't be. M. would never recognize me if I didn't identify myself. Then again, she might not recognize me either way if Adgur A. never mentioned me. Maybe we knew each other before, in which case I would recognize her. But in this scenario I wouldn't recognize Adgur A.'s M.,

The Shore of Night | 317

but my old friend M., who will overshadow his, and my entire idea would go to pieces.

As for what might come next, I didn't think about it. And why such a wild thought popped into my head in the first place, though as I tried to explain above I had to continue Adgur A. one way or another, I don't know. I don't like the way I explained things above. There are elusive quantities here. Fate, a wind-up mechanism, paths that for some reason definitely intersect instead of remaining parallel for the foreseeable distance—not into infinity, since the geometry of our world sooner or later connects all paths, meaning, of course, all destinies. But not all meetings can take place within the parameters of a single life, not to mention those eyes in which the memory of Adgur A. lies. Maybe I deceived myself. Maybe all this was the deeply buried echo of something I had once read or heard or seen, something that passed through other hands, now devoid of its original freshness. In short, not mine at all. I agonized over this for a long time, feeling not only discomfort but a sense of complete failure, and I'd already stopped believing in that light or heat. Isn't this all just self-deception?

And yet something within me resounded demandingly. Behind everything that had happened to me recently, I saw a sign—maybe even less than that, just a hint—but precisely not someone else's, not borrowed, but mine.

I decided to find M., not yet realizing why or what I would say or do once I located her. Unable to explain my own actions clearly and unequivocally in the spirit of the clarity and precision of a mathematical formula, I decided to rely entirely on my feelings, to follow my heart when my mind was powerless to plot the trajectory of fate.

*I still can't tune in and march in step. As a child, I never forgot
that we were playing at war but it wasn't real. Now it's the other
way around. The war is real, but I still can't believe it. During the
day, we're too busy to think for long about any one thing. There's
an upside to this: We're freed from the tedious and difficult need
to always remember ourselves. Our "I"s dissolve into something
huge and faceless. It almost looks like happiness.*

*But at night, when a howitzer screams so alarmingly in the
distance, I understand quite well the unimaginable horror into
which we've all plunged. Before, at the close of my childhood,
I experienced something similar, except that horror was
associated with life. I knew that I was alive, real, and that was
simultaneously joyous and terrifying. More terrifying, even. It
was an unbearable black torment gently dusted with fine grains
of light. And that there could be anything here resembling light
at all puzzled me. I was afflicted with a huge, incomparable
fear of existence. Death was also right there. But death, as
usually happens at that age, I placed far beyond the mountains.
Inevitable, according to adults, but—as my heart told me—
unlikely to have any direct relation to me.*

*Now everything is happening otherwise, recklessly and
frantically. It turned out that everything wasn't behind the
mountains but just around the corner—both life and death so
close that it's impossible to distinguish between them, and they
overtake us, breathing down our necks, throwing us first into
the cold, and then into fire. Yesterday, the Kid was still alive, but*

*today he was killed by shrapnel. He fell into the sleep that he
loved so much while he was alive. But now it's forever.*

*O, cowardice! O, absurdity! These human words flowing from
that first Word, confound it! The 'eternal sleep' is a euphemism
worthy of a bum, cheerfully passing through life with his eyes
closed and his ears plugged.*

*The Kid, despite all his passion for that lazy pastime, is in no
way satisfied with his 'eternal sleep,' I'm sure. And neither are we,
his friends, nor his father, mother, brother, sister, or his girlfriend
Saria, about whom he never spoke but who we knew was waiting
for him in Gudauta. We would have liked for the Kid, giant and
powerful, to lie snoring closeby so we could know for sure that we
could wake him up if we needed to and that he, smiling, would
lazily open his eyes.*

*I'm off-balance, which is why it's so hard for me to throw my
eyes open wide and look at the truth of what's happening to us.
If in war, on top of the inconceivable noise and fatal fury, there
is some underlying meaning then, probably, it's just that it drags
a person out of the mud of petty everyday life and shows him the
unthinkable brevity of his allotted time. War sweeps away our
complacent tendency to live our lives day by day.*

The old man stood a trustworthy distance from me and in
a muffled voice splashing with saliva, the indignant droplets
of which fell onto my face, uttered his nonsense about the reasons for the offensive and shameful collapse of the Country

of the Soviets—those were his words, "Country of the Soviets"—fraught with catastrophe about which, due to a lack of intelligence, those hawks overseas didn't bother to think. Our spark has been lit, a worldwide fire lies ahead, and soon—"Sooner than we think, young man!"—it will blaze so furiously that only a single cinder will remain of this, our ball of fools.

I imagined the lively blue globe—with its seas and land, cities and villages, forests and desserts, people and animals—hurling itself in a frenzied rush across the universe, smoking and stumbling, like a man running out of a burning house and trying to throw off the flames that have engulfed him. As he runs, however, the flames flare up and consume him entirely. Having burned for several desperate meters, he then falls lifeless. The earth won't fall, it'll keep hurling itself forward, and on the way the globe will eventually shrivel into a black pebble.

And suddenly I was thinking of other globes hot and elastic not with air but the tender elasticity of a woman's living flesh. I thought about Natela. She was probably tired of waiting for me and would greet me, as always, sullenly from under her brows like a deceived, offended child. Even though she was no longer a child, not even a young woman but a woman on the threshold of maturity beyond which old age begins. Old age, the approach of which Natela confronts with increasing horror day by day. The wrinkles are fine, barely visible, like the trace of a smile about to disappear, but that's enough for Natela to spend hours contemplating her face in the mirror with indignation and despair, constantly comparing it with the portrait of her mother standing nearby in a simple blue frame. Her mother's face was streaked with wrinkles.

I didn't understand why Natela held on to this particular photograph of her elderly mother, taken during her illness and on the eve of her death, rather than a younger image of her. Perhaps she was preparing herself for the bleak future?

She looks at her mother and there's so much pain in her eyes that I feel sorry for her. I say a few comforting words, as a rule meaningless in such instances. Natela is ready to forgive me everything, but that isn't what I guessed to be the real reason for her grief. So as not to upset her more, I start talking about how difficult it is to lose a mother. What can I say to her besides these banal words?

The weight of her horror before the onset of old age disappears when we make love to each other. Natela doesn't experience anything but the fact that she is once again desired tells her that she's still young and, perhaps, that it isn't her mother's fate that awaits her, but something better and longer-lasting. After all, her mother wasn't old—only forty—even though in the photograph she looks to be in her eighties. Natela says that it's because of the illness. In the span of two years, she turned into an old woman. She died in terrible agony, from a rare form of cancer. She felt like something alien, hard, and predatory had settled inside her and started growing and she constantly put her hand to her stomach, then to her chest, her sides, sometimes her head to indicate the location of the monster moving about inside her. It was everywhere.

Natela often talks about how she cared for her mother, how she suffered for it, that it had seemed to her that it was she who was dying instead of her mother. Her mother died a long time ago—Natela had only just finished school—but still she can't forget how she had suffered. She keeps asking: Why had her mother been condemned to go through such inhuman pain, why had she been so punished?

I tell her it wasn't a matter of punishment. Her mother had been seriously ill and that explained everything, it was from that which her suffering had stemmed. But Natela doesn't want to hear this. She's gotten it into her head that every illness is sent to someone for their sins; even an ordinary runny nose has divine origins. Her mother had also committed some transgression, though Natela knew nothing about it. "You're being cruel to her," I say. "No worse than God," she replies.

Her love for her mother is built on this mixture of pity and unconscious cruelty. Sometimes, I think she hated her. Children are also punished for the sins of their fathers, she's told me more than once, without revealing which fathers and which sins she had in mind. She means, it was not difficult for me to guess, that her womanly failure and hence the misfortune of her entire life is predicated on her mother's guilt before the heavenly Father. This is where I usually fall silent. I realized a long time ago that it's impossible to convince her otherwise.

Natela, despite her panicky fear of old age, also wants to live for a long time, an incredibly long time. She loves all the various stories about centenarians. Having seen some old woman on TV with her long cigarette holder, forgotten by death, emerging from the smoke in her wrinkled glory and talking about her long hardships on the path of life, Natela will listen in fascination with an envious and admiring gleam in her eye. There were several such celebrities in her family who had lived past one hundred, included in various foreign and domestic books on the phenomenon, widespread among preliterate Abkhazians. The only confirmation that they had rattled along so long was their own memories. In the absence of documents confirming their exact date of birth, they correlated the milestones of their lives with certain historical and natural events that sunk into their memories of childhood: The Russo-Turkish War, the first wave of migrants to Turkey and the countries of the Middle East, the unprecedented blizzard of 1911 nicknamed the "Big Snow."

I can't understand Natela. To live a long life means to inevitably grow old and, with such a genetic inheritance, to grow old and ugly. But she, contrary to logic, in spite of the one who doomed her mother to an early and painful death, wishes to live a long, wrinkled life. What she would prove by this remains unclear. Given her long-lived roots, she seems doomed to languish for decades to come. But she herself makes the effort to do this because the climate, food, and life today are not the same as they were during the times of her well-favored elders, and these conditions are not conducive to the living of a long, healthy life. True, her efforts are purely cosmetic in nature: Powder, various creams, gels, and monthly, or even more often, panic in the face of the mirror. The rest of her "healthy lifestyle" remains unchanged: She smokes the same way, citing our old women puffing away as examples, forgetting that they usually didn't inhale, thereby saturating their lungs with cigarette smoke.

Sometimes I ask myself if I still love Natela. I don't know. I'm at a loss trying to remember the feelings I had for her, except that passionate desire to always possess her. But I can't recall those others.

Natela doesn't experience pleasure in bed. She told me about this herself when I was still madly in love with her: "I'm frigid, no man has ever managed to turn me on, and neither will you." This was the main argument she provided against my advances. She said that she doesn't love me and is moreover incapable of love at all. What kind of love could there be when the body is cold as stone? I didn't believe it and continued to pester her. I really loved Natela and couldn't understand how it might be possible for such a beautiful woman to experience nothing with a man. Once, I pursued her all day. Wherever she went, so did I. She decided I had lost my mind—the city was small, many people knew her and knew me, some were curious, some cast puzzled glances after us—but she's afraid to raise her voice. What if I were to suddenly do something idiotic? Gritting her teeth, she endures it all. When I recalled all the stupidity of that day later, I blushed to the roots of my hair and felt sorry for Natela.

But I was like a man possessed. A dying man in the desert thirsts after a gulp of water, and I thirsted after Natela even more. Just one touch, nothing more, then the passion would leave me. But she insisted with cruel obstinance: "No!" We parted on that "No!" I lost all hope and went home with such a burden on my heart that I thought I wouldn't be able to bear it.

*Seriously, I'm embarrassed to admit now that I thought this iron thing was capable of protecting me in my entirety. Firstly, my head and the brains inside it, then, with that primary organ securely covered, the skin and everything else under it, beneath this thin and pinkish shell, my bones and my blood, flowing continuously inside of me, keeping me awash with its life-giving redness. And I put on this thing, heaped this unfamiliar cargo onto myself and was myself surprised at such an ingenious method of self-preservation invented long before my time.*

*But I was mistaken. I've been as naked and defenseless as the moment I was born. Nothing could protect me from life.*

The thought entered my mind that only a book, in which the others, those same time-killers, and I featured, could become a framework for my life and destiny. It was moreover necessary as the only possibility for understanding something about myself and to survive, to resist. But survive what? Resist what?

I'm going to speak plainly. I'm a generous person and am not disguising my intentions, unlike certain other cheapskate writers. Some of these misers will hide their scant thoughts so deeply, organizing them with such magnificent and majestic accompaniment, that you'll gasp but, in reality, the meaning is a soap bubble no larger than the eye of a needle. Using a simple example, I'll explain what it is that I must survive and what it is I must resist. It must be remembered that this doesn't come from any literature, although I've read *Horror* and *Nausea*; instead, this is original, something I've truly experienced and which kept pace by my side here along the streets of Sukhumi.

The street, down which I started with a very decisive and purposeful step, no longer remotely resembles its former self. More than a year of continuous shelling and bombing has distorted it beyond recognition. At its side sit dilapidated houses which remind me of an old, shabby, drunk woman with a cigarette in her mouth and an insolent look . . . In a word, the street is like a grimace of despair now when I walk along it. The sun is shining. It's all happening at once: I'm walking and the sun is shining from on high. What a coincidence. It's not out of pride that I'm on the same level as the sun or, rather, near it, as some might scoff, but it's a coincidence of life circumstances.

I destroy the street with each step while the sun in the sky, unlike me, blindly devours the day. But by the time I reach the end, the sun will have burned out a piece of the day so tiny that, having reached the end of the street, I can hardly feel that decrease in the light and the sun for me will remain nearly as bright as at the beginning of my trek.

A pathetic example, but so eloquent. I, this man, walked down a street—a whole street—and took several irrevocable steps. Water off a duck's back! Nothing above moved in any perceptible fashion, there was no sympathetic gaze, no friendly guiding hand. But I digress.

The sun is shining. There are people around, as always. People surround me. But with each step I take, I break their brotherly circle. They close it again, and I open it again. My entire journey is a closing and an opening, a breaking and connecting, going beyond the boundaries and returning to the delineated limits. I want to go beyond the dubious brackets into which people put me. But this isn't the main thing as it is almost always. But what I want to talk about is rare, with earth shattering results.

There's no turbulence in my brain. The clarity in my head is dazzling. I see the world in all its colors and details. Here, Beardy sneaks in, muttering under his breath, "Night, I'm on your shore . . ." as he remembers a recent game of backgammon, at which he's a reckless and terribly unlucky player. Here's Macho, with a folder under his arm and sombrero on his head, standing sad and alone in front of the intercity. Then, a doe-eyed beauty passes by, a telephone operator, an old spinster with a reputation for whoring around or a whore with

The Shore of Night | 327

a reputation for being a spinster, I don't know exactly. And here, an honored worker, dressed immaculately in the old fashion, with a suit and tie of the Party color; and another, of the post-war litter, in metal glasses and a suit of a fashionable color, that is to say, light like the president's . . . In a word, I see the world around me brightly, in detail, which once again speaks in favor of the idea that it's all hunky dory up there in my brain, that it's safely protected by a bone sphere and in the darkness inside it's ticking away like a clock. But it's getting harder and harder for me.

The street fills up, people pour in, the circle shrinks. I stop. The world returns to its borders, but the question is: Why am I here and where am I going? Is there anywhere for me to go? I have no answer. People mill around: two-legged, two-armed, and, most amazingly and unbearably, two-eyed. If they were without eyes, these black circles in the center of an oval, it would be easier. But their glassy eyes—black, brown, light blue, dark blue, green, and more—look at you, although you didn't ask them to. They're peeled and that's that. There's no way to walk down the street unnoticed. Someone's piece of glass will catch sight of you and call out; in someone's memory, there will be a place for you, too. Even if no one ever calls you to mind later, somewhere in the depths that even the recaller himself doesn't know about, you will remain. And all simply because one summer afternoon you were walking along the streets of Sukhumi and a stranger also happened to be on this street, with that same piece of glass meaninglessly rotating in the globe of his skull, capturing and appropriating much of its surroundings.

Why so much? Anything it comes across: the short, dark-haired man in the stall with a wide variety of goods, from the red and yellow Brooke Bond to the gray-paged and faithful Republic of Apsny; a portable bench with a rainbow of cosmetics, all those Rexon and Kiki things, various little items from the Celestial Empire, like bobby pins, hairpins in the shape of large, silver-winged butterflies, handkerchiefs, nail polish, huge white chunks of humanitarian soap, which old wives get by pulling strings; and the owner herself, a purple-haired girl with a crass, boorish look; a group of young people, thin and fragile, squatting, with eyes dazed from weed; a fat, red-faced man in black silk trousers and a snow-white, short-sleeved shirt, casually slamming shut the door of his foreign car, his entire appearance reminiscent of some outlandish animal; a flock of lighthearted students from the medical school, scrawny and bow-legged, clad in miniskirts and platform sandals, with tattered books under their arms; and an old woman . . . In a word, everything that falls into its path.

And, because I'm exposed and recalled in this way, because I'm meaninglessly reflected in these glassy surfaces and shoved into someone's memorable guts, I feel terrible. I'm walking naked through the streets of Sukhumi, scratched at by countless eyes.

Then I remember her and almost set off running. Now it's no longer the chaos of the street that flows over me, but something soft, pliable, and this soft, pliable thing absorbs me completely into its warmth. For a short time, order is established in the world, things line up in comprehensible rows, and stop merging into a hopeless, continuous blur. Natela!

*It rained today. The sky darkened instantly, clouds slowly floating above us like huge, ragged, black ships. Lightning*

The Shore of Night | 329

*flashed like a sharp dagger and water gushed down from the sky.*

*Rain has always unsettled me. In its dull noises skulk hopelessness and sadness. Sometimes thunder and a blinding flash of lightning will bring a little variety to this heavenly stream of Heraclitus—now everything is turned upside down, and the same water pours over us which shortly before rose as steam from reservoirs, rivers, and seas. The Greek Heraclitus was right in form, but in essence he was wrong: No matter the unique elegance of the clothes in which you dress an old woman's life, beneath them it's the same—toothless, blind, wrinkled, bony. In short, ugly to the point of nausea. Heraclitus should have stood in that river longer instead of fearfully jumping out, having barely wet his feet.*

*I'm completely in this stream, up to my neck in it, and I'll speak frankly. It's not so bad, it's even great when the Heraclitus stream pours down from above. The exclamation point based on intonation—that very "!"—is not something I'll be adding. Its proud, narcissistic posture does nothing to convey all the bitterness of my words.*

*Over these past few months, I've aged. If only I could be scrubbed white, if I could scrape off these rough, boorish bristles, I might pass for the age I am on my passport. But I know for certain that a frail old mean, nearly a corpse, took possession of me long ago. An old man who, from the wrinkled top of his bald head to his broken, uneven nails, is an animal in essence. He eats, he sleeps, he defecates . . .*

*The rain has stopped and suddenly there's a rainbow in one half of the sky. Enough already! We jerked the breechblocks of our machine guns, sending a cartridge into the chamber, and pointed the muzzles at the rainbow's arch—and let's shoot at every hunter who wants to find out where the pheasant's sitting.*

*I, too, succumbed to this general indignation and fired off half a clip. I don't know about the others, but I aimed at the foremost part of the bloody arc. Knock it out of the general formation!*

*But then it got worse, much worse. Clouds floated out from behind the mountains and into the blue, blue sky after the rainbow cleared. An invisible celestial trumpet had sent them out with such mercilessness towards us that tears welled up in my eyes because of both the beauty and my own self-pity.*

*The idea of shooting at the rainbow came to me while we, tired and wet, were walking along the road with our heads down, no one paying any attention to what was happening in the sky. There were other things to worry about besides a rainbow, and no one would have wasted cartridges on such a meaningless gesture, nobody would've thought of it . . . Well, no normal, sane brain would have. But I saw it. My soul ached sweetly, and I saw before my eyes how the guys might raise dozens of guns to the sky at once to begin spewing bullets at their sorry human lot. A thing of beauty. The seven components of light squirming before a few armed people who didn't agree that nature is eternal*

*and that the disintegration of light into seven elements isn't*
*a final disintegration at all, only a temporary one for the purpose*
*of creating beauty while they, human beings, will disintegrate*
*forever while nature so brazenly, cynically flaunts its power over*
*and indifference to them. And people can't think up anything*
*better than confirming their powerlessness with some mosquito*
*bites.*

The sea was incessantly whispering about something of its own, long since incomprehensible to the human ear, and Adgur A. and I slid along the surface of these sounds. We were again in the unconscious grasp of countless things said, thoughts that had faded and lost their original shine. We were talking about our motherland. Maybe for Adgur A. this was a hot and blazing topic. Probably. He spoke with the words of others, but they came out as his own, hard-won through his own skin. I was a little tired of all this, since we were in Amra and I preferred the noise of the sea and the silence of the mountains. For Adgur A., the sea and the mountains symbolized the two primary components of our spirit: mutability and rigidity.

Abkhazia is both a coastal and mountainous country. To those approaching by sea, it is clearly mountainous—the mountains rise higher and higher from behind the arc of the horizon and, having reached the shore, such visitors find themselves nearly at their feet. The mountains begin right at the edge of the sea and rise sharply upward. When these restless travelers go deeper—or rather, when they rise farther—into our country, then they will see only the docile surface of the sea. In our people, two irreconcilable elements have also been joined together and the rich, variegated nature of this combination is often unbearable for us, rendering a hefty pressure on our spiritual stores, finding its way out in desperate, suicidal acts. And the beauty of our country is in this same combination, richly variegated, which has always attracted the hostile eyes of others. The whole life of an Abkhaz is spent battling foreigners, possessors of greedy eyes. By the time those greedy eyes have returned to their familiar, boring, gray landscapes, the Abkhaz has already started fighting with himself. All that was best in him spent itself on repelling foreign predators, while everything petty, envious, and spiteful settled at the bottom of his soul to disturb the consciousness that grew clearer in times of danger.

"But after this war, it'll be different," continued Adgur A. "We can't keep tripping over the same stone. Now is when we build our own state. We will be free."

These days, he was often in a suitcase kind of mood; he wanted to leave Abkhazia. Where and why he didn't know himself, but at every meeting he resolutely declared: "The die has been cast! I'm leaving in the next few days!" The "next few days" came one after another and still Adgur A. wandered around Sukhumi or sat in Amra all day. Despite his lack of employment—he didn't work anywhere, having left the publishing house, "away from all those senile people preoccupied with their mediocre manuscripts," and now considering himself a free artist—he displayed periods of frenetic activity. He could be found in the least expected places of Sukhumi, and Abkhazia too, with the least expected people, from university professors to ex-cons. And everywhere he "weight" was no lower than average: the professors heard him respectfully and the criminals clearly considered him one of their own.

"A motherland is, first and foremost, a vise," he used to say. "A motherland isn't a mother but a stepmother. It demands so much from us. Well, fuck it . . . I want freedom. That's why I'm leaving. In just a few days."

Adgur A. put everything on the cold, glittering rails of logic, and everything went smoothly for him. A mosquito wouldn't even touch his nose. He agreed to the point that for the common good, one mustn't love one's motherland, but hate it.

I no longer remember what twists and turns his monstrous logic took to bring him to this paradox, but it had sounded quite convincing.

Adgur A. always dressed differently from others. He seemed to be wearing the same thing as everyone else, but it looked unique on him, with a family crest. His jeans were like any jeans, but, look closely, and you'd see they didn't fray like everyone else's, in unusual places not predicted by the movement of the human body, and they were beautiful, and the brand wasn't one of those whose names were everywhere, blatantly swarming up to meet your eyes. His shirt was a fashionable color for the season, but it managed to fit him perfectly, and his shoes . . . In short, his difference from the others was conveyed through his clothes. He'd also had a hand in this. He carefully chose these items, a fact he no less carefully hid from his acquaintances. In the Abkhazian mentality, a man shouldn't pay too much attention to himself, especially not his clothes. Adgur A. covered up this "flaw" of his by some deliberate sloppiness or negligence. Perhaps the shirt was slightly, almost intentionally wrinkled, the shoes covered with disingenuous dust, or the sleeves of his jacket were torn for a little while and he walked around for some time, as if not noticing those coquettishly fraying threads . . . But none of this could conceal the high cost and fastidious selectivity of the things that he wore.

Some cynicism in his discourse notwithstanding, Adgur A. was a respectable young man and followed our customs strictly, even with a certain foolish consistency.

All of our customs are, one way or another, connected to funerals, weddings, or feasts. Adgur A. knew everything that concerned these things with an enviable completeness. Some old people, who had forgotten much over the long years, raised their heads in interest when he brought to light something obscure, be it a word, toast, or ritual. He was often a friend of the bride or groom at weddings. This is an honor and a big responsibility. One must know, by heart, the entire complex and boring ceremony and the strict sequence of toasts because there are dozens of perked up and not-entirely-friendly ears around and the slightest mistake will instantly invalidate the entire ritual. You must be able to drink with dignity and not get drunk. You must respectfully listen to your elders, answer them with emphatic respect and, finally, you must be able to speak, which is the most difficult part. Dozens of ears looking for well-trodden paths that will set no one's teeth on edge; only a bright, memorable word! The relatives of the bride and groom are numerous and all the important ones must be described accurately in just a few words, outlining their entire life trajectory in bright colors. We mustn't forget the younger branches of the mighty family tree. Without overfamiliar condescension, we must predict for them a worthy continuation of the work of their fathers. And some bits about their glorious ancestors. What a tangled knot! Adgur A. successfully unraveled it.

In fact, Adgur A., being such a supporter of these traditions, would ridicule it all mercilessly in conversation. He called our customs a tedious and absurd pastime. You can't reject funerals and weddings, but their scale and splendor ought to be stripped down to an almost ascetic framework such that only that which still breathes with freshness and genuine feelings remains. But he could be seen at the funeral of an old man, a distant relative, no further away than a shabby mountain village, where he was mournful, almost inconsolable. Even those who claimed it was affectation were pleasantly impressed, and those with a nationalist bent said: "Our foundations are that strong—some denier you are!" It is not surprising that he paid tribute to the memory of the deceased. Something else is surprising. With such a distant branch of the family, you don't have to trouble yourself much. But these seemingly little things are the essence of this custom, its viability. Your father left the village and settled in the city. Now it's no longer the custom to send mourners. Everything can be found in the newspaper or the television. Then someone died in the family's former village, not a relative at all, not even a neighbor, simply a resident of the same village. Custom explicitly requires lamentation for the deceased. When you hear about his death, you don't feel anything, you're already up to your neck in work and you don't have time to be distracted. But what will those who know that you, generally, come from this same village, and who consider you a fellow countryman, say? You drop everything and you go. You can, of course, not go, weasel your way out of it. Adgur A. never shied away. He was straightforward, like our customs.

"All our—Abkhazians'—strength went to either repulsing greedy, bloodthirsty invaders or to endless feasts and funerals. This is the vicious circle people have lived inside since ancient times: wars, funerals, feasts. This is our cross and our share!" Adgur A. usually began this way.

"What else could we do?" I picked up the topic and so began our game. "Someone was always coveting our land, and the Abkhaz couldn't close his eyes day or night, he didn't know a quiet life—always ready, always on the alert. So when there was a respite, he lost himself in long feasts."

"All that is gluttony, just gluttony, splendidly and grandiloquently furnished."

Adgur A., as always, joked. In his words there was nothing of his own that came from the heart, just a mental somersault, as he called it. At some critical depth of the conversation, however, we forgot about the game. The masks fused to our faces and the roles we took on called for death in earnest.

"And you still believe the legends," Adgur A. continued with affected pity. "The legend is just a lie. People see their own imperfection, uselessness, the invalidity of their existence, so they come up with a beautiful dream, someone else's necessary and meaningful life. Time passes and new generations, equally unnecessary and flawed, replace them, and here we are today saying, 'Glorious ancestors.' We judge by a handful of heroes fashioned by the popular imagination. They didn't and couldn't have existed. People don't change, they just come up with new words."

"You're talking nonsense. You're exaggerating, deliberately reducing everything to the everyday life of our people as if that's their entire essence. A custom for you is just a ritual, but you don't notice what lies behind it—its meaning and its purpose."

"It's not worth a thing, believe me. It's people like you, who have some kind of mental itch, looking for some special meaning in everything, that have forgotten how to see with their own eyes. A person needs to refine his animal essence, so he learns to gorge himself with some panache. Look at our weddings, our funerals. Over there a corpse is rotting and we're eating and drinking. And you want to excise this baseness from us, as if it has no influence on our highs. No, my friend, the high and the low are connected, as they say, by inextricable bonds. And the high, I think, isn't even a high at all."

"How?! What about heroism, self-sacrifice, honor, and generosity?!"

"Bullshit! All that's from folklore. There's no spirit in customs. People invented them so they could tolerate each other. And you pile onto them, poor things, such an unbearable burden—spirit!"

*We're climbing up a gentle slope when suddenly a machine gun fires at the top. Its hysterical, furious bark made us all throw ourselves to the ground. We lie down, not moving. Any centimeter to the side could cost us our lives. The bullets scream. Some of us "catch" them. Moans and cries can be heard. I came across a small depression where it seemed a little safer. My neighbor to the left was wounded, and my neighbor to the right, but I'm still holding on. Suddenly, someone forcefully pushed me in the side, hoping to drive me from my spot. I look, and he's a boy, his face still free of blood, his eyes dazed, and he's poking at me. What could I do? I gave up and moved. Then a bullet hit him, and he screamed in surprise, threw his head back, twitched, and died. A moment ago, in that spot where his head is now, my head was*

*there. If I'd stayed there a little longer, would the bullet have
hit me or missed me? After all, it was probably released after he
laid down in my space, though this hardly changes anything if it
was already in flight. In both instances there's an inconceivable
interlinking. We moved, the machine gunner moved, an
unimaginable pattern of small movements formed and the
bullet, flying along its inevitable trajectory, hit the unlucky
boy in the head.*

*Fate is a strong thing in hindsight. When everything has
happened and nothing can be changed, it's easier to determine
the ending, to see the signs of such an ending in the
lead-up.*

His life was woven from the past: Gone, disappeared, irrecoverable. And in the library he was busy with the past. He
took a book at random and opened it to the final pages, where
there was commentary and notations, and he read the brief information about the life and affairs of various people who were
honored to be included in it.

Though they say that the average life expectancy used to
be much lower than it is now, many of them lived in an aura of
glory and honor into old age. Especially marshals and gener-
als, despite the deadly nature of their profession. They really
displayed a bulldog grip, clinging to life. Beslan imagined this
sort of dashing general, confusing names and events, once
without a shadow of a doubt—without even raising a decisive
eyebrow—sending his soldiers to death and now tooting his
own horn about it. Boasting about defeats and victories, about
minimum casualties in terms of manpower and equipment on

The Shore of Night | 339

his side versus the enormous damage heaped upon the enemy that predetermined the outcome of the battle.

But he envied this myopic, self-important knuckle-dragger whose body was completely covered in scars from his wounds. His unworthy—or perhaps worthy, who could say?—life was captured in just a few dry words. He went down in history and became part of it. Beslan could disappear anonymously; the future didn't promise him immortal lines. Even as a notation in someone's work, there would hardly be a snug little space for him. Not even a footnote. Like that brave soldier managed to deal with his life, so Beslan would deal with his. Surely the soldier went to bed each night with a sense of accomplishment and fell asleep easily, like a baby. In the morning, he got cheerfully to rush again into the struggle for existence and to fulfill his important duties. (Just as Beslan was reborn every morning). And here was his reward: a few lines in a book.

*Winter has passed. I'm still alive, which surprises me. Whether it's nice or not, I can't say. Or rather, I couldn't until I smelled the flower. This lilac-tinted little fellow, unlike its plump domesticated compatriots, was fragile. It was wild and fought for its life in the untamed forest. Everything about it was small, especially the smell. Only by moving it closer to the nose, almost pushing it into the nostril, could one catch the aroma hidden in its body. But what a barely perceptible aroma this was!*
*I remembered the distant happiness that was either with me or not. I felt joy that, it seems to me, was not there where the scent transported me. The recollection of that day when I first experienced the scent of that flower made the long past into the*

*present, as if I had carried the happiness of my first meeting with*
*that intoxicating scent of the world all these years, had forgotten*
*it, and the flower had reminded me.*

*The flower was plucked and, then, drunk through my nostrils,*
*it wilted before my eyes. It dried up, fizzled out, and its six*
*pliantly opened petals, releasing all of their aroma, faded away.*

*The flower's dead.*

*For a long time, I remembered its piercing scent, which my*
*mother may have experienced when she carried me under her*
*heart, and which had already reached me then, so that now*
*I thought of it as a paradise lost.*

*Winter has passed. I'm still alive. Before the flower I didn't*
*muse on whether this was a pleasant thing or not. But here was*
*this flower. And death became terribly pleasant to me.*

I'm sitting in the library, forgetting about my own life and busying myself with others. I'm learning how to become Adgur A., his continuation—in deed, in fate. Sometimes, however, my thoughts jump from the books I've been reading to my neighbor, the old man. He's laid out piles of *Pravda* in front of himself, donned glasses with lenses so thick that, for a normal eye, distort the world in a strange and absurd way and, silently moving his thin, bloodless lips, he boldly floats along the patriotic waves of Party decrees and resolutions. Sometimes he removes the glasses, wipes his eyes, watering from his efforts, with a handkerchief and then, giving them a well-deserved rest, looks at the ceiling for a while, dare I say it, offering my head for the chopping block, dreamily. Or does it just seem

The Shore of Night | 341

that way? Could it be that he's tired? A man usually dreams when he's tired of life. When he's in his prime, he's decisive and rude. The old man is tired, that's for sure. So, he's dreaming. Most probably about something impossible.

I would give a lot to swap places with him, even for a moment, to become him, his decrepit body, decrepit mind, decrepit soul. After all, I can't avoid that widespread decrepitude— if, of course, I'm lucky. If I'm lucky, I'll become ripe for death, just as this old man has been for quite some time. The weaker his knees, the more uneven his gait, the quicker he goes to the end, running, running briskly, running headlong into it. He quickens his pace like a stone thrown into an abyss. There is probably a universal law of gravitation towards death.

As I left the library, the old man spoke to me. I've been waiting for this for a long time, because old people are sociable and they like talking to their hearts' content. They can hammer away at the same topic for years. If you remind them of that they'll blame the forgetfulness of old age, but you shouldn't trust them. They're cunning. They're not as forgetful as people think and as they'll say themselves when it's useful. They've not made sense of their own lives and, time after time, return to what they consider to be its main events. Constant, boring reprimands aren't capable of changing anything. After these wordy outbursts, old people calm down a bit, growing dull before our eyes. Then they gradually build up their strength, accumulating memories in themselves in order to discharge them into the first available ear.

The old man, as it turns out, was also deaf. It's not surprising, although in my phrasing there is an element of surprise, as if it's not a requirement for old people to be hard of hearing. That's why old people are old, to have more flaws that remove them from reality prior to death. Through the gradual disappearance of the sounds, smells, and colors of this world, they become familiar with the other world. But weak hearing has one positive property, too. It forces you to be closer to your interlocutor in order to make out what he's babbling on about with such delight. Look, moreover the somewhat-deaf humanity, in an effort to hear each other, will merge into a single whole. Now that's égalité and fraternité for you!

Because of the above-mentioned reasons, the old man stood so close to me that I felt his decrepitude with every pore of my soul and body, felt to what insulting degree he was corroded by life. And the smell coming from his was indescribable, a smell of decomposition mixed with acrid sweat because he was straining to delay the time running madly through him, at least by a little. Beads of sweat appeared on his body as a result of this effort. It filtered through the old man's skin. (If this seems to someone to be in poor taste, then I put it to the taste of this hypocrite, this "average quantity," this forever tiptoeing servant of decency and similar nonsense. After such crap as the war, in which we all ate to the fullest, there is nothing in life at which I'll turn up my nose. Every word I say is an antagonism, a protest against everything established and thoughtlessly taken for granted. But my worst enemy is literature, or what is meant by it. Everything convenient, trustworthy, harmonious, and cowardly—usually called "good taste"—sickens me to the point of nausea.)

Wrinkled skin was thrown over his bones, abundantly dotted with warty, hairless moles of all shades, spots of pale brown. What a juicy fig for the waiting worms! A year in occupied Sukhumi had knocked ten or twenty kilos of weight off him and now he was hanging in there thanks to Red Cross

The Shore of Night | 343

lunches, a thin, tasteless gruel given out daily. Once I gave him a couple grand, and he thanked me at each meeting for an entire month. I was ashamed. To get rid of him, I pretended to be in a desperate hurry, but he still wouldn't let go of my hand, holding it in his, grateful and sweaty.

But all that came later. Now, he started from afar, testing the water with general questions: What's your surname, what's your name, what do you do, are you a relative of so-and-so . . . I, as befitting of a young Abkhazian, answered briefly and respectfully, but my mind was elsewhere—on Natela's smooth, immense bottom, the snow-white elasticity of which I would kiss and bite to my heart's content, burning with passion.

The old man wouldn't let go, wouldn't let me stick to what I wanted. Not maliciously, but because of his talkativeness, which directly followed from the dull loneliness of his life. He took me out of my role as Columbus, reprised many times, discoverer of the inexplicable charms of Natela, of which I was destined not to get my fill. The old man, according to his documents, went by Mikhail Stepanovich, although his real, native Abkhaz name was Satbey, son of Mancha. (Such a distortion and translation into the Russian manner is a common phenomenon; one needed to meet the standard so as not to bother "big brother" with the inconvenience of pronouncing wild, native names.) With streamlined words, he assessed the situation of the country and its people. He pronounced "people" clearly and with a capital letter: People. Country, oddly enough, was lowercase: country. When he replaced it, not with intent but for the sake of variety, with "motherland," it clearly took a capital letter: Motherland. Then, he went through the governments, with alternating values of "g": if the government was from the past, then "G"; if it was current, then "g," or something even smaller.

> *Since a single life cannot be avoided, and two cannot exist,*
> *I write.*

I don't like my birthday. I'd rather sleep through it. There's nothing to be particularly happy about. My soul is rather sad and vile. It would be better for it to go unnoticed. But that's hardly possible with us!

Before I was even born, they began immediately to feverishly write me into ledgers thick and thin, into various documents and papers, as if they were afraid I might slip back into my mother's womb and writing was the only way to keep me here. I was paperworked, shoved into some text, perhaps more significant than *War and Peace*.

After learning to read and write, I began to fill out the countless questionnaires slipped to me by a caring society myself, and with no less zeal, where that eternal day was confidently indicated, when I had the honor of being plunged into life.

I come to work in the morning at about ten o'clock and these fools gather to congratulate me on the occasion. Twenty-five years! The cooked up a lot of nonsense and ruined the day beyond salvaging. The spinsters gave me a book, apparently the first that found its way into our kiosk: *Deserts of the World*. It was, however, voluminous and colorfully decorated. I decided not to lose any face and borrowed some money from the accounting department against my future salary to take them to a restaurant.

I wanted to go on a bender. On the evening of my birthday, I bade farewell to my youth in a fog of wine vapors that

The Shore of Night | 345

filled my heart with an incomprehensible delight. Seeing the world optionally, unsteadily, through a haze—this has, to put it in an old-fashioned way, its charm. To one of the spinsters, from whose blurred features (the world was swimming around me) I assembled with my overactive imagination a dusky, eastern beauty, a latter-day Schererazade with sweet, milky flesh, a huge backside and wasp-like waist, I confessed a long secret love, the torment of sleepless nights, and unquenchable passions. "Have you never noticed how I cast furtive, longing glances at you from behind the instruments?" I whispered in her ear while we danced. She didn't notice. Everything about her evoked a hot wave of tenderness in me, even the way she blew at a naughty curl that fell loose over her forehead trying to cover her right eye, not to mention the touch of her small, dense breasts.

I think I also confessed to a longheld, secret love and glances from the behind the instruments to the other one, but I can't remember exactly.

We were the last to leave the restaurant, even after the big spenders, those who like to linger in such establishments with a certain touch of mystery on their bulldog faces. Three tables away sat a group of people not quite young any longer, headed by a long-maned man, approaching sixty, with the impudent, crass face of a born scoundrel. I wasn't being especially noisy, but I was loud enough—indecently loud for being so close to them. They kept shooting me puzzled looks. I was so brazen—the drinks were clouding my head—that I gave a toast in their honor. They politely thanked me, but I didn't receive a toast in return. They got up and left. When they passed by our table, one of the younger men—their leader hadn't looked in my direction once throughout the evening; I didn't exist for him—grumbled: "And in the motherland you can't even have a relaxing evening!" Scum, I thought, your motherland is just somewhere to come relax, when somewhere in Moscow you're making money hand over fist, and I called out: "Hey, you . . . !" Neither the leader nor his retinue turned around at my voice. They walked out primly, accompanied obsequiously by the waitresses and the manager, to the Volga, waiting for them at the exit in the approaching night like a white spot. Afterwards, those same waitresses instantly wiped the sycophancy from their crass, well-fed faces and, muttering under their breath in dissatisfaction, noisily walked past our table several times, making it clear that it was time for us to go.

The spinsters were pleasantly surprising. They were slightly intoxicated and turned out to be quite cheerful and easygoing . . .

I was completely drunk. Everything around me was drowning in fog, preserving the feeling of unreality about what was happening. While my head was filled with an unbearable buzzing, I also felt an extraordinary peace of mind.

The next morning I didn't even wake up in a hungover stupor, no. I sobered up overnight, with no consequences from the previous day's bender. I had the feeling, however, that a certain milestone had been irrevocably passed, and my heart ached all morning. The reins had been dropped, time rushed forward at full speed: I was past the threshold of twenty-five years old!

I arrived to work late. Invar Tamshugovich looked at me sternly and made a remark. I could barely contain myself. The spinsters were busy at the instruments. When Invar Tamshugovich was around, they tried especially hard. Suddenly, Adgur A. showed up with his usual expression of concentration and circumspection, which began to irritate me. After the previous day, I was gloomy. I didn't look at the girls. I felt ashamed. Adgur A. realized that I wasn't in the mood. I think he decided that I wasn't very happy to see him, but I had no particular desire to convince him otherwise, to talk about the drama I was experiencing in connection with the waning of my youth. (The only time I allowed myself this weakness about my own age. What came over me then? Why was I suddenly sniveling about this? 'It happens'—the typical answer in such cases. Then, after a meeting with Natela, I understood what had caused my depression then: I wanted to love, and my longing for love was awakened in me by that very same spinster to whom I had whispered such nonsense about my imaginary suffering.)

We had almost nothing to talk about. We went to Amra more out of habit than anything else and, perhaps, in the secret hope that doing so could still salvage something. But there was nothing by then that could salvage any of it.

(Our dissonance here is described as something accidental, a consequence of my fleeting mood. But that's not it. People usually break up without stormy scenes hashing out the relationship, doing so instead quietly, sometimes shyly hiding their eyes from each other. Nothing connected us except the habit of speculating on abstract topics, and that can't last forever, eventually becoming boring as sooner or later all topics will have been covered far and wide and then repetitions begin. In a word, everything degrades into banality.)

> *They bombed the "sushki." Suddenly, they jumped out from behind a hill, gleaming silver in the sun. The sky was a painful blue. Especially overhead. At the edges, the blue fades, not*

*carrying itself through, although it seems that it should flow down along the slope of the sky to its hem and thicken. Here, it's on the contrary—it's thick just above us, like at the bottom of a huge cauldron.*

*There was silence, a sleepy stupor. We lazily exchanged words, achieving an impossible brevity: we understood each other with an interjection. We settled down inside an unfinished house near the river. Some laid on the ground, setting down mattresses, others on bunks made of planks . . . Lower down, across the river, there is a suspension bridge on cables, the bottom covered with wooden planks. Armored vehicles couldn't pass cross it, only cars. Nearby, however, a few meters from us, was a ford. So they launched SAMs and then dropped four bombs. They jumped out from behind the hill so unexpectedly that no one had a chance to understand what had happened or to react. If a bomb had landed on our house, or even a SAM, it would've killed everyone. The bridge was blown to smithereens.*

*When they shouted "AIR!" many dropped to the ground, covering their heads with their hands. One unlucky guy went straight into a pit of slaked lime and there was laughter when he crawled out.*

*The anticipation of an explosion. I'm sure it'll happen, but there's still an itch in my soul: What if it doesn't? What if it lands near you? Will it be quick? And you lie there without raising your head, a chill running down your back from furiously running goosebumps, as if you've been doused with ice water. In this waiting, there is a moment of emptiness, a complete exclusion from life. There's nothing inside you or outside, not even the coming explosion. It doesn't exist, just as there is nothing around you. A moment of bliss: you don't exist.*

*But it wasn't us they were bombing, even though the bridge and the ford were just a stone's throw away, and we couldn't count on the accuracy of the sushki. This time, they lobbed all four bombs into the riverbed, capturing both the bridge and the ford. All that remained of the bridge were the cables, and the ford was also gone.*

*A smoking splinter crashed down next to me. I then took it into my hands. Weighty, still warm, it laid fiercely in my palm, cooling off gradually. By the time we came back to our senses, the sushki were over the hill, the sound behind them. It remained for a moment as a thin, long thread, and then became quiet.*

*The day dragged on tediously. It's summer. The night is no longer than a chicken's yawn and the day, like an ox, lazily trudges along. Everyone already knows, however, that summer nights are much shorter than summer days. It is known, but whoever mused on it and felt it freshly, as if for the first time, when on the primitive human brain it suddenly dawned, emerging from the dense darkness of thoughtlessness, that in the summer the day is much longer than night, that in the summer there is lots of light, and for a long time ... Well for that person it was like the surprise and discovery of childhood.*

*The sun slowly climbed higher and higher then, just as slowly, having passed midday, sank into the sea. Night was falling. That's all ... It seems simple, but what's behind it all? And it's not at all boring; I made a slip of the tongue earlier. That's how it seemed to me during the day. And then the remnants of my discontent took me by surprise as soon as I took hold of the pen. It's night now and the day that has passed doesn't seem so long to me anymore. On the contrary, it was annoying short, lived through. It seems beautiful to me; irrecoverable and thereby beautiful. It's the night that seems long to me now. I'm in a hurry to greet the dawn and in the morning I'll lament the passage of night.*

*The sushki flew away and we shook ourselves off, ranting and raving. An expert in cursing swore at them with relish. We had some fun and then remembered about lunch ...*

Everything I write is an attempt to continue Adgur A.'s existence. He is me, with my boring baggage of formulas and theories. (This is a general belief, and so it is: Formulas and theories are boring. Because they aren't invented but are already contained within the matter of the universe, they need only be fished out. Fishing a small creature from a river, lake, or sea is no small feat. Anyone with a fishing rod is capable of such things. With different skills and equipment, one can fish theories and formulas out of the matter of the universe, which is a very tedious task, I assure you, despite the lifelong and even posthumous glory awarded to the undertakers of such tasks.) With this unimportant, downright dull inheritance,

The Shore of Night | 351

I introduced him into writing. My style is similar to his. This is the style of a period of apprenticeship, meticulously reading into letters and learning its secrets. I can only preserve him once I've gotten to know him.

I didn't manage it in life. He walked past me almost like a stranger. And in the texts of his that remain, he was more than he was in his communications with me; more, perhaps, than he was in life at all, even in the sum of everything he said, thought, and felt, in the sum of all his relatives and friends, in the sum of everyone who ever saw him, thought about him, or remembered him. In the sum of all this, he was not as clear and real and himself as he was in the things he wrote.

Often, I was frightened or, if not frightened, then I felt a chill: To discover myself so clearly in what was written, in the structure of each phrase, in every word, in their connections, to be so exposed! I preferred namelessness and obscurity. I tried to walk through life as unnoticeably as possible, along its insignificant, shadowy edge, in its twilight. I didn't long for immortality—neither in print, nor physically, nor in any other way. Physics answered this need of mine, and here my efforts didn't change anything in the world, only revealed what the world already contained within itself before me, after me, without me—its own rules of the game.

Adgur A. demanded something else: To come up with the rules of the game for himself, to carve out a world according to those rules, and this world—most amazingly, considering the rules had been dreamed up by himself—would be one to one with him.

Perhaps this isn't all so astounding, so unexpected, if one imagines that the world, also at that zero point, having broken free of its suffocating tightness, began to scatter, made up rules for itself—that is, for its entire future trajectory—to the very last atom, to the most dilapidated way station past which it, without even thinking of stopping, will rush like a hurricane. It outlined and wrote it all out, not giving up, following its chosen route and it cannot each time, no matter which time period we examine, help but coincide with itself.

Whether I intended to take this route is a complex question. Here, formulas and theories reveal themselves as powerless and shyly fall silent. However, I suspect—and this suspicion of mine is part of what was made clear to me that one day in the university dorm, in the evening, when the twilight, cold, and sunset laid a quiet melancholy onto my heart (it was March 6, the date forever imprinted in my memory)—that I was also plunged into reverie somehow and the hyper-focused and careful movement of the world along the thin blade of its constants is to ensure that I wouldn't accidentally fall off-course like a foolish chick falling from the nest.

I've grown increasingly cold to physics, to everything scientific. Adgur A. provided a daily example of the retreat into language, into wakefulness, trying to shake off the sweet sleep of existence. Having settled down by the water with a rod, he was going to catch not a fish but something else or, more precisely, something that didn't live in the reservoir at all. "You're weaving a veil with your perception of the world, and you're going to get cataracts!" He used to say, classifying me among that hopeless breed of people who have reduced the meaning of life to a foolish accumulation of education. The dispute about physicists and lyricists was just an echo around us and meant little in our skirmishes.

To continue Adgur A. in text.

I read through what he wrote and try to glimpse him behind the words, which didn't come to his mind by chance or
were recorded after painful rumination, the real him. Or else
embrace his letters so that, having grown accustomed to them,
I feel like I am him.

*More and more I turn to the notebook, which has suddenly*

*turned out to be so spacious. I haven't even filled half of it yet.*

*Yes, I write small, not like usual—large, sweeping—to save*

*the pages, though no one knows whether I'm destined to fill the*

*notebook or not. A question like "To be or not to be?" But it*

*has different coordinates, clearer and more justified than in the*

*case of the plump, red-cheeked, wheezy, and underachieving*

*prince. And who needs this? To whom is this addressed? I don't*

*know. Is there someone looming in my imagination—a future*

*heir?—into whose hands these notes will suddenly fall, by the*

*whim of almighty chance, to weave a hopeless pattern of fate?*

*Someone who isn't too lazy won't just leaf through them casually*

*out of curiosity but will read, page by page, carefully, delving*

*into the text and imagining. It's best—for the purity of their*

*perception—that this so-and-so not know me, never having*

*looked upon me in person, never having ever heard my name, so*

*that no one can tell him about me in meager, indifferent words.*

*Then I'll reach him whole, closer to myself. My appearance and*

*the events of my life will not be a distracting obstacle.*

*I know it would be better for me to remain with my friends, to*

*listen to them eagerly, remember their eyes and voices. Not even*

*remember, really. After all, who can say who will survive whom,*
*whether it's worth remembering at all. What's more important*
*is what connects us, and this is so overwhelming and new for me*
*that I can find no other name for it than joy.*

How many times had she, as a child, imagined how her mother would die, crying bitterly both out of pity for her, who had gone into an irreversible night, and out of pity for herself, now alone forever in an empty world. Everything turned out differently, however. She couldn't squeeze out a single tear, standing still as a stone over the coffin, in black from head to toe as her attentive aunties had dressed her. These same aunties were outraged by Natela's behavior. They kept urging her on: "Cry! Cry! It's shameful! What will people think? You're not a little girl anymore . . ." One of them even pinched the rebellious girl to rouse her from her shameful insensibility. She pinched painfully, past what attentiveness called for, and Natela, who didn't understand her guilt and generally understood even less of what was happening around her, rebuked the opportunist with such a hateful look that she walked off indignantly.

Her soul seemed to have become numb, not even numb; it was like it had evaporated from her, leaving an illegible scum on the walls of her heart. She was bereft and looked at her mother as if she were a stranger unconnected to her in any way. Her mother lay in the coffin just as if she had found that exact cozy place for which she'd always been searching.

Natela was surprised by the calm serenity that there was now on her once lively face. Death had even smoothed out her wrinkles, and Natela wondered if the wrinkles had come from her constant attempts to find out what her mother had wanted to tell her in the end but never said.

The Shore of Night | 355

I didn't think about going to the sea. I had always found the spread of naked bodies, the smug complacency of naked flesh, to be revolting.

I didn't think about going to the sea, but every person I ran into, whether acquaintance or stranger, kept coming up to me with important news: The sea, you see, is unusually warm today; something like this hasn't been observed in quite a while. Global warming!

They conspired, weaved networks, set lures—friendly, obsequious, brazen.

I couldn't resist. I went to the sea and saw the same sickening image I'd seen before: poor relative trying to find room for herself near the water, on this narrow strip of sandy shore covered with naked bodies. Not entirely naked, the so-called private parts were hidden behind underpants, swimsuits, and swim trunks. Therefore, complete unfeigned nudity was not enough for the picture to be completed. Let both young and old—and there were more old people, as the sea is useful to them, and with their thirst for life growing over the years, they will never deny themselves anything useful, even if it's as indecent as lying naked on the sand—put their shame on display.

The world is old and decrepit. It will somehow hobble to its death. That's all it has the strength for. Like that old man—this, by the way, is Mancha Satbeyevich—wandering towards the water. He put his hands forward. He wants to touch the water first, to feel it, but his legs got there first. When the water approaches his weak, empty loins, sadly outlined in his knee-length shorts, the old man, scooping up the water with his hands, rinses his chest, neck, and face. After this preliminary meeting, sniffing at each other, this procession into the depths of the sea continues. The water reaches his waist, his thin breast.

Here, the old man stops, looking sadly in front of himself for some time, thinking about something, then suddenly sharply bends at the knees, crouching down and plunging headlong into the water a couple times. Snorting contentedly, covered in droplets flowing down his emaciated, bony torso, he wanders wearily back. Once upon a time, he'd emerged from the primordial waters into the light and it was not exhaustion but jubilation on his face. Now, he has emerged from other waters, again towards the light, but above the surface of the sea, into which he half-heartedly submerged several times and whose suffocating embrace forced him to hastily reemerge. What awaited him was not that old, jubilant light, but the dim twilight accompaniment to a final darkness.

Old folks, old folks everywhere. Everywhere you look—faded eyes beneath shaggy, gray brows, distrustful and angry. Everywhere you look—wandering shadows who with all their plodding strength hate the world that has brought them to a beastly state and which they have inevitably carried with them for many years, with scars and wrinkles and a crust of accumulated salt in their joints, drawing them nearer and nearer to the edge of the abyss. That's what is scary—the meaningless, gaping maw before them.

The lures are set all around and I naively fall into them. To everyone who smiles and diligently invites me to the sea, I nod, smiley, thank them for the information, so timely and important. I am one with their cunning. In the embryo, tailed and nimble, in the impenetrable liquid darkness of the uterus, blindly but purposefully scurrying back and forth, in that embryo my soul had barely grown warm when I was grabbed harshly by the world for the entire long path of life. But those around me, those same captives, made their benevolent

The Shore of Night | 357

contribution to my captivity and capture. They marked and corrected my path with watchful milestones such that in the end I would plunge into a disgusting, lukewarm body of water called the sea.

I stepped ashore. The sand crunched underfoot, perhaps out of longing for its great brother the desert, far away and dryly turning yellow under the scorching sun. The sea, like a fetus in its mother's waters, tossed and turned, dissatisfied in its bed. It didn't make much noise, splashing discreetly at our feet. But I felt the wary, hostile eye with which it watched me.

I undressed and went to it, anticipating its salty taste on my lips.

Mancha Satbeyevich didn't notice me. I am also not burning with the desire to approach him. I don't want to see someone I know naked at the beach.

I move through the city, hot from the summer heat. My shirt sticks to my back, chummy, while the angry sun blinds my eyes, and the city slowly and inexorably drowns in the molten air, gradually turning into a ghost. On familiar faces, flickering every now and then with tedious repetition, something similar to a smile of greeting, shines palely, then immediately fades away, and the faces return to their former tired and indifferent expression.

What more is there to say about this day, through which I walk as if half-asleep? It keeps moving farther and farther away from me. Nothing can delay its hot march into oblivion even slightly.

At night, lying in bed, I will glance back and survey my vanishing life, inadvertently amazed. How did I manage not to suffocate in this empty and alien day? For some time, until I forget myself in an anxious, sweaty sleep, I'll be haunted by the airless corner into which I'll be placed to die a long, cruel death.

But gradually, I begin to dress the day that's passed in different clothes and the further it retreats into the past, the dearer it becomes to my heart.

From here I inevitably conclude that my life is woven from the past. I don't have a present as such, but I have an enormously swollen past that floats onto my present and absorbs it without a trace. What about the future? A remade past, in which the same joys can be expected that, in fact, did not exist in the past but which my imagination—always on the lookout for the unshakeable, reliable, solid—constructed for it. Or am I so lamely lagging behind events, hopelessly delayed in experiencing them, that I dress up the emptiness left in their wake, making it brighter? Maybe I really was ... Not happy, that word is hopeless from the get-go, in the sense of that end point after which you hit a blank wall and fall silent in confusion ... So, not happy, but calm and confident in the unknown past, with coordinates X, Y, and Z? Perhaps that's why there's such sadness for it and such a desire to return to it? To get it back?

I move through the city like a disincarnated spirit. Everything my eyes see evokes no more feeling in me than the mirror that reflects them. In the unbearable heat my soul remains cold. Meanwhile I see people, above and behind them the merciless blue of the sky, houses, the intersection of streets and their lonely lives between alleys, various living creatures—dogs, cats, birds ... All of it enters me through an indifferent pane of glass and settles into my depths, at first a little lost, apprehensive. I know, however, that soon it will violently and demandingly break through to the surface and it will be the only thing to occupy me, this seemingly vanished past along

The Shore of Night | 359

the edge of which, it seemed to me, I strolled apathetically, skimming over it with my gaze. What a load of crap! My pupil instead slid and devoured space insatiably; my ear—how clever—hungrily absorbed voices, sounds, noises, and my nose—Oh, God! . . .

*I know that I'll leave this world with pain that I could never become a tree. That tree which has grown into my dreams. My lot was to be a man, not a tree. I was deprived of the ability to return to my origins. Yet, occasionally, I felt within myself the soul of a tree, the soul of a river.*

*(Sweet, honeyed, high-falutin, pseudo-sad. Some worldly coordinates. "I'll leave the world"—where does this knowledge come from? Nothing can be known for certain, but here I am, writing endlessly. Half-truths, self-deception, false hope. But I don't wash away these lines. Behind them lies my "I" in its moments of weakness its common places.)*

I'm trying to finish a line started by Adgur A., but I can't. I can't understand what he was trying to say. The line is like this: "The divergence and formation of things, their scattering into nooks and the loneliness of proper names . . ." Absurd, so memorable. Adgur A. loved to dress up the least pretentious idea of Sukhumi promenade regulars in such flowery prose that it immediately dropped dead. Its clothes turned out to be unbearably heavy. We had a game where we would figure out what this or that person we met was thinking about.

Sometimes he managed to revive an apparently hopeless and outdated thought and it suddenly became young and fresh. He called it "raising the world from the ashes of words," "restoring originality to words," and things like this, all of which sounded a little wild and ridiculous to me as a physicist. Words were superfluous; the world didn't rest on them. And thought could be expressed in formulas—contained, unequivocal. Words led away from the essence of things. They were used to weave and weave a veil. Such extravagance, part timidity, surprised me.

But this happened rarely. The thoughts of the people of Sukhumi were similar one to the other, like two dead people. They revolved around eternal southern themes: female curves, both above and below the waist (though still mostly below) and the rise and fall of local pencilpushers. And Adgur A. wasn't always on such a good trot, despite his convoluted verbal and mental labors. It was beyond his power to extract anything worthwhile from the pickled brains of Sukhumi residents.

Giving up on his attempts to mold, in his words, something human from a herd of nitwits, he sadly looked around from the great heights of Amra to the promenade, along which a variegated and multi-tribal crowd was scurrying about. Below us, the green sea quietly lapped at the rusty piles with their black shells and the sounds of the splashes insidiously penetrated the soul, singing tales about the distant, vast ocean and uninhabited tropical islands. From the nearby hills tightly crowding Sukhumi, thick greenery trickled down. Behind it, high in the sky, the melancholy Chumkuzba glittered with snow.

This was typical discourse. But back then it seemed to us that our self-abandon and ardor provided a justification for everything: our ignorance in many matters, and the impudence

The Shore of Night | 361

with which we disparaged authorities (both exaggeratedly and deservedly). And little thoughts, dragged in by the ear, piebald from the mixture of blood, kicking, not wanting to be led to a stall that wasn't theirs . . .

During the time I was away, Sukhumi—already not mine—drifted even further and greeted my return with indifference, if not hostility. I was assigned to a local university, where I was supposed to work for at least two years. But on the very first day I had an argument with the head of the lab. Invar Tamshugovich decided to give me a test to find out if I was a good fit—this after I had a Tbilisi diploma and a transcript without a single C in my hands. And after the order for my appointment, signed by the rector, a funny old man, an intellectual and a partier, had already been issued.

I, of course, understood this as hostility and was offended and disrespectful. Invar Tamshugovich didn't expect such a rude response, was taken aback, and ran out. He had wanted to display his strict and responsible approach to recruitment in order to cast a cloud over the mess going on in his lab.

He had a habit of rushing like crazy through the halls of the university, always preoccupied, with an expression of deep thoughtfulness on his face that immediately disappeared the second he opened his mouth. He spewed such nonsense that my ears turned off. Even with the grandiose mimicry abilities of Invar Tamshugovich, it wasn't endurable. At the very first words, his face suddenly, with relief (after all, it was quite a strain to portray a scientific thought!) settled into the homely expression of a simple man, far removed from science. He was minding his own business, and his desire to fit in, to meet demands, and to keep pace had stupidly distorted him both internally and externally.

There he would go, running along a gloomy, filthy corridor that smells of damp. Running past the laboratory, he would suddenly remember that he's the boss and, wanting to catch us off-guard, he would pull the door open so hard it almost broke off its hinges, sticking his head in to stare blankly at us for two minutes, no less . . . We, too, were in complete, unanimous silence and, I suspect, no less stupidly—the law of imitation, triggered with even greater effect due to the surprise—we looked back at him. Then, have made sure there's nothing amiss, he would slam the door shut with unimaginable noise and run on.

Natela lives alone. She's never had a husband, nor any male friends. Enough girlfriends and acquaintances to sink a battleship. Sometimes she talks about Asida, once her closest friend, but she left Abkhazia immediately after the war. She was either a childhood friend or from university and, according to Natela, is slowly losing her mind due to spinsterdom, the forced burden of many Abkhazian women.

All day long Natela stands on the second floor of the market, selling other people's things and making her living in this manner. An educated woman, she worked before the war as the deputy director of the House of Culture, enlightening the masses.

I never have money, but when it suddenly appears—from my mother, or one of my rare friends, basically the same kind of riffraff as I myself—then I give it to her. I feel obliged, but there's no force here. I don't even think of appending to her the role of a kept woman, and anyway she'd never allow it. She accepts the money easily, without taking any offense, but she'll never ask for it herself. Though she ought to be content with what she manages to scrape together by selling people's things.

She dresses averagely, but with taste, uses perfume sparingly, and hasn't bought any books for a long time. She would never take money from me, but evidently she doesn't have a choice. I suspect she's saving it up for something important, most likely to leave, which she hinted at once but I ignored. I visit her twice a week, not more than that, and I'm drawn to her less and less. She probably thinks it has to do with her age and accepts my cooling off as natural. Her fear of old age isn't connected to men's perceptions of her, as it is for most women. For her, the fear of old age is all-encompassing. It's a real curse.

After two, the bazaar closes, by three Natela has settled her affairs—the primary among which is to take the goods to the storage facility in exchange for a receipt—and then she's free. Until six in the morning the next day, time drags on agonizingly slowly for her. She doesn't know what to do with herself. What saves her is the TV, cigarettes, and me. She's happy about my arrival, though she doesn't show it. Natela has gotten it into her head that, since she's deprived of the primary feeling that makes a woman a woman, it isn't fitting for her to have other feelings. And if they suddenly arise within her against her will, then it means they're not real, but rather imitation, hypocrisy, or both. That's her habit. That's why she never talks about her love for me and why I've never asked if she loves me. I already know she does, but she's afraid to admit it.

Natela's living situation is poor. Two small rooms with a table, four chairs, two spring beds (on one of which her mother died; Natela never sits on this bed, instead covering it with a dark blanket, as if in mourning), a sofa, two armchairs, a coffee table, a vanity, a wardrobe, a credenza, and a TV. The most necessary things, nothing superfluous. And everything is already outdated, old, though not the feeble decrepitude of old

364 | *Daur Nachkebia*

age, rather strong and thoroughbred, a dignified kind of old. There were several shelves of books. Stevenson, Dumas—she adores them and talks about the day she acquired ten large red volumes of Dumas as the happiest day of her life. Tolstoy, The Brothers Karamazov, Shinkuba, Iskander, Gogua, Hemingway, Salinger . . . For a long time, she loved Chekhov, but one day found him to be boring and pitiless, and got rid of him, not just without regret but even with relief.

The bathroom is at the end of the corridor. The stove, at which she cooks, is right behind the doors.

Natela loves cleanliness, but in her rooms there is always an acceptable disorder. A pink robe hangs abandoned on the back of a chair, an open volume of Dumas with a bookmark depicting a thick-beaked, colorful parrot lies on the bed, next to an ashtray with a half-smoked cigarette, a slightly curved gray cylinder of ash looms dangerously large but not yet crumbled into dust. There may be other acceptable disorder, but each time Natela's hand is recognizable and with these little things she firmly entered my life. Her daily habits became not simply a part of her, but a part of me, and all this is inseparable from us both.

If she has something to eat, then she'll treat us, but more often we limit ourselves to a few cups of coffee and even a shot or two of homemade vodka. Then we play backgammon, cards, and chess. I'm touched by the childish seriousness with which Natela plays, with furrowed eyebrows, pursed lips, and forehead wrinkled in thought. As if a wrong move on her part, especially rather, a loss—God forbid!—the health and lives of at least another hundred thousand people depend on her. Tenderness boils over in me and I take her hands. She keeps reaching for checkers, pieces, cards, and with a light movement (this lightness is given to me by tremendous effort) I pull her towards me. She looks at me, and each time it seems like there's bewilderment hidden in her eyes: Who is this who touches me softly and carefully? Why is he touching me so softly and carefully? What is he thinking about what he's going to do with me? But this feeling of mine is fleeting. Instead, she looks inquisitive: Am I really still desired? Does he really love me? Or curious: What has he come up with this time? What kind of caress will he employ this time to warm up my frozen womb, melt my hopeless ice? There is also fear in her eyes, that someday all this will end, that she'll die quietly and routinely, and then no one will ever again gently and carefully, as if afraid of scaring off her distrustful, desperate heart, pull her to himself and then embrace her as if he wants to strangle her, kiss her tirelessly with hungry lips, that no one will ever try to heat up her body and soul with their warmth, never tear her away from a now-sickening game with a light movement.

She gets up lazily, as if reluctantly, and sits on my lap. And when, reluctantly and lazily, she rises slightly and pushes her chair away . . . When her arms, legs, breasts, eyes, mouth, all of her, separated from me by several endless centimeters, suddenly move closer to me, blocking the light from the window, and I can touch her . . . This movement of the body raised with such languor, its reluctant, lazy approach, the sweet fading of the heart, its landslide down to my yearning loins . . . And the expectation, the fear of not meeting, of separation forever, right now, suddenly, at this moment everything is full of meaning, everything is immortal, everything is jubilant. I begin kissing her madly, drowning in her mind-blowing scent, while at the same time I undress her. I take off the always rebellious, harmful dress. I take off her bra with the always intricate clasps, mercilessly soaking up time. I take off the pliant panties, thin and cool, the touching of which always stirs up a powerful tenderness within me. My hands rest of the curve of her wide, pliant backside . . . In my mouth, her rough, stiff nipple . . . I spread her legs, so abundant, so alive, so white . . . And I slowly enter her, enter the dark, wet warmth . . . And the yearning of my loins slowly enters the dark, wet warmth . . . And I am one with her, we are one flesh and soul, we have shaken off the unnecessary "I" . . .

I love Natela . . .

Natela and I talk little, not because we've already discussed everything, whether about ourselves or others, about the past, future, present, about life and death . . . We've learned to value silence. We passed our love through the sieve of long conversations and were left with the most valuable thing: That time when words aren't necessary in order to be together, to never forget each other.

Sometimes, however, she breaks through and begins to talk about her life in the sort of detail I wouldn't wish to know. How she was madly in love with a classmate, how she surrendered to him one night on the seashore near Kelasur, what a mistake she had made by admitting to him that she'd felt nothing from their intimacy. It was a shock for him that he was unable to get over. All his efforts coming to nothing. Natela realized too late that she had to fake her feelings in order not to lose him. But that meant deception on her part, and she didn't wish to deceive him, she couldn't. He gradually cooled to her and finally, as is usual in these sorts of cases, married one of her friends.

That's how Natela's first love concluded. She no longer believes in any kind of love that leads her to a bed.

The tragic story of a beautiful woman who feels nothing.

But most of all she talks about her mother. This is a never-ending topic. She never reminisces about her father. I don't even know if she had one. Even if there had been, he was lost without a trace in Natela's constant thoughts about her poor mother who died while still relatively young.

Her name is Madina. I learned this from Mancha Satbeyevich. They're distantly related, almost a prerevolutionary connection. Either his great-great-grandmother and her great-great-great-grandfather were brother and sister, or perhaps the opposite way, but their families are intertwined and originate from the same root. Her friends, when inviting her for coffee, called her something else. Chincha, a bird. Madina, however, is of a decent height and couldn't be called thin—she has just the right amount of fleshiness. Apparently, the nickname has stuck since childhood. "She's a good girl, with a good surname, good parents—everything is good for her," said Mancha Satbeyevich. "But she's deprived of happiness, poor thing. What are the young folks thinking these days?"

During the war, Madina was a nurse. An overdressed hag and her idiot friend, positioned like Cerberus at the entrance to the library, told me about this for some reason in a whisper.

Could she be that very same M. about whom Adgur A. wrote? There are a lot of coincidences here. The name begins with the same letter, she was a nurse, the age seems appropriate . . .

Mancha Satbeyevich habitually surrounded himself with piles of *Pravda*. He licks his wrinkled index finger, turns the page, and scans it with dim eyes, looking for an encrypted message hinting at the imminent collapse of the USSR. Having found one, in his opinion, he would carefully read it, then read it again, then make a copy of what he called the 'supporting words.' His notebook, of course, is red, with a gold inscription: "Glory to Communist labor!" It was apparently a trophy from a Party conference or industry meeting, of which he sat through many during his life.

He had lots of such records. Once he allowed me a secret glance into his notebook, neatly covered in precise handwriting. Each section, usually a thesis, is indicated by a Roman numeral; the subsections —Arabic; the subsections of subsections —Russian letters in alphabetical order. As far as I could understand, the confirmation of thesis goes from section to subsection and further downwards: In some subsection "Shch," you could find irrefutable proof of a statement from subsection 79) of section LXI.

I said hello and went to my usual spot in the corner. Near my feet is the upper portion of a window from the lower floor. Sometimes I like to take a break from what I'm reading and look down at the passersby scurrying along the busy Prospect. It's especially good when it's raining out and there are few passersby. When it rains, the city becomes beautiful and sad, despite the reputation it's acquired for being a sunny, southern resort town.

Many acquaintances pass by, not suspecting I'm only two steps away and watching them. I wonder if anyone is thinking about me now? For no apparent reason, I suddenly remember a complete stranger, whom I may have seen only once, but who for some reason I recall. Does he experience anything, too? Does he receive some kind of sign? After all, with my memories I'm still connected to him somehow; he occupies a certain place in my thoughts and heart. This is how, with invisible threads, we are connected with many others. And do

The Shore of Night | 369

these threads mean nothing? Or do they mean something, having an influence on our destinies?

Madina dived into the magazine. Judging by the colorful cover, it was a women's magazine. She raised her eyes to me a couple times, squinting myopically, and then lowered them.

*I, like many others if not all, tried to grow out my beard. But as soon as my face begins to get lost in the reddish stubble— I have black hair, but at a certain length my beard suddenly turns reddish, with sparse shoots of gray, making me somehow two-faced—I hastily, with an almost superstitious fear, shave it off. After a while, I again want somebody else's alien expression to stare back at me through the looking glass, and I let my beard grow out again.*

"So, what you're saying is according to the laws of nature— an overripe fruit, with a wormhole and everything. All it had to do was fall and lay there, which it did, to the joy of many. I'm not pretending to be Newton here, whose head and fluffy wig this fruit honored with its illuminating blow. I was confused by the unexpectedness of the process. If the fruit is overripe, then its fall is to be expected, but here everything happened all of a sudden."

"They tore it off!"

"Yes, they tore it off and didn't even let it ripen."

"Sooner or later, it would've ripened."

"In a thousand years, when Communism would triumphantly embrace the planet with a ring of universal happiness and prosperity! The earth wouldn't even need a branch then. The sun would simply become a yoke, to say nothing of our fruit. It was just filling up with juices, it was still green—not a single one of the great projects had been implemented, they were just getting started. The peoples were uniting into a new community and were just about to move on to 'each according to his needs.' But the envious and hostile environment, which had been sending storms and threats for seventy years, that day pulled the skin of the tempting serpent over itself, and, with its hands on our community anchors or, better yet, wankers, tore it off—after all the storms and threats, it had remained on the root branch of the great idea of the brotherhood of man."

"The environment didn't have anything to do with it. We ourselves are to blame."

"We let our guard down, underestimated the strength of the enemy, got dizzy with success. We forgot the tenets of those who were there at the beginning."

"It was probably that they bequeathed the wrong thing and had the wrong beginning."

"You're speaking blasphemy and sacrilege, friend. Believe my experience—people should live as a team, elbow to elbow, shoulder to shoulder . . ."

"And walk in lock step with those on your left . . ."

"Friendly, brotherly. Would humanity have survived if it scattered from the caves as individuals, I ask you? No, people would have died from hunger, cold, and other misfortunes that can only be overcome together. First children and old people, then others—the world would be empty. There would be no civilization, no culture. Without communism, humanity is doomed."

The lives of all, about whom Natela has been talking in detail for a long time, were grim and hopeless. After a good but short period, they ended in the most disastrous ways, as a hideous mixture of the characters' personal flaws and the fate that chased them. I was scared and depressed when I left her. I looked for signs of fate in the external world—from the shapes of clouds to random yelps from the street. Everything around me gave hints and warnings. Something was coming. It was definitely a conspiracy plotting around me. It was a matter of my vigilance whether I keep drifting down the hostile river like a feeble wood chip or find a way to prevent the strikes that targeted me.

But Natela believed that people docilely follow their own tragic end. Most interestingly, they understand everything, feel everything in advance, some of them even attempt to change their lives. However, the devilry of fate is precisely that all the paths are entangled in a tight know of inevitable end, to which lead all the roads.

Overwhelmed with this desperate prison philosophy, I looked around unsettlingly, looking for signs, prompts, and warnings. My endeavors did not succeed as every sign signified lots of things, so I could not deduct a rigid scheme like Natela in her stories. The future was unknown. It did not come out of the present or the past, which was even more unknown. What did it even mean? What did it conceive, and how did it develop? It was impossible to know any of that.

Exhausted, I stopped searching and told myself: Let it go as it goes. You'll meet another Natela who will bring back a structure and purpose to your life.

I have to meet the bus today, it's Sunday. My mother wakes up early since our village is far away from Sukhumi. To arrive there by the time the market opens, one has to head over early. She leaves her bed at the crack of dawn, puts the prepared meal into a bag, and then carries it to the bus stop. My father starts the fireplace, grouching about that they shouldn't send me any food, so that maybe hunger will make me remember my home. Nimbly packing simple snacks—one or two wheels of cheese, a jar of matzoon, herbs, about two kilos of nuts—mother scolds the cows for giving little milk and blames father for his heartlessness.

Lighting a cigarette from a firebrand, father grins. "Is it me or your son who is heartless?"
"It's not the boy's fault, it's the blockade."
"The blockade keeps him in the city? What a thing to say . . . Here is so much to do, but he sits around in Sukhumi . . ."
"He didn't study so he could hoe your corn . . ."
"My corn! What a thing to say . . ."

Sometimes my mother, an aging woman who did not complete her education because of an early marriage, writes me cramped letters by her fingers better fit for collecting tea or milking a cow. Usually, she writes when some neighbor or relative dies. She sends me money for a ticket because missing the funeral is not allowed. I miss it, and mother gets offended. Father takes it easy and philosophically, although he never read any philosophy. He tends to measure everything on the scales of reason, which generous God gifted him openhandedly, even too much. From time to time, it looked as if he was completely heartless, unable to accept it if people treated traditions too loosely. But those who followed traditions too passionately, father considered shallow people, as they usually turned out to be. His approach was to stick to a custom formally in such a measured way so that nobody would suspect or, moreover, blame him for inobservance. The fact that his kid, that is me, was the bird of a feather warmed his icy heart, speaking candidly. This is what explained his soft attitude to my apostasy. It gave my slow-witted mother a reason to reproach him for pandering to me, if not for secret conspiracy against her.

It did not bother him that his kid, this bird of a feather, followed the same custom, only established by nature not people. But I already said that my father was not a fan of abstract speculations.

Mother carries bags to the bus station. Father handles the cattle. He would be embarrassed if people saw him sending food to his son.

In the morning silence, the bus can be heard from a distance. It rumbles along the bumpy country road slowly, wheezy, and with frequent stops. When it crawls out of a bend in the road, mother raises her hand shyly, even though the bus would stop anyway. It slows down. She fussily passes the bag through the opened doors, cursing the war and the Georgians in my defense. Then she stays there till the bus disappears after the turn. Why? Perhaps she is embarrassed to go home immediately. The passengers might imagine that she only wants to make her bag the others' responsibility and go about her business. Or maybe the actual reason is that she is seeing off the bag. At first, she sees it off for real, till she can see the bus. Then in her thoughts. In about two hours, when mother is distracted from her work for a moment, she says with relief, "He's probably received it already." Then she continues working with peace of mind.

Having good health and a light fondness—no more than three shots a day—for *chacha*, the strongest double-distilled grape vodka, father approaches old age, which apparently will last as long as it did for my grandpa, his father. My mother, always a concerned, fastidious, and gaunt woman, is getting old alongside him. Housekeeping and "what people will say" are her never-ending worries.

They age in a cold house built at the end of the sixties. The two-story stone boxes went into fashion then. Following Stalin's slavery, the easing of the Thaw let peasants breathe more freely. For some small money made by collecting tea leaves, growing tobacco, and silkworm farming, people pulled down their ramshackle *akuaski*—wooden stilt dwellings considered a relic of the dark past—to build other houses, of blocks. Two homes under one roof! This is how they justified their vanity. Because what if not vanity could explain erecting those huge, often unnecessary, buildings.

I spent the whole day at home, staying in bed till it bored me. Around noon, I stood up, flung on a robe, and moved myself to Magbulia's couch, old but nice. By the evening, I relocated to the armchair, also old but nice. Generally speaking, everything in Magbulia's flat was old but nice, of solid totalitarian material, made to endure if not eternally, then definitely at least a millennium of communism.

Today I decided to take a break from my search for the exemplary life and did not get to the library. Maybe I won't go tomorrow or the day after. Maybe I won't show up there for a week, driving Mancha Satbeyevich to a mild panic—so many days without sharing his rock-solid evidence with someone! But my search is also music to the old man's ears. I am sure that a stirring thought about the new generation reviving lost values ferments in his tainted brain, so it cheers him up to look at me, a young man. In fact, I live someone else's life every day. I don't want to come back to my own.

But what about Madina? She'll notice my absence and start thinking of me. I don't care how long she'll be thinking of me. Like I am thinking of her constantly. I can't explain why I'm doing that. I'm just thinking. That's it. My head is barely involved, yet it's the head which is supposed to do the thinking. It seems like I'm thinking with my whole body. In my thinking of Madina I reach unity with myself.

Most of the time I read the same Hawking. I closed my eyes when they got tired and started listening to the voices and sounds from outside. Sometimes, I would take a nap. Sometimes, I imagine being a seashell washed ashore, where it has to stay for years, decades, or maybe centuries, until someone's foot—belonging to the future me or the future Mancha Satbeyevich—tramples it down, so the seashell falls apart and turns into sand.

Night arrived. Since I've been mixing sleep and wakefulness the whole day, I couldn't fall asleep for some time.

It's hard to understand a suicide at war, where death is everywhere anyway, so you just have to be patient to wait. Why did Adgur A. pull such a trick at the end? What did he want to say? Every gesture, every word must mean something, he said. So, what meaning did Adgur A. put in his last gesture while throwing his helmet away?

Maybe he was imitating Trakl, Mooney, or those nameless thousands who rejected their bodies in the middle of a fight and exposed themselves to bullets? What happened to him? His will for life broke? Reason overcame self-preservation or discovered a truth incompatible with life?

At war, I never had the thought to stop the senseless motion via bullet. I knew that the motion would continue even without me. Also, that question of "where am I in all of this and what is 'I'"? *I must survive, and everything will go differently, anew*, I thought. Adgur A. didn't think the same way. He was a captive of the endless repetition of the same things. Being an original writer, who made his difference from others the purpose of his work, he wanted to be different in life, too.

Brekhalovka. Regulars and idle onlookers. Around noon, officials of every caliber drop in. Wearing ties and white short-sleeved shirts, they come to show themselves and talk to people. The people do not pay much attention as they are busy. Several domino teams gather under the huge cypress trees. The players are mostly silver-haired, but the new generation, a lot of noisy youth, stick around as well. Ten people are watching the four players. The clock is ticking, a "fish" beats a "goat." At the tables under the blazing sun, someone plays chess. There are a lot of drama and advisors. When moves are made backward, some of them allow it while others don't— they argue themselves hoarse. A bad move causes denouncing comments. The loser proves that he had the win. No one believes him, much less sympathizes with him.

The frayed Amra is close. It didn't manage to push away from the shore and set sail on the oceans of the world. Such things happen when you take root too deeply. From time to time, the real players, the ones who play for money, walk out of the gap between concrete slabs that surround the unfinished hotel Abkhazia. Inside there was a *kumarkhana*, a game room. The players of different leagues have crowded together and organized a table for playing *seka*,[1] *nardi*,[2] *beibut*, and sixty-six.[3] Sometimes, I watch them. Friendly folks, they even invite me to join. But I remain silent and don't interfere.

It smells like the sea. The splash of a wave can be heard through the players' roar sometimes.

"Why this sadness and where does this pain come from?" If I am not mistaken, someone asked this back in the old, glorious, or rather, just olden times. Everything that was destined to exist began with this question. A poet, a balladmonger, a verse maker, a bard, blast him.

I laugh, shedding tears and tearing my guts out. There is no question stupider than that. Like "to be or not to be?" Where does such sadness come from? Who knows. Who will tell me where it originates, like a river, and why, as it expands, it floods everything around?

I loaf around the city like a shadow.

*I am the author of a few published stories and many unwritten novels. I find comfort in the hope that the unwritten is worth something. Is it not enough?*

*B. N. claimed that every law of nature will be discovered one day. The laws make sense only because of the individual who discovers them. In eternal dimensions, science is senseless. Salvation lies in the humility and curiosity that drives a true scientist, and not in the ambitious desire to supersede others.*

*B. N. had a different theory. If the world is eternal, then the creation of unique works is impossible. Sooner or later, at different ends of the universe, independently of each other, all books will be repeated word for word, and not just once, but many times, an infinite number of times. Thus, God jealously reserved the role of creator for himself. If the world is temporary, then creativity is possible—the world won't have enough time to discover a law that has been discovered just by you or to write a book that only you alone have written. Here God shared a piece of his creativity with man. Only he knows why he did it.*

*I am for eternity! In such a case, my unwritten books will be written by someone else one day. I have the boring task of transferring them to paper, and only for the sake of being named their author before someone else. Is it worth spending your life on this?*

*I don't even want to live so much. I want to watch, to float around the earth as a disembodied spirit and peep at others' lives. If nothing else, a stationary observation post might work— to be, let's say, a mighty tree, and better for as long as possible, better if for eternity. But B. N. said that the universe will most likely vanish too. It will fall apart. Time itself will slow down and eventually fall lifelessly like a horse driven into the ruins of space. The world will burn out completely. A great night will come. It's only morning now. A tiringly long day lies ahead.*

*So, there is no need to talk about real eternity. As soon the universe disappears, all books, written, unwritten, published, unpublished, manuscripts, which for some reason are not afraid of fire, lost and found, will disappear with it.*

*Let it be this way. I agree with those ten to the hundredth power of years (the monster from B.N.'s stories) after which the visible will be dismembered to the last brick, to the last particle. I wish I could stand like a tree all these years, noting the decline of the stars.*

*I came to see. There is no other reason why I loaf around here yawning of boredom. If there is another goal, show it to me, pull it out from your stingy storerooms, present it with a genuine seal. You can't?! Because there is no true goal. In every pocket, hidden or not, everything is shallow.*

*At war I live for real, not like before. I explore life from a different perspective, that is, life appears for me in its actual shape, not dressed up in comforting words. I don't need to make anything up because I feel everything like it was for the first time. Everything is fresh, new, sharp, and real. The rapture in battle and on the verge of the abyss is familiar to me. I can still stand it all. That's what surprises me. I know what to do if there comes to be too much of life so that I can bear it no longer.*

*This is what I call watching. I look at the guys around me. I didn't know any of them before. In tiny Abkhazia that's possible only if you've been away for years. But it seems to me that on the streets of Sukhumi, in Amra, at funerals and weddings, I've seen all these faces, that their dissimilarity refutes that they belong to one tribe. I know that most of them won't survive this massacre. I don't know if I will make it myself. But seeing them—fearless, kind, cheerful, real—is worth being with them.*

At such moments, his silence scared Natela. She took his head with her hands and turned it towards herself. Looking into his eyes, she asked him, nearly falling into a scream, hysteria, sob, tears, dog-like whining: "Where are you? Where did you go? I need nothing from you but to hear your voice, just talk to me about anything you'd like: your father, mother, the war! Talk to me! I need your voice more than your cuddles."

Taking on a calmer tone, as if she had pulled herself together, Natela delivered the longest monologue:

"I've always known it. I've expected it since my early childhood, as soon I recognized myself as a subject separate from others, as soon I started recognizing relatives' faces and being afraid of the faces of strangers . . . Since that time, I've known it. I've expected that something bad will happen to me, that my life will go down and down to the bottom—that I'll never live happily but always in trouble, that I'll always be in pain, and nobody will love me so that as long I live, as long I see my childhood premonition is fulfilling itself over and over — and if let's say yesterday I felt quite good and today that feeling somehow continues, then tomorrow or the day after tomorrow I'll have to pay for this accidental 'quite good' feeling a double or triple price and everything will fall to ruins, ash, and despair—but now when I feel quite good I turn my face away and pretend as if I felt as usual—and all of this just to stay clear of new troubles—although those hungry troubles, as I already know, are waiting in line impatiently, scaring my knee to twitching and my stomach to spasms—but the trick of turning my head away and closing my eyes doesn't help, so my heart beats out of tune, exposing itself to the sunlight, the noise of the rain, and a morning breeze when I'm walking to work along the embankment, the play of light on the surface of the sea, or the smile of a familiar stranger's girlfriend, or the song of birds soaring into the sky that is so clear while remembering you—Yes, yes, you first of all—my stupid disobedient heart starts beating rejoicingly—every morning I start all of this anew, with a hope—how this hope endures and where it

The Shore of Night | 381

comes from is a mystery for me—but soon after the day terminates this all and the night drives it into pitch darkness—but somehow in the morning after waking up I want to live again, so I'm walking towards the day, or rather life lurking in ambush, because everything I'm doing or not, everything that's happening to me or not—all this has been called life since my childhood where it was always light and delight and anticipation of when real life would start—but it still hasn't started and there are just crumbs from someone else's table instead—after all of this you can just lie in silence, like I mean nothing to you, I'm just a thing you've used and left till next time when you want to play—your whole male kind is heartless, a person means nothing to you, but I have a heart and want to be happy—say something, don't be silent, just don't be silent—when you are silent like that I'm afraid my heart drops and it becomes empty and frozen inside—there is a vast knowledge behind your eyes, so when you're silent like this I think that you're plotting something bad—but it will turn against you and ruin you . . ."

Beslan looks at Natela, but she understands that he neither sees nor hears her. *Why does he need me,* she asked herself. *Does he need me at all if he leaves me alone to freeze, if he's able to go away suddenly without grabbing me, warm and soft, under his arm?* At such moments, her heart started beating, so she could no longer ignore its questions, hopes, and pain. Goddamned heart! She understood already as a child that it would be better to turn off her heart, to wall it up in her chest, otherwise everything would be very hard for her.

Whoever I've talked to, I never could distract myself from the guts hiding inside them. Like many others who are occupied with things like consciousness, the motherland, or independence these days, he talks about the sublime. But I see only disgustingly warm and self-satisfied guts curling up in his paunch.

One of my worst childhood memories. A cow that broke her leg was slaughtered at home. My grandpa slid a razor-sharp knife along her stomach, from the neck down to the udder. I still hear the subtle, chilling sound of the skin being cut. He dumped the cow's entrails, as one piece, into a woven basket. I could barely resist the urge to put my hands into that steaming, warm, gray ball with its blue veins.

They make undulating movements, pushing shit through themselves in order to get filled with a new helping of fresh stuff. Meanwhile, their owner talks my ear off, covering all this obscenity with his skin and clothes. He couldn't care less. Jumping from one topic to another, he keeps babbling, although he should better fill his mouth with water and stay silent, huddling himself up in a corner.

I can't forget about the guts. I also can't forget that sometimes all this is clothed into a beauty so astounding it becomes difficult to breathe. Here she walks proudly and independently, as if it's not the guts but a sunset in half the sky under her delicate white skin, that dizzyingly fragrant cover. Why do I want to cry for her? For her flickering shadow?!

Once you get to know someone at the distance of an inch or less, their underwear appears before your eyes in all its ugliness. A man is just a piece of meat. But I almost forgot about eyes! I am not talking about the soul that hides inside till death; this is beyond my competence. The soul is the great unknown, the formulaic X included in all equations yet unextractable from them. It has not yet been captured and measured by the machines; its mass, volume, and momentum remain unknown. A serious scholar would not support a dubious hypothesis lacking that data.

Did you notice how cold and soulless one becomes once he puts on his sunglasses? The explanation is surprisingly simple, even primitive: We do not see his eyes. Hiding your eyes behind nontransparent glass, you can do whatever you want—an alibi is guaranteed, no evidence. No matter how white (pale?) her skin and how narrow her waist, no matter how sensually she moves, it is the eyes that hit the target and knock it dead. The scurrying eyes, greedy, fussy organs made of glass, look but never get enough. Her eyes not only look and see, but they pierce you to the bone with a sharp, cold dagger of anguish. The mere fact that she exists at all, two-legged, two-armed, and two-eyed, is already enough to howl in inexplicably unbearable pain that suddenly grips the heart. And that moment when she casts her careless, proud glance at you . . .

Eyes are something. I'd prefer that everyone, especially the women of this city, blinded by sun, wear sunglasses. A city in dark glasses. The ignorant would seek environmental explanations: The south, subtropics, rampant sun. I would know the actual reason: This is a precautionary measure against two bottomless pits waiting for you at every step.

This idiot moves on, having missed a grandiose event. The shining beauty sailed past us with unfurled sails, breaking the monotony of existence. How can one resist pathos! Beauty in which the guts hide till the time comes. Hours and days pass, bringing closer the moment when the guts crawl to the light, reducing the miracle to their fetid essence. It's not too long till that moment. Beauty is fleeting, but imperishable. It is beauty's involuntary carrier who is perishable. He is subjected—no matter how many trivial regrets there are about it—to aging, slow or rapid, to steady necrosis, not to mention various perils, such as illness, or accident.

(I confused myself. I can't complete a thought to clarity. I tried to say that guts will take over sooner or later. Although beauty is eternal, its former carrier will be taken over by guts. This is what I wanted to say. Now I can probably get out the study brackets.)

Beauty is the shortest moment, after which time stays indivisible. The infinite particles that compose the world are the particles of beauty. This can be revealed only in such moments; further contemplation is a crust of emptiness and tediousness.

I do not forget the worms that will sometime devour beauty. This is unbearable. This is what pins me to the bed every morning, keeping me from getting up. Sometimes I stay in bed the whole day. I'm lying with my eyes closed or staring at the ceiling. Sometimes, I listen to the concerned voices from the rear yard and find out what is going on in the world—who's been robbed, killed, who smashed his head driving a car into a roadside pillar. I lie there as if not having any thoughts, while actually I want to howl.

My interlocutor divulged his secrets at a gallop, oversharing what he thought before and after bedtime, what appeared in his disturbing dreams, what he chatted about over a cup of coffee or with himself alone. An idiot; he lived a full life, always busy with something. Notably, he was not busy with himself or his empty, boring life, but with the high-flown—the motherland, the people, Georgia, Russia—in a word, fateful things.

I listened to him with a half an ear, keeping the chatter of a busy person away from me. My gaze weakly clung to the uncontrollably melting image of the stranger who plunged me into despair. At the same time, a shadow of meaning dawned before me. The city, the crowd, the day, and I—everything suddenly became important. Everything emerged from the chaos, the senseless whirling, everything became isolated and rooted in something all-encompassing. Peace descended, there is no other way to say it, no matter how old-fashioned it may sound.

(I'm lying; it's possible to say it differently. Out of laziness, I summed up my condition in a certain way. I took advantage of someone else's experience and descriptive cliché. But someone else's experience and articulation, despite that the author was also a bipedal and upright, can't fully express what I feel).

Now the annoying talker seemed to be nice, a bit reclusive but a good person, sincerely concerned about Apsny and the Abkhazians. He discussed the delay or even complete impossibility of recognizing us as an independent state in the next hundred years. But this is not a problem, the patriot continued bravely, we can endure without external help, maintain the army at such a level that if the Georgians dare to come to us, they will get punched in their teeth again.

I was thinking about how to abolish the guts, so that only the shell could remain to exhaust the content entirely. I thought I knew how to do it. Adgur A. gave me a hint.

*Where is M. now? She wanted to go to the Eastern Front to see her family. Has she made it? Helicopters haven't been flying since December 14th, and there is no other way of getting there. She talked about her younger brother a lot, who fought there. She worried about him.*

*That night on the Gumista shore, I gave her a hug and even kissed her. Then we loved each other. Without words. Greedily. As if we would be taken to execution soon.*

*We decided to swim in a river. I would rather avoid describing it because I'm afraid of striving after literary effect. We were naked; there was M.'s white body, which was hard to see in the night dark, so my inquisitive imagination completed it. There was a cold stream.*

*(I must say something about the river, my first love, my consoler—the nearby tree, also my great love and consoler, goes next—I must say it without the fear of stepping onto the beaten path, the well-worn road, the plowed field, without skimping on exalted words. Sparing no time, which I almost didn't have anyway, since a day here—when you bring your body and soul more or less intact into the night, enveloping the earth after the sunset and then plunging your body and soul into a life-giving sleep, that is, for a certain period of time removing them from existence—takes up such a hefty chunk of time that an ordinary day would never digest, choking on it and vomiting it out with blood. I'm not going to unfold a thoughtful treatise with a set of names and quotes from those who put a lot of effort into education, natural science and cognition—I'm not a fan of grabbing other people's crutches at every mental stumble. I love the river to bits, to knee-trembling, heart-fluttering, unearthly delight and joy. The backwater under a steep bank, the deep place of the river, where it flows slowly, as if in thought, is full of enticing, charming mystery for me. Most of all, I would like to be a stone at the bottom, where the waters would flow above me unceasingly.*

*"Bury me at the bottom of the river" would be my last will and testament, if such a thing in war makes any sense.*

*But what I love especially are the forest creeks. I love these quiet, modest beauties, murmuring through the thicket with their thin bodies.*

*A riddle: Why are the river's sounds so sweet, and why do I want to listen to them forever, while the rain disturbs and torments my heart unspeakably?*

*The body consists mainly of water. Perhaps, the soul too.*

*How dull would the earth and human life be without rivers and trees?)*

*We had a moving intimate conversation that would be hard to imagine under different circumstances. The night, death is just four steps away. Having known and thought of each other for a long time, but now brought together by fate, we talked about ourselves and life in a way that you couldn't during the day. Far away from impossible, ghostly death; eye to eye. I wrote it down in its entirety, without any changes or polish, straight away. Perhaps, it has been already written into our souls in the past. This page-long text outweighs all available literature from Homer to the opuses of modern scribblers; it is deeper and more truthful than anything ever written. There is no praise for me here, nor is there any for M. We spoke in words that came from unknown, unsuspected depths; they were inside us long before we were born. We were free and happy.*

(Then everything is blurred out. Even with a magnifying glass you couldn't make out the words, thickly and carefully crossed out by Adgur A.'s hand, mercilessly changing its mind.)

*We haven't seen each other since then.. Will I meet her after the war? I'm sure nothing will happen between us again. In the ghostly light of day, we would rather pass by each other as strangers, not even slightly nodding our heads as a sign of secret agreement that strangers do not need to know. We would not carry on our secret with a proud feeling of being doomed forever to loneliness. What happened between us then—both love and conversation, or rather, love and words, words and love— belongs to the night. It cannot be pulled out into the light, for then everything will be covered in darkness; everything will cease to exist.*

Natela decided to leave. "There's nothing to do here," she said. "We'll be sitting in blockade for a long time, cut off from the world." That same friend, Asida, who, according to Natela, is quietly slipping into madness somewhere in Moscow or the Moscow region, has settled down well and is now inviting her to "try her luck."

Nothing holds Natela here, so she is leaving. She asks Beslan to look after her apartment and gives him the keys.

"Nothing, absolutely nothing, is holding you back?" he asks, stung by how easily Natela is giving up everything and going to God knows where.

"Definitely not the motherland . . . And you don't even love me anymore."

"What gave you that idea?"

"I see it, it's easy to notice. The way you have been pronouncing my name recently is enough . . ."

"And how do I pronounce it? You're making that up!"

"Not like you did it before. I'm not making it up."

"Natela! Natela! Natela! Want me to continue?"

"Don't, it's not the same."

"I don't understand. Maybe I lost my voice, or it's just changed. Why would you think I don't love you anymore?"

"You don't know yet, but I know it . . . I love you but I never told you. I believed I mustn't impose myself because I'm not a typical woman. But now I can say it. What happened between us was a mistake. It's not your fault, but mine. I'm leaving and you should marry someone and have kids. There is nothing better in life."

Beslan stays silent. He doesn't know what to say and is unsure if he still loves her. In a few days, he might start missing her a lot, as he missed her during the war. She spent the entire war in the village with her maternal relatives. Reluctantly, but driven by an urge to share with someone and ease her heart, she spoke sometimes of that period as the most terrible time in her life. So many young people killed! How to live on after seeing that . . . Something has broken inside her. The core, which had not allowed her to bend until now and because of which Beslan rightfully considered her a strong person, broke during the war. It was no longer the same Natela. "I got five years older in one year," she said, looking at herself into a mirror and seeking the evidence in her new wrinkles. Her experience did not affect her appearance in any way. Beslan did not find her aged, but it was clear that something had broken in her.

Upon arrival at Ingur, Beslan's battalion was commanded to settle in the village of Saberio at the foot of the mountains, where they had to take control of the hydroelectric station.

It was early October. The nights here were not the same as on the plain, closer to the sea. They were fragile, glassy, and chilly. The stars looked out with eyes wide open. After everything that had happened, unexpected silence tuned his mood differently. The anxiety and sense of danger—not for himself, but for others—suddenly went away, and peace enveloped him with the desire to keep everything half asleep, for a long time, if not forever.

But he could not forget Natela. Not a day went when he wouldn't think of her. He thought of her more often than during the war, when the future seemed to be a terribly long way away, if possible at all. His desires usually did not encroach on this longitude for more than one or two days. But the future arrived in an instant. It dawned at once, and on his still-intact body, even, except for the difficulty he had with bending his elbow due to an arm injury that could be counted as an inevitable mark of war and a soul frozen by luck.

Sometimes he suddenly woke up in the middle of the night, amid the snoring and restless sleep of his friends, amid the extraordinary deafening silence carefully guarded by the mountains hanging above them. Heavy premonitions tormented his heart. He heard gossip about Natela stuck in Sukhumi or even killed. His timid attempts to find out about her fate—he could not afford a serious search in their situation—yielded nothing. He could only dream of hugging her, soft and warm, of inhaling the smell of her body, imagining with what fury he would love her, as she would stay indifferent as usual, cold to

The Shore of Night | 391

everything he did with her. Well, let this never cool him, he would always love her.

He often saw her in dreams, and then spent the day with the feeling of her being close, hoping that she was alive. Sometimes some wild thoughts come to his mind. He imagined that if she died, he would dig up her corpse and make love to it. It did not bother him that the corpse would be cold, numb, and possibly decomposed. He felt the same passion for her corpse.

Service was pointless, but he could not leave his friends without an excuse. When some sort of next shift arrived, from their faces and new uniforms, Beslan realized that they were still wet behind the ears and that they would engage in looting, but on a large scale: Dismantling a factory, plant, a workshop, with the commanders' approval. He rushed to Sukhumi.

He traveled for almost half a day, because the truck in which he was sitting not only carried the goods looted in Gala and the suburbs, mainly wardrobes, sofas, chairs, but also pulled a trailer full of seven or eight captured cars—Ladas, Volgas, and even an antediluvian turtle Zaporozhets, a total junker, scrap metal, just a shell, but potentially useful for something on the farm. The driver went slowly, with frequent stops due to engine breakdown, a broken cable that halved the caravan, or an encounter with a familiar hunter after prey. Moreover, the road was clogged with endless herds of buffaloes, cows, bulls, driven from the Mingrelian Gali District to the rest of Abkhazia. The drivers shouted at the cattle to stay in line, and the cattle meekly obeyed.

Scruffy and dressed in dirty, sweat-stinking clothes, he climbed the familiar creaky stairs and knocked on the door. In the most intense days of the war, his heart did not beat so wildly: He did not feel fear, as others do not feel physical pain, but there was excitement.

She opened the door, saw him, and grew numb. She looked haggard, but her eyes, which had suffered a lot, were alive. They stayed in silence for a while, then they hugged, and Natela whispered warmly to him: "You are alive, alive . . ." She hugged him but not as before. She did it with special tenderness, as a real woman can hug. He thought that the suffering which she had experienced had aroused a dormant sensuality in her. But he was wrong.

Then there was a crazy week when he loved Naleta as before.

Today was a fruitful day—eleven names. Beslan, as always, asked Madina to bring him a book with such and such a letter, such and such a number after the first one on this shelf. When he came to them for the first time, signed up and went up to the reading room, she did not understand him. She asked him again several times, and when he explained it in more detail, she was surprised, even finding his request strange: "No one has ever made such a request." He spun a tale about researching the accidental patterns that exist in nature, and for the sake of credibility he named several big names who have made significant contributions to this field of contemporary science:

"The arrangement of books on shelves in connection with their texts and the distribution of certain words and letters on certain pages will help to reveal these patterns all over the world—from a lonely atom on the universe's outskirts where no guardian of the law would even look, meaning the lonely atom is free to do whatever it wants, to the most complex systems like a human, even if he is sick of life as a man, or a woman—people—that is, a person even if he is sick of life as a man

The Shore of Night | 393

or a woman, old people and children and the universe itself; that is, that lonely atom on the outskirts of stars and galaxies, black and white holes, dark matter, a person, even if he is sick of life as a man or a woman, old people and children—here I deliberately omit the rest of the earthly creatures crawling, swimming, flying, walking; I deliberately do not talk about the dead who died long ago or recently settled in fresh coffins in fresh graves, I don't want to spoil your cheerful mood, because I see you are a cheerful person; that is, you see joy in life but the suffering of illness and death you consider to be misunderstandings that quickly pass no matter who they happen to— because the list would be too long and I would bore you by reading it from A to Z, from Z to A, and erratically—that is, in random order—and I would not want to bore you, this is not one of my tasks, this is not the goal of my stay here today, of my visit to your cozy library, a treasure trove of book wisdom and many years of book dust, you already manage to tire yourself out of visitors in a day, you might not have many visitors, just a handful of devotees, but there are books around you, in which heroes do not lie as dead letters and words, waiting for a reader who will revive them as some smart aleck might think, they live even when no one reads them and influence you, imperceptibly drawing you into their existence—So, all of the above and that which has been omitted out of the desire not to bore you, is subject to certain patterns, which we must break down, you can ask why all this is necessary and how to find out how a lonely atom on the outskirts of the universe lives and breathes, because you can't get to it in any way . . . How to find out what governs a person who is disgusted with life—if he is disgusted with life, is he even living at all, or pretending—after all, to reach his ice-cold heart without breaking it into shining fragments that would immediately melt from our warm empathy is difficult and your question is appropriate; that is, I would say even a good question—this is what politicians usually say when they don't have an answer to a question raised starkly or a question posed correctly or a question posed starkly—you understand what I'm confused about, three stark questions—as is generally accepted in the thinking world, this is half the correct answer . . . So, your first question: Why is this all necessary?"

At this point, he lowered his voice and bowed his head to Madina, making her automatically bring her head closer to him, but within the limits allowed by an imitative impulse, and then, having come to her senses, she pulled away, but out of politeness, as unnoticeably as possible: "But I don't know, madam, the answer to your sacramental, rhetorical, inimitable, murderous, crushing question. 'To be or not to be?' also remains unanswered, hanging in the air for so many centuries in the loneliness of its sacramental, rhetorical, inimitable, murderous, crushing demand. Since that question has not yet been resolved by the human mind, unambiguously and without equivocation, then I, sinfully, sometimes think whether the question mark '?' is the whole point, whether it is the answer to all questions . . ."

Madina did not believe in his gibberish but did not say anything. She looked at Beslan in a friendly manner, taking everything as a joke. At first, she asked herself if he was deranged. Then she found him a little strange, but this strangeness was expressed only in his unusual choice of books, and nothing else. Generally, he was normal.

The book that Madina brought turned out to be chubby. It was the memoir of a famous politician who drowned his whole life by an unfulfilled vanity that made him malevolent, the poisonousness of which was reflected in his rat-like face. His comments were plentiful. The author compensated for his life's failures, although from an outside glance he was very successful. He occupied a high post in some European state, and the number of celebrities with whom he'd had the chance to meet, talk, have lunch, share his bed and take pictures, could make any ordinary man salivate with envy.

Mancha Satbeyevich was not there. His presence always distracted Beslan, as he felt uncomfortable with Mancha's indignant exclamations, interrupting the silence with the regularity of a newspaper page, from his frequent absences to the bathroom—his bladder was weak—from his smell, which doused Beslan as he passed by, from his clumsy attempts to make Madina laugh during the breaks she arranged for herself. Moreover, he was always eager to set on Beslan's ears as soon as, drifting into thought, he took his eyes off his book.

Beslan delved into reading and, before the library closed, managed to change his mind, and imagine the lives of as many as eleven people, long dead, who lived from 23 to 87 years of earthly life.

"Young man, I want to tell you something."

Her face expressed extraordinary affection and care. I felt embarrassed. At the same time, through the sagging skin, wrinkles, cream and powder, the impatience of an inveterate gossip showed through.

We walked away to the dusty bookshelves, and she said in a half-whisper, but so that her young, moronic friend could hear (if one is going to be an ally, then it is to the end), looking at us and grinning with wide, crooked teeth:

"Young man, I like you so much that I can't help but warn you. Madina was a nurse in the war and was wounded in the stomach; she will never have children. I feel terribly sorry for her, she is so good, you can't even imagine how good she is! You can't tear it away from your heart, that's how good she is . . . !"

The ugly girl echoed her with a nod of her head and a smug, anticipatory smile. She is, thank God, healthy! She can give birth to so many babies, as long as there is someone who wants to hobble her, take her in his arms and time after time, in the sweat and persistence of righteous labor, cover her and sow her fertile womb with his hot seed!

The wretch was waiting for me to speak, but I remained stubbornly silent out of spite. She stared at me in bewilderment, then became embarrassed, which, honestly, I did not expect. But she pulled herself together quickly: she squinted; her eyes flashed angrily; she turned around and sat down heavily in her place. The moron felt that something had gone wrong; her friend had screwed up. She instantly removed her stupid grin from her face and looked at me with hatred, which made her face even stupider, although that had seemed impossible.

Without saying a word, I turned away and went up to the reading room, where Madina was sitting at her desk, buried in a book. Walking up the stairs, I felt how rapidly the disappointment and dull anger were rising behind me. Of course, I was irrevocably crossed out from the list of "sweet, nice young men" and blacklisted as an "arrogant and self-confident troublemaker." I was also classified as an "unfortunate morphine addict" using the elderly woman's words or the "junkie," as the younger would say.

From that day on, they barely greeted me. They nodded coldly, as if I were an old acquaintance who had screwed them over.

We get to know so many different people in life—cold, warm, clean, dirty, soft, or harsh. And is it really possible that as soon as we wash our hands, nothing remains from these touches, that we wash away everything that briefly connected us with those people?!

She still remembers her hands. Dry and bony, her mother worked hard with them all her life. Sometimes it seemed to her that she could smell their scent, that it was still lingering on her fingers . . . She remembered her mother as if she were alive. But what was imprinted in her memory most vividly was not mother's appearance, but her touch, her skin. She could not believe that the soul has nothing to do with the body. After all, maybe there is no soul, but only a body? She remembers only her physical mother. She does not exist outside of her body for Natela. Will she ever meet her mother again, like an ethereal shadow? It won't be mom anymore . . .

Her fingers were cold. The warmth of life that she remembered from childhood had faded in them. With what trustfulness she placed them in her palm! She used to sit by the bed for hours, holding her hand. She falls asleep, wakes up, and Natela still sits, not taking her eyes off her. If mom dreams about something, she recognizes it by the slight trembling of her fingers, the shuddering of the body, muttering . . . Or maybe it's not a dream, but just nerves? Natela wants her mother to dream about something, so that her dream does not look too much like death . . . All of her is in every particle of her body. And in the fingers too: They seem to live an independent life.

The argument did go on. We changed our outfits, trying to be different and go beyond our selves. I reproached Adgur A. for equivocal behavior.

"Any smart person must follow the existing social order, at least outwardly. It's stupid to be a black sheep."

Another time he answered differently, saying that he only wanted to see where one's commitment to social guidelines could lead to. Each time, he meticulously wrote down his feelings, then compared them, so he got a kind of a emotional diagram. But in its curves, he did not see any spirit of which I spoke. What he saw was a boring repetition. Where the diagram led to is unknown; its meaning is unclear. It certainly led to emotional fatigue. Customs, like people, wear out and become obsolete. Alternatively, he could answer that he had many reasons, different each time, to follow customs. Yet he did not see any hypocrisy or discord between his behavior and words. He never experienced any inner discomfort.

We climbed down from Amra into the city, slinking towards night. People were milling around, colorful vacationers in groups, enchanted, as if they had suddenly found themselves in Eden. They timidly walked along the boulevard. "Everything seems unreal to me, fictional," said Adgur A., "and this city, with its inescapable twilight melancholy, and this sky, suddenly darkening, and this incomprehensible country given to us by God . . ."

We had talked about these things more than once. Not about the commonplace "life is a dream," but about this invincible feeling that had gripped us recently, when our relations with the Georgians became heated to the point of the impossible. Adgur A. gave this his own, as always paradoxical, explanation: We feel the impending danger in our gut, the beast that

The Shore of Night | 399

still lives in us feels it; that is why all our sensations are heightened—we began to see, hear, feel much more than before. And we had finally seen our country. We'd seen how unbearably beautiful it is. We couldn't believe our eyes; we couldn't believe that under the sky such beauty is even possible. If so, it's all a dream. We actually had woken up. But what we saw is beyond our ability, so we ran back.

I said the opposite, that Abkhazia has never been as real as it is now, on the verge of trouble. If war happens, the country will rise dazzlingly authentic from the ashes. I considered our dreamlike experience a self-hypnosis, an effect of books, a brain twist. With his sophisticated casuistry, Adgur A. tried to prove the opposite: that I, too, saw everything as in a dream, only that through many years of studying physics I had drowned out the primordial subtlety of my feelings and clouded the clarity of my consciousness. It cannot be that in other rare moments, when meanings, the essence of things are captured with clear focus, I do not feel the unnecessariness of everything that happens. These minutes were like awakening. The final, irrevocable awakening will be death. Death will shake off the extraneous from us, everything that stuck to us during our earthly life. But even before death, it happens that the current suddenly carries us to the surface of the sleep in which we are immersed. It will endure, maybe for a moment, but that's enough. The truth will strike us like lightning: everything is a dream. Have I really not experienced anything like that? I haven't experienced it. Adgur A. started in a new circle: For children there is no difference between sleep and reality, and who is closer than them to the world's source and truth? Then, growing up, and therefore moving away from the source, packaging the world into words, we lose the frankness of a child's perception. What had perceived the truth directly, suddenly scattered into five incorrect senses. We help this to happen by accumulating other people's thoughts from books.

I wrote it down as I remembered it, in my own words. I threw out the names and theories that Adgur A. mercilessly piled up to make his fiction sound convincing. I think he won't be offended by me for this—if he can feel anything where he is now. On this shore of life, as he used to say, you need to keep one feeling unquenchable—the feeling of life. All the rest go overboard. Let it hiss and fade away into the abyss of a fraudulent world. He considered everything a fiction, including himself: "I was invented by someone sluggishly . . .", ". . . clumsily", ". . . stupidly", ". . . out of spite" —always in different ways, because a day never repeats, and every hour of life is unique. People in this "every hour" are different. They flow like that notorious river. Words are not enough to describe the special features of the days. But every day will be called a combination, a combination of words. So, eternity can be given a name.

Natela left, taking her mother's picture with her.

I went with her up to Psou. I was empty and exhausted. All the words that I had prepared before going to bed evaporated by the morning. During the night, I am defenseless, open, my soul is naked, I feel something and find some words to express it. I was gentle with Natela from a distance, lying in my lonely bed a few blocks away from her. I never stay at hers. It's uncomfortable, and the neighbors, who are fewer because of the war, can see everything. They moved into deserted Georgian apartments and houses.

She lived in an old communal house with a grimy courtyard. When I go up to the second floor along the creaky wooden staircase, as old as the house itself, if not older, all the neighbors see and hear me. As soon as I put my foot on the first bottom step—for some reason the creakiest one—their curious ears and eyes immediately take up an observation position at the windows behind the folded curtains and at the keyholes. The bravest ones might even step out of their apartment, allegedly for their own purpose, and walk up and down the porch. All of them are female individuals, the owners of very curious ears and eyes, or maybe their husbands are just hiding better. Even before the war, "well-wishers" informed my family that I was "ruining my young life by getting involved with a whore." My mother, as befits a mother, raised a fuss and almost sent a delegation to Natela's relatives with a demand that she "leave the boy alone." My father stopped her. She was afraid that I would marry Natela, blaming her for making me forget my parents. "Harlot! She's bewitched him!" During the war, she made a vow that she would forgive me everything as long as I stayed alive. To fulfill her vow, she had to sacrifice a white goat, without a single black hair . . . Now she no longer talks about my marriage, Natela, or anything. But this is temporary, I know. Soon she'll start to pester me with talks about marriage and kids, saying that it is the right time for me to start a family. After all, I am the only son, who will get the farm, the house, the estate, and the garden. Who will look after the graves where seven generations of our family lie.

I woke up as usual in the morning. My soul is hiding and my words have evaporated. I remembered them, but they no longer had that fire, sincerity, and tenderness that I had put into them at night.

We were on the bus the whole ride but didn't say a word to each other. It was early morning, the bus was full, mostly with women going to Psou to trade. Tangerine season! Many of them wore black. Some women pinned one or two small, mournfully framed photographs of their dead sons to their chests. Their faces looked tired. Their eyes carried inconsolable grief. Sometimes I sneaked glances at them, feeling guilty because I was alive and those guys were dead, laying in the ground.

During the day they make several trips across the border. Having bought tangerines on this side, they will transport them—in wheelbarrows or bags—across the bridge to the other side to sell them at a higher price. They come back if the tangerines start rotting. They go on until dark when the border closes. The next day, everything begins anew early in the morning: Humiliating walks back and forth through the mud, under the shouts of customs officers, standing in slow lines, bargaining here to give at least a little, and there to not give in. Nothing can be done about it; they need to feed their surviving children, grandchildren, and unemployed husbands. They need to organize funerals and anniversaries. On the birthdays and the days of their sons' death, they need to gather their friends. They need to take care of the graves, place a stone of some kind. All this is only so that others don't forget the dead; so that people don't think that the dead are gone completely; so that everyone can see they are remembered.

After work, the mothers fall asleep wearily. Finally, before going to bed, they have an opportunity to think about nothing their sons who were killed at war. They reproach themselves for thinking about these sons rarely during the day, and, for that, they ask to be forgiven.

Mothers cannot make peace with the death of their sons. Me either . . .

Sometimes, discouraged by my silence, Natela looked up at me expectantly. I stood over her like a stone statue. But when I caught her eloquent gaze, something instantly jumped between us—a charge, a spark, and I loved her in that moment, and was afraid to part with her. She lowered her head, and the charge disappeared completely into my indifference, not even indifference, but my soul's numbness. It seemed to me that the mechanism of fate had been set in motion and that I was powerless to stop it. One thing ends, another begins, and there is no return to the past. It's impossible to keep what must go. If you grab it, it will carry you away, cut you off from the present, and therefore from the future.

We parted the same way we acted during the ride—silently, like old acquaintances who understand each other without words.

*They die when there is little life.*
   *When there is a lot of life, they kill themselves.*

I've walked Madina to her house. For the first time, I made it to the end of the working day, despite that it was difficult to get rid of Mancha Satbeyevich, who always leaves early and invites me to walk along the promenade. He has had the habit of daily walks and collecting gossip since the time of his voluntary military service. He even invited me for some wine at his place, "My nephews have sent it to me, no water or sugar, just like what our fathers and grandfathers drank." I promised I'd definitely come and taste his wine sometime soon, and that I'd walk along the promenade with him, talking about important matters of local and global significance, with the obligatory discussion and condemnation of the key figures involved in those matters. But now, pardon me, I can't, I'm busy, I lied, with an extremely entertaining smart aleck and heartbreaker, who, thanks to these two characteristics, has been elevated to the very top. I learned about him from an extensive source, to which I was forced to turn, contradicting my rules, because the smart aleck and heartbreaker aroused my keen interest.

The old man is observant with the trained eye of an old informant. He noticed that I mostly read biographies, but in abridged form, in notes or footnotes, and asked what kind of interest I had in the compressed destinies of other people. Wouldn't it be better to take a full-length volume, like something from the series *Lives of Remarkable People*? Without thinking too long, I named my reason. The footnotes usually have the essence of the person's life. When studying a "passable" biography, you learn what to pay close attention to, what to highlight with special care or ignore silently, because there is a great danger of drowning in trifles, insignificant details, with which, like the bottom of a ship overrun with various living matter, every life is overgrown.

The old man was pleased with my promise and loquaciousness, which he clearly regarded as a sign of special affection and trust in himself, especially trust, with which fate had not spoiled him. In general, today he is in high spirits, not as gloomy as on other days; and a living light seems to have appeared in his eyes. Apparently, he found new evidence of an internal and external conspiracy against the Soviet Union.

Heartbroken and depressed, he set about unraveling the shameful mystery of the death of the largest and mightiest empire that history had known. And he was always seething with indignation at the traitors—they couldn't wait for the time when the USSR, gradually cutting off the republics, shrank from one sixth of a landmass into a medium-sized country. They betrayed humanity, its future, and through their efforts the empire was knocked down. But the search carried away the searcher: The initial revelatory impulse faded over time, and now he rejoiced at any confirmation of his guess, no matter how tiny it might be. 'I was right!' he exulted in his soul, rejoicing at his sagacity, his fitness for duty, but outwardly keeping a sorrowful expression on his face, especially when he spoke to me.

Madina and I walked out together, escorted by the indignant and offended gazes of her friends. They did not expect such impudence and shamelessness. Madina felt somewhat awkward, and she lowered her eyes as she said goodbye to them. I looked them straight in their faces, and because of this insolence they themselves had to lower their eyes. Tomfoolery! Why did I do that! I did not protect Madina from their evil tongues; on the contrary, I added fuel to the fire.

We walked along the Prospect, chatting about nothing. The street was easy for me, not as usual. We reached her house. She lived at the end of the Prospect in a nine-story building. We said goodbye.

"Meet me under the Clock."

"That crazy one?"

"Yes."

"People might see us . . ."

"Well, let them . . ."

"Maybe somewhere else? Like in Penguin."

"Meet me under the Clock, and then we'll go to Penguin to grab coffee and ice cream."

"Okay."

Sometimes I lie down and wait for sleep to extinguish me, when all of a sudden, I hear a dog bark. It comes from somewhere far away. The lonely, distant barking is especially unsettling. It hits my whole body, so that every cell responds to it. I lie tense, cold sweat appears on my forehead, my heart is hidden deep in my chest. I can't hear it. I'm waiting for something, but I don't know what. Maybe for the end of everything and the beginning of a completely new, unprecedented thing that I have been anticipating all the time since the war ended? Is that ordinary barking in the middle of the night a herald of the coming renewal of the world?

None of the pack answers the dog, and this is strange. This means that something has gone wrong in their brotherhood, and now it is trying to remind everyone to whom its voice reaches about that former union.

It pours itself out for several hours, finally becoming exhausted and hoarse.

The answer is silence. The dog pack does not even think of supporting their brother, the dog pack is against it: Let everything remain as it is. But then it would be necessary, according to custom, to answer the distant call—stretch out your head, tense up and bark, and this should be picked up by everyone who hears. In this friendly chorus, the dog's melancholy will speak out and go away.

The unanswered, lonely barking is truly new. I fall asleep with this comforting thought and with a secret hope: What if tomorrow morning . . . ?

*Our mountains have always given me a feeling of silence. They stand and remain quiet. All the literary metaphors with which*

*the poets have crowned them (grey-haired, proud, majestic)*
*I can connect to. For me, the mountains pushed those metaphors*
*aside like a stupid and annoying human attempt to name the*
*immense silence and serenity that they kept within themselves.*
*I always felt like a stranger in the mountains. It seemed to me*
*that everything around me tensely froze, stopped life in itself and*
*was waiting for me to leave. And when the forest rustled and the*
*sky crackled with thunder, when the lightning-fast, unearthly*
*light overtook the world fleeing into the night, into darkness,*
*I felt even more uninvolved in the high and secret life of the*
*mountains. Everything here was different, everything was in its*
*full expression, minted and inevitable: colors, smells, sounds*
*were pristine. I am their distant fuzzy echo, their irreparably*
*broken fragment. Only in the lowlands could I find what is called*
*peace of mind. I replaced the hot and destructive breath of the*
*world with the cozy warmth of everyday life, among the named*
*and therefore supposedly known things. But my soul remembered*
*the shine and ringing, so after several days, I, bogged down in*
*the named world, thought with longing about the mountains as*
*something long familiar, close, but, alas, forever lost.*

Adgur A. never mentions her injury. Maybe she was injured later, after their meeting or after his death. Or maybe he didn't know, she didn't tell him, and that night he didn't feel or see the scar on her stomach.

I think about Madina. I imagine what she is doing at this moment, what she is thinking about. Maybe she remembers me? Or the war? She hasn't gotten out of it yet, and it's unlikely she will. I didn't get out. Although women are stronger than men . . .

She is a woman of few words. Her whole life is within her eyes. I had never seen such eyes before, perhaps because I don't like looking into other people's eyes and don't want them to look into mine. What the first and most important thing about them is, I haven't figured out. The eyes are the most amazing and most dangerous human organ. Draw a circle and depict two black dots on it resembling eyes— and something alive is looking at you, looking and looking, trying to say something. The Other is much more tolerable if it has no eyes.

Madina's eyes are bottomless, directly connected to her soul. But any eye, if you look into it for a long time, becomes a dead glassy pellet. It loses its meaning, like a word repeated many times. Where does the life, which had been shimmering before, and in Madina's case shining through her eyes fade away to?

Madina, I will never look into your eyes for so long. That means you won't either: There is no way that I could look into your eyes without you looking into mine. We will warn ourselves. In life, you have to do everything with half an eye, with a squint.

*I ran with everyone, and it seemed to me that we were running as one huge Something. This feeling of unity with everyone arose in me from the very first days of the war. As time passes, it has not weakened even slightly, but on the contrary, has intensified. I have never experienced a more joyful, intoxicating feeling. The same blood flowed in us, the same heart beat, the same will guided us, and we fulfilled it obediently and gratefully. If there is a God, sitting in heaven with a white beard and terribly kind eyes, then, I am sure, he hints about himself in precisely such moments—when you, among everyone else, run to the forest, from where they are cutting us off with heavy fire, like corn with a sickle. Nothing is important in life, in the universe. Your head is turned off. It does not weigh you down with the unnecessary burden of thought—you are free. You notice something else: suddenly the sky has gone somewhere high, and for some reason it's tilted and blue. You feel the cold wind blowing over you. You hear the desperate shots from far away and the bullet whistles around. But all this seems to be due to the inertia of a past life, due to the residual memory of yourself, your body. You have already rejected your body, in any case. It is the body that now carries the bright and joyful part of you. It is separate from your substance, a thing in itself, everywhere and nowhere.*

*I made it in one piece, but I know: If a bullet had caught me and killed me on the spot, I would have been dying in the same joy that I experienced before—in a single impulse with everyone reaching the safe edge of the forest.*

What was Adgur A.'s last gesture about—when he took off his helmet and threw it away? Was it despair and the consequent decision to run away from the surrounding horror for good? Or was he following the text, when suddenly it dawned on him how he should complete his journey? "Life has become too much," he writes. But isn't this an excuse? I have not yet been able to understand his train of thought. Maybe grass really is to blame? He got stoned and was carried away to the wrong place, away from reality, where he did not want to return. Or, on the contrary, he slowly swam out of the dope, found himself at the same place from whence he had swum, and got overcome by despair. Then he took off his helmet and threw it away. In this case again—despair. Looks like there's no way to get rid of it. A keyword. Then another explanation arises: Despair had been gathering in him for a long time, drop by drop. Now a whole sea was raging inside him, and the text had suggested what gesture to deal with it. It was by removing his helmet, that is, exposing his head (he wanted the bullet to hit the head, the main culprit-organ). Although it was enough to stand for a while at his full height, he would certainly have "caught" the sniper's bullet in other parts of the body and would probably have been killed.

But he wanted to make an unusual point. His own. Baring his head for a bullet.

Mancha Satbeyevich suspects something. Recently, during our meetings, he has been looking at me conspiratorially, spelling out his borrowed wisdom: "Get married, procreate, there are few of us, and the war has taken away so many of the best..." A clear allusion to Madina and my feelings for her, which could not be concealed from an old-school volunteer chekist. He did not serve officially but was very kindly treated as valuable secret personnel. For a long time, he did not dare to share. He hesitated to do it while his pride poured out of him. Maybe it was not his pride, but he just wanted to lighten his burden, take a load off his soul.

Noticing his urge to share his secrets with me, I assumed that I would hear a lengthy, heart-tugging confession, with a couple of inserted adages that like a red thread tie the old man's simple life together into a single whole. But he remained strong and walked around mysteriously, carrying his secret knowledge in his skull until I earned his trust. I think I earned it, but I might be mistaken. He did not utter a word about his past. In the end, Mancha Satbeyevich finally gave up. He didn't have enough courage to remain unknown Mr. X. He confessed, looking at me as if he expected me to crash onto the ground in surprise. But I remained standing still and indifferent, and this disappointed the old man a little. His confession disgusted me. He understood this from my facial expression and added hastily: "Don't think about it, young man . . . I handled only notorious scoundrels, natural-born snitches, who killed innocent people out of envy and malice. I made not the enemies of the people sing, but the enemies of man . . ."

"You mean, you made them scream?"

"No, their songs were bad, like their souls!"

And he began a long story about how he did it. It was interesting, but I still didn't believe him.

He gave me unequivocal hints, but I didn't understand. After greeting me, he immediately added in a half-whisper: "There are enemies all around, the legal bodies are not doing their job . . ." Sometimes, Mancha Satbeyevich pointed to someone, apparently a Georgian, and say: "An ardent nationalist, he hated us all his life, he collaborated, and now he walks around as if nothing happened. I'd like to know why the legal bodies are not doing their job! In the old days, for this he would be . . ." His eyes sparkled with accusation, condemning the legal bodies for their lack of vigilance, loss of shape, and for God knows what else. Mancha Satbeyevich, who knew the legal bodies' kitchen, could easily present them a substantial bill for their shortcomings.

412 | *Daur Nachkebia*

Busy with my observations, I sometimes looked with curiosity at the old man, who bowed his bald gray head over the *Pravda* pages, that were partly yellowed, yet partly retained their original whiteness.

Mancha Satbeyevich's struggle with history—truly heroic, I would say, at the limit of his aging strength—was impressive. It would even be more accurate to say that by revealing the lies and corruption of a short historical period unfolding in unprecedented scale on as much as one-sixth of the earth's landmass, Mancha Satbeyevich revealed time itself, which, by any means necessary, breaks forward like a shaft, without souring in place, covering itself with a patina, or growing into the mud. So, time went on, cruelly and mercilessly stepping over the most sacred thing—people's faith in justice. All fundamental values fell in one night. The faith that had been ripening for centuries in the hearts of the oppressed fell too. What will happen to humanity? Will it continue to rush headlong towards the abyss, or will it come to its senses, stop, and descend to a simple worker, nameless author of all the best that exists in this world under the sun?

"I don't envy you, young man. You will live in a terrible world," the old man prophesied more than once, taking me by the elbow in a friendly manner. "We've outlived our time, and, I'd say, not in the worst way. It's time for us to go . . ."

I thought how to immortalize him, in what footnote to include him, in what words to justify his presence in the text. Only I can do this. Or not? Will Mancha Satbeyevich really end up in a book? Will his name suddenly appear in some footnotes or comments in the future? It's possible. Some historian in the future, rummaging through archival dust, will come across him, inscribed in many documents, starting with the birth certificate and ending with the death record. He will include him in his work. Someone will read it and maybe think for a moment: Who was this Mikhail Stepanovich? How and why did he live? By what design and necessity did he idle away his life for some number of years? If there is no photograph of him in the book, which is most likely to happen, since Mancha Satbeyevich is a vanishingly small figure on the scale of history—but who knows . . . If there is no image, the reader will draw his portrait in his mind, based on the meager lines. His image will depend on those lines and words.

I had some money, and I took him to Narty.

"You won't believe it, young man, I forgot the taste of mămăligă with beans. I haven't eaten it for a hundred years!" Mancha Satbeyevich said, happily devouring food with both cheeks. "You can't live like you want on my pension. I am a respectable man! Who would have dared to do this to me in the past? Nobody needs old people . . ."

A man and a woman, apparently a married couple, tanned, in light shorts, with a foreign expression on their faces—open, simple-minded and smiling—were sitting under a canopy in the courtyard and eating Adjarian khachapuri. The first vacationers were beginning to arrive, many at their own peril and risk.

The only reason we are interesting to the world is that we have a coastline of over two hundred kilometers. On this coast you can build a lot of five-star hotels and resorts for low-income tourists, numerous and voracious like locusts. Clean up the beaches. Drive the natives away from the sea, at least beyond a five-kilometer zone, so that they do not become an eyesore and do not frighten vacationers with their wild appearance. The most handsome and intelligent will be selected for service: Waiters, maître d'hôtel, elevator operators, guides, strippers, and prostitutes. Athletic men will be dressed in Circassian hats and put on display in supermarkets to advertise various products. After tiresome righteous labors, humanity will blissfully stretch out on the sand under the rays of the generous southern sun.

Money will come to us. They will buy us entirely, if they haven't done it already. Many are waiting for it. Many are looking longingly at the North, sometimes timidly and furtively casting glances at the prohibited West. So, come and take me. I don't need much. I haven't developed an appetite yet. I don't need a jacuzzi-shmacuzzi. An outhouse in the outskirts over a stinking cesspool is quite enough. But I desperately need a car. Preferably, a comfortable foreign car. It alone will console me, dispel my melancholy, give me a feeling of freedom and strength, the fulfillment of a dream, and I will rush like a catechumen along the bumpy roads of my beautiful hand-sized homeland until I crash into a roadside pole, a tree, or an identical car with a suicidal driver as hard as I can and smash my brains on the windshield. On the day of the funeral, on the great day of grief and meeting with relatives, friends, acquaintances, the car, or rather what is left of it, a pile of twisted metal, will be covered in black and put on display in the yard for everyone to see. It is possible that later this pile will find its last refuge at the grave—not as an edification, that is, this is what recklessness leads to, but as an envious reminder that a suicidal crasher was honored to spend his short life driving a cool car, traveling around his hand-sized country along its length and breadth.

From our booth, Mancha Satbeyevich kept casting curious and at the same time alarming glances at the married couple.

The Shore of Night | 415

I decided—the old sinner, a cool drink of water had turned his head.

"A beautiful woman," I said.

"Ours are more beautiful, no one has such white skin like ours . . ."

"But you clearly like her. You can't take your eyes off her."

"I'm looking at her husband. He is also a security officer. At first glance, they are all so simple . . . Watch him—but carefully, don't scare him away. If he notices surveillance, he will immediately cower and become like everyone else . . . Watch, and you will agree with me."

I had no desire to find out whether the red-haired fellow, whose jaws were grinding food, moving up and down, was a security officer or not.

"You see, he looked at me too. Feels familiar . . ."

"They are the only hope," I said, to change the topic.

"We can't survive without them. Now the Georgians won't leave us alone."

"I meant the tourists."

"Let them come, they don't mind the sea and the sun, you see how many of them we have, even too many . . ."

"And let them leave their money here. Is that what you want to say?"

Mancha Satbeyevich nodded his head (his mouth was full) to express agreement. He ate greedily. He chewed his food long and thoroughly. I have noticed this greed for food in old people. Not just greed, but the exceptional status they assign to meals. They chew with concentration, even thoughtfully. They want to extract all useful things from the food without leaving a trace.

The waitresses were bored. There were only one or two visitors.

"It was crowded here before."

"Everything was different before." I tried to set the old man up for positive memories.

But the heat and the amount of food Mancha Satbeyevich had eaten made him sleepy and drowsy. He stared blankly at some point, not having much desire to stir up the past.

We stood up and I paid. He humbly thanked me and walked home towards the ruins of the Dioscuria restaurant. He lives near the post office, not far from the library—alone as far as I know. His wife died a long time ago and his children moved away. The old man was forgotten. Or he never had them, neither a wife nor children—I still don't understand. His surname is rare. I've never even heard of it. He has almost no relatives. Mancha Satbeyevich talks about it as the biggest failure in his life, almost a tragedy. There was no one to stand next to him, to lend him a shoulder, to put a word in for him to the high authorities. In his family, there was nobody reputable enough whom Mancha Satbeyevich could mention to make other people treat him with respect—this way trying to compensate for their previous indifference. His mother's surname was extinguishing. It smacked of the same primitive savagery and loneliness as his father's surname. Otherwise, Mancha Satbeyevich would have made a dizzying career and would hardly be standing in line for free soup today. "If only I could get through 1937 and subsequent years, keeping my head intact . . ." he adds after some thought, not without regret descending from the sky-high heights of the career ladder to the terrible land with its "troikas," Siberian frosts, and Magadan.

The Shore of Night | 417

I headed over along the promenade to Akop's Place. It was late summer, and the approaching fall could be already felt in the air. The growing yellow and red colors, the shadows—for some reason it's only in fall that you notice how long your own shadow is—the smells, sunlight, suddenly gentle and even sad, especially in the evening. It was calm and light in the heart.

Beardy rushed past me. He recognized me, nodded, but didn't stop. Apparently, he was in a hurry to get to the game. He does not go to the *kumarkhana*—there are gamers there whom he despises for their cheating and impudence. He always plays fairly and for small stakes: He told himself that this month he will place such and such a bet—kill him, but he won't back down. He will lose as always. And, as always, he will passionately and for a long while explain his loss as fatal bad luck. He described backgammon succinctly: The tragedy of a single move. Let's say you desperately need to make du-shesh. But instead of a thick dotted blackness—the eye barely noticed it, the mind couldn't yet make any estimations, but the heart was already jumping, jubilantly expanding into the entire chest—it's a pity to lose at checkers: ekibir—du-yak.[4] Indeed, he always says how he gets the rarest combinations. Probability theory restrains them to the far corner. Chance does not even think to look there, but if it does, it's only to comply with the rule that provides for this exception, or just to make fun of people like Beardy.

He puts so much soul into every move! In particularly bad spots, Beardy actually casts a spell over the checkers, gently whispering something to them. He hesitates for a long time to make a move, but then plucks up courage to throw the cubes. Then with the cowardly edge of his palm he cuts them off. His move does not count. He takes the checkers and starts his divination again. Rolling the dice with his hard, strong fingers and whispering kind words, he throws it, but fails. Instead of a desired number, the worst one appears. It ruins the position on the board, leading to immediate loss. His opponent says dau, dauba-se or dauba-char—usually, without even getting to the last one. Beardy is careful, and also doesn't care much about money. He bites his lips and moustache while swearing. The stakes are low, but it's not about that. Beardy fights fate but loses again and again.

He jumps up angrily, almost throwing away the checkers with which he was so gentle and affectionate a moment ago. He waves his hands, inviting everyone to witness the curse hanging over him, "You've seen it, haven't you?! My mother used to say, don't play, son, it's bad for you. She died with those very words. A fool! I didn't listen. Jackass, it serves me right!"

Next day after his loss, Beardy is silent and frowning. When asked to play, he responds that he has quit. With his arms crossed over his chest, he indifferently watches the others play, swaying rhythmically back and forth, sometimes rising on his toes. Likely, he has no money as he squandered everything yesterday. He never plays for show. This is also his principle, just like playing small bets. Having accumulated some savings—he works as a loader at the market and can be seen every day from morning until two, in an apron to his toes, a naked, hairy, muscular body covered in flour dust—Beardy again rushes to fight the fate,\ which has haunted him all his life for not listening to his mother.

It's not that Beardy can't play. In nard he is like a fish in water. However, he follows the rules too much and doesn't accept risk. Perhaps, the desire to calculate everything, to exclude chance—in a game where almost everything depends on

The Shore of Night | 419

which side of the dice lies upward—is what brings him down. And yet, with a little luck and a long game, he will beat anyone. But he is terribly unlucky. If everything he says is true, then there is no doubt that doom really hangs over him, and the strangest things happen to him which even avid experienced players, who are accustomed to chance's unpredictability and playful, evil displays, do not believe. All his stories are like that one when he got du-besh five times in a row, couldn't figure out the easiest and most obvious move and, of course, lost the game. He has a lot of such stories, each better than the last. He can spin them all day and night, savoring his bad luck with special aplomb.

Yet Beardy does not stop trying to change his fate. He is persistent. After all, the whole meaning of his life is in the game. Only by playing, he can prove to himself and others— above all to himself and his mother, whose condemning gaze he constantly feels on himself from somewhere above, as he confessed to me once when he was drunk. Despite all of this, heaven hasn't given up on him completely. A bit of good luck, a little joy is in store for him too, poor guy.

He astonishes me, the modern Sisyphus with small dice cubes no less heavy than the stone of the ancient Greek, for he invested in them no less than the meaning of his whole life.

Mancha Satbeyevich's past is dark. He entered the reading room hunched over, concentrated, with a pitiful, obsequious smile on his face. His dark and repulsive past perched in the hall. This was the feeling I had every time. I could even feel the fetid smell of his past. It followed him on the streets, menacingly towering above his head. I can't say whether the past haunted the old man, depriving him of sleep and peace, or whether he carried it with him everywhere, carefully, devotedly, lovingly.

I considered his self-justification about the selective nature of his work delusional, when he pawned those who betrayed others, obviously innocent. But I have no proof that the old man informed on his neighbors, friends, and relatives. Perhaps, judging by the happy, but not carnivorous sparkle in his eyes when he inadvertently throws out a nostalgic remark about his past, he did this solely out of his personal disposition, but in no way out of anyone's coercion, not out of fear or a desire to please, for casual or official profit. Even if he didn't lie, then I still don't know everything he experienced. I don't know what considerations he used when choosing his next victim. Although it sounds wild and implausible, he could really be a kind of people's avenger, which he wants to assure me of, and caused troubles only to scoundrels. It is possible, although difficult, to imagine such a failure in a well-thought-out and well-established mechanism of mass extermination. The idea of fair retribution, supposedly initially included in the mechanism, was sometimes implemented, despite everything.

I admit, he could be wrong about his new victim. What if that was a decent person, a good family man, a loving husband and an affectionate father, reputationally untainted, who did not deserve Kolyma and Magadan? Or the same kind of Robin Hood as Mancha Satbeyevich himself? But if Mancha Satbeyevich voluntarily, with a deep awareness of his duty, invaded the area of the forbidden, then he must answer for it himself. Let the bumps of the afterlife land onto his wrinkled bald head. I can't help him with it. I see a pitiful, weak old man, who, perhaps, on top of everything else, carries his own hell in his soul: Remorse, late repentance, and so on. He wanted to

The Shore of Night | 421

survive at any cost. The thirst for life was so strong in him that no prohibitions or obstacles mattered. I see how he is now: He needs warmth. I'm becoming sentimental, so I'll stop talking about this. I cut him some slack.

Let's imagine another picture. When Mancha Satbeyevich was still Mancha, a barefoot and snotty-nosed boy, then a rural Komsomol member, he took off his rawhide boots made of buffalo skin and for the first time put on boots with real soles, which were unusually tight, and girded himself with a wide army belt, a gift from his older brother. He idolized the goat-bearded Iron Felix and dreamed of becoming a security officer. But it didn't work out; fate tripped him up. Either he came from wealthy peasants, or his father acted unreliably in 1921 by reacting to collectivization without any enthusiasm, or he himself had flat feet, urinary incontinence, sudden diarrhea, or other ailments. In a word, his way to the halls of officialdom was barred. So, he decided to carry things out semi-officially, in the darkness and shame of denunciation.

Or he didn't have the spirit for it, and is now composing his broken, failed life. The fulfillment of a dream is beyond moral principles.

I largely invented Mancha Satbeyevich's past. I invented it from the scarce details that he told me. If I treated the dead in the footnotes the same way, why should I treat the living differently? No, I don't paint the dead and the living with the same brush. There is a significant difference between them, and I know what it is. I thought about it. That's how my restless mind works. I can name many external and internal features that will allow a less experienced one or someone who has never bothered his brain, but who unconditionally believes his eyes, to instantly distinguish the dead from the living.

I also know that if you pierce someone with your gaze, going to their depths, down to the smallest units, down to the quark, then you will not be able to distinguish the self-satisfied dead from the restless living.

But I don't know what to do with this knowledge. Nothing comes from it, or nothing happens, so I will not develop this topic further.

I didn't want to know Mancha Satbeyevich more than my eyes have seen. I didn't want to plunge into the darkness of his life. Sometimes, he hinted at his informant past. It was only because, in his words, he had it and always carried it with him, hiding it deep down in his lonely heart. He had nothing else in his life.

Beslan was surprised that even after several days Natela's departure did not cause in him the storm that he'd expected. The only thing was that, at first, he felt unusual while returning home at night. Something was missing. As if the established order or ritual had been violated. His soul did not even think of yearning for her, but his flesh languished with exponentially growing force. Time after time, his imagination depicted Natela's charms, her supple living flesh, her dizzying smell. Sweetly, feeling some longing in his groin, he remembered how she surrendered herself entirely to his undivided power, detachedly, as if her soul was not there. There was so much faith in him for her selflessness. Sometimes he felt afraid: A woman older than he was, who had some life experience, trusted him, only yesterday a boy. His shoulders, back, and body ached from responsibility. She trusted him like a teenager, a schoolgirl who had fallen in love for the first time, and not with anyone, but with her strict teacher. The deafness and muteness in terms of bodily sensations made her completely helpless. She gave up

The Shore of Night | 423

her body, renounced it, looked at it from somewhere on the side, like a soul, having soared away, looks at an abandoned dead body. She was terribly silent.

After some time, after the carnal lust, sleepless nights, a lot of cigarettes, his melancholy suddenly subsided, and his flesh was reconciled and cooled down. He stopped dreaming of her. Before that, many nights in a row, when he fell asleep, tired of memories and imagination, Natela appeared in a dream. He saw himself with her so vividly that, upon waking, he could still feel her warmth in his hands and experience her scent. She was more real and desirable than she had ever been for real. Then she sweetly tormented him all day. He was in love with her image, revealed in a dream. It was very real.

And yet this was not the storm that he had been waiting for and that he secretly feared. Because if his melancholy had become extreme and unbearable, he would have gone after Natela. But this idea has never entered his head. It was as if his heart had nothing to do with physical longing, did not join it. It remained lonely, deaf, unconscious. This surprised Beslan. He didn't even think whether Natela had settled down, whether everything was going well for her. He didn't even think to call her. She gave him the phone number of her friend at whose place she planned to stay until she found something. She gave the number "just in case," although she guessed that this case was unlikely to come to pass.

Beslan explained to himself that his heart did not participate in all this only because his contact with Natela was physical. The feelings of the heart were absent, replaced by the habit of always talking to each other because it was uneasy, awkward, even a little scary to remain silent while being close, together. In moments of other silences, Beslan felt that everything was unreal and useless. Who am I? Who is she? Why am I here? She's a stranger (as if others were not). What can connect me with her? Unanswered questions jumped inside his head. At those moments he freed his tongue, constrained by the awkwardness of the situation, to hide the blinding fury of these questions in his voice and words.

But Natela needed him. She constantly told him things, often in few words, omitting unimportant or inconvenient details, which is why her stories always suffered from excessive brevity and blank spots. Beslan was not always able to complete them.

This thought first came to him at the intersection of two streets—one more or less dressed in concrete, running from the railway to the sea, and the other unpaved, sprinkled with gravel, uneven, with puddles from the recent rain. Here was a crossroads of the melancholy which suddenly gripped Beslan. He was targeted by it. Such sadness and hopelessness were so spread thickly, all around him like tar, that he wanted to shoot himself. This was the only way out of the deadlock at the junction of the two roads. This thought came suddenly and unexpectedly like melancholy. In past, it had never fired, but, apparently, it was loaded, and the trigger was also cocked. But now was the time. Maybe the air was special after two days of rain with only short pauses. The belated fall heat was washed away and at night, and especially in the mornings, it became chilly. Maybe the light from the setting sun was especially soft, gentle, sad, and colored everything around accordingly. Maybe it was because for a few seconds he found himself completely alone, although not far away there was a five-story building and there were probably people living in it, hidden by the walls. The other, busier streets were also

The Shore of Night | 425

visible in all four directions. The cars and pedestrians scurried there. Suddenly, everything disappeared. He found himself in some sort of void. It was a short but terrible moment. Beslan's hand unconsciously reached for the Makarov gun, which he always had under his jacket hung behind his belt. Had he stayed a little longer—even for the time necessary to pull it out, cock the trigger, put it to his temple—he would have been left lying as a corpse at the crossroads of seven roads. In fact, just two miserable underdeveloped streets, the names of which were unknown to him. They were so short that they would hardly have been worthy of names. Leaning on the mature streets, they completed themselves. He would have remained lying there, holed by a nine-millimeter bulldog bullet. But Beslan, as if spurred on by someone's authoritative voice, ordering him not to dare, hastily and even timidly put his hand in a pocket and slowly (he wanted to be sure whether this desire was a random impulse or not, and whether it would catch up with him again; it didn't catch up with him) went towards the sea.

Sometimes, passing by, Beslan looked into the intercity telephone station. He walked around the boxes, hearing fragments of conversations—"hello!", "how are you?", "goodbye!"—with which people fill the emptiness of life. He also wanted to enter one of the telephone boxes, pick up a cold handset, and then, after a long conversation, put it back, warm from his palm, ear, and breath. But Beslan had no one and nowhere to call. Natela had left his life. He did not dare call her. Feeling the foolishness of his position, he hastily left the call room.

He saw one weirdo several times there. After the war, people from the mental underground suddenly crawled out of their dark holes and flooded Sukhumi in unexpected numbers. Clearly, he was one of them. They usually meet in negotiated places, as if by agreement they have divided the city among themselves and perform some service. (Their service, apparently, was to ensure that the townspeople see the mark on the scale with their own eyes, dangerous even to approach, to cross, moreover, that they avoided it, and Sukhumi looks normal in a general sense.) There are also pass-through passengers, who march through the streets, waving their hands, or lively talking with an invisible interlocutor, making impossible grimaces, and sending curses to someone, or trying to shake hands with everyone they meet.

This one was of the locals. Usually, you could find him near the telephone room.

He is dressed poorly, but neatly, not without panache, but at the same time clumsily. A short, wide red tie of a bygone fashion, a bright shirt with some sort of South American pattern, and a sombrero. This gave rise to calling him Macho. All year round, yellow shoes with worn-out heels, a shabby red jacket, worn off-white jeans, and a signet shining on his left ring finger. He has a thin mustache, a stroke of mascara turning black above his lips. He is always clean-shaven and smells of cheap cologne. In summer, he wears sunglasses. He always keeps a rather plump folder on a thin belt, made of faux leather. Nobody knows what's in that folder.

He entered the telephone room with confident firm step. With the same firm step, he walked towards the order window, where a cow-eyed telephone operator sat. She looked at him smirking but didn't say anything.

"Can I have a call?"

"You can," said the cow-eyed operator, not at all surprised by the inappropriateness of the question. Apparently, this was not the first time.

The Shore of Night | 427

"Wherever I want?"

"Yes".

"To Japan?"

"Yes".

"And to South Africa, to the Cape of Good Hope?"

"Yes".

"And to Cape Horn?"

"Yes".

"And to Australia?"

"Yes".

"And to Georgia?!" he asks in surprise.

"Yes . . ." She says, adding, taken aback, "You must have permission."

"And you said 'everywhere,'" he said not without malice. "However, I don't need to call there. Unlike others, I don't have anyone there . . . Does everyone get permission?"

"So far no one has complained . . . Don't delay the line, write the city and phone number." She pushes a piece of paper and a pen towards him.

He moves away from the window and, looking around cautiously, as if afraid that someone might peep, writes down the country, city, and phone number. Then he carries the piece of paper folded in four to the window, pinching it with his fingers so that it does not splay out from the grandiosity of the secret it contains and doesn't peep out for everyone to see. The operator opens the "secret," then begins to look for the country and city in the thick reference book. She can't find it.

"You're at it again!"

"What?!"

"There is no such city here, and there is no country either . . ."

"It can't be!"

428 | *Daur Nachkebia*

"It is!"

"There are so many new things around . . . they had to appear by now!"

He is disappointed and almost crying.

"Nothing has appeared and nothing will appear!" the operator mercilessly cuts him off.

"But I need to call!"

"Then call."

"But you say that there is no such country and no such city!"

"Call somewhere else."

"But I dreamed of this city, this country and this number!"

"Go to sleep again, maybe you'll dream something else, closer and more real."

"Please look again!"

"Mister, you're stopping me from work!"

Several people had gathered near the window while Macho was finding out whether the country and city he dreamed of actually existed or not. Waiting for their turn, they started to complain.

Macho walks away with his head down.

Beslan watched this scene more than once and always with a mixed feeling of resentment for the unfortunate Macho and fear of what was hidden behind this seemingly simple incident.

*In the morning, we walked past the cemetery. The sun had not yet risen, ripening for a long hot day somewhere behind the mountains. Its light was timid and weak, but it did draw a clear jagged silhouette of the mountains in the sky. The fog spread all around, the trees stood out from it like ghosts whose legs had been*

The Shore of Night | 429

*lopped off. It gradually dissipated, melted, but not entirely, only in shreds, illegible scraps. Little by little, the heavy materiality of the world surrounded us predatorily, as if taking aim. In the gorge, which became visible from the height of the village, the thick fog lingered for a long time. We couldn't hear the river from here. Flowing out of the fog where the tightness of the gorge suddenly disappeared, it continued motionless and leaden along a narrow and short valley, only to be squeezed back again by the hills.*

*A few hours ago, when the night began to enjoy bringing all its darkness down on us, we crossed the river, cold and fast. Like most of us, I kept my boots and clothes on when we entered the water. It turned out to be for the best. Some of those who took off their shoes slipped on smooth stones and fell down to the water, unable to resist the current. We were equipped solidly: a machine gun, dispenser magazines a "bra" tightly wrapped around the chest, a helmet, grenades hanging on the belt like unbelievable grapes, a mukha,[5] or even two. With cargo like this, falling into the water would end badly. (I prudently carry grenades in my pockets. It might sound funny or even stupid. But there is always a chance that, if a grenade is dangling on a belt, the safety pin will get caught on something and explode. But this is so unlikely that even if I had wandered all my life and a little longer through our impassable thickets, I'd hardly met a twig grasping enough to catch the ring and pull it out. And yet, knowing about the insidiousness of fate, I did everything I could to out-trick her.)*

*I was lucky, and everyone crossed the river wet but safe.*

I haven't dried out yet. When the wind blows, my pants stick to my legs giving me an unpleasant chill, reminding me of the river. Once upon a time—it seems to me that it was a long time ago, like last year's dream—I wanted to flow with it, and when I thought about its dark waters in quiet deep places, I felt good. I was almost happy. Although I no longer know what "happiness" means. I wanted only one thing: to dissolve completely in the river, as if I had never existed. I didn't want to die in the dark waters, but to be a river, so that I, a biped without feathers, would not be heard or breathe, so that I would be irrevocably removed from any form of memory.

Now I crossed the river that I had dreamed of, and its waters, having slightly touched me, partly flowed away and partly remained in my shoes and trousers. They will dry out. The river will merge with the sea. Our brief contact—when I was crossing the river, holding the machine gun above my head, and when the river flowed foamily and talkatively around me—will vanish too. The river's serenely clear fluid soul and its warm body that wanted me will disappear as well, leaving no visible trace beyond in my finite memory. For the river, my warmth was an accidental and ridiculously short-lived touch. Maybe it didn't even have time to notice it. The river was colossal in age and size, but I was small. My warmth was insignificant to it. I spent with the river only a few moments. I remembered the river and the joy I felt while I was with it. My feet carefully stepped on the stones and carried me to the other bank. I surrendered to the river with all my heart. I imagined that it was waiting for me, and now it takes me in such a tight, loud grip because it yearned for me. It is in a hurry to remember me, because it knows that I will soon leave, and we will part forever. Painfully, I felt something important was going to happen which was not about to happen at all. I went ashore. The water began to flow off me, and the good things I felt flowed away with it. Nothing changed either around me or in me. I gradually returned to the same state of mind. The feeling of unity with the river, with its mystery, was gone. I was already suspicious of all this. I felt even somewhat embarrassed for my delight.

Then we climbed the slope, dark and menacingly hanging above us. The higher we climbed, the paler and more inconspicuous the stars became, as if they had been thrown into a muddy stream. The powder of the Milky Way disappeared. Then other weaker stars faded too.

We went up to the flat outskirts of the village. To be more precise, the village was still quite far away, but many paths, clearly trodden not so much by wild animals as by patient cattle, indicated the proximity of human habitation. It encouraged us: The goal is just around the corner. But at the same time, we were wary, because danger was getting closer to us.

Only a few stars remained in the sky. There were more on the west side, but they hung sadly and hopelessly. It seemed that the light of the rising sun had driven them away to this edge of the sky.

The group sent ahead to check the surroundings returned with surprising news: The village was empty! Located on a narrow plateau stretching along the river, the village was the farthest settlement north of Sukhumi, further away there were mountains. It was pointless to mount a defense here—the terrain did not allow it, and the residents withdrew in advance.

432 | *Daur Nachkebia*

Silence. Our barely sounding steps are drowned in it. The night goes further and further, backing away like a crustacean, with its eyes closed. At this pre-dawn hour, when life is so impossibly new and feels like an outlandish and unrealizable dream, we trampled past the cemetery, barely disturbing the heavy damp dust that still covered the dewy night.

The road was going up. When it and us with it tiredly climbed up the hill, crosses and cemetery fencing appeared from the fog on the right. Under the watchful gaze of the faces in the portraits from the gravestones, we trudged on.

It seemed to me that their eyes were watching us with some kind of gloating, self-confident impudence, arrogance. I couldn't get my head around the feeling that the dead, long turned to dust, were somehow superior to us. It was written all over their faces that expressed reaction not to the moment the picture was taken but, as each of us thought, to our camouflage-armed, multi-legged procession. The faces in the portraits lived their own lives, and their owners, who had rotted in the ground, somehow continued through them. The dead seemed to say: we have snatched away from eternity a fatty and tasty morsel—our life. Here it is, under the oval of our faces, fitting into the dash between the dates of birth and death. What could be more convincing and clearer than this dash. You still must snatch your share from eternity with your teeth. There is a dark unknown before you. We have already experienced it. The advantage is on our side.

But with their inevitable dash, or rather a dash of oblivion, they barely scratched the body of eternity, have bitten it toothlessly. The only thing they got was the perpetuity of a gravestone. Eternity, fully equipped and cold eyed, rustled past

The Shore of Night | 433

ponderously and detachedly, just as we rustled past, briefly noting with our tired brains the crosses and twisted fence of the cemetery.

We rustled past. But after a while I returned.

We settled into houses that had survived the shelling. There were the fresh traces of life that had been passing here in anxious anticipation only a couple of days ago.

An empty house, with things abandoned in a panicked rush. They picked up the most necessary things that would still be useful. But here, it seems, the mess was carried out by our people, those who visited here before us. No war story could pass without an image of heart-melting toys, and a girl in a torn dress, with her huge questioning eyes and a one-legged doll in her hands. It was really there—no girl, only toys lying everywhere—because war has a bad taste. Recently people have lived here, walked, talked, ate, breathed, in a word, did everything that people are supposed to do. They even had thoughts. They also had feelings, more complex than those of a casual and familiar nature. So-called mental life took place in them—a thing, I tell you, unimaginably uncanny, slimy, disgusting, shameful, and indecent. But man, an animal by nature, is doomed to this additional weight, to this dirty work of the soul—spirituality. Why not simply enjoy the unpretentious pleasures of bodily existence, follow the natural urges of the flesh in spite of and against the soul?

The house is empty. The inhabitants have left, others have come, but the house is still dead.

After a sleepless night, most of us fell asleep. You could hear a discordant snoring. I was about to pass out, but as soon as I closed my eyes ovals, crosses, and metal bars appeared in front of me.

I went to the cemetery where the dead jealously keep their secrets under the stone slabs.

The sun had already risen and was blazing over the mountains. In my head, there was a haze of unsteady thoughts inspired by the night march. Something was wearily wandering around in my skull, blindly poking at its walls. But I've climbed the hill, the fresh morning breeze has touched me, and my head has started clearing up.

The cemetery was mixed. There were Abkhazians, Georgians, Armenians, Russians, Jews, Greeks. I had a hard time making out the inscriptions on the gravestones. The voiced names seemed to make both the life and death of those lying under the stones more real. The faces looking at me from the pictures acquired a sound component, which spoke about them no less than their eyes. I couldn't make out one last name. It was half erased, so it couldn't name the grave's owner properly. It was a not-so-old man wearing a papakha.[6] He looked at me with almost the same expectation which he once had looking into the camera lens. At that time, he was probably assured that the impartial eye of the heavy apparatus pointed at him, around which the rogue photographer was fussing, would capture and preserve his mustache and sadness in his eyes for eternity. But what did he expect from me now, why is he looking unblinkingly? I didn't know his name, so there was no way he could become close to me. There was only a face, eyes, papakha, mustache, but no name. In the sounds of our names, there is more of us than in our bones and meat. Maybe we are born just to have a name they call us. His name merged with black stones and was silent. The mustache man tried to break through the granite muteness and reach out to me. He succeeded: The longer I looked at him, the more familiar, dearer

The Shore of Night | 435

to me he became. I felt so sorry for him. He walked the path
that I still have ahead much earlier than me. He already knew
some things. But he did not give me any signs from his distance. There was not even a hint in his eyes, which looked sad
and at the same time cold. His eyes demanded that I clearly explain to him what had happened with him that was so loud and
burning and why it ended so quickly, in one breath. Probably,
death, where he is stuck, is very boring. But life is something,
and who, if not the living, can explain it.

*What could I say to this persistent mustache guy? Don't think too
much, my friend, and continue to rot. You've been very successful
in doing it the last half a century. I can't help you; I understand
less in life than you. It seems like it's easier for you because
you've been trampling the ground longer than me. There's such
hopelessness and sadness in your eyes. You knew it quite well with
this bitch who fooled you so badly. Sadness in the eyes develops
like wrinkles. It requires time.*

*You also, it seems, spoke about offensive brevity and haste.
There's nothing you can do about it, brother. What was destined
came to pass. You were carried in a coffin on helpful and joyful
shoulders. What else could they do with you? They took you
away from sight. No one needed you anymore. You disturbed
everyone: Relatives, neighbors, acquaintances, even those who
did not know you but accidentally heard about your death and
felt uncomfortable, annoyed, as if you had done something
indecent, shameful, let's say, farted in public. You created great*

*inconvenience for everyone, man, and everyone couldn't wait to forget you as soon as possible. Now you want me to remember you, you impudently climb into my soul, you are looking for a place in me to continue your existence for some time. After all, while I think about you, consider that you continue to live. You want me to carry you on my back for the time allotted to me, as if without you my load is not enough. I have figured it out for you. You don't care what life is, you just want to live in any form, to prolong the memory of yourself, even for the briefest moment.*

*The dead man grabbed me with his bony hands. He impertinently stuck to me so that I would leave the cemetery with him, hidden him deep in my memory and, perhaps, in my heart.*

*I left not alone. I took him with me, and on the way, I imagined what he thought, what he wanted, what he lived. I tried to become him. From the scant information—a mustache, a papakha, sad eyes, a few wrinkles, and an insatiable thirst for life—I constructed his fate. It could not exactly coincide with what his real life was. But that didn't matter. He existed, and the gravestone confirmed that. I just tried on one of the possible clothes in which, under a different set of circumstances, he could have gone through life. I made up the path of this life, sometimes straight, sometimes intricately winding, labyrinthine, changing the attire of my hero. I was curious to see how a slight move of the path sometimes led to a complete change in the traveler, both externally and internally. Let's say he was a highwayman who killed more than once and finally fell at the hands of*

The Shore of Night | 437

a bloodthirsty avenger, or a lawman's bullet overtook him. In
this case, something stony, hard appeared in his appearance.
I attributed the obvious sadness in his eyes either to late
repentance, or to an involuntary sign of a latent internal struggle
which had little in common with repentance. He was not aware
of his sins. Another force spoke through him. It was not his soul
that ached within him, but something else—more likely, a regret
about the brevity of life.

Maybe he was an unremarkable person with a boring,
gray fate. He was born, seemed to live, and died for real. What
depended on him? He was caught up in such a frantic stream
that he only had enough strength for a few hand waves. But
the stream that carried him away did not even notice that. He
managed to make the incomprehensible trinity of birth, life, and
death so ordinary. Not only from an external perspective but also
for himself. He was so boring. He lived life as a duty, without joy.
And he died as unnoticed as he lived.

Maybe he was a man who had fully experienced the
bitterness of life. A man who lost loved ones and friends.
Everything was difficult for him, failures followed him all his life.
On top of this, health problems and a premonition of an early
death. But he managed to take a wife and give birth to his heir.
This was the only bright spot in the darkness that surrounded
and filled him. He died with the understanding that he had
succeeded in something. His seed had sprouted. A drop of light
would remain from him. Clutching the hem of his wife, who

was fussing over him as he died, his little son cried over him constantly whipping his snot with his dirty sleeve. In his features, he recognized himself with hope and inexplicable, bone-chilling horror.

Well, why do I need him? He has been dust for a long time. His bones are in the dark belly of the earth, while I am still alive and stomping in my heavy, dusty black boots. In a few minutes, I'll be with my people. I will eat something, most likely condensed milk with bread, which already makes me sick, although a stew, no matter how much adjika you add, makes me even sicker. Then I'll fall asleep.

But for now, I keep thinking about that mustache stranger. Something connects me to him. I can't understand what. He seems to be superfluous and random on my path, and yet he holds me tightly. It's as if he whispers to me, "I'm not a stranger to you ..." It's not even just him who whispers, but all the graves. The dead in different voices whisper to me from under each gravestone: "We are not strangers to you ..." The whole cemetery whispers, "We are not strangers to you ..."

I laid in each of these graves. In the one that looks pre-revolutionary, with a plain stone cross at the head. Also, in the luxurious one with a massive marble slab and a marble bust of a middle-aged man, already bald, large-faced, with a double chin. In that modest one, too: An iron fence, granite tiles with life dates. I lay in each one, already rotted into dust, forgotten by

*everyone who knew me and loved me. They, who knew me and
loved me, also turned to dust long ago.*

*During life we pass each other by. I have always thought
little about myself. I thought more about others, lived their lives.
Not in the compassionate sense, I'm not that kind of person.
But in my phantasy. I imagined someone else's soul, always
an abyss. Falling into it makes us feel united, overcoming our
loneliness.*

He thought about Madina more and more often. The questions poured out at him: What is love? How to distinguish real love from fake love? Is it possible to fall in love not immediately, but over time, becoming more and more ignited by another being, previously a complete stranger? Passion—not even passion, rather habit, which Beslan called a vocation—to weigh everything, measure, explore with an armed eye, take it apart and, having conjured over the corpse, put it back together again, in a word, the scientific approach did not let him go here either. It silenced the voice of the heart with all sorts of doubts.

But everything told him that love is a sudden illness which cannot be started on purpose and cannot be cultivated through any sort of self-hypnosis. Something similar to what he had with Natela at the beginning until everything went downhill and turned to dust. But it is different with Madina. Or is he deceiving himself? If, over time, Madina becomes his beloved, won't he become cold to her the same way he cooled towards Natela?

Every day he thought more and more about Madina.

*My notes would unlikely interest anyone. Not to mention whether
anyone would even find out about them. I don't really care.
A thorough or articulated thought is not as important, or rather,
not as inevitable, as a written one. I feel free after
I write something. It is the most general description of my
writing experience. One can call it a duty. Having fulfilled
a duty, everyone feels calmer. So do I.*

*My notes are the fulfillment of such a duty. There is no war
in them, no blood and dirt, although I seem to be an eyewitness.
With my eyes, I see what is happening around me. But I don't
crawl out of my cocoon. I don't encroach on what is beyond
my gaze. I get snippets of reality from other people. I imagine
how everything happens in real life, but I can't vouch for the
authenticity. We are moving forward. We are climbing
a mountain, then descending into a gorge, crossing a river. All
this in order to recapture Sukhumi from the Georgians. They
hold it solidly. The rest of Abkhazia is under their occupation too.
I know this for sure. I don't want to know more.*

*Speaking in B.N's words, I am the infinitely small value, an
unremarkable insignificant detail in a mechanism, exceeding
me in size and power many times over. But I am the detail
with greedy eyes. I look at everything and everyone from my
dark corner. I don't miss anything. But I can't say I memorize
everything. Why overload yourself with memorization?*

*I fought in several battles, but I cannot describe them. I can
only tell you about my feelings: how scary it is at first—your legs*

*and arms go numb, it seems like you will never move again, and*
*then you suddenly become insensitive and do what you need to*
*do. You shoot, kill, run if necessary, you hide your head and spew*
*out curses all the time. I shout them as loudly as possible, in all*
*your cracked voice, hiding the resentment for your fate. But how*
*to come up with a realistic representation of what is unfolding—*
*it's impossible.*

*Any description lacks something essential. The description is*
*like a background, but another thing emerges in the dimensions*
*not characteristic of our world. If I only could convey this 'other*
*thing,' its breath. In this case, literature would gasp out its life.*
*The writers, not those who just tell stories, attempt to convey this*
*other thing and waste piles of paper and their mental recourses.*
*How much nerves and time! A lot of time and a lot of nerves.*
*Literature is still an ongoing process, and unlike the reading*
*audience, who have long lost faith in the ability of literature*
*to chew and put something else into their mouths, the writing*
*fraternity is not diminishing. It proves that something else has*
*not yet been captured in words, not squeezed into a text, even if it*
*is three times a Nobel laureate.*

*If every person dies on a bridge when he comprehends*
*something else or is on the threshold of that comprehension, then*
*literature suffers the same fate.*

What were Adgur A. and M. talking about? Did Adgur A.
esteem their conversation too highly? Obviously, as he wrote

the next morning when he was still under the sway of the preceding day's events, he saw their entire conversation as full of unusual content and meaning. But why then did he cross out most things so thoroughly, keeping only his astonished, even bombastic assessment? When did he cross things out: The same morning or a few days later, after re-reading it and thinking it through? What was he suddenly afraid of? Maybe he didn't want to make things known to others? This is a mystery. Maybe everything they said to each other out of passion and with such romantic ornamentation—the war, the night, the stars, the river—the next morning seemed to him like nonsense? Maybe, it was simply a failure, which especially often happens to writers who occasionally work at night. You scribble with inspiration, childish glee, endless self-joy. But when you read it in the merciless light of day, you see just the delirium of a graphomaniac, which makes you feel embarrassed. Your face burns with the heat of shame. A similar thing happened to them that night: They succumbed to the deception of the night and spoke as the highest truth what the night had whispered to them.

But he still retained his assessment. This means that this was not nonsense, but self-disclosure to such limits that cannot be trusted even to paper. It must remain in a verbal form and should not be written down. In the end, the person who writes is an exception, perhaps, a soul dislocation. But the person who speaks is everywhere, he is the one who truly lives, he is evident. People don't always say smart things to each other. More often it's the opposite. But the words are full of meaning for them. The words bear an imprint of peoples' personalities, fate. People live by what and how they say. The latter, 'how they say,' is even more important. In general, words are spoken not

The Shore of Night | 443

to convey meaning. When it happens, people are indifferent to each other and are only interested in words. What's needed to be conveyed is a feeling. That's why a person talks. What is important is not what is said, but how it is said, in what voice, for what purpose.

Beslan could not stand it and shared with Mancha Satbeyevich his doubts about his past. He was so cruel—apparently because of the sour wine, to which the old man treated him, bragging about his nephews' attention and care for him. Beslan asked directly: "Do you have blood on your hands, Mancha Satbeyevich?" Surprised by the sudden question, the old man shuddered. He looked at Beslan coldly, even with a veiled anger. But quickly pulling himself together, he smiled obsequiously and muttered through his teeth: "No, young man . . . You still don't understand what was happening then. People were given a choice: Good or evil? By choosing, they helped the triumph of justice. I assure you, none of the guilty escaped punishment. There were no innocent people, everyone was guilty . . ."

"And you too?"

"Some less, some more. I'm less than you think . . ."

"You say strange things, Mikhail Stepanovich. Explain yourself."

Beslan felt that he had drunk too much but could not stop. After the war, he hadn't drunk like that for a while. A petty thought came to his mind: Had the old man put something in the wine? There was such a fog in Beslan's head. But, ashamed of his absurd suspicion, he quickly pushed it away.

"It's difficult to explain, but it's possible. Life was at the limit, on the edge of the abyss, as the poet said. Everyone wanted to survive, but at what cost? A great test befell the children of men. They faced the question: What is more precious to a person—his life or his conscience? Both life and conscience are given to us by God. I believe in God, although I have never admitted it. You understand that it was impossible to believe in God then. And I did not believe by command. That is, I didn't believe in words and not in deeds. I believed in God deep in my heart. Everything I did was measured against him, by asking for his advice, consent, and blessing. So, both life and conscience are given to us by God. We have to choose what is more important. He said: For whoever wants to save their life, will lose his soul. You can lose your soul only by living according to your conscience. He spoke, but we didn't listen. The body is visible, tangible, olfactory, it breathes and lives, it is close, it is so dear, and we cannot separate ourselves from it. But you cannot touch with your hands either the conscience or the soul. A person prefers the body, that is, life, or rather, the tiny life of his body, ridiculously short-lived, but he destroys the soul. Out of his stupidity, cowardice, and lack of faith, he exchanges eternity for the momentary, the fleeting, the transitory. This is mind boggling! Stalin was an instrument of providence, a plague that God sent on people to test them once again. Those who have passed the test are walking in heaven. They are blessed to have eternity in their pocket. But I think there are not many of them. The majority are languishing in hell. Not even in purgatory. Death awaits them, eternal death . . ."

"And where do you think Stalin is?"

"This is a difficult question, young man. I have thought about it. But my knowledge of theology is clearly not enough to resolve it. Common sense says that if he was an instrument of higher powers, then all guilt is removed from him. But here it may also be that Stalin was God's instrument not directly,

The Shore of Night | 445

but by his own will—just as every trial in life is an instrument. Then he too will burn in hell. Then again, it is difficult to believe that God could conspire with a mortal in order to test other mortals. We are all a test for each other."

"Even you and me?"

"Yes, us too, can you imagine? I am old and decrepit and already have one foot in the grave, but it is no coincidence that we met. I don't know what you will take away from meeting me, your future life will show that, I will no longer know about it, but it means a lot to me. I never told anyone what I told you today. Now I feel better. I have carried this load all my life, and it was hard, I assure you. But I reported it, and now I can . . ."

"Die?"

"You guessed it, young man: Die. It's easier to die when at least one soul knows the truth about you. After all, the two who knew me by sight had already died. In my documents, I went by a pseudonym."

"But God knows, isn't that enough?"

"God! He is inconceivable. But I am still alive, and a man speaks in me. As weak and mortal as you. I appeal to a man."

"Do you want me to put in a good word for you with him?"

Mancha Satbeyevich winced with annoyance at the vulgar simplification. Beslan felt ashamed again. Beslan did not expect the old man not to be as simple as he seemed. But, on the other hand, looking for the reason for the collapse of the USSR in *Pravda*? After all, for that, one's brains had to be pretty scrambled.

"No one's word, no one's recommendation would help there. They don't accept people into the Party!" The old man smiled at his joke, but it didn't touch Beslan. It wasn't a good joke. The old man removed the smile from his face, realizing that he had made a mistake with this joke. "I don't need your intercession, I can speak for myself. But like everyone else, and you one day, I will not have to say anything. As you rightly noted, up there everything is known about us. Our most secret thoughts and desires are known, not to mention our deeds. They don't hold any judgment there and don't weigh anything on any scales. Our soul has barely left the body when everything has already been weighed, measured and a decision has been made. This decision is not subject to discussion or appeal. Neither you nor I will be able to correct it."

*Why does he always nail me down?* Beslan thought. As if in a friendly manner, but in fact with intent? Does he want to say that he and I are one and the same? Is he identifying himself with me? We are inseparable, that's what he wants to tell me. He wants to say that the same thing awaits me—a collapse. What is his life if not a collapse? So, he stood up on these ruins and started talking about God, about conscience! When his unwavering hand signed denunciations, he probably didn't remember about God. He put him in a corner, with His face to the wall. But now, on the threshold, he suddenly remembered, he wants to atone for his sins.

Beslan thought through all this, and for the third time that evening he felt ashamed. Wine is to blame, he said to himself. He didn't believe himself and wondered in fear whether he had really changed so much.

"And yet, everything is not as smooth as you have presented it here, dear Mikhail Stepanovich. What does justice have to do with it? How could scoundrels, rapists, and murderers stand in a fraternal union with decent people to contribute to the triumph of justice?"

"On the gates of hell is written: 'Suum cuique.'"

The Shore of Night | 447

Then there was a long argument. They raised their voices while drinking more wine. The old man almost cried. Beslan even blamed him for the last war: "People like you made it happen, and then sat down quietly!"

"I couldn't get out of the city!" Mancha Satbeyevich justified himself, humiliated.

Beslan did not know that the old man had been in Sukhumi during the Georgian occupation.

Beslan was disgusted by the old man.

Those were times of the fullness of life because life was held by the feeblest tenure. Any wrong step or awkward word could ruin it. A overbearing power hung vigilantly over everyone. The secret recognition that he, pathetic, insignificant, had received a little of this power and the fate of several people depended on him, filled Mancha Satbeyevich with a keen sense of self- fulfillment. He could drink a lot and not get drunk. His head remained cool. His eyes tenaciously caught the slightest change in the face of his interlocutor. His ears noted all the shades of the speaker's voice. He unmistakably, with some kind of animal instinct, determined when the speaker was lying, and when he was telling the truth out of his stupid sincerity.

Now that same wine has loosened his own tongue. His obsequious smile, his humiliated self-justification, and his theory about the triumph of justice through denunciations and betrayals—everything disgusted Beslan.

*How did I not notice all this before?* he asked himself. He could not find an answer. It turned out that the old man had simply wrapped him around his little finger with his pitiful appearance. Beslan became his next victim. Bravo, old fart, you're still in shape. The young can't mess with you!

Macho. I have never seen him so out of control. I've heard, however, that twice a year he loses his temper and bursts out like a bubbling volcano. At such moments, he spouts nonsense that you can't help but listen to. A quiet and cautious man, who usually avoided his own shadow, suddenly became a protest against people, fate, and God. ". . . I can't get through to anyone. They don't answer my calls, and you still walk here as if nothing's happened, measuring the ground with your confident feet, forgetting that these feet will eventually lie in the darkness of the earth, gnawed by death, and no one will see that they are so white and fragile; the earth will cover them with eternal darkness, no one will ever dig them up and say that these are the bones of such and such, and it was not in vain that he walked on the earth for so many years for so many years, it was not in vain that he ate, drank, copulated and defecated, and sometimes thought, loved, suffered and then no one will love you, no one will feel sorry for you and cry for you—you have forgotten all this, all this has disappeared from your holey heads, your mind has flowed out along with your soul and therefore you will also be forgotten—none of you cares about my suffering, my pain, you are all focused on yourself and, at best, two or three people, your wife, father, mother, children and you don't care about anyone else, you don't care about the strangers, but they are not strangers, they are people too and they have a heart, I also have a heart, look, it's beating, I hear his voice, look how my chest rises and falls, this is my heart, I have a heart —you know that? but there is no God, he was here, but then he cowardly left the world, looking at the work of his hands, he left us alone and hid somewhere behind the clouds, sometimes he looks at us from above in horror, he sheds burning tears for our fate, but he does not interfere

The Shore of Night | 449

anywhere, he has no strength for this, he's too old and sick, he's sick of us, he's waiting for death to get rid of himself and of us, but we don't let him die in peace, we yell and scream, we talk on the phone, although it's impossible to get through to anyone—have you tried calling somewhere? I tried but nothing worked for me, there is no such city and no such country, and the number doesn't exist, they told me. If you don't believe me, go to that window where the beautiful cow-eyed girl is sitting, all made up, rude and unceremonious, and she will tell you that there is no such city and no such country and no such number. She told me that five minutes ago and get the hell out of here (she didn't say the last thing) but I'm sure she thought it, like she's tired of me. I come here almost every day and she probably thinks I'm crazy, but I'm not crazy, I just look the way I behave, I have documents in my folder, they confirm that I am sane, look how many of them I have, a lot of them, a stocker I knew was happy to give me this paper, although he didn't have a stamp, but look how beautifully he signed it, if you don't believe me, look here, there is his personal data with his family registration address, marital status, then his wife ran away from him, he beat her out of love, his birth place is indicated here, although there is no date when he died, but all passports lack that, although they promise to introduce new more advanced passports that will indicate when their owner has died, and I welcome this decision, it's time to bring order to this area! But before it wasn't written there and they roughly knew who would die when—I've been collecting them for a long time, going to different offices and medical institutions, wherever I went, they gave me a piece of paper with a stamp that I was in my right mind, my mind did not leave my head and I didn't lose it, but as it is, I fit my mind entirely, and when she said that, I believed her. Maybe I shouldn't have believed it? But why would she deceive me? All these people in the telephone boxes are talking to someone, I even heard the words they spoke to the person on the other end—hello! how are you? no, I don't have more money, still have some from the last time, you better come here, it's not like that, now here there are less robberies and murders, and the sea is unusually warm, it's been sunny—I miss you, Natela, I loved you, I love you even now, but you left so unexpectedly without saying anything, without warning that you may come back but you don't know, I can't go to you, my old parents can't stand it, and in general, why do you live there, you don't even see the sun properly, but it's warm here, summer is coming, the sea and I—but I don't believe that they are with anyone—they say they are talking to themselves, but they don't let me check—is the person talking on the phone actually talking to someone else invisible and distant, or is he talking to himself and has he secluded himself just to talk to himself out loud? I was told that there is no such country, no such city, no such number. Then what did I dream about?

Addressing himself to a crowd, one moving stream except a few curious people standing there and silently looking at the short man, Macho's monologue is accompanied by indescribable facial expressions and passionate dancing movements. His hands are always moving, as if he wanted to sculpt words out of thin air, turning them into something tangible and volumetric, so that they would penetrate and burn him. He takes the most diverse funny, absurd, monumental poses—each one with the same goal of conveying the confusion and tension of his preverbal soul. Sometimes various historical characters can be recognized in his speech. One can notice them in the

The Shore of Night | 451

timbre of his voice, the characteristic phrases, gestures, and facial expressions that made those people powerful to fool the gullible public, greedy for spectacles and terrifying stories. It's difficult to say whether he does it intentionally or is driven by his unconscious. However, he drives his listeners to colic, they cackle, laugh and from time to time shout out with delight the familiar names they recognize: Napoleon, Lenin, Hitler, Stalin, Khrushchev, Gorbachev, Yeltsin . . .

They bracketed their lives brutally. Inside those brackets were dates, the first and the last ones. Some managed to squeeze into them a fair amount of time, the so-called rich, long life. I can imagine the honor, hypocritical noise, and feigned grief with which they buried others. How envious they had been feeling.

Was there some secret here, or did everything happen according to that unreasonable animal instinct called fate? The hero has collected the years, without thinking much, just trusting his body as it is wise and would take you out. How can I calculate this from the meager data I had: The dates, supposedly, the main ones, a few remarkable lines that the tight-fisted author did not skimp on?

Everyone takes the most important things with them to the grave. It would be better to put only one date on the tombstones: The one that the deceased considered central in his life. That date exists in every destiny, the greatest and the most banal. I don't understand what the point is of indicating the date of birth and death. Who needs this? If the deceased lived a short life, is a passerby supposed to shed a hypocritical tear? If it's long, are you supposed to take it as an ideal? Maybe, it's all about identifying the period that the deceased supposedly took from eternity and supposedly made his own.

He is its private owner. No one will be able to appropriate this period because he filled it all with himself and no one will be able to squeeze in there. Is that it? Then it would be necessary to indicate only the age, let's say thirty-seven, or forty-three, or eighty-six. But no one thought of it. Everyone keeps putting there the dates of birth and death. In my view, it's better to have one date. There's more intrigue in that. It's not so straightforward and banal. Let's say, someone has it engraved as if on tablets: 1949, August 1, 4:41 p.m. This was the year, day and hour when he finally decided to resort to betrayal: To inform on his friend, neighbor, beloved, father . . . But no one knows about it anymore. It can be even more succinct: 4:41 p.m.—let not all cards be revealed.

But who would dare to reveal the truth about themselves? During life or after death—it's a hell of a lot. Everyone would lie to embellish and sweeten up their worthless lives. The dates in the wills, I guarantee, will be tied to events of ridiculous importance, like marriage or the birth of an idiot son. Some will be mistaken voluntarily. Only a few people are given the chance to know their life. Closing our eyes and covering our ears, we rush past life, sometimes without ever looking into its eyes.

Will I succeed in what others have managed casually, without blinking, sometimes even with some grace, as I can judge by their biographies? Is this a deceptive easiness? The life lived by others always seems easier, more bearable than your own.

The day will end, night will come. Then it will change into morning and another day. Night will come again. After all, they will not bring anything. Boring, stupid alternation of light and darkness. I am included in this cycle against my will. Nothing can be done about it.

The Shore of Night | 453

Here is Madina. She has buried herself in a book. She lost herself in the text, and people around her, including me, ceased to exist for her. A typical way to kill time: Disembodied, having forgotten yourself in lasting oblivion, you are wandering somewhere in unknown lands. Destroying time, smashing it to smithereens, turning it into dust is man's pipedream. A book is one of the ways to do this. Non-embalmed corpses, books of all colors and shades, of different formats and sizes stand in a row. We take them, skim them, read them. Our time, allotted to us in vast storerooms, decreases exactly in hours and minutes frozen in the corpse of a book.

But killing time is the same as killing yourself. The old-fashioned expression "the soul is yearning to go somewhere," baseless melancholy, sometimes gnawing at even the most petrified hearts, is nothing more than evidence of a person's desire to jump out of the seething stream of time that carries him into the unknown. Jump ashore, shake off the droplets. And then . . . ?

*Ideally, the text should be as simple as possible, even primitive. "Born, lived, died." The rest is the minor details. But nothing is ever clear with the second member of the triad: Did he really live or just look at the world through the meaningless eyes of a trembling creature? A detailed text would be needed to describe "the path of life and spiritual quests."*

*In reality, everything is simpler. If someone, even for one moment, was pierced by the feeling of the great mystery of existence, so much so that it made him numb, and the great horror and great joy overwhelmed him all over, then we can admit that he lived. Once is enough.*

*Man has come up with too many words. He is drowning in them. They are like a weight around his neck, pulling him to the bottom. The abundance of names distances us from the essence of things. This is not my idea, and it was said a long time ago, as far as I remember. We no longer see or hear the world as it really is. The world is obscured by a bellicose army of words. The Golden Age managed to live with a minimum of speech. Or maybe there were no words at all. An ideal world is a world where words are not needed, where they have long been thrown into the trash heap and forgotten. All human actions had clear, distinct contours. There was no difference between a word and a deed. Then every action began to acquire new words to justify the world's decline. Having eaten from the tree of knowledge, man replenished his previously meager vocabulary. Literature began then.*

That evening I unexpectedly got the blues, although this was not part of my plans for the next hundred years. I got emotional in the most shameful way.

No, I did not show a sudden momentary weakness with a single gesture. Speaking about the next hundred years, I guarantee that no matter what happens to me or to anyone else nearby, even if the whole world suddenly breaks loose, not a single muscle will tremble on my face, no treacherous moisture will cloud my vision.

("Treacherous moisture", "momentary weakness", "not a single muscle will flinch". The reader, I hope, can guess why

The Shore of Night | 455

I am acting so impolitely and ill-mannered. If he does not immediately pick up on what I am so rudely, indecently leading to, then I'd generously give him a hint. I don't want to dress the world in new words and thereby make it more bearable than it is. In order to make the world bearable, we cannot do without new words. Humanity is engaged in the invention of new words with manic constancy. We need to come up with more of them, squeeze them into text, and then, you see, the world will appear not as a bared beast, but as a fluffy one. However, Adgur A. has already written about something similar.)

I went to a cafe on the promenade. It was raining. I felt worse than ever. I thought hot coffee would dispel my despondency. I sat down at a table in a dim corner, away from prying eyes. There weren't too many curious eyes: A girl at the counter and a bully at the table close to her, apparently the owner. Of course, he deliberately folded back the edge of his jacket, showing a gun sticking out from his belt. In the evening in a post-war café, he couldn't live without it. He was sitting confidently, self-sufficiently, at peace with himself, drinking coffee and smoking. I almost envied him.

The girl smiled sweetly at first, but when she heard that it was only a cup of coffee, she could not hide her annoyance, turning sour, her face changing.

I took a sip. The tart coffee pleasantly burned my tongue and palate.

There was something unnatural in the silence that reigned around the three of us. We were neighbors but were sitting too far from each other.

She listened to music quietly. It barely reached my corner. Her lips silently repeated familiar words. Her head swayed slightly following the melody, as simple as the girl herself was.

He sat upright. Under a confident and arrogant expression on his face, he hid his discomfort and readiness for any turn of events.

Did he fight or not? It doesn't matter to me, and it's impossible to figure it out now. Touch anyone, and they would choke with anger: How dare they offend the defender of the Motherland, who shed his blood for freedom! You will never hear this from real guys. But there are too many fake heroes.

The girl started singing along to the melody in a louder voice. She turned to another track that had no words but an unusually piercing sound. Maybe it just seemed so to me. But what does it matter whether it was Mozart or someone less important?

I listened to her, frozen, forgetting about everything in the world. Suddenly something moved in me. My chest felt tight. A lump came to my throat. The melody sounded for about five minutes, no more. I did not move and did not touch my coffee. (It was music. You can't learn it by heart. But there are poems that make you want to die.)

I didn't know what to do with myself. I was caught unaware.

The meaninglessness of the world and life was revealed to me. It was so piercing! It became clear to me that pain is the only law in this world. I wanted to cry. For them, my brothers, who lie in the damp ground. I know they would not forgive my belated cowardly tears: They did not die so the living would cry for them. But my heart was in pain, and I wanted to cry.

They are gone, and they will never return. No way, ever. They will no longer be able to fill the space around them with their bodies and voices, thoughts, and feelings, with their warmth. Neither can we. We are only able to add a few lines they left unfinished. But even those lines are unlikely to be the ones they had in mind for presenting themselves to the world—to its apathetic, indifferent, deaf ears.

Mancha Satbeyevich fell ill. He was not in the library for several days in a row. The familiar picture lacked a gray head bent over files of newspapers. It lacked the glasses perched on his nostrils, and his puffing, which occurred when something pissed off the old man. Irritated, he would raise his head and look around at the library visitors in search of support for his indignation.

It was usually he and I in the library, but also Madina at her "boss's" desk. At first, each time I caught sight of his gray head shaking disapprovingly, I involuntarily looked back at him. Then I got used to it and ceased paying attention: He raised his head too often, like someone cocking a gun in anticipation of danger.

I asked Madina if she knew anything about our elder as I jokingly called him in front of her. I thought that at least an "open secret" would bring us a little closer. Madina always smiled, and my heart felt warm.

As it turned out Mancha Satbeyevich ended up in the hospital.

Adgur A. would hardly have been pleased with such a plot move. Moreover, he would have torn him to pieces with the unprecedented annoyance into which he fell when he caught someone faking or simplifying a task. Natela's mother was also ill, so now we have got the second patient. Is it too much for a short text? In order to maintain a certain plot, fabula, and stylistic balance, I will have to leave Mancha Satbeyevich alive. His illness will be some trivial, ridiculously ordinary thing— let's say, a strangulated hernia, hemorrhoids, sciatica, or appendicitis.

458 | *Daur Nachkebia*

Although our funeral deserves to be captured. It is something: The Abkhaz farewell to the deceased on a journey with one end. The living fuss so much with the body, which has finally found its long-awaited peace. It would be best to hide it in the ground, away from people's eyes, and let it slowly decay, in the depths, disintegrating into anonymous atoms. And we . . . Apparently, our relatives cannot do otherwise. They call this the last farewell to the deceased, confident that they will never meet him in the dank, dark place to which he suddenly and irrevocably left.

At first, this is what I thought: that the old man would die from a sudden illness, as he himself believed, and with the frustration of a man who had been betrayed from the most unexpected side. In fact, he died from the exhaustion of life in himself. It shrank to a small entity resembling an octopus that settled deep inside him and corroded him like rust.

But Natela's mother also died from a formation that settled in her and devoured her from the inside. Therefore, we will send Mancha Satbeyevich to the next world in another way. Let's say he will have sudden cardiac arrest after he finds final and indisputable proof in *Pravda*, and his head, having solved the riddle so brilliantly, collapses on the newspaper. Or, after solving the mystery, he will have a stroke. His head will fall on the newspaper, and blood will flow from his nostrils, staining the words that finally and indisputably confirm what he was looking for. In order not to bother Madina, we can do all this to him on the street, on the way home, to the library or to the promenade, on the Prospect, at the busiest hour, among the crowd. Driven by sympathies and curiosity, the crowd would immediately gather around the fallen old man. He was walking briskly, squinting in the sun, a smile of senile contentment on his face, and suddenly he went limp, sagged, his legs giving way. They will shower him with attention that he never received during his life. Or it will happen on a side street with a few passersby. The old man will not be found immediately, but after some time, which will give compassionate onlookers a reason to speculate in their favorite, non-binding subjunctive mood: "if . . .", "so that . . .", "if only . . .", and then finish with the even less binding "apparently, it was destined . . ." If we want not to bother anyone at all, including the victim himself (if possible), then we can conduct this whole simple operation at his home, in his own bed, late at night. That is, we will send Mancha Satbeyevich to the afterlife deep in the night, when he is sleeping quietly in his own bed, having no disturbing dreams, premonitions, or worries. That is, in a dream.

One good morning—when sun shined vulgarly, the birds chirped vulgarly, and in general, cats, dogs and other creatures showed the usual vulgar cheerfulness of the pre-human animal world—the old man's body, which had long ago lost all sensitivity to small things, but was still sensitive to radical changes in himself, signaled that "Amba!" was approaching with a slight tingling sensation in the right side—almost like that for Ivan Ilyich. The malfunctions that had accumulated over the years turned Mancha Satbeyevich into a corpse.

I'll go to the funeral and see her there. She may be the only one who truly feels sorry for the poor guy. Until he actually dies, I don't know whether I will feel sorry for him or not. Madina is almost in mourning. The dark dress attractively highlights the whiteness of her skin. If only she had also put on a thin black chiffon scarf that fell over her shoulders, gathered it under her chin and held it lightly with long thin fingers with long nails painted bright red. Framed by thick darkness, her face becomes gentle, detached, unearthly. I can smell the light scent of her perfume. I wish I could bury my head in this soft, intoxicating whiteness.

Mourning suits our women. It makes them somewhat mysterious, inaccessible if you like. Unusually sexy. Mourning reminds us of death. How far is it from love to death?

But Mancha Satbeyevich is not a close relative to deserve a chiffon scarf. It's unlikely that Madina would ever put on a chiffon scarf, no matter how close the deceased is to her. She is too modern for that. Only the elderly wear a chiffon scarf as a symbol of deep sorrow and grief.

Standing in a semicircle near the coffin, the women are weeping. Distant relatives are seated on the benches behind them. In the coffin, pale and shocked, lies Mancha Satbeyevich. The faces of the dead always express some shock from the sudden change that has happened to them. His facial features that were always thin are even more sunken and faded. The nose with its sharpened hump retained the proud posture of his lifetime. I have noticed this common feature of the dead: A hooked nose.

The coffin stands in the small hall of his three-bedroom *khrushchevka*.

The women are all in black, with appropriate sorrow on their faces. A mourner or a group of mourners appear. They wail, showing everyone their great, inconsolable grief. At the same time, their curious eyes glance at the visitors: who is who, how is he dressed, with whom did he come. During breaks they whisper, sharing impressions, discussing this or that, wondering through which family branch someone ended up here. Sometimes they even laugh. A typical ancient old lady is here too. You can meet her at any funeral. Wrinkled and hunched over, she is some relative long forgotten by everyone, including the deceased during his lifetime. But she always comes on this occasion.

In general, I noticed that there are an indecent number of old people at funerals. They can hardly move their legs, but they hobble to accompany their brother. I once saw an old woman with two sticks. She entered the courtyard, where an open coffin with a dead man was displayed under a canopy. She was like a boat that was about to set sail, but she immediately raised a terrible cry, which, given her physical shape, was not only unexpected, but impossible. She even threw away her sticks to free her hands to scratch her cheeks. When she had scratched them to blood—the first sign of bleeding was enough for everyone to acknowledge her impeccable commitment to the ritual—the women that came with her, proud of the knowledge that their delegation had risen to the occasion, gratefully handed her the sticks. Old people cry at funerals with copious and sincere tears, partly mourning their own close passing.

The ancient old woman beautifies the funeral with her lamentations, performing a disappearing custom of seeing off the deceased on his last journey with heartbreaking screams while scratching your own cheeks. She laments about the premature death of Mancha Satbeyevich: He did not have time to accomplish everything that he could and planned; but he also did a lot in his short life. This all is about an almost ninety-year old man. He left us for a place from which there is no return. He will meet his family and friends. Many of them moved to that world before him. They left our world, full of evil and hatred, for a better one, where there is light and goodness. They left the world of lies for the world of truth.

Madina also mourns, but not as ostentatiously as those next to the coffin. She stands silently, and her silence is special. It makes her more desirable. I want to stand next to her and be silent with her about the frailty of everything earthly and the brevity of love. But is she silent about this? Where did I get the idea that Madina is silent about the brevity of earthly things and the vicissitudes of love? There are no clear indications that sweet, sad, and mournful Madina is busy with eternal questions instead of simply observing a funeral ritual. But she is silent and thinking about something. About what?

In such cases, I think indecently little about the deceased and his afterlife. Watching the living, doomed and curious crowd surrounding the dead man is way more interesting. At Mancha Satbeyevich's funeral, I will think about Madina, secretly admiring her. I will think about her warm, soft, living flesh, and probably identically soft, warm, living soul. I will think about it with longing for an unattainable distance.

Then the deceased will be taken out into the yard. Obliging youth from the relatives and neighbors will lift the coffin and lean it on their shoulders. Numerous advisers will tell them where and how to turn the coffin, how far to raise it, how to lower it so that it does not catch on the railings, or the deceased suddenly falls out. The youngers will carry it down the narrow flight of stairs. A crowd will have gathered in front of the house, coming to pay their last respects to Mancha Satbeyevich. Those who have already paid stand at a distance in boredom, patiently waiting for the compulsory post-funeral treat. After all, you have to send the old man off with a bowl of beans and a few glasses of wine. They are invited by people who serve the funeral. Those people know the custom by heart and do not let anyone mess with it. Gently but firmly, if necessary, persistently, because according to the same custom it is necessary to refuse, they invite guests to the table. People sluggishly and as if reluctantly follow the servants of custom, who instructively repeat: "It is impossible otherwise, dear ones, this is what our fathers did, and what the dead man himself loved! Believe me, his soul will be restless if you do not raise your glasses." Therefore, there are some number of drunk people in the crowd. They try their best to stay upright on unruly legs and feign attention. They more or less succeed, although their faces are sometimes distorted from belching. They ate a lot of hotly seasoned beans and sauerkraut, which was prepared hastily due to the pressing deadline and was just beginning to turn pink. They also drank a lot of sour wine.

The coffin will be placed on a table. A small procession will be organized. His whole life was given to his Motherland, his memory will remain in the hearts of all who knew him, the speakers will say eloquently. The old man's patriotism will be especially emphasized. They will lie about the responsible posts that he once held, and how in these posts he thought day and night about the good of his people. They will talk about what a blow the last war was for him, how he did not leave Sukhumi for reasons of principle, how much suffering he endured from the Georgians, and how miraculously he survived. The crowd is indignant and takes pity on the old man.

On this wave of shared pity, an unscheduled talker, a drunk one in khaki riding breeches and worn-out knee-high leather boots takes the floor and talks nonsense about how they still remember Mancha Satbeyevich in his native village, how they were worried about his fate during the war, knowing that he stayed in occupied Sukhumi.

Despite his age—although he could not be considered an old man by Abkhazian standards—he was a man in his prime. But, you know, years of hard work for the benefit of his native people . . . so, despite years of hard work . . . that is . . . in a word, he was engaged in undermining the enemy from the inside. Undermining from within. At his age! While Mancha Satbeyevich was alive, the villagers slept peacefully. They knew that there was one close person in the city whom they could contact at any time of the day or night, and he would help. "Farewell, Satbey son of Mancha, may the Almighty place you in paradise," the drunk man will say in the end. Then he will go up to the coffin and kiss the dead man on his cold forehead. Then he will wipe away the tear that has welled up with a calloused peasant finger, wave his hand—all is dust!—and return to his place, creaking with his dusty boots.

The old Russian neighbor lady intersperses her speech with genuine tears, which she wipes away with the end of a simple gray scarf tied under her chin. In general, women are not supposed to give speeches over the deceased, but this is a special case. She talks about Mikhail Stepanovich's generous soul, always attentive to the needs of ordinary people. She remembers what cheerful jokes Mishka made every time he met her alone on the stairs. Who would have thought that he would leave us so early! May you rest in peace, our darling!

At sensitive moments, speeches are interrupted by loud sobs of inconsolable relatives. The ancient old woman is the most zealous of all: "Damn me! Damn me!" she hits herself on the forehead. When she raises her hand to hit her forehead,

The Shore of Night | 465

the wide sleeve slides down and exposes her arm to the elbow. The arm is entwined with thick blue veins and dotted with many light brown spots. Her hand with crooked gouty fingers and swollen joints looks unnaturally large, as if from someone else's arm. She squeezes it into a weak, thin fist and hits herself on the forehead. The men, the relatives, sternly shake their heads, realizing the severity of the irreparable loss, both for the family and for the entire people.

I decided to visit the patient. He was accommodated on the first floor of a dull, shabby city hospital. I entered the department passing a small courtyard with a dried-up fountain lined with multi-colored pebbles. In the middle, there was a lonely gray stone bird, either a crane or a heron. Apparently, healing moisture that alleviates suffering was supposed to ooze from its broken beak. The corridor is dark and gloomy. It smells of dampness and bleach. Its coldness and melancholy pierced me to the bone. The space heater kept the room a little warmer: The spiral smoldered dimly, without turning into full-fledged red. But this room was gloomy too. The only window covered with white curtains faced a large, solid, uneven, gray stone wall. The daylight sneaked into the room like a spy. Mancha Satbeyevich had a roommate, another patient, an overweight middle-aged man with a huge swollen belly. He was sleeping, and you could hear his heavy, intermittent breathing.

"Young man, years of hard work don't go away without a mark. Now my time has come. This can't go on forever. From a certain age, each of us lives in constant anticipation of death. One day our worst fears come true, and they drag us to a cemetery. Life is a risk, a big risk, my young friend. You young people are in a hurry to live. When we are in a hurry, time passes slowly. But in old age it's the opposite: we are in no hurry, we want to hold on to life, but time is like an unbroken horse, which is ripping away from our hands . . ."

He's lost weight, although he is not seriously ill, as far as I know. It's probably stress. If we judge with a sober mind, and not with the instincts of aching flesh, which power controls him entirely now, then why should he continue this burdensome work? Isn't it better to lie down and quietly shrink into a decent corpse? His curiosity makes him wonder what will happen tomorrow. Will everything really be like this, just without him? Is there still a need for it? He holds on, holds on tightly.

All his life, Mancha Satbeyevich served as a minor bureaucrat in a minor department of water, gas, or insurance. During his lifetime he wrote a pile of redundant pieces of paper: Requests, responses, statements, rejections, petitions, appeals to a higher authority, instructions from a lower authority, minutes of meetings, extracts from minutes, reprimands and dismissals, incentives, award orders, leaves of absence. He lived somewhere in the corner, in the shadows, rarely came into the light, or, one might say, never did. However, this was his life. He lived that way, and it was to his advantage. Wasn't Mancha Satbeyevich impeccable in his earthly nature, a real guru? An unrecognized guru who lived in a small coastal town on the outskirts of a vast empire. It was destined for me to meet him, to learn from him the art of life, and then preserve it on paper, so that future generations can drink from this life-giving spring of inexhaustible wisdom.

Funny. But . . . he didn't doubt for a minute: Everything that happens around him and with him is actually happening and is happening inevitably. He never wondered whether to go this way or turn another path. He did not try to predict

The Shore of Night 467

his future. He never lingered at the entrance of his home, not knowing which way to go. Maybe this is the highest wisdom? The fact that Mancha Satbeyevich is not even smart but rather stupid only proves that wisdom and intelligence are not the same thing, as was already discovered a while ago. You have to live long enough for everything in you to burn out. It might smoke, like from an extinct, tired volcano. But when you have real wisdom, the sky above you is cloudless, because you are empty inside, and nothing will ever be born from it. Wisdom is sterility, an internal vacuum. Natural and other forces in you have dried up. You are no longer able to create. You only exist.

Then it occurred to me. The wizened old man (let's sweeten it up for the last), who sits pathetically at the threshold of eternity, has indecently, I would even say, disgustingly thick skin. Otherwise, he would not have lived to such insulting years. He would have long ago gone to rest in his cozy grave. Did he also have those nights when monstrous fear squeezed his heart, and he could not close his eyes? Those nights, when the distant barking, common and usually unnoticed during the day, sounded like a trumpet, so that he needed to cover his ears?

I cannot believe this, with all my purely human (after all, we are from the same tribe) condescension towards the pitiful fate of Mancha Satbeyevich. Maybe at the dawn of his misty youth, when the foreign, fresh smell of the world fogged his brains and drove his heart wild, something similar happened to him. A sudden melancholy fell like a drop of poison into his day, which had strived for harmony with the world, and serenity was gone. But he recovered from this misfortune quickly, as soon as the dawn had passed and a full day of life had arrived.

The old man always slept well. It has been his habit since his foggy youth. He boasted to colleagues who complained about poor sleep. As soon he climbed into his lonely bed, he fell into an endless abyss until the next morning. He never had any dreams. Unable to relate, he listened to those who talked about their nightly wanderings in God knows what places, where they met their long-dead relatives and acquaintances, as if it was something common and experienced by everyone.

His colleagues did not believe him and quietly envied him, thought Mancha Satbeyevich.

His tales about the noble informant-avenger, which I almost believed out of pity—all these were his attempts to use me to break into the future, to get there untainted. He partially succeeded. He was firm in his past and had no intention of giving it up. I lived and am still alive—it was written on his face. He secretly triumphed, believing that he had managed to deceive and defeat fate. Even though he was born and lived in such a terrible time, he made it to an advanced age.

"The only thing I regret is that I didn't have time to solve the secret of the USSR's collapse. But I was so close . . ."

I tried to console him, saying that he would still have time to sit in the library, leafing through his favorite Party newspapers.

I put money under his pillow. The old man didn't want to take it. He muttered something about attention. I left. I won't come here or the library again. If the living can't live, books won't teach them how to do it.

I secretly hoped that I would meet Madina. She must visit him sometimes to fulfill her family duty. It's also obvious that she genuinely feels sorry for the old man. Why shouldn't fate arrange it so that she and I end up in the hospital at the same time? Let's say I come, and she is already sitting with him, or vice versa—she comes, and I'm right there. We look at each other in surprise and slightly confused. Trying to get away from the awkward moment, we show exaggerated concern for Mancha Satbeyevich, bombarding him with questions about his well-being: "Where does it hurt? How does it hurt? Maybe lie on the other side?" He answers with unnecessary and lengthy details that we ignore. We pretend to pay the greatest attention to which side hurt yesterday and which side today.

Then, having said goodbye, wishing him good health and strength, we leave the room. Passing the fountain with a bird of unknown origin, we exit the hospital and find ourselves on the street. Then we go together.

*None of those who have reasoned about lofty matters inaccessible to the human mind and have repeatedly slipped God into the hands of the gullible public as a way out of a dead end (where any discussion about "meanings" necessarily leads) has really understood the beauty of death. Total death, without residual ash such as a soul, memory, a tombstone, an obituary, or a book. Although it was said long ago that it would be better for a person not to be born at all.*

*A man's cowardly cunning appears here naked. If a person is not born, then where does he go? What's his address? Where to look for it? With the hope that one can be without being born, this formula is uttered. Otherwise, how can it be better for someone who doesn't exist at all? Or is it the weakness of words?*

*There is no need to leave a notch. It's unnecessary to try too hard. Waste of time.*

*I, still alive, am depressed that my ashes will smolder in the ground for a very long time. After hundreds, thousands, millions of years, the substance from which I am woven—the only thing that is truly immortal until the final disappearance of the world, which N.B. often talked about as an immutable truth—my substance may become part of another body or several other bodies.*

*This all ends up in the idea: my flesh is not mine at all, I kind of rented it. It's like clothes that I can wear and throw away. I can do it for a long time, as long as it is fresh and fits me, as long it has not become wrinkled, before I pull it off to put on something else. I can change my outfit whenever I want. This is my natural right. For communal purposes, I should not be limited in doing so as if in the name of God. The unpronounceable feeling, not recorded by any devices, tells me: I am free in my body, and this is my only real freedom. I believe that by breaking a vessel we spill the contents, so I can spill my soul and it will flow into the sand without a trace.*

*Maybe this is our only real freedom?*

*I would want desperately not to leave any imprints, even for the shortest time. Even if B.N. is right, and sooner or later I, like everyone else, like the entire world, will be erased without a trace.*

*After all, it is possible in another way. B.N. also spoke about this, that the world (what a horror!) is eternal and will never*

*perish. A dizzying and scary prospect: it is possible that someday*
*I will be reassembled all over again. Eternity has enough*
*intelligence and time for that.*

I say farewell to Adgur A. I free him from myself and myself from him. I take off his skin, which was almost attached to me. The dead want to be left alone, but this is incomprehensible to the living. The living believe that they are obliged to remember the dead, as if memory prolongs the life of the dead. The dead want one thing: To be forgotten once and for all.

I think that Adgur A. wanted to find his soul in the war. But there was too much life in the war. The soul cannot stand too much life; it's harmful.

I couldn't finish his line. The stories that he'd mostly finished don't count. I only corrected them in accordance with his plan. But he entered my heart and took root in it. He rooted deep. Now it's not so easy for me to remove him. There is no "delete" button to erase a person from your heart without a trace. (I will never erase Natela, who left in my heart a sweet, aching emptiness.)

How can I explain that his notes had such an effect on me? Why did I get it into my head that I should continue him at least in text? How can I reconcile my ongoing life with his, already ended?

The only connection was Madina. But is she the same M. about whom he writes? I never asked her about a certain Adgur A., once my friend, a writer, who either died or committed suicide in the summer of '93, not far from Sukhumi, during our last attack on the city, and who wrote in his notes about a certain M., his pre-war acquaintance, and his beloved during the war. He hides it under the feigned coldness of indifferent lines, sparingly describing their meeting at Gumista.

He didn't dare to do it—this is not entirely accurate, or rather, completely inaccurate. My initial orientation toward providence, with which I began my non-search for M., remained throughout this entire story. I never once wanted to break my word to rely on chance, and it is exactly what I didn't dare to do. But even when I met Madina at the library in some autumn rainy evening, when Sukhumi is sadly beautiful and all its parts, from Kelasur to Gumista, are permeated by the wind, and the black (lowercase "b") sea noisily beats against the granite shore, when the embankment is deserted and something aching presses on your heart, and you want to dive into this bad weather, into this wind, the evening, when I said to myself "it's her!", I didn't mean M. I meant something else: Another one. I didn't recognize M. in her. I felt that it was a meeting with the one for whom I had been looking, the missing half from whom I was once separated either by malicious intent or by misunderstanding. Suddenly, my emptiness was filled to the brim and the rib fell into place. All this is described simpler with one word, but I don't want to use it. It may not be a coincidence that it sounds so similar to "blood,"[7] which I so hate.

Having learned that her name began with "M," I started to doubt my first feeling and again saw the hand of providence in everything, now associated with Adgur A., not with me. Chance led me to abandon myself, which was natural, since I dared to continue someone else's unlived life. While in my own body, I got another soul, someone else's. It felt like a punishment, because two people were fighting inside me—Madina and Adgur A.

The Shore of Night | 473

But I still tried to continue Adgur A., although my feelings for Madina gradually forced him out of my heart. How could I continue him, even on paper, without giving him a place in my heart? It would be a stillborn text. Only one thing could save me: If Madina turned out to be M. But I could not talk to her about him. This would violate all the rules of the game I had started with fate. It would be dishonest. So, I relied on chance again. That chance that was more like a miracle.

The three of them—Beardy, Macho, and Beslan—are standing at the counter in Akop's Place. The outline of the Amra jutting out into the sea is visible not far away in the unsteady early evening twilight. It's a little cold and drizzling autumn rain. The regulars have long since left.

They talk, listening carefully to each other, without interrupting, and sometimes nod their heads understandingly.

"You won't believe it, but they told me at the telephone station that there is no such city, no such country and no such number!" He opens the folder, pulls out several sheets of paper covered with the names of countries, cities, and telephone numbers, and shows it to Beslan and Beardy. They look at the paper, think it over, but say nothing.

"Well, now you see that I am not asking for anything impossible. I just need them to connect me, and then I know what to say. I have a speech prepared, that's it!" He pulls out another pile of papers to show them. "I can't call anywhere. Every night I dream of different countries, cities, and numbers. The next morning, I write them down exactly, word for word, letter for letter, number for number. Unlike some, I am sane and have a good memory. Do any of you remember the names of all the participants in the first World Cup? I remember them and I write them down neatly—you saw how good my handwriting is, how all the letters are tilted at the same angle, they argued with me, they didn't believe me, but a fireman I knew had measured all the letters that I wrote under his dictation, I wrote them at maximum speed, which surprised him, he dropped his jaw and started respecting me, he even gave me a certificate saying I'm normal—so, I come to the telephone station to fulfill my duty—after all, it's not for nothing that I dream of these countries, cities, numbers, I definitely have to call and say, and I have what to say, I showed you it—but there in the window sits that uneducated fool, who doesn't know any country except for Abkhazia, Russia, and Georgia, she brazenly declares that there is no such country, city, and number—the number is really long—I haven't seen such numbers in my life—it's because they do things differently, they have gone ahead of us—but I will never believe that there is no such country and city, they exist but they don't want me to contact them and they are also persistent, they don't lag behind, they chose me, it's not my fault, every night they send me a signal to get in touch, and I'm trying to do my best, I know I'll be told that after I do it, everyone will feel good, everyone will love everyone, but they won't let me in—and I'm starting to think that no one talks to anyone on the phone, it's all a deception, a conspiracy, and people in the call boxes pretend to be talking and that's why they don't allow me to call so that I don't reveal the deception—in the boxes, they talk about everything that they don't dare say in public, looking into someone's eyes, they speak into the phone. I pass and hear snippets of conversation between different people with my heart: Natela, come to me, I want to hug you and hold you close to me, you are so far away, and I am so lonely, are you really gone forever? Only after losing you did I understand what you had meant in my life,

The Shore of Night | 475

Madina was just a self-hypnosis, I got into my head that I had to continue the life of a dead person—is this really possible?—the dead are dead, they cannot be resurrected, and it is unclear whether they want to be, I suspect that they don't—He loved only M.—besides what he wrote, I didn't know anything about her, and I decided that it was Madina, she fought in the war and was wounded—in a word, she fitted his description—although he didn't say anything about her wound—it probably happened later—and I decided to love her without even knowing if she was the M. about whom my friend wrote, she had the opportunity to finally become close to Adgur A. but maybe I just wanted to make amends for my guilt before him? Then I lost interest in you, my mind took over my heart, I'm a man of science, and now I yearn for you—for your scent, breasts, ass, voice, and for the depth and sadness of your eyes—the rib did not fit anywhere, but a gaping wound remained—Natela, come to me and drive away my melancholy, no, you are not cold, you have a heart and this is the most important thing—I am beginning to understand it now—my friend helped me with that, he had a heart, but he hid it deep and only showed the edge of it in his writings, and this was his major mistake—he and I never became true friends, he looked at the world with half-closed eyes, squinting when they should be wide open, the war is to blame, it taught me to hide from life not because I was afraid of death for myself but because I was afraid for the person in myself, I was afraid of living to death along the way, having lost the person in myself, so I began to study other people's lives, not just what they thought, but what they did, and then I figured out whether it would suit me or not, no one else's life suited anyone's fate, I didn't want to and couldn't repeat my friend's life, Mancha Satbeyevich—you won't believe it—helped me in some ways but most of all you helped me, despite the fact that you have a dark vision of life, you've lived and a living heart beats inside you, it knew everything about what awaits a person—I have not been able to keep a living heart until now, and I thought about my father and mother, I will go to them and stay for a long time and there is no need for something grandiose to happen, we are alive and we have a choice—this is already grandiose—I made an incorrect choice—I wanted it, maybe I was deceiving myself, but I wanted it—I offended you deeply too many times, I never seriously talked to you about your mother, I always brushed off your questions with some platitudes, I didn't try to help you, I thought that everything had already been said, nothing new could be added, and you had to come to terms with it and forget your mom—after all, we will all die someday, there is nothing new in this—but you thought, in your naivety, or rather stupidity, or rather heartlessness, you behaved as if your mother alone had died and bequeathed to you only old age and not something that would help you live—I thought that old age was everyone's lot, so what was the point of suffering in advance—I saw you suffered, and I thought that you were living incorrectly, I didn't understand you, I didn't find the right words to tell you to console you—I even thought that comfort was akin to deception, but you were right when you said that I don't love you—or rather, that wasn't entirely right—I behaved as if I didn't love you, but I loved you—after some time, I became deaf to you, I wanted to know other people's lives, to collect or scatter my own life—rather, scatter it because I could no longer live as before—I was missing something, and you were nearby, I wasn't afraid of losing you, although sometimes I thought about it as a future possibility—but I didn't do anything, fate would decide everything, I said, and it was wrong—there is no fate, but there is the person—every day he must make a choice, and his fate depends on his choice, I thought—and I admit it was nice to think like that, to hide behind the formulas that govern the world—I thought that we are all prisoners of matter and the movements of atoms, that we can't change anything, all our attempts during life instantly depreciate death and movement, a bad property of matter—in imitation of that bad property, man constantly moves too, and I began to hate any kind of movement—what is it for if everything is predetermined? My heart has finally closed—but this started long before the war, which reassured me in my attitude towards the world—I got fixated on Adgur A. and M. as an opportunity to cope with my life, but it was all in vain and now I'm alone, but I'm capable of loving again and I love you Natela, I will always love you—you say, 'get married, have children, always be with them until you die, don't give up, teach them the good things that you know, teach them about life, there is nothing better'—maybe you're right, I don't know that yet, I'm afraid to give someone life yet, I didn't manage to give life to Adgur A., despite that it's a bit different from what you say, but I believe you Natela—once you asked if I needed you, remember? That day when you suddenly let go of yourself and before you always kept yourself in control, you wanted to become a person without feelings and you almost were one, because you rarely allowed yourself to talk about your feelings—but on that day something happened to you, it seems that it had been building up for a long time and finally burst out in a stream of words, you fell upon me, you also said sometimes you look like that, I'm scared, there's so much knowledge in your eyes— where does this come from in you? Before the war, you didn't look like that, or I didn't notice. What could I say? The war has nothing to do with it, but you wanted to think that the war changed everything—and what I'm going to tell you now will explain a lot—although you might call it self-justification—it's something I've never told anyone, even Adgur A. I just gave him a hint, I told him the date, the sixth of March, a significant date in my life, but I didn't reveal the details of my spiritual upheaval, I couldn't find the right words, and I'm unlikely to be able to explain it to you, so it's better that I briefly tell you the consequences, which sound like this: After March sixth, I ceased to care, not that I didn't care at all, and it's impossible—probably even suicides don't get to that point, maybe they care more than anyone else, that's why they kill themselves—but it was different for me anyway, I knew that I would never die and with such knowledge it is almost impossible to live—immortality would be the most difficult and unbearable test for a person, everything gets boring quickly—the immortality that killed me on the sixth of March was real—each of us feels immortal, the oscillation of the pendulum between such faith and disbelief is the essence of human life, but for me, this feeling broke the surface of consciousness and took the shape of a conviction—at first, I took a long time to get used to the fact that in my immortal movement towards the unknown—the feeling of the unknown and incomprehensible arises immediately as you realize your immortality—I will be everyone who has lived and those who will live, that is, you will become or have already been everyone you meet, even the most wretched, the ugliest—even a bum who reeks from a mile away of piss and shit—from here the merciless conclusion is drawn that one must love everyone indiscriminately, and it is only possible to love them as oneself, no more and no less, this

The Shore of Night | 479

is the hint and meaning of the great commandment—there is no 'I,' people invented that—but I hid this knowledge deep in my heart, I did not develop it, I did not derive a 'philosophy of life' from it, it did not give me any joy, it did not satisfy my existential hunger, I obeyed it as a law of nature, just as I obeyed the law of gravity, I lived like everyone else because I understood that knowledge was nothing—it doesn't add anything to earthly life; earthly life doesn't need it—even if knowledge wins complete victory, people will live as stupidly and meaninglessly as they have lived until now—the only thing is that I got rid of any kind of fear once and for all, therefore, during the war I was fearless to the point of frenzy, I am not afraid of anything or anyone, and your fears seemed funny to me, I was indifferent to them and never found words of consolation— maybe if I considered it necessary to console you, I would have found them, Adgur A. wanted to get rid of his instincts, to get rid of his animal bodily nature, so that there would be nothing left but spirit—I almost achieved that, I lived in a world where the very word 'hope' had already been a useless corpse, everything was clear to me, and I did not understand why people complicate everything—if sometimes I was a 'person,' then out of forgetfulness the so-called heart, that is, my instincts, had escaped the supervision of a cold mind, but that was before—people say different things in private, and I don't particularly want to hear all this . . . But what can I do? The ear hears, the heart remembers . . ."

"I always hear my mother's warning voice. Every night she comes to me in a dream but does not say anything. She sits down in front of my bed. She is wearing the gray dress in which she lay in the coffin. She asked to be buried in this very dress, once given to her by my father. She looks at me, looks sadly, but doesn't say anything. She doesn't even reproach me for not listening to her and continuing to play backgammon. I don't lose anything special, but all my life she reproached me for my losses and debts. Although they happened, especially in my youth, they were so insignificant that I managed them quickly. My mother didn't have to work hard to get me out. Yes, I didn't tell her about my losses. For a while, she didn't know that I was playing at all. But you can't keep it a secret for long. Some neighbor told her eventually. I have always been careful and knew how to stop in time. I am not interested in money as such, but I am not interested in taking one round either, when the opponent doesn't care whether he loses or wins, does not play with all his strength, does not take risks, and the game turns out deadly dull. But most importantly, with such a game I will not be able to find out what was assigned to me from above. Money is a temptation, a test for all of us. Playing for money is the most significant test, a test of the ability to remain human under great temptation. In a normal game, whether you are lucky or not does not play a special role, unless you and your opponent are in a life-and-death fight. Sometimes, out of some incomprehensible choice, a person might want to win over just one particular opponent. Even if he normally loses to everyone else. Those battles turned out fiercer than ones with a huge bet. Nobody thinks about it and doesn't apply it to their life. But when money is at stake, you already make every throw with a special attitude. You already pray to God to help you. When it goes wrong and you don't get what you asked for, you understand that heaven did not hear you, and even if it did, it refused to help. This is worse. When they don't hear, there is a hope of shouting out to them. But when they don't want to hear, all hope dies. What did you do wrong? Why are you not worthy of fulfilling such a simple wish: So that at the next throw, you could get a du-shesh, and not a lousy, mocking du-yak, as it usually happens. No, zara fall as they like. I no longer ask God, but zara. They have replaced God. Chance rules the world. I came to this point with my mind. It was then that I read Einstein's quote that God does not play dice. Yes, God does not play, but we do. He taught us the game. I never succumbed to the power of money. I managed to stop in time, at least it seemed so to me until recently. But I see it, and it's impossible not to see it at the market, I used to do something else, even at one time I had a lot of money, but the war ruined everything. I see that today money has become everything, and for the sake of money people are ready to do a lot, it doesn't matter what the amount is, and for the sake of a little thing they can go to great lengths of villainy. Until now, I considered playing small to be my virtue, but I asked myself: Is this really a virtue? After all, the mercy of heaven, luck, in my mind, means winning money, even if only a little. Is the joy I experience at those moments really less than the joy of winning big sums? Probably not. Worse than that, my joy seems to derive from my battle with fate. Isn't it enough to confirm that heaven favors you, and after the next win, take it and leave the game forever? But I keep playing. This means that I deceived myself by covering up self-interest and innate gambling with lofty words. I wanted to convince heaven that I am entitled to something, and I wanted to find out why it's always denying me this something. It turned out that all these years the heavens were saying: This is not for you, give up hope. But I didn't hear, I didn't want to hear. They didn't hear me; I didn't hear them. It's always like this: We want to be heard, but we stuff our ears with wax."

## 482 | *Daur Nachkebia*

"So, you say to get through by phone or, if you wish, toss out the required point, but you need to get through not to someone else's city, but to someone else's heart, and then the number that will make you happy will appear, even though you and I don't believe in happiness—first of all, I myself never believed in it, I thought it was fiction, but now I understand that I was once happy, except I didn't realize and didn't appreciate it—it's impossible to go back there—Natela left forever, she had to leave, she said there is no return to the past, let's not deceive ourselves—I can only remember you and I'm grateful to you, I know I was once loved, and it means something in life—my mother loved me, although she left me alone without saying anything about how terrible and at the same time good life was, she did not try to hide her suffering from me, in any case, she did not tell me an encouraging word and she was lost in all her pain, but she still loved me, and her last words were 'I'm leaving you alone,' it was said with concern for my future, and she didn't say anything else—I spent a long time feeling offended by this, but I was stupid—Natela always did everything right, she was afraid of old age, which is not wrong—life wouldn't be real if you weren't afraid of anything—if you forgot your mother, forgot the pain she suffered while dying—reconciliation with it is impossible, as soon as you reconcile, you die as a person, you can be a person while suffering—I said goodbye to Adgur A. nicely, by saying that the dead want to be forgotten, I myself forgot that while the living belong to the tribe of the living, the dead will live in them, I even thought of ending this whole story so beautifully, thick-skinned—I will run my finger by the slightly rough scar on her smooth matte belly and Madina will bashfully turn away and look to the side, putting her left hand under her head and hugging me with her

The Shore of Night | 483

right hand—I'll look at how the scar just above her navel, in a semicircle, descends down into her sweetest nether regions, I'll ask if she knew some-such Adgur A., she will say that she didn't know him, now I know that the sheets filled with small handwriting in which there is an attempt to continue Adgur A.'s short and voluntarily interrupted life will remain unfinished— they will lie in the desk until one day during house cleaning Madina will burn them along with other unneeded papers— I wanted to say goodbye to him forever, unequivocally hinting that I would not write further—this would be the moral of my story: The uselessness of writing and the impossibility of an encounter—I wanted to forget him because the burden of his life was added to the burden of my life, it was not easy for me to bear two lives at once, one life is already too much for a person, I did not have enough for both Natela and Madina, but I no longer wanted Madina to be that M. and, therefore, I didn't develop a friendship with Adgur A. It was my fault, I lived in another world, in a world of brilliant formulas that explained life unambiguously without unnecessary fictitious assumptions—within these formulas my 'I' was delineated, it consisted of almost eternal and almost indestructible atoms, they could be measured, weighed, even seen—but Adgur A. lived in a world which was constantly in danger of destruction—there was nothing reliable, everything was shaky, foggy, deceptive, and it turned out to be impossible to connect two such different worlds, even after I saw with my own eyes how fragile a person is, how metal crushes and breaks him—though he is also unusually strong, and it is impossible to defeat him, I was convinced more than once that he could be killed but not defeated—it does not bother me if it was said by someone before me, I acquired the courage to speak well-known truths, in my case it was not difficult, because I was only discovering what nature initially contained—I was, in general, a plagiarist, my mind, a derivative of the same substance as the universe, penetrated into the structures of which it itself consisted—like that snake biting its own tail—but Adgur A. also went towards the same thing except he did not have time, maybe he managed to get there, and his last gesture meant humility—yes, humility, I can't find a better word—it meant that Adgur A. had come to terms with life, with the fact that he was a human being, and in order to make sure that he was a person he decided to prove to himself that he was mortal; he succeeded through death, thanks to death—death makes us human; we have no other way to be human—he has come to terms with the fact that he is a person—that is, he repeats and reproduces—and there seems to be a contradiction here; in any case, every reader is hopelessly stuck in arithmetic with the indisputable 'twice two equals four' —with the severity of a schoolteacher, we will edifyingly say that everything is not as smooth as it is sung and will triumphantly point out gaping gaps of semantic inconsistency here and there, but we will show this stillborn pedant his place and wipe his nose, because the individual Adgur A. is mortal—although in fact he is not mortal, he thinks that he is; let's forgive him for his sullenness—this is, again, a completely acceptable individual delusion—in a word, he did not want to develop his style, considered it unnecessary work, not worth it—here is a jump into something of which a dry-wit, stillborn pedant could not have dreamed: Having realized your individual mortality along with the fact that you are cut from the same cloth as others, you gain immortality— I may say it vaguely, friends, but I couldn't find any other words or put them straight—I think there is no point in looking for

The Shore of Night | 485

them . . . What is important is the feeling, which is always inde-scribable—something put into words is already a lie."

During the war, Adgur A. and I could not meet. I was on the Eastern Front, and he was on the Gumistinsky Front. He died. I want to believe that his death was quick. In any case, from what I know when a bullet hits the head, death occurs instantly. It turns you off, like turning off the light. The dark-ness comes from all sides. This is how it seems. But I think, it is more important that the world plunges into darkness. Ev-erything around instantly disappears: Maybe this is not my death, but the death of the world? Infinity emerges from the darkness of an unsolved problem. Reasoning leads into the vast distance of unprovable consolations, which a weak heart desires so much. In peaceful times, I would not wish anyone an immediate death. In any case, I don't believe that it is the best, because it is not conscious and without pain. How much of this is even true? How do consciousness and pain manifest themselves at death's door? How fast are they? Who knows. It was not for nothing that Caesar dreamed of such a death. But in war you have to die quickly, all at once, to not be a burden to your comrades. He was killed by a bullet to the head. Do you know how powerful a machine gun bullet is? You need to feel this for yourself. I was wounded in the hand. My hand, the left one, as you can see, is not okay. I was spun around like a top by the blow and thrown back several meters. That was a sniper bullet, a larger and more powerful one. The bullets are beauti-ful when they lie in the palm of your hand, filled with the solid weight of the death they bring to you.

Slender, the bullets make you feel like a rocket which is about to soar into the sky. One of them, made at some military factory and stored somewhere for years, one day was loaded into the chamber by someone's hand and killed my friend. In general, he was not a friend. We did not have time or were made of different dough. Although, thanks to his notebook and my inexplicable desires, I see that we had a deep affinity of souls, our root systems were intertwined and fused a long time ago. But the branches in their quest for light . . . I won't intellectualize, and I'll cut it short: We never became friends, we didn't fall in love with each other. Adgur A. had his own theory of darkness. He said: "It is complete darkness out there. But due to his lack of imagination, a man cannot think of complete darkness, nothingness. This gave rise to the idea of immortality." I still hear his voice coming out of the darkness where he went. I don't understand what he's talking about, but I feel sorry for him. Or rather, it's not a pity. He chose his own death, and my pity is ridiculous, useless. But it hurts me. Do you know why?

He decided to walk along the promenade, past Penguin, Narts, Akop's Place. The sea, lead-gray, almost calm, but still noisy in this deserted silence, was beating against the shore. The seagulls, exposing their bellies to the wind, hovered over the waves, sluggish as jelly. The cold rain fell in quiet, thin streams.

In all this, Beslan recognized something familiar, even native. As if all this had already happened to him: Maybe in a dream, or maybe in a distant past life, but it happened for sure. This is how he had already walked along the shore, pierced by a cold wind and washed by a thin stream of rain. The smell was the same—the sea, the fish, the dark abyss. Where was he coming from then? Where was he going? Where was he rushing off to? He couldn't remember. But he remembered that he was not going to a warm, cozy home. Rather, he was in a hurry to keep up with the rain and wind, to walk through them as much as possible, to not arrive anywhere they seem to be waiting for you. It's always like this: In the rain and wind. Past each other.

An unfinished port. Huge logs, the dead memory of the forest, lie on the pier, ready for loading.

Near Akop's Place, it is empty. The tables under the mighty cypress trees stand lonely and bored. Gathering in the foliage into large drops, the rain plops onto them and breaks into pieces. The droplet world shatters into small fragments. The pier is laid with thin, narrow, partially rotten, and broken boards. The supports are rusty. The pier goes into the sea like a skeleton.

Blown by a gusty wind, Beslan reached the end of the pier. Kelasur, Sinop, Turbaza, the wooded hills above them were visible through the glass of rain pouring between them and the distant beloved shore.

The return took too long. A chill gripped his soul. The warmth is leaving it. It's leaving all the time. It cannot be stopped.

It was not possible to separate my heart into two halves—living and dead. I should tie it into a knot and move on. But for what? Where to go? Where does it end? Will it never end? Will the rain continue to pour, separating you from your beloved shore in the distance?

## Endnotes

1 https://ru.wikipedia.org/ wiki/%D0%A1%D0%B5%D0%BA%D0%B0.

2 https://en.wikipedia.org/wiki/Nard_(game).

3 https://en.wikipedia.org/wiki/Sixty-Six_(card_game).

4 Du-shesh, ekibir, and du-yak are the combinations in the game of nard.

5 https://en.wikipedia.org/wiki/RPG-18.

6 https://en.wikipedia.org/wiki/Papakha.

7 The word the narrator avoids is "love" (*liubov'*). In Russian, it rhymes with "blood" (*krov'*).

Printed in the USA
CPSIA information can be obtained
at www.ICGtesting.com
JSHW021956111024
71521JS00002B/6